A
CREATIVE ODYSSEY

The Story of Floyd and Richie

By Richard L. Rotelli

Copyright © 2001 by R. L. Rotelli

All rights reserved. No part of this book shall be reproduced or transmitted in any form or by any means, electronic, mechanical, magnetic, photographic including photocopying, recording or by any information storage and retrieval system, without prior written permission of the publisher. No patent liability is assumed with respect to the use of the information contained herein. Although every precaution has been taken in the preparation of this book, the publisher and author assume no responsibility for errors or omissions. Neither is any liability assumed for damages resulting from the use of the information contained herein.

ISBN 0-7414-1011-7

Published by:

519 West Lancaster Avenue
Haverford, PA 19041-1413
Info@buybooksontheweb.com
www.buybooksontheweb.com
Toll-free (877) BUY BOOK
Local Phone (610) 520-2500
Fax (610) 519-0261

Printed in the United States of America

Printed on Recycled Paper

Published April, 2003

This book is dedicated to
Angela,
my mother, the woman behind Richie;
to my Aunt Selma who gave the extra push it took
for me to get working on this story;
and to my wife, Pat who more than anyone else
knows the effort it took to complete
and who shared the work of its development.

CONTENTS

	PROLOGUE	1
1.	SUMMER - - 1944	5
2.	LIFE IN ITALY - - 1912	17
3.	TEXAS - - 1909	21
4.	RICHIE'S EARLY DAYS (THE ROARING 20s)	29
5.	RIDING THE RAILS - - 1909	43
6.	RICHIE IN THE LATE 1920s AND EARLY 1930s	52
7.	THE WHEAT FIELDS OF NORTH DAKOTA - - 1909	63
8.	BACK IN LAMPASAS - -A BUDDING ARTIST 1909 – 1923	75
9.	MADAME EDITH ROWENA NOYES GREENE AND ROY GREENE- - 1875 – 1923	100
10.	FLOYD COMES TO FRAMINGHAM - - 1923	118
11.	RICHIE, LENA and DICKIE (and the Trailer) 1933 - 1937	154
12.	FLOYD'S TRAVELS IN HIS CAR - - 1932 – 1933	164
13.	THE ARTIST RETURNS - - 1933 – 1943	199
14.	LUCKY POINT - - 1945 – 1949	227
15.	FLOYD'S NEW BASEMENT APARTMENT 1949 – 1950	273
16	FISHING IN WAUSHAKUM POND - - 1950 – 1959	304
17.	IN FLOYD'S OWN WORDS - - 1952 – 1955	348
18.	THE FINAL YEARS - - 1956 – 1966	391

PROLOGUE

I first became aware of Floyd Walser when I was nine years old and he was about fifty-six. Of course from my perspective he was an old man, but the fact that he was paralyzed, with the use of only his right arm, fascinated me. I knew that he had once been a Texas cowboy and I believed that he was thrown and trampled by a wild horse, resulting in crippling injuries. I was to learn later that although he was thrown from a horse, the dreaded disease, polio did the damage. By the time I got to know him, his legs had atrophied to resemble thin sticks with his feet permanently bent and totally useless. His left arm was similarly very thin and unable to move on its own. His left hand was only able to grasp objects if the fingers were forced to open or close by manipulating them with his right hand. Once something was in that hand, it was held as if in a vise. The fact that he somehow had managed to become a well-known artist who worked in just about every medium from pencil and charcoal, to pastels, oils, watercolors, and etchings was nearly unbelievable. He gave art lessons to many residents of my hometown, including most of the little kids, often entertaining them with stories of the "Wild West". As I grew older, I began to learn more of the captivating story of his early life and of how he came to reside in my neighborhood as the protégé of famous musicians.

But the part of the whole story of this courageous and talented man, that, for me makes it really special, is how his life was eventually touched so dramatically by my father. Until my dad, Richie, entered Floyd's life his mobility was severely restricted and his daily activities considerably limited. Richie was a natural at inventing things and was as creative at what he did as Floyd was creative in the world of art. Fate would bring these two remarkable men together at a point in

Floyd's life when he was worn down from all the years of struggling to get around in his little room. Just getting out of bed in the morning took him nearly an hour. Once he had managed to push himself into his chair, it was a significant challenge to get around the room without help. His chair, equipped with four swiveling casters on its base, was an old living room easy chair. He propelled himself around the uneven wooden floor by shaking and thrusting his upper torso while pushing or pulling on whatever was handy with his one good arm occasionally aided by his cane. Richie's inventiveness was to change all that while simultaneously opening Floyd's life to a level of freedom he had not known for many years.

A dictionary definition for odyssey is "… a long wandering or voyage usually marked by many changes of fortune" so it seems very appropriate to incorporate that word into the book's title.

This then, is the true story of Floyd and Richie and many others who touched their lives, told from many memories and much research material, and with the help of many people who knew them. It is a story of courage, creativity, determination, and a love for life.

The material contained in this book is based upon many sources; much of it actually witnessed by the author and others. A great deal of it is the result of research, which involved discussions with relatives, and friends of both Floyd and Richie. A considerable portion of the background information on Floyd and the Greenes is from newspaper clippings and other archival material found in various places, including the Framingham (Massachusetts) Historical Society and Museum.

To the extent possible, the material presented here is factual and accurate. However, several parts of this story are presented in a fictionalized way. In those places, I have striven to provide the reader with what I believe could actually have occurred and with dialogue, which is probable, although clearly not an exact rendering of what took place. Particularly the chapters on riding the rails, the experiences in the wheat fields and Floyd's travels in his car have a heavy component of invented dialog and situations. However, even these portions are based upon solid research and are presented in a way to be both entertaining and informative.

CHAPTER 1

SUMMER
1944.

It was summer again. Time for my friends and me to find new mischief and adventures. We were good kids. Kind of simple-minded and naïve, especially compared to the high-octane, precocious youth of today. We didn't have TV quite yet and the world certainly seemed simpler and slower paced. The fact that World War II had been raging for the last three years and that the decisive battle of D-Day at Normandy had just occurred didn't seem to really affect us much. We were kids. Even when the brother of one of our playmates was killed in action, the reality of it all was still obscure. We saw our share of war movies and watched the newsreels between feature films to keep up to date on how The Allies were beating the crap out of Hitler as well as the progress of the fierce fighting going on in the Pacific. But we were far more interested in Bud Abbott & Lou Costello, and those wonderful serials where the hero's life was put in peril, if not wiped out for sure each and every Saturday. No matter how much it appeared that our hero could never get out of the situation the writers put him in at the end of each episode, he always found a way to triumph. In many ways we lived in a sort of make-believe world, where we could have adventures just by mutually inventing them. We often made up situations and pretended that we all believed the nonsense, allowing our active imaginations to entertain us, sometimes to the point of scaring ourselves.

Home for me and my Mom and Dad was the top floor of a two-family house on Dow Street in Framingham, Massachusetts. What a great location this was! What kid could have asked for a better place to grow up? Just down Nipmuc Road, which came right off Dow Street across from our house, was the sandy beach of a good-sized pond known as Lake Waushakum. Pronounced Wah-SHAKE-um, its name

Waushakaum Pond and my neighborhood. My house was at "X" on Dow Street. The Greene's old house where Mr. Walser lived was at "G".

in the time of the Nipmuc Indians who had lived along its shores, had variously been recorded as Washakamaug or Shakum. It meant "eel fishing place" evidently due to the abundance of those snake-like fish that could be caught there. Over the years, for a variety of reasons, the eel population had dwindled so there were not too many of them squirming around in there. It was small compared with other lakes, at just under 90 acres in size, and really was classified as a pond. We always called it, "The Lake". It was about a three-minute slow walk past Fair's Icehouse; a place loaded with ice packed in hay. It was amazing that the ice could last all through the hot summers. We still used ice in those days in our iceboxes. Not too many folks had refrigerators yet, although this was just about to change dramatically, making the demand for ice diminish significantly. Unfortunately, Fair's Icehouse burned to the ground one exciting night. I remember watching the inferno from the front porch of our house, feeling the heat on my face even from that distance, and wondering how a place loaded with frozen water could burn so ferociously. My folks were watching the spectacle with me, and my Dad said something about having seen this same fire 12 years earlier. I didn't understand that at all.

If you walked along Dow Street at a right angle to Nipmuc Road, you would very soon come to Lake Avenue, which paralleled the lake. This street made a sharp right turn parallel to Dow Street, and became Cove Avenue, so named because the lake curved around into a cove just out behind this street. The concrete foundation of all that was left of The Cove Ice Company's icehouse after it met a similar fate as Fair's, marred the view and gave us a place to roam around playing war games. If you ventured out behind the concrete pillars which used to support the Cove Ice Company's long-gone icehouse, you came to the smallest part of the lake, not too surprisingly known as "the cove". Out a little way from shore was a small island, which, for reasons that were never known to us was called "Monkey Island." I once overheard a teenage boy say to his girlfriend, "Let's swim out there and monkey around." But I'm sure they never did because the water was way too full of weeds, snakes, snapping turtles and lots of other stuff you wouldn't want to tangle with. Continuing on Cove Avenue, you came to Winthrop Street, which headed off past the other end of Dow Street and got you to The Memorial School, where we went from first grade through Junior High, and to Hollis Street. From there, downtown Framingham (and the Hollis Theater) was easily within reach of a few more minutes of spirited walking. So that was our block, our turf, the area where we could play at practically anything.

One of the things that made it so terrific for us was that the Anna Murphy Playground was right there. It was on the corner of Lake Ave. and Cove Ave. and ran quite a distance, about half the way, along Cove. There was a chain link fence behind our house, which ran all along one side of this wonderful playground. We had our "secret" ways of defeating this fence, ways that got more creative as we grew up. At the Lake Avenue end of the playground was a clay tennis court enclosed by a tall fence. Not once did any of us attempt to play any tennis there. Nobody in our gang had a tennis racquet, or any idea about how the game was played. Besides, in our minds this was a sissy's game. Not far from the tennis court was a shed where summer activities for small kids (like us) were conducted. There were swings on heavy metal pipes, a sliding board, seesaw, jungle gym, and a sandbox. On hot summer mornings you could hear high-pitched sounds coming from that part of our world. These were the sounds of excited kids having great fun, their happy shouts blending in with the rhythmic squeaking of the swings and seesaw. The largest part of the playground was taken up by a baseball field, complete with backstop, pitcher's mound, and paths of clay to run the bases. Real bases were brought to the field by various teams and taken away with them when they left. We just used somebody's glove, a piece of wood, a dead bird, or anything handy. Far off in distant left field was a smaller softball area, or at least that's what we used it for. Only when the bigger kids where playing baseball was anybody at our "softball field" in any danger of getting conked on the head by a fly ball.

One of the most interesting things, and at the same time a little scary to me and my pals, about the area across Lake Avenue from the playground was that a strange, crippled old man who was an artist, lived in a big old house set back in the woods near the lake. He was known to us only as Mr. Walser, sometimes called "Tex", and rarely called by his first name, Floyd by the adults in our neighborhood. The old house that he lived in was owned by Mr. and Mrs. Greene. We knew that the Greenes were well-known musicians and that Mr. Roy Greene was the conductor of something known as The Civic League Orchestra. Mrs. Greene was reportedly a little strange, sick much of the time, but probably very famous. We rarely saw the Greenes, but occasionally, Mr. Greene would hire some of us to do odd jobs around his house. Little by little, we would get to know Mr. Walser, finding out that he sometimes gave art lessons to what we figured must be some of the bravest youngsters in town. It turned out that it seemed as though half the population of Framingham at one point or another took art lessons from him. We very quickly learned that we had nothing to fear from this remarkable man, and in fact, we enjoyed spending time with him.

The houses on Dow Street were close together and many people were related. Just about everyone in the neighborhood knew everyone else. The lion's share of the population was made up of people who had immigrated to America from their homes in Italy to make a better life for their families. Several of the oldest children in these families were born in the old country and made the long, slow passage to America by boat with their young parents. Italian was spoken in these households, although as soon as the kids started going to school and otherwise blending in with other neighbors, English began taking hold. Many of the "old folk" really didn't want to speak anything other than their native tongue, and would go to great lengths to avoid using English words when it was so easy to stay with what was so familiar. Eventually, their kids would be the driving force which got them speaking broken English at first, then a very acceptable version with occasional Italian phrases or words thrown in for good measure. There were a lot of people who weren't Italian, but there was no doubt that this was a neighborhood of people who really cared about one another and looked after each other's needs. Just about every family, at least the Italian ones, had large vegetable gardens in their back yards. It seemed as if everyone was good at farming. I sometimes wondered if the name of our town might have been an accidental misspelling of "Farmingham".

My cousins (a Belloli family) lived right next door in a stucco-sided house that their father, Joseph had built. They had five boys and one girl, but the ones I hung around with all the time were Henry, a few months younger than I was, and his brother, Sonny, who was about a year older. (I was 9, going on 10.) Eddie, nicknamed "Bananas", was part of the big-guy group and whenever we tried to copy some of the things they did, we got in trouble. Bigger brothers Tony and Carlo were, as far as I was concerned, grown ups, as was big sister Corinne. One of the things I loved about my cousin's house was the grape arbor in their back yard. We used to play in the sweet shade of that grape vine and when we thought no one was looking, we'd sneak a few of the ripest, juiciest grapes I've ever eaten. There were grape arbors at my house as well as my grandparent's, but Henry and Sonny had the one I liked best.

On the first floor of our house lived the Bortolussi family, a family with the mother, Eureka who was called Rica, the father, Fred who worked at Dennison Mfg. Co. where my dad worked, and one child, a boy named Freddie. He was born just two days after I was. Although we were not related, Freddie and I were real pals. So the principal gang was Dickie, as I was known then, Freddie, Henry, and Sonny. You didn't often see one of this bunch without the others. There was one other full-time member of this gang who deserves to be mentioned. That was Henry's faithful dog, Major. He always enjoyed being with any and all of us, but

Summer 1944
From left to right: Freddie, Dickie, Henry(standing), Sonny, and Major

First day of school, 1944
Freddie, Henry, Sonny (in back), Dickie, and Major.

there was no doubt that Henry was the one he would do anything for. Sonny was a year ahead of the rest of us at the Memorial School, where we learned various important life lessons, like the three "R's" and how to dance with a girl.

One hot morning as I was slowly savoring my daily eggnog (man, how I loved the way my mother made that cold, delicious drink with plenty of vanilla flavoring) I heard Sonny come running and stumbling up the back stairs of our house. When he got to our kitchen screen door he shouted, "Hey Dickie! Come on! We've got a job. Mr. Greene will pay us each 25 cents to rake up a bunch of leaves around his house and dump 'em down by the cove. Let's go!" With a quick "O.K." from my mother, I ran along with Henry, Freddie, and Sonny diagonally across the playground to the big old house by the lake where our job awaited us. I was thinking that 25 cents for raking up a few leaves was a pretty good deal. It only cost 12 cents to take in a movie at the Hollis Theater.

Mr. Greene was waiting for us with large rakes and huge dropcloths. He showed us just what he wanted raked up and where we should dump our hauls. He instructed us to carry the dropcloths full of leaves out toward the cove and to dump them over the edge of where his land dropped off to a lower level, where it met the lake. He was not much taller than ten-year-old Sonny was, but even though he spoke softly and with a pleasant manner, we all respected him and would do whatever he needed done. He asked us to be as quiet as possible, since Mrs. Greene was not feeling well and was resting out on their veranda. (They had a veranda. We had porches.) The job wasn't too difficult and we finished it up in less than an hour. When he brought us our pay, he asked if we would like to do some chores for Mr. Walser, whom he called "Floyd". We eagerly accepted since the lure of another 25 cents in our pockets was too much to ignore.

We really hadn't seen Mr. Walser up close before and we were all a little nervous, worried that we might stare at his deformed torso with his legs nowhere in sight. His left arm was there all right, but it was tiny and didn't work at all. He did have a strong right arm and hand, which he used to enthusiastically shake hands with each of us in turn while he smiled with a sort of scowl while saying, "Howdy". He sat strapped into an old upholstered living room easy chair equipped with casters on its bottom. After a while, I realized that he indeed did have legs. Crossed over each other and folded under his upper body, they were mostly hidden by a blanket, but I could see that they, like his left arm, were shriveled and useless. With a lot of effort he could make his chair go in the general direction he wanted it to by sort of jerking his pear-shaped body and pushing or pulling with his cane. How could this man possibly be a well-known artist whose paintings, sketches, and etchings had won critical acclaim? As the weeks and months slowly rolled by, we would get to know Mr. Walser much better, and our admiration for the man increased by leaps and bounds as we began to understand some of his life story.

Later that evening, while my mom, dad, and I were having supper, I talked pretty much non-stop about the interesting day I had. I talked a lot about Mr. Walser and what a strange creature he was, but how I really liked him and thought that I might want to take him up on his offer of art lessons in exchange for doing odd jobs for him. I wasn't really all that interested in fine art, but I did want to learn how to draw cartoons, and he didn't actually come right out and say that was a dumb idea, so maybe there was hope. I also went on and on about how beautiful it was out in the woods near the cove: the majestic pine trees (Mr. Greene said that the area used to be what he called a pine grove), the wild blueberry bushes, and the water of Lake Waushakum softly lapping at the shiny stones at the edge of the lake. And there were flowers floating on the surface of the lake! Beautiful white ones with big green "leaves". (I learned later that these "flowers" were water lilies.) All of this seemed like another world, not just a place that I could walk to in five minutes.

My dad listened very closely to all I was saying, which was not the usual response from him, and had a sort of dreamy look in his eyes. He finally said that for quite a while, he had been aware of just how special a piece of land it was out where I had been dumping leaves that afternoon. I almost fell off my chair when he said, rather matter-of-factly that he had decided to try to buy that property and build his dream house on it. My mother was not shocked to hear this, so I guessed that they must have been discussing this for some time. I of course, had never thought about ever moving out of our home. It was perfect for me. Why should we move?

This two-story house we lived in was built in 1921 for my grandparents, their two children and other relatives. My grandparents along with then eleven year old Richie and his kid sister, Selma originally lived on the first floor, along with my grandmother's brother, Angelo, his wife Amedea, and their baby boy. The upper floor was occupied at that time by my grandmother's other brother Joseph, his wife Maria, and their baby, Corinne. During the first few years there was a lot of moving about within these two floors, with other relatives coming and going as their urgent needs for a place to stay just could not be ignored. This over-crowding led to both uncles building their own homes on either side of this madhouse. Both families happily moved into their new homes before the plaster was dry on the walls, and with lots more work to be done.

My grandparents and my dad's sister, my Aunt Selma, now lived right next door to us on the other side from my cousins, Henry and Sonny. It was their father, Joseph, with help from his brother Angelo who built that cozy dwelling in about 1930. The house was really modern and had some nice touches, like an ironing board that folded out of a little door in a wall of the kitchen. They also had a ceramic tiled bathroom upstairs that I thought was pretty fancy. My grandmother's brother, Angelo, with his wife and family now lived in the next house along Dow Street, making it seem to the casual observer that everyone was related.

In the back yard of my grandparents house was a large vegetable garden, stretching all the way out to the chain link fence of the Anna Murphy playground. In that garden, they grew the best tomatoes I had ever seen or tasted (except for the ones grown in most of the other back yard gardens in the neighborhood). Also, my grandparents grew lettuce, carrots, beets, potatoes, beans, peppers, cucumbers, squash, corn - - in short, just about everything. They also kept a bunch of chickens in a coop in a fenced-in area. Lots of fresh eggs were always available, as well as an occasional fresh chicken. The only thing I didn't like so much about what looked to me to be a huge farm, was the few times I was called upon, usually in the blazing heat, to help weed between the veggies. Ugh! Hot, sweaty work was not exactly what I dreamed of doing on nice summer days.

At that time I had no way of knowing of the interesting history of the land where our houses now stood and where we had those bountiful gardens. Back nearly three-quarters of a century earlier, in 1867 nearly 200 acres of land, much of which bordered the shore of Lake Waushakum and included where my Dow Street home now was located, had been purchased by three remarkable young men known as the Sturtevant brothers. They were gentlemen of means and were well educated, with the second brother, Edward having graduated from Harvard Medical School in 1866. He never practiced medicine, but Dr. Sturtevant became an agricultural scientist very interested in scientific research. When the brothers purchased all this fertile land, they began the development of "Waushakum Farm" which soon became well known as the site of a series of "... brilliant experiments in agriculture, which are models in experimental acumen and conscientious execution." In 1875 Dr. Sturtevant set up the first lysimeter to be used in America. This was a large closed metal box buried to be nearly level with the surrounding soil surface and was used in a scientific way in water quality experiments and monitoring, measuring the percolation, or drainage of water through soils. He presented its records at scientific meetings both here and abroad, of over four years of its use.

The brothers Sturtevant had a significant herd of dairy cattle and conducted considerable research on the physiology of cow's milk. But the research they did on corn would probably have interested my relatives and their friends the most. Dr. Sturtevant spent over 20 years investigating the maize plant and shortly before his death in 1898, published a work entitled "Varieties of Corn" in which he extolled the virtues of a marvelous sweet corn he called "Waushakum Corn".

Dr. Sturtevant built a beautiful, 10-room residence for himself and his large family on two and a half acres of land on the corner of Winthrop Street and Wood Avenue. He planted several beautiful shade trees and much ornamental shrubbery on this property making it one of the finest homes in the area. There is little doubt where he got the name of the street that this house faced. He was born in Boston and when he was just a child, both his parents died. He and his two brothers were then brought up by an aunt who lived in Winthrop, Maine, his father's birthplace.

Now in the mid-'40s, with so much changed in the world since the time of the Sturtevants, the fertile soil in our neighborhood was still producing worthwhile crops. Both of my father's uncles, in addition to their natural capabilities as home gardeners, were very skillful carpenters and cabinetmakers. They both earned a good living plying their trade, but they were passionate about making music. Large brass band instruments, like a Sousaphone, tuba, trombone, as well as clarinets and saxophones were played, usually in a basement, 'til the wee hours. Playing in local bands provided a great way for these men to enjoy their full creative potential. My dad clearly inherited all the good carpentry and cabinetmaking genes, but didn't come close to picking up any musical interests. However, his natural abilities in making things, honed to perfection by the coaching of these fine craftsmen would serve him (and others) well in years to come.

CHAPTER 2

LIFE IN ITALY
1912

My dad, Richie, was born in Parma, Italy on March 27, 1910; the first child of Luigi Rotelli and Luisa Belloli. His full name was Riccardo Carlo Pasquale Rotelli; his second middle name commemorating the fact that he was born on Easter Sunday. The economy of Italy was in terrible shape at that time and it was extraordinarily difficult for the average citizen to barely make a living. The custom, perhaps even the law at that time required that a new bride must move with her husband into his family's home. Luigi's father, Marco owned a large farm which produced primarily wheat and grapes, plus fodder for the animals, cattle, horses, pigs, chickens, etc. as well as fruit trees.

Life for Luisa was very difficult in this large, very hard working family. She had a frail constitution and was often ill, but she strove every day to keep up with her share of the work. There was no lack of chores for her to do. The rough and tough nature of all her new relatives was foreign to her since her own family was far more genteel and although also very hard workers, were deeply religious as well. Her father did a lot of work for the village priest for several years. Although Luisa had not moved from her own hometown, it must have seemed to her that she was in a very different place.

When Richie was nearly two years old, Luigi and Luisa were blessed with a second child, a boy whom they named Raimondo. I recall my dad telling me many years later that his father really liked the name Raymond, since the components of it in Italian meant "King of the World". Although Luisa felt the strong need to nurse her little baby and to stay with him as much as possible, she had to leave him and Riccardo each day with the older women of the family while she went out to the fields to work in all kinds of weather, just like everyone else. Lacking the means to keep food fresh for more than a short time, it was not unusual for these hard workers to occasionally become sick from spoiled meals. Little Raimondo, who was not yet six months old, was unable to assimilate what he was fed, and died.

Heartbroken over their loss, the young couple knew that to stay in such miserable conditions was simply out of the question. They were sure that if they could get to America, they would clearly be able to live a much better life and would be able to properly provide for young Riccardo as well as any other children that God may send their way. They were not afraid of hard work, but also recognized that their only real skills were as farmers. They were sure that there must be many farms in America where they would be well paid.

Luigi mustered up the courage to ask his father for the money it would take to sail across the seas to that wonderful land of opportunity with his wife and young child. He had been dreaming about making a new life in a place called California. This was an unbelievable thing for his father to be hearing. Shocked that his strong young son could even think about leaving the family when there was so much work to do, he roared out his uncompromising refusal.

Unwilling to give up what now burned inside him as more than a dream, Luigi solemnly approached the kindly village priest. With his young wife at his side and holding little Riccardo by the hand, he must have touched a sympathetic chord within this man of God. Perhaps it was the many years of work around the church provided by Luisa's father. Or possibly a deep belief that this young family was worthy and in serious need. Whatever the reason, money was loaned to the grateful couple, who gleefully promised to pay it all back with interest.

It turned out that California was simply too far away from Parma to be reached with the money they now had in hand. They barely had enough to sail to New York City where an uncle of Luigi's was now living. To conserve as much of their meager funds as possible, they booked passage in the steerage section of a modern steamboat.

Once they were underway, and the stormy seas made the boat pitch and roll violently, Luisa became ill. After days of seasickness, they had no choice but to move her out of steerage and into the infirmary, where she spent the entire trip. This move took a large bite out of their dwindling bankroll. By the time they arrived in New York, Luisa had realized that her seasickness was amplified by the fact that she was pregnant.

When they finally arrived in New York, they found their way to the uncle who was waiting for them. He was really of no particular help to the new Americans in finding them any work. He did however, suggest that they would probably do OK if they went up to a place in Massachusetts called Framingham. He knew that there were quite a number of Italians from northern Italy who for some reason had settled there. He gave them the name and address there of a man he knew to be reliable and trustworthy. So, without any ability to read or speak English, off the three of them went by train to Framingham.

Their new mentor was indeed a wonderfully kind man; a baker named Cavagni. He allowed them to stay with him for a few months until Luigi was able to find work and rent a place of their own. As time went on, Cavagni's Bakery would be well known for miles around as the best place for Italian bread and pastries.

This then, was the real beginning of the new life that Luigi and Luisa had dreamed about. Since there really was not much of a demand for skilled farmers at that time in the town of Framingham, Luigi, who was very strong, quickly learned a new trade. He became a "Chipper and Caulker" at The International Boiler Works on Waverly Street which was within easy walking distance of home. He would continue to work at this very physically demanding job in a hot, dangerous and noisy environment for many years. He could not have realized at the time that he would be sacrificing his hearing with each passing day at the boiler works. Luisa was content to care for her children, with baby Selma now part of the family. She was able to plant and tend to a good sized garden loaded with healthful vegetables in the small back yard of their modest home on Coburn Street. Soon she would enclose a small group of chickens there as well. This location was just a short distance from where I grew up on Dow Street.

CHAPTER 3

TEXAS
1888-1909

Half way around the world from Italy, Floyd Niles Walser was born in Fayette County, Texas on January 29, 1888. He was part of a large, active family, with two brothers, three sisters, and an older half-brother named Tom Ivy. Lillie Edna Walser had died at the age of four before Floyd was born. They all were raised on a farm, known as The Walser Farm, just outside of Winchester, Texas. Here they profitably raised a variety of crops in the rich soil and kept a small herd of livestock mainly for their own use. His dad, Daniel Nathaniel Walser, known as Nathan was rough and tough and demanded lots of good, hard work from all his offspring. Floyd's mother, Mary Ann (Criswell) Walser who was known as Mollie, was small in stature, but was respected by all in the family for her serious-minded attitude and obvious love for her family. She was capable of any and all tasks that a pioneering woman of her time could be asked to perform, and yet was thought of by her children as not only a force to be reckoned with, but as a priceless treasure to be cherished. Floyd's brother, Benjamin, known as Benny Haden and about five and a half years older, seemed to be his father's favorite and in Floyd's eyes could do no wrong. Floyd quickly learned how to handle horses by watching Benjamin ride, and by seeing that his big brother had absolutely no fear of any horse, no matter how wild and untamed it happened to be. Without ever letting on, Benny was in awe of "little" Floyd's innate ability to soothe the nastiest of horses as well as his knack for making handling them look so natural and easy.

Riding and caring for horses were very important skills in this family, as was hunting for game such as deer. As a youngster, Floyd would be filled with pride and was awed at the sight of both of his parents returning on horseback from a short hunting trip. Floyd, Benny and Tom would see who could guess which one would be carrying home a deer tied to their horse. Very often, each of his parents would have one, but the good-natured jesting between them about just who had shot which deer usually left the kids arguing for days about which parent was the better shot. It really didn't mater much, since the extra food that would be derived from the successful hunting excursion would be what cheered up everyone.

The Walser "clan" from which Floyd was descended was a hearty bunch who traced their roots all the way back to 13th century Switzerland. The upper Austrian Alps contain a valley known as "Der Grosse Walsertal", or the big Walser Valley and nearby there is the "Klein Walsertal" which is the Little Walser Valley. These locations are even now promoted by the Swiss National Tourist Agency as having some of the world's finest hiking trails. These trails, which were developed by the Walsers as they migrated during the 13th century into the area now near Liechtenstein and Mittelberg, Austria, make up what is still known as "The great Walser Route". The early Walsers had all been hard workers, used to long days in the fields and they valued family and friendship. A further example of just how close-knit they have stayed is evidenced by the fact that the European Walsers even have a dialect of the language that is still diligently kept alive in parts of lower Germany and up into the Austrian/Swiss Alps.

Floyd's great-grandfather, Frederick Walser, (1817 – 1847) served in the First Regiment of North Carolina Volunteers during the Mexican/American War, which took place from 1846 to 1848. This regiment was stationed in Saltillo in northern Mexico and although they did not participate in the ferocious 2-day battle of Buena Vista just to the south, he did see plenty of action. The Walser family had a great deal of pride in their war hero.

Floyd's "formal" schooling was long over, having quit after only completing the eighth grade in 1901. He was a good, although not especially gifted student, who enjoyed learning geography and literature. His classes in geography fueled his wanderlust and made him want to see more of this great land than the hill country of Texas. Thinking of himself as a rough-and-tumble cowboy, sort of rough around the edges, he was surprised to find that he loved to read. He remembered nearly everything he read in whatever books interested him. His brother Ben excelled at mathematics, to the point where the headmaster of what these boys both jokingly called "The Winchester Academy" pleaded with their parents for Ben to continue with more schooling, especially in math. However, there was far too much work to be done on The Walser Farm for Nathan to allow one of his most able-bodied workers to be off at school.

Floyd had always pitched in and done as much of the daily farm work as he possibly could, crawling out of bed at dawn, and doing whatever was needed. Many days he spent in the saddle of his favorite horse and was a very accomplished rider. He also enjoyed the challenge of taming the wild horses he would sometimes find. By sundown, he was ready to unwind with whatever book was at hand.

His mother enjoyed books and encouraged a very young Floyd to discover the adventures that could be had by reading. The toughness and no-nonsense attitude displayed by Floyd's father was balanced by the sweeter, calming influence of his mother; although he knew that if his mother ever heard him use any kind of foul language, such as hell, or damn, he would be in for a peck of trouble. She also encouraged all her offspring to play musical instruments. Floyd's older brother, Ben had learned to play the banjo quite well. He also was an accomplished fiddle player, and could play a mean guitar as well as the harmonica. When Ben attached his harmonica to his banjo or to his guitar so he could play these instruments at the same time, Floyd must have thought this was a little too much showing off. Although Floyd couldn't quite match Ben's musical talents, he did learn to strum a fairly hot banjo. The sisters, Erie, Lena, and little Clara, all younger than Floyd and not wanting to be outdone by the guys, also played instruments and would often blend their voices angelically in song.

The Walser household must have been a fun place on winter evenings. It was to be young brother Tansey, however who would truly become an expert fiddler in years to come. He was the one who eventually would be sought out by folks who had weddings or other occasions and who wanted "the best fiddler for miles around". When Tansey was in his teens and beyond, he particularly enjoyed playing his extra lively fiddle at the many "42" parties held at church socials and family reunions. That popular domino game ("42"), invented by a couple of Baptist youngsters in1887 in the tiny hamlet of Trappe Springs after they had been chastised for playing cards, has been called "the National Game of Texas" and has never lost its appeal. (The fact that Tansey had so much musical talent may have somehow been preordained. His middle name was Showalter, chosen by his parents in honor of his father's sister Carolyn's husband, Anthony Johnson Showalter. Born in 1858, in Virginia, A. J. Showalter was a music teacher, author and publisher who studied music in England, France, and Germany. In his prolific career, he published over 130 music books, which sold more than a million copies. One of his best-loved compositions, sung in Baptist churches everywhere, is *Leaning on the Everlasting Arms*.)

Years later, Floyd would enjoy the memory of his mother and father singing gospel songs and the old favorites together as they did their chores around the place and after supper in the evenings. Learning to pipe in at the right place on some of those old tunes was something all the kids loved to do and Floyd was especially thrilled by the challenge of adding his voice at just the right spot.

While Floyd was still in early grade school at the one-room Winchester Academy, he discovered that his Pa really liked to gamble. One day, after their father had been unusually jovial, practically dancing around the place with his Mollie and promising the kids that *better days are a-comin'*,

Benny Haden took Floyd aside. The older brother swore little Floyd to secrecy. Then, when he was sure that Pa was in the barn and away from the front of the house, Ben guided Floyd to the front porch. Lifted high on Ben's strong shoulders, Floyd was told to reach behind a board which was nailed to the inside part of the beam that supported the porch roof. Fearing that he might be putting his fingers into a wasp's nest or something much worse, and that his big brother was just planning to have some perverted fun at seeing him in pain, he refused. Ben promised him that no harm would come to him and that if he would just do as he was told he would learn a secret. Floyd pulled himself higher and peered around behind the board. Then he saw it! A small moneybag tied up with a string. Ben told him he would hold him up long enough for him to untie the bag and look inside. Floyd had never seen gold pieces like that before! He didn't count them, but he could tell by their weight that they represented a lot of money.

With the bag tied just like it had been, and carefully put back exactly as it was found, Floyd was lowered to the porch. The boys were sure that their Pa had put the gold up there to hide it from the family. Ben told Floyd that he knew that lots of times, on the weekends, Pa would ride into town and be gone all night. Sometimes the next day he would be in an awful mood and you'd better stay out of his way. On those days, everybody got extra chores to do. But once in a while, like he was acting on this day, old Daniel Nathaniel would be everybody's pal. Those were the times when he must have won a lot more than he lost at his "secret" nighttime poker game.

So now these two brothers could pretty much tell in advance when they were in for a rougher day's work than usual, or when they could probably get away with almost anything. They agreed to keep this discovery just between the two of them. They were sure that if their brother Tansey or the girls found out about their secret, no good would come of it. They certainly were not about to tell their older half-brother Tom

Daniel Nathaniel Walser
circa 1895 - Texas

Right: Floyd Walser
age 20 - Texas

Floyd's home in Lampasas, Texas in 1910
His mother (seated) with his brothers and sisters.

Ivy about anything as important as this. Who could tell how he might use this information?

Unfortunately, as seems to be the case so often when it comes to gambling, the stockpile slowly diminished and the extra happy days seemed to disappear.

Floyd managed to enjoy spirited games of baseball with kids of his age whenever some of them rode their horses over to his place, or when he could quietly gallop off to their territory. Whenever he got back to his chores after a few innings, he found that there somehow was more to do than when he left.

Whenever Floyd and any of his brothers or friends would ride their horses into town to run errands, they would take a little extra time to set tin cans on fence posts at random along their way. Then on the ride home they would see who could shoot the cans right off those posts while at full gallop. It was rare for anybody to actually hit the target with a six-gun while being bounced in the saddle so much. It was agreed that after passing ten or so untouched cans, they would go back, come to a complete stop, reload and then blast each tin can target to oblivion. They all felt that this was good practice for defending themselves against all manner of danger. In addition to poisonous snakes, and wild animals, there still were some unhappy Indians in these parts. There also were very few laws to discourage highway bandits. At that time and place, a lawman was not a common sight, and there were people all around who felt as though if they saw that you had something they liked or wanted, they would just take it from you by force. Being proficient with firearms was considered by every able-bodied young man as one very important skill.

But now, in 1909, things were very different in Floyd's life. His father had died nearly eight years ago, coming down with pneumonia after working for days out in a cold downpour that seemed as though it would never end. Within a few months of Daniel Nathaniel Walser's passing, the family moved from the farm outside of Winchester, Texas to the town of Lampasas, Texas. Floyd's mother had relatives in this developing town. Being a frontier woman in every sense of the word, she rapidly took charge of her family and sold the farm and the farming equipment. She loaded up the wagon with household goods and the children and headed off for Lampasas.

Floyd loved this little town. Its famous mineral springs were popular with Indians long before white settlers arrived. Approximately thirty-three years before Floyd was born, a certain Mrs. Hughes in 1855, was miraculously healed by the waters of Lampasas Springs. The news of this event spread rapidly, enticing the few landowners at that time to begin to promote their town as the "Saratoga of the South". All this notoriety led to rapid growth, so by the time the Walser family moved there in 1902, it was a bustling town with an electric generating plant, a small telephone system, water works, and a population of almost 6,000. After spending his early youth out on the farm near Winchester, Floyd must have been enthralled with the activity and liveliness in his new hometown.

After having spent seven years in this exciting community, Floyd felt the pressure to earn more money for his family and was actively seeking better paying work. An opportunity, which appeared to provide just such employment, was found. The wheat fields of North Dakota offered high-paying jobs that would combine Floyd's natural abilities with horses with what appeared to be a lot of hard work. Thinking of going to such a distant place must have also appealed to his desire to see more of the world. A tall and handsome young man of 21 now in 1909, he felt that he could do just about anything he set his mind to.

So, with a tearful "so long" to his beloved mother and his three brothers and three sisters, he took as many of his possessions as practical, hopped on a freight train and headed north with Fargo, North Dakota as his destination.

CHAPTER 4

RICHIE'S EARLY DAYS
(The "Roaring Twenties")

Richie was one of those people who, if life had been a little different, could have risen to the top in the world of technology. He had a natural talent for all things mechanical, was fascinated by cameras and photography, and had an intuitive understanding of how things worked. His father thought all he needed was a little schooling, and then he should help with all the chores. He took him out of school after he had completed only the sixth grade, even though at least one of Richie's teachers made a special visit to his home to practically beg that he be kept in school. The teacher talked at length about all the natural talent he saw in the young boy, especially in the areas of mechanical drawing, penmanship and arithmetic. It was many years later that Luigi would realize that missing out on so much schooling was indeed a big mistake. Richie would always do his best to read whatever books interested him, work on his spelling and penmanship and practice drawing and printing. His younger sister, Selma, who was a very bright young lady, sailed all the way through high school and then took several college-level courses in the evenings. (College itself was financially out of reach.) She would go on to have a very successful business career. Even though she was two years younger and behind Richie in grade school, there were many times she would provide coaching and assistance at reading and writing for her brother.

When Richie was about eleven (in 1921) his father needed a dependable way to get a good sharp edge on his cutting tools, especially his scythe, which he used to cut tall grass in fields for a little extra income. Together, Richie and his dad scoured magazines looking for ads for grinding wheels. They found and ordered just what Luigi was looking for. It was a strange-looking sharpening contraption that worked by pedaling it like a bicycle to rotate the large carborundum grinding wheel. The only problem was that it came completely unassembled and required a good bit of ingenuity to get it all together so that the person sitting at it and furiously pedaling could safely sharpen what needed sharpening without getting caught in the works, or having the whole machine fly apart. Realizing that he was not up to the task of getting this infernal device together properly by himself, Luigi enlisted the aid of his young son, who with no apparent effort, assembled it with ease. He surely got it together right, since I remember seeing this strange looking machine in our basement on Dow Street, not understanding until very many years later how it was born.

While not yet into his teen years, Richie was fascinated by the whole concept of radio, marveling at the thought that all sorts of music and voices were somehow in the air and that with the right components, put together the right way, you could listen in. By carefully following plans he found in a magazine, he built his own little crystal radio using the then famous "cat's whisker" technology. It really worked and he could hear Rudy Vallee crooning his famous songs. His sister remembers seeing him connected to his radio by its headphones, smiling happily while sound asleep. She also recalls vividly that while the assembly of his radio was in process, she would be vigorously shooed away if she got too close. When it was fully completed and the novelty had worn off a bit, Richie allowed her to listen by donning the headphones. She was simply not impressed with the reception and never bothered with it again.

When Richie was about 14 or 15, his father bought an automobile. Not really for Richie, but since Luigi had been very good at riding horseback, but had no plans to ever drive a car, you had to wonder who this machine was for. Although there is no record of just what make this car was, it may well have been a Durant coupe; over 55,000 of them had been purchased in 1922, its peak production year. While his father was at work in the boiler factory, slowly losing his hearing,

Richie would start this infernal contraption, make it go forward and backward without stalling it too many times, and dream about one day taking it out on the open road. When this got boring, he decided to see what made it work. In a fit of enthusiasm and with no manuals to guide him, the engine was methodically dismantled, piece by wonderful piece. All the marvelous engineering! What clever linkages! Bit by bit, the engine's innards were spread all over the grass next to the chassis. Wow, this was unbelievable! OK, now it's time to put it back together, before Pa gets home and finds out what's been going on here. Almost all the pieces were in fact reassembled. The ones that did go back in place went into all the right places. But there were these weird little parts, that seemed like they must have dropped out of something else. It turned out that they were shims, and they performed a vital function in allowing the engine to work. Fortunately, one of Richie's favorite relatives, a young man who later would own his own automobile service station just happened by and saved the day by insisting that the engine not be run until it could be dismantled again and these pesky little parts put in where they belonged. Luigi couldn't understand why his son was not interested in driving the car back and forth that evening as he so often did. But by the next day, after the repair was surreptitiously made, the car got a good workout.

The world of photography captured Richie's full attention for several weeks. With some of his earnings from odd jobs he did around the neighborhood, he bought a camera and a roll of film. He took pictures of everything; the cat, the house, the grapevines, his sister, close-ups of some flowers and anything else that caught his eye. To save the cost of having his pictures developed at a local store, he quickly built a darkroom out of a closet. It is not known how many rolls of film were lost to the learning-by-doing method. Eventually, he had it worked out so he could reliably develop all his film with excellent results. He even thought about setting up a little business developing other people's pictures at rates that could not be beat by the stores downtown. Luigi had way too many jobs for him to do each day, so he never launched his enterprise, but always thought he probably could do it later. Maybe.

Drawing and sketching fascinated him at an early age. He had a natural talent for drafting and would spend some of his spare time teaching himself how to prepare multiple views of mechanical objects. He would follow the instructions he found in a variety of engineering drawing textbooks and was especially enthralled by preparing what are known as auxiliary and section views. Freehand drawing of a variety of subjects also came easily to him. When he happened to notice a drawing his sister, Selma, who was in junior high school at the time, had just made for geography homework he asked her what it was supposed to be. She replied that it was obvious that it was South America, and she was surprised that he couldn't tell by looking. She had taken all of about 2 minutes to draw it and was all set to turn it in the next day at school. Richie, who had not gotten to that level of schooling having dropped out early at his father's direction, told her in no uncertain terms that what she had prepared was simply not acceptable. He sat down at the table and proceeded to show her how to make a drawing of South America that actually looked like that continent instead of the strange shape she had drawn. His sister pleaded with him to not make it so good or the teacher would never believe that she had done it. She stood behind him, watching how he was doing the sketch and listening as he explained his technique. The next day Selma handed "her" drawing to the teacher whose reaction was as she had predicted. He said it was an excellent piece of work, but he doubted that she had drawn that map. She was made to stay after school that day and to draw a fresh map right there in the classroom. It was fortunate that she had paid attention to what her brother had shown her, since she was able to draw a reasonably good rendition with a result a notch below Richie's work, but convincing nonetheless. Her teacher was satisfied, and when she reflected on the episode, she realized that she had indeed learned a bit of drawing technique after all.

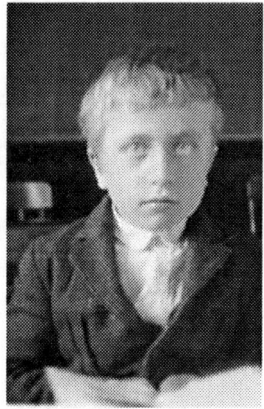

Richie in first grade eager to learn about everything.

Richie's family in 1914. Luigi, Selma, Richie and his mother, Luisa.

Richie at 16... studying a book on photography.

...in his father's car, ready to roll.

Even as a little kid, Richie displayed a natural talent for gardening. Of course, the fact that his parents had a vegetable plot that was really more like a small farm in which they grew everything they needed, and then some, meant that he couldn't get out of the many chores it entailed. But he really enjoyed the smell of the rich loam and he never minded having lots of it jammed under his fingernails. This appreciation for growing things was to stay with him his whole life. When Richie planted something, be it any kind of vegetable or flower, it grew. Actually it flourished.

His first real, paying job was at a small diner known as Gibbon's Lunch in downtown Framingham. Here, a very grown-up acting Richie at the age of 14 was employed as an all around worker; cleaning up the place, doing the dishes, and generally being useful. It wasn't long before the owner realized that this was no ordinary kid, and soon had Richie developed into a somewhat passable short order cook in addition to his other duties. Being located on the corner of Concord Street and Waverly Street and next to the railroad depot, there often were droves of customers flocking to this well-known diner in clusters when their trains would pull in. The little restaurant would quickly go from mostly deserted to overflowing with hungry people who were all in a rush to be served. At times such as these, the young inexperienced worker would try his best not to get knocked over or to bump into the boss or the other helpers. It didn't take him very long though to develop the sense of timing and rhythm to cook up the orders shouted to him and to get them mostly right, occasionally ad-libbing an ingredient here and there. There were very few customer complaints about the food when "the skinny kid" was doing the cooking.

Years later he would enjoy telling us about one particular customer who really frightened him. This was an old man, or at least old in Richie's eyes, who came in on a regular basis, but always when the diner had few other customers. Due to a never revealed tragic event in this man's past, both of his hands had been replaced by shiny metal hooks. The man's voice was deep and gravely, and when he spoke it seemed to Richie to be a stern warning to do exactly what he wanted done - - immediately. His order was always the same. "Coffee. Half and half!" The first time Richie encountered this man and his intimidating manner, he didn't understand what was being ordered, so he filled the cup only half way, hoping that would please this strange person. It most definitely did not! The customer slammed both his hook-hands angrily down on the counter, bellowing out his disapproval. The owner quickly came to Richie's aid, fixing the coffee order by filling the rest of the cup with cream and whispering, "That's half and half." Then this unusual customer demanded that Richie lift the cup so that he could manage to get one hook into the cup handle and the other one steadying the bottom so he could bring it to his mouth growling, "It damned well better not be too hot, kid."

The next time this unique customer came in Richie was prepared, and served him properly without being asked and managed to make small talk while doing so. Other times if "hook man" came in for his coffee and Richie was away from the counter, the raspy voice would demand to know, "Where's the kid?" When Richie eventually left Gibbon's Lunch for a better job, the owner really missed him.

In spite of the fact that he had not learned to swim, surprising considering his proximity to the lake, he was captivated by sleek canoes. He quickly learned to smoothly and apparently effortlessly guide these unstable craft over the calm waters of Lake Waushakum. There was a good-sized canoe rental establishment housing over 50 canoes not far from the sandy beach, just down the street from his house. Even though Richie was only about 14 or 15, Charlie Roy, the owner of this place hired the youngster to work at renting out and repairing his canoes. Mr. Roy was more than pleased with the inventiveness shown by this kid in coming up with all sorts of clever and neat repairs. When asked where he had learned to do the things he did, Richie was hard-pressed to admit that he was just making it all up as he went along.

Richie, and his father, Luigi, always were very close and shared a dynamic relationship. There was no doubt that they loved each other, but my father was always striving to get his dad's approval by inventing, assembling, and otherwise building things that could be useful.

Luigi and Luisa operated a "Mom and Pop" type of general store, which was located right next door to their house. Richie was especially helpful in setting up many innovative ways to make the little store easier to operate and maintain. Years later he would recall making the sausages that they sold very successfully. He had to go into Boston to the butcher's to get the pork for the spicy and uniquely flavored links he would make. He remembered that several of their customers were in every week to each buy ten pounds of his specialty.

The little general store was moderately successful for about five or six years, but was eventually torn down to make room for what was to be home for Luigi, Luisa, and Selma once Richie married and moved into the top floor of the original two-family house.

Richie was a real dynamo, always up to something and interested in just about everything. He kept his body in good shape without going to a gym or working out on any exercise equipment. In those days, no one thought about purposely working up a sweat in a gym after a hard day of honest physical labor. His father kept him constantly at work on any number of chores, hauling, lifting, carrying, and carting. He became rather proud of his manly physique and thought of himself as a young Charles Atlas, who was famous then as a body-builder, "the world's most perfectly developed man". This image got a real boost and moved into high gear when he got a job at the age of about 17 or 18 operating a pneumatic jackhammer. Although he would forever be unable to hear high-pitched sounds as a result of spending long days breaking up all sorts of things like paved streets and hunks of stone (with no hearing protection at all) he looked more and more like the famous Mr. Atlas. He thought it was great fun to impress the girls at the local country fairs that had the old "Ring The Bell With The Sledgehammer" carnival game. When this muscled young man stepped up to that attraction, he would wait until he had a good-size audience and then smash the sledgehammer down with enough force to not only ring the bell at the top of the pole, but practically dislodge it from its mount. One booth at a nearby carnival had an attraction where you could win a doll as a prize for driving a large spike into a railroad tie. The catch was you had to do it with four or fewer blows of a hammer. The fewer whacks you needed to take, the better the doll. Most people had a hard time getting the spike all the way flush with the wood in fewer than six mighty swings. Not Richie. He made it look easy with four, and sometimes did it in three unbelievably well aimed smacks. The operator of this booth pleaded with him to stay away from there. Far away. He would soon be out of prizes if this muscle man didn't leave him alone. Richie said, "Well how about if I switch and use my left hand?" The nervous guy thought there was little chance this customer could be ambidextrous, and even if he were, what would be the likelihood of him being able to do this unbelievable feat left-handed? Once Richie had wowed the whole crowd by winning dolls, left-handed or right-handed for most of the girls, he considerately obliged by moving on with adoring fans watching to see what he might do next. Very few of the girls' boyfriends were at all interested in challenging him to stop showing off.

One of Richie's best pals in his teen years and beyond was a handsome young fellow named Mario Trombi who came from very similar roots and lived nearby. Mario was similar to Richie in his fascination with building things, but it was always Richie's ideas that sparked their adventures. Probably their all-time greatest collaboration was *The Iceboat*. Living practically at the edge of a lake, these two were always looking for ways to do something exciting on it or in it. The fact that neither one of them knew how to swim just was not important to them, since they knew that whatever they did, they would not be in any danger. That is, if they gave any thought to that aspect at all. One of them managed to get his hands on a used motorcycle engine. It was unbelievably powerful and was not equipped with any kind of muffler; so when it ran, people all over the neighborhood would wonder what the devil that racket was. It didn't run at all when it was first acquired by this duo, but shortly after Richie began tinkering with it, it was running smoothly, if not quietly. What to do with this marvelous machine? There were no chassis, wheels, handlebars, seat or any other items which would identify this engine as ever being part of a motorcycle, so what could they make it into? Since it was the middle of winter and the lake was solidly frozen over, the idea of skimming along on the frozen pond in the most outrageous iceboat ever seen was suddenly the obvious answer. They were consumed with this idea, dreaming about it day and night. They worked out a few sketches of how they could mount the engine to a frame with ice skates bolted to its bottom. They needed something to provide the thrust to make this into more than just a noisy curiosity. Somehow, somewhere, an old airplane propeller found its way into these budding aeronautical engineers' hands. It probably came from Teddy Gould's Airport, which was just a few miles away and was a favorite hangout for both Richie and Mario who loved to watch all the latest airplanes take off and land. It is fairly certain that this old, beat up wooden prop was of no value to anyone at the airport since it must have survived (just barely) a wreck. After many failed attempts, it was successfully attached to the old motorcycle engine which was by now mounted on a platform of two-by-fours and other boards which resembled nothing ever seen by anybody who had ever seen an iceboat. The propeller was mounted in such a way that it would push the "iceboat" and its rider swiftly over the ice. To prevent it from accidentally ingesting the rider, or hapless low-flying birds, a screen was fastened all around it.

All of the assembly of motor to framework was done in the warmth of the basement of the house next door to Richie's where his aunt and uncle lived. They knew he and Mario were up to something down there, but they had no idea what it was. They definitely were unaware of a rebuilt motorcycle engine in the basement of their home. Poor Aunt Maria, who one day was alone in her kitchen, never expected to hear what sounded like a major explosion followed by a house shaking roar which seemed to last forever. The two pioneers had just started their invention "for a minute to be sure it worked" before they took it outdoors where it was so cold. By the time they shut it off, and they would swear later that it was only running for two seconds, Aunt Maria was already out of the house and running for shelter toward the chicken barn. They apologized over and over again until they finally had her reasonably calm, at which point she began to tell them in no uncertain terms that they were no longer welcome to use her basement as a proving ground for such a ridiculous and dangerous contraption. Even when they calmly pointed out that they had the foresight to remove the propeller from the engine before starting it, she still would not yield. Later when her husband, Uncle Joe came home and he found out what they were doing, he became enthralled with the whole idea, but also insisted that further testing be done elsewhere. He did, however, get so interested in this whole crazy contraption, that he provided his skill with woodworking to help build the wooden framework, making it a bit more like what one might imagine a real iceboat would look like.

It developed that the propeller was very unbalanced and also needed to be shortened. Using available hand tools, Richie and Mario whittled away and sanded until it looked about right to them. It was now time for a trial run out on the ice. History does not record who was the first one to realize that the cellar door opening was several inches smaller than the completed iceboat. Once they understood that there was simply no way to make the doorway larger, without incurring the wrath of the homeowners, they set to work separating the engine from the framework. The major components were rejoined outside in the bitter cold. Eventually, they carried this amazing machine down Nipmuc Road until they came to a good place to get it out on the ice. With Richie straddling what would pass for a seat, and hanging on to whatever parts could be hung on to, Mario started the engine. Before he could even figure out which way he was headed, Richie was moving; slowly for the first couple of seconds, but then accelerating at a furious pace. With the wind in his eyes he could barely see, but the thrill of traveling so fast and still accelerating was a wonderful sensation.

For this first run, they did not take the time to put in any kind of steering mechanism. As he rapidly approached what looked like a part of the lake that was not completely frozen over, he must have suddenly remembered that there were no brakes on this goofy thing. No problem. Just shut off the engine. With that done, Richie waited for the thing to slow down and stop. It showed no sign of slowing at all. Powerful lessons were being learned, but survival was most likely the main thing on Richie's mind. With the engine stopped and the propeller not turning, the hiss from the steel blades against the ice was the only sound. Richie thought he could hear God telling him to lean to one side. Leaning as far to his left as he could, he gradually began to turn away from what appeared to be open water. It was fortunate that the ice was in fact solid, and only wet since Richie and his crazy machine were still gliding smoothly and slowly, and by now with a large audience of baffled skaters, all the way to the far shore. With the ice boat and Richie finally stopped, Mario came running, slipping and sliding on the ice, whooping and hollering out of sheer joy. Richie looked up at his pal and with total reverence said something like, "I heard God telling me to lean to my left. It didn't really help, but I was saved. The ice stayed solid!" Mario shot back, "That was me yelling at you to lean. Everybody on the ice started yelling it too. You were just damned lucky!"

Being out on the solidly frozen surface of Lake Waushakum on bitterly cold winter days was not limited to the escapades with the iceboat. Although there were plenty of daring rides all over the lake by Richie and Mario, plus a growing number of admirers, many of whom were cute teen-aged girls, the speedy machine finally wore out and broke down. Then Richie got a job working for the Fair Icehouse Company.

When conditions for cutting ice were just right, Mr. Fair would set off a loud whistle, which was mounted on the roof of the icehouse. At the sound of this whistle, which signaled, "We're cutting ice!" men from all around the neighborhood would drop whatever they were doing, call some pals who might not have heard the whistle, throw on heavy winter coats and boots and gather down at the icehouse. These men would work in shifts to cut large thick sheets of ice out on the lake within 100 yards or so, of the building. These immense, eight-foot wide slabs were guided through open black waterways by grabbing them with long handled hooks and slowly pulling them through these temporary canals to the base of the building. Once there, the sheets of ice would be sawn into cakes two feet wide and about four feet long. A clanking old chain-driven contraption powered by a sputtering gasoline engine would hook on to the bottom surface of one of these cakes and nudge it, against its will, up a ramp. Workers with special grabbing bars would manhandle these unruly monoliths into the appropriate opening in the end of the icehouse. Starting at the lowest level, the icehouse would eventually become filled to its roof (about 50 feet high) with rectangular blocks of ice insulated from each other by several inches of hay, pitch-forked in by other workers. This technique allowed the ice to last all through the following summer, when demand for its cooling properties was at its peak. In addition to the hay, extra insulation against summer heat was provided by having the exterior walls of the structure filled with sawdust. Richie worked long, cold days (and nights) at whichever of the positions needed an able bodied hand. The work was strenuous, dangerous, and difficult. But he never complained about it while he warmed himself back at home with some indescribably delicious, piping hot homemade soup and pasta. His mother always knew just what he needed after a long shift on the ice, but was always amazed at how much he would consume.

CHAPTER 5

RIDING THE RAILS
1909

In the late spring of 1909, Floyd Niles Walser, a ruggedly handsome 21-year old man with an athletic build, tossed a large canvas bag stuffed with the items which defined his life at that time, along with his old banjo, into a boxcar in a freight train which was headed north, and hopped aboard. His destination was Fargo, North Dakota and the wheat fields where he was told he would earn good money for some hard work. His plan to get there was to keep heading north on whatever freight train was available and was chugging in that general direction.

This was the start of his journey to what he thought would be at most a few months of high paying work. With the death of his father over 8 years ago, there just wasn't enough money being earned by the others in his family to provide the quality of life that he felt that his mother and the rest of the family should be entitled to. His two older brothers, Benny Haden, who was now 27 and who had been married almost 6 years and their half-brother Tom Ivy, who at that time was 31 were really the only ones, in addition to himself, who were bringing in any real money. Of course nearly all of the money that Ben was earning was needed to support his own growing little family. He and his wife Viola (Jennings) were the proud parents of four-year-old Daniel Abishia and baby Agnes Ruth born last November. Tom was also kept busy providing for his wife and himself and although they had no children there was little to spare to help with his mother's expenses.

Sister Erie had been married for a little over a year now to handsome Eddie Ross, so whatever wages she may have been earning at the time would surely have been principally earmarked for their needs. Floyd's twelve-year old brother,

Tansey, as well as his other 2 sisters, Lena who was 15 and his favorite, little nine year-old Clara, simply were too young to earn any significant wages, although they did what they could. They all did many chores around the Lampasas homestead. The "drill sergeant" of this bunch was his mother, Mollie. She combined all the qualities needed for survival as a widow with a young family in the West at that time. She was a tough, hard worker and had a real talent for getting the most out of her family without breaking their spirit. Having relatives nearby was the main reason for her selling the farm in Winchester after Nathan died and moving her clan to Lampasas. They were helpful to Mollie and her family at first, aiding in getting them set up, but they were of little real continual help, since they had their own daily problems to deal with.

So, filled with high hopes and expectations of earning more than he could around home, by working extra long shifts in the wheat fields, Floyd was on his way to Fargo. It was far too long a distance for him to travel there on his horse, although he really wanted to. He knew that he and his steed could make this journey in less than a month if the weather stayed good. He also knew that having such a fine animal with him there when he arrived would be a real asset. But he also knew that such a trip through areas that until very recently had been considered "Indian Country" had plenty of extra hazards. Freight trains were now running all the time, and although they had absolutely no conveniences, were not guaranteed to make it to their stated destination at any specified time, and were not totally safe either, this was the means of transportation he chose.

Never having actually stolen rides on railways in this manner before, he must have felt somewhat apprehensive and perhaps a little uncertain about just what may lay in store for him. But his spirit of adventure was in high gear. He had heard lots of tales of other men, some called hobos, using the freight trains to "beat the road" and get themselves out of their confining home towns and into adventures and jobs in exciting places. His mother most likely argued against her headstrong son's desire to head north for several months just to earn a few extra bucks. And such a dangerous, and illegal way to travel! However, she must have soon realized that he was going, no matter what, so she undoubtedly did her best to provide him a "roadstake", or enough cash to get at least a few good meals along the way. He never was a big fan of hardtack, the old hard sea biscuit made with flour and water, but she managed to stuff several of these "treats" along with a small canteen of water into his bag.

Among other items in his "duffel" bag, such as an extra pair of boots, a couple of changes of clothes, some soap and shaving stuff, was his prized six-gun. It was a Colt Cattleman single action .45 caliber handgun with a mean-looking 7 ½" long barrel. This was the style gun carried by the likes of Jesse James, Pat Garret, Bat Masterson, and nearly all the famous gunslingers. Many years later, as Hollywood popularized the "Old West" it was seen time and time again in the hands of famous stars such as John Wayne and Clint Eastwood. Frequently strapped to his side or tucked into his waistband and loaded for any emergency, but now nestled into its holster in his bag, it was both a source of comfort to him and a serious probability of an accident waiting to happen. Since by this time he was expert in the use and care of his "Peacemaker", as this particular weapon was known, he most likely kept only five bullets loaded. This six-shooter, like all single action revolvers, had to be cocked by pulling the hammer back. When the gun was uncocked, the hammer would be in physical contact with the chamber beneath it. If that chamber were loaded, then a sudden, sharp blow to the hammer would cause the round to fire. Such a blow could be the result of dropping the gun, tripping and falling down, or a variety of other mishaps. He had heard of some bad injuries and damage caused when some idiot had failed to pay attention to this safety precaution. So there was little doubt that he kept the chamber under the hammer empty of ammunition.

There is no detailed record of Floyd's slow journey north by what must have seemed to him to be an endless progression of freight trains. He probably jumped off trains when he was hungry or not sure of his location, figured out which newly arriving freight most likely would get him closer to his destination, then toss his bag and himself aboard his new habitat. When he needed a little extra money to buy a hot meal or even a sandwich at one of the depots along the route, he would most likely sit near the ticket window strumming his banjo. The few coins tossed into his hat by appreciative travelers were all he would need until the next stop, wherever that might be. He probably learned very early in his journey how to avoid the eye of the railroad "bulls" or police officers whose job it was to prevent hobos from hitching free rides on their employer's property. There's little doubt that he also learned that many of these bulls wouldn't bother you if you didn't look too wild or stupid.

Since this method of transportation was potentially hazardous and definitely unreliable, to say nothing of uncomfortable, it is possible to conjure at least a part of this adventure as having contained an episode such as what follows.

It was day three of Floyd's journey from Lampasas, Texas to Fargo, North Dakota. Another day when the dry, dusty heat could almost be tasted and his bones shaken like a gambler's dice in a cup by the constant lurching and clattering of the freight train as it labored north. The thought that maybe this wasn't such a good idea after all was beginning to haunt his short dreams. Would he really be able to earn the kind of pay that would make this torture worthwhile?

As the long string of boxcars slowly ground to a halt at another strange location, it was time to again figure out if he should stay put, or get off and try to find a train that might, somehow get him to Fargo sooner. At least the car he was in offered a little bit of comfort since he had plenty of room to spread out his bedroll. Also, so far he had not been bothered by any other "passengers" and had the entire empty boxcar to himself. While he was evaluating whether or not to get off, a filthy old bag came tumbling in right next to him through the partially open door next to where he was sitting. Then, crashing about, cursing and smelling vile, in rolled a man even filthier than the bag he had just thrown in. With dirty, stringy hair down to his shoulders and an unkempt beard with what looked like most of last week's food stuck in it, he was not someone Floyd would have chosen to ride along with. It was impossible to tell his age. He didn't even seem to notice that there was already somebody in this particular boxcar, or if he did notice, he really didn't give a damn.

Floyd was just about to get off the train, figuring that the stench from his new companion would soon be too much to take, when with a sudden banging lurch and surprising acceleration, the doggone car was moving forward again. He settled back, resigned to simply ride along peaceably until the next stop, and then get off and put some distance between himself and this stranger.

After a few minutes of silence, the new arrival looked him square in the eye and in a threatening, gravely voice said,

"What you carryin' in that sack, boy?"

"Just my stuff", came out in a strangely high-pitched voice that made Floyd wonder if it was really his own voice that he heard.

"Where y'all headed?" said the stranger in a way that was more a challenge than a question.

"North," Came the quick reply.

"That's a mighty fine lookin' sack. Betcha some real good stuff could be in there," replied the strange-looking character in a voice that was a raspy whisper.

Floyd was now believing that this guy sitting on the floor across from him with his back against the wall was surely intent on robbing him of the few dollars he had. He had never actually encountered anyone before now who made him the least bit nervous about being robbed or beat up. His thoughts quickly went to his six-shooter, which was peacefully tucked away in the bottom of his bag, under the banjo. He had never shot a person, or even considered the possibility of such a horrible deed. He was pretty sure that he would never be able to pull the trigger on someone, especially at point blank range, face-to-face. What an awful problem! As he was trying to figure out how he could easily get his peacemaker in his hands to defend himself in case this nut really was a threat, the man reached out his right hand and announced,

"My name's Willy. I been ridin' the rails longer than I care to remember. Proly since before you was born. What's your name fella?"

Floyd shook the hand in front of his face and replied, "Floyd. - - Floyd Walser. From Lampasas, Texas."

Willy stretched back, shook off a cloud of dust from his hat and said,

"This your first time travellin' courtesy of the railways? You look too young to have been at this game for long. How old are ya, anyways?"

Feeling somehow less threatened, but not understanding just why, Floyd opened up a bit and said,

"Yep, this sure is a new way to git around for me. I'm headin' for the wheat fields of North Dakota for some work to try to make some good money for my family back home. I just turned 21 and I figure it's time I really earned my keep. Where' you headin'?"

"Oh I'll be heading west in a couple more stops, to see my old Ma. She been sick, I think. I'll pick up some jobs in towns along the way; proly get me some hot meals from the good folk I meet in the jungle."

Becoming more interested in this strange person and quickly growing less concerned about being threatened, Floyd said,

"Jungle? What jungle are you talking about?"

Willy let out a hearty laugh, which brought on a fit of coughing, which in turn caused another cloud of dust to rise. When the coughing seemed to have stopped, Willy explained,

"There's a whole lot of stuff we side-door Pullman experts say. We say "Jungle" when we mean hobo camps around the outskirts of towns next to train stops. We stay there as long as we need to. I'll tell ya, there's some of the best folks I've ever had the privilege of spendin' time with in them jungles. Some of them "Knights of the Road" as we like to call ourselves, will share an extra bed roll, or split a cup of coffee, or let you use their razor - - whatever. How many folks you know do that? I've been on some boxcars with as many as 30 other bo's. Damn good travelin' times."

By now, Floyd was comfortable with Willy and was more interested in learning some tricks of the trade than in figuring out if he would have to put a bullet between his eyes. He knew he would never be able to do that, so why dwell on it? Besides, this old guy was interesting to talk to. Floyd reached into his bag, groped around and said,

"I've got some hardtack in here. Want some? I wouldn't mind getting some tips on the best ways to get to where I'm goin' without gettin' myself killed."

"Sure, I'll take a piece of hardtack. Thanks. You know don't ya that it's damned dangerous to try to jump on a moving freight train? I've seen a fella once almost have his arms pulled out when he ran along side a moving car and he grabbed ahold of a railing to try to pull hisself up in. Damn fool was lucky. I heard later that he was in a horsepital for a long time, but he lived. There have been others who tried that idiot trick and wound up under the wheels of the train. You ain't seen nothin' uglier than the sight of some poor mother's boy what's been runned over by a bunch of steel wheels that don't even feel a thing."

Willy was beginning to enjoy tutoring his young student of the rails.

"You got to be real careful that at some stop, 'specially if you're sleepin', that the train crew don't lock the damn doors on ya. It's easy to freeze or die of thirst in cars that can be left at the side of the main track for weeks at a time. I used to carry my own railroad spike and wedge it into the door space just so's this couldn't happen. Now I'm just careful. Some of the bindle stiffs I've met have been guys kinda like you, goin' to work a harvest somewhere. Good guys, usually. But every once ter a while, you're gonna meet up with some mean bastard who'll cut ya as soon as look at ya. You'll learn pretty quick."

With that, Willy leaned back, pulled his hat down over his eyes and within a couple of minutes, was snoring loudly. "What a strange guy" thought Floyd. "It's too bad I was frightened by him. He's O.K. How will I know when I meet up with someone who isn't?"

After a couple of hours, during which time Floyd dropped off to sleep too, the train slowed, nearly stopped, then picked up speed again with a jolt waking both travelers.

As if no time had elapsed since Willy's last comments, he continued.

"Some train companies have real mean bulls. That's what we call the railroad police. You've got to watch out for them, or your trip could be over for quite a while. But if you get on the Union Pacific, now that's easy ta ride. You can ride anyplace on the train and the crews don't bother ya at all. But don't go thinkin' you can ride in just any old car anyplace. Stay the hell away from the tender right behind the engine. If you go through any tunnels you'll think you've gone to hell. The smoke blowin' back at ya will choke ya so's if you don't die, you'll wish you would. If that don't get ya, you'll proly go deaf from the noise bouncin' at your ears."

Willy slowly stood, straightening out his arms and legs and reminding Floyd of the rag doll his sister, Clara played with. When Willy had managed to finally stand up nearly straight, he tilted his hat back and added,

"And for the love of God, when you do get on a boxcar, be sure it's a empty. What might look to you like a collection of boxes you'd want to snuggle up against to sleep, can shift and fall on a person. Squash ya flat."

The train now slowed and this time came to a full stop. Willy reached into his bindle and brought out a tattered old paper. He handed it to Floyd and said,

"Here, kid. This'll help ya find your way around some of the stops between here and Fargo. It shows some of the rail lines and their stations. It's a little out of date, but it could be useful. It shore was for me - - for a long time. I think I got the damn thing memorized by now. You may as well have it."

With that, he stood up, stretched to work out some kinks, reached over and gave Floyd a big bear hug. "Good luck, kid." He was out of the boxcar and moving away before Floyd even had a chance to thank him.

CHAPTER 6

RICHIE IN THE LATE 1920s and EARLY 1930s

Richie continued his innate style of exploring just about everything that caught his interest. And he was interested in so many things. But the fact that he was a good, strong and dependable worker was of real value to his small family. In the 1920s in the U.S. and around the world, there was a rapid increase in industrialization. This in turn fueled growth in the economy and things really did seem to be "roaring". By the time Richie was about 18, in 1928 he and his pals not only found jobs that paid reasonably well for guys without much formal education, they also were able to find fun things to do in their spare time. Of course one of the fun things was centered on the latest auto to be acquired. Usually it was one of the older fellows who managed to come up with a "new" car. Whenever one of the young men in Richie's gang did show up with something new to them, they would all check it out from stem to stern and took great pleasure in tooling around the neighborhood in it.

By the time Richie had turned 19, although the economy was still going strong, things were about to change dramatically. Wages had increased along with consumer spending, and stock prices were rising. Although no one in Richie's family or circle of friends was in any way able to invest in the stock market, since they were really just getting by, this boom period did influence those with money to spend. Billions of dollars were invested in the stock market with many people speculating on rising stock prices. A large number of "ordinary" citizens felt that there would be no problem with buying on margin. What those folks would do was to buy stock on credit with confidence that its value would only rise. They would put a down payment on the stock with the expectation that in a few months they could pay the balance of the initial cost and receive a sizable profit as well. The stock market was becoming in essence a speculative pyramid game, in which most of the money invested wasn't actually there. Some people, caught up in the race to make a killing, invested their life savings and/or mortgaged their homes and found other ways to cash in what had been safe investments to ride this crazy bandwagon.

It was truly fortunate that Richie and his family and friends were "unsophisticated" enough so that none of their hard-earned savings were dumped into the frenzy of the time. However, the stock market crash, which followed in October of 1929 had repercussions for everybody. By the time that all the turmoil had resulted in what was called the Great Depression, thousands of investors, many of whom were simple ordinary working folk, were destroyed; financially ruined. By the end of 1929, stock values had dropped by fifteen billion dollars. Many of the banks that had gone along with heavy speculating of their deposits were wiped out by falling prices. A "run" on the banking system ensued and factories and businesses also failed.

The impact of this financial disaster on Richie and hundreds of thousands like him was that jobs became very difficult to find and the whole sad economy was a mess. This was to be the case for pretty much the entire decade of the 1930s. But being young and high-spirited, Richie and his pals simply worked at whatever jobs they could find, helped a lot around their homes and continued to enjoy the excitement and adventure to be had in tinkering with and driving whatever autos became available.

The automotive industry had been going hog wild all through the '20s, with hundreds of innovative manufacturers all trying to cash in on the public's love affair with what had started at the turn of the century to be "horseless carriages". Now this was big business with advances in engineering and styling coming along rapidly. It was possible in the early 20s to actually buy a car by mail order, although regional dealerships were most often used. Richie loved everything about cars, especially the engines and transmissions. He spent hours disassembling and then rebuilding parts of these mechanical marvels that were sometimes available in junkyards. He soon learned how just about every part of an auto worked and even entertained the thought that he could build one of his own someday.

The humbling and nerve-wracking experience of getting his driver's license was something he never forgot and in later years would often tell me, and eventually his grandchildren about the traumatic episode. He was just 16 at the time and really had been driving his father's 1924 Durant coupe for quite a while. Most of the time he would keep it in the back yard and driveway area, but once in a while he'd take it for a spin around the block, shooting along Dow Street, turning left on Winthrop then left again on Cove Ave. 'til he got to Lake Ave., then left again on Dow and he'd be back in his yard. He wasn't too pleased with the hand brake on this car, but then he didn't have to stop until he got home, so why worry? Luigi needed his son to do many errands for him including going in and out of the markets in Boston to get provisions for his general store. Richie needed his license at the first opportunity.

In April 1926 a few weeks after his 16th birthday, Richie found himself in the driver's seat of this noisy four-cylinder machine prepared for his driver's test, with a mean-looking and short-tempered Registry inspector seated beside him. This was crucial. Vitally important. His dad needed him to officially operate this car. He must pass the test. To say that he was a bit nervous would have been completely missing the point. He was petrified that something - - anything - - would go wrong. He sat there with the engine not running waiting for the inspector to tell him what he wanted him to do. In response to the gruff question, "What's your name, kid?" he stammered a quick reply. "Rotelli - - Richard, uh, I mean Richard Rotelli." The response was, "Well dammit kid, which way is it? If you don't even know your own name, how in hell can you expect to get a driver's license?" Richie did his best to assure the red-faced man next to him that he did know his name, then sat there waiting for direction. Eventually he was told to "Start the damned car! Do you think I'm going to give you a license just because you're so smart? Let's go!" With trembling hands and his heart pounding in his chest, Richie started, then stalled the car. He immediately restarted it with a great grinding of gears and an exasperated expression on the face of the man next to him. With the car now chugging along the street, Richie was starting to relax just a little when he was told to speed it up a bit and turn onto the next street which curved steeply uphill. He was doing fine now. Suddenly, the order to "Stop!" was shouted at him causing him to jamb on his brakes and stall the car. He was told to restart his engine and proceed several yards further on the steep hill and then stop again. That darn hand brake! He had an awful time keeping the car from rolling back as he let out the clutch and operated the gas to go forward, but he managed it, somehow. But after he had to stop on what seemed to him to be the steepest hill he had ever seen, he knew he would not be able to keep the car from rolling back this time. Noticing a solid curbstone at the edge of the street, he smoothly rolled back, turning the steering wheel so that the car was crosswise on the street until his rear wheels were right against the curb. He then quickly and efficiently drove up the hill to where the street leveled out and executed a smooth three-point turn when directed to do so. Old Mr. Grump-face then told him to drive back to their starting point, handed him the all-important piece of paper and simply walked away. He had done it! No problem! He realized years later that the inspector must have been very much aware of how poor the brakes were on that car and really did him a favor to allow him to get his license based upon his ingenuity in overcoming what should have been a reason to keep the car off the streets until the brakes were fixed. And fix them he did.

By the time 1930 had rolled around, Richie was not only a very accomplished driver, he also was well acquainted with the inner workings of a surprising number of different automobiles. He always was particularly impressed with any car made by Walter P. Chrysler who had been president of Buick and then moved to Willys. He had started the Chrysler Corporation soon after acquiring Maxwell, and launched the DeSoto in 1928 to compete with Oldsmobile and Pontiac. Styled similarly to a Chrysler, it sold for $885. When De Soto introduced a straight eight in 1930 with a 9½-foot wheelbase, it was billed as "the world's cheapest 8-cylinder car". Of course, the "Dependable Dodge", which had in the early 1920s been produced at the rate of 1,000 cars a day and was second only to Ford, was one of Richie's favorites. His idol, Mr. Chrysler, bought out the Dodge Company in 1928 for $126 million.

Richie loved everything about all those cars and many others. He was in awe of the Marmon's improved 8-cylinder engine introduced in 1929, although the prices for new Marmons were way too steep for him. He really fell in love with the Cord L-29 introduced in November 1929. It had front-wheel drive, was rakish and beautiful and really ahead of its time. It had an advanced 8-cylinder engine that developed 125 horsepower. His experiences with this fine auto were mainly through magazine articles, since less than 5000 of this model of these wonderful cars were built, having been introduced just as the country was plunged into depression.

Perhaps most of Richie's puttering around and experimenting with all aspects of autos had come from the most popular of them all - - Ford. Over 15 million Model Ts were made from 1909 to 1927, making it the best-selling car ever. (At least until the VW Beetle came along years later in 1949.) One could buy a Model T Roadster in 1925 for the sum of $260. This may have been one reason why the Depression never fazed Ford, managing to sell 4.5 million cars in four years and outselling Chevrolet (another of Richie's favorites) by nearly 2 to 1.

Another auto that captured Richie's interest due to its engineering excellence and innovations was the air-cooled Franklin. The fact that the famous aviator, Charles Lindberg owned this car made it all the more appealing to the young auto enthusiast. Richie learned that in 1915, a demonstration of the efficiency of the air cooling system was conducted. Mr. Franklin himself had driven one of his cars from Walla Walla, Washington to San Francisco in low gear without its overheating.

Perhaps his favorite car of that time, however was the Reo, which by then had been in production in various forms for nearly 25 years. 29,000 of them were sold in 1928 with sporty models and such appealing names as the Wolverine and the Flying Cloud. He was astounded by what Reo, who had pioneered in the development of what was called "syncromesh", later introduced in the 1933 model. It was a two-speed automatic transmission!

One of Richie's friends had made the observation that there seemed to be cars for every letter of the alphabet. As far as Richie could tell, this was nearly correct. Except for a few foreign cars or perhaps one or two that had never amounted to anything, the only letters of the alphabet that were not the first letter in an auto manufacturer's name were the letters Q, X, Y, and Z. They figured that if any of them were ever to invent their own car some day in the future, it would have to start with one of those unused letters. As it turned out, nobody in his group ever had to worry about coming up with such a name.

In 1931 Richie and a few of his pals, usually including Mario (of iceboat fame) enjoyed spending summer evenings and occasional weekends driving around in their latest "hot rods" and trying to impress the girls in Framingham and surrounding towns. The guys must have thought they were pretty "cool" or whatever the phrase was for "debonair" at that time. Most of the girls probably thought they were show-offs, but enjoyed the free-spirited, fun-loving attitude that usually came along with the various autos and their "devil-may-care" drivers. Richie, by all accounts, was one of the most spirited and exuberant of the bunch. He confided to me many years after the fact, well after I was out of my teen years, that one of the things he thought was a lot of fun, was

Richie in 1931 strikes a dashing pose to impress Lena.

Richie's pal, Mario (of ice-boat fame) about 1930.

Richie and his girl, Lena in 1931.

to have his open-top car full of kids, drive it into a field, and with it still running, get out and run alongside. He would pretend that he couldn't get back in and at the last moment he would hop up on the running board on the driver's side and get back behind the controls. He swore that he never let the car go too fast and always had everything well planned out. But he would scare the daylights out of the female passengers, who most likely thought the crazy rides with Richie were a hoot.

One shy and cute young girl he met on one of his frequent joy rides with his pals really caught his attention more than any of the others had. She lived in the neighboring town of Natick and seemed somehow particularly angelic and special. It took him a couple of days to get the nerve to actually speak to her alone and find out her name and where she lived. She was Lena Ortenzi, and had just turned 16 years of age that July. She was not allowed to be out very late and was never out without several of her friends, most of whom were almost as shy as she was. Once Richie had discovered where her house was, he would drive directly there and pretend to be casually cruising around the neighborhood. On his lucky excursions, he would find her somewhere nearby and nonchalantly, as if it were unplanned, coast right up near her and stop to chat. She always seemed embarrassed by the attention he paid her, but secretly thought he was cute.

Thinking he had to do something dramatic to really get her attention, Richie installed what he called a "cut-out" into the exhaust pipe of his car. With this ludicrous contraption built in, the muffler, which was a far cry from really silencing the engine, could be by-passed completely. This was advertised as a way to maximize the power of a car. Fire engines allegedly were so equipped and they sure as heck were noisy, but got to a fire pretty fast. The way Richie's cutout worked required a heroic kick down on a lever he installed sticking up through the floorboards of the car. This bypassed the muffler and made the car sound unbelievably loud and powerful. He knew it was probably illegal to operate such a peace-disturbing noisemaker. But it surely would get attention. He knew that the bridge over the railroad tracks just a few houses from where Lena lived had high metal walls on both sides of the road. He figured that the extra reverberations caused by those perfectly placed walls would only enhance the effect he was going for.

Of course he experimented with this wacky device and impressed the guys with the sound, so he knew it worked just fine. However, he was careful to use it rarely, and always away from anybody who knew him. When he actually drove his cutout-equipped car to Natick and approached the bridge to where his favorite girl should be if she were home, he had second thoughts about actually using it. What if it really scared her and turned her off to him forever? Or what if her parents should be home then and figured he was a blooming idiot? With his good friend Mario at his side egging him on to, "Blast it, Richie. Blast it!", - - he did it. He really didn't notice the two young girls walking peacefully along the side of the road in the middle of the bridge when he kicked the cutout's lever and stepped on the gas pedal. Amplified by the metal walls on the bridge, the roar was an explosion; a terrifying sound that ricocheted back and forth and seemed to be coming from everywhere at once. The poor kids who had been walking along, minding their own business, jumped into the air, screaming and hugging each other, probably thinking the end of the world had come. Richie (and Mario) felt terrible about causing such fright in the innocent girls. He disengaged the cutout, turned the car around and drove straight back home where the next day he removed the stupid thing from the exhaust system of his otherwise pretty nice car.

Richie's infatuation with Lena continued unabated. He discovered that the name, Lena was short for Angelina, which in itself was the diminutive of her "real" name of Angela, which no one ever called her. Her parents, Domenic and Immacolata thought the world of him. They liked the fact that his parents were hard-working, honest Italian immigrants with backgrounds and interests similar to their own. They also saw that he was a bright, well mannered and easy to talk to young man who no doubt had a good future ahead.

Domenico Ortenzi had grown up in the town of Paganico Sabina, in the province of Rieti just northeast of Rome, Italy. Living and working conditions in his home area were poor at best and he dreamed of a new life in America. He set sail for the United States from the port of Naples, on the ship Montevideo, one of over 1200 passengers, arriving at Ellis Island on April 11, 1907 at the age of 25.

His first work in the new country was in a coal mine in Pennsylvania. He hated the oppressive working conditions and after a cave-in that claimed several of his companions, he left that job for good. After settling in the community of Natick, Massachusetts, his dashing good looks and charm had made him a very attractive bachelor, thought of by the local unmarried young women as quite a catch. Immacolata Paganuzzi was a teen-age worker in rice fields near Parma, Italy and was from a large, poor family. She sold her beautiful long hair to help raise enough money to book steerage passage to the New World and also wound up in Natick. With no skills in the English language and without a real job, it was she who caught the eye of this prize catch.

Lena had two brothers; Nick was about two years older, and Joe, who seemed to be her mother's favorite, was a couple of years younger than she. Her kid sister, Rose was about 7 when Richie first showed up and it was very often Lena's responsibility to look after her while her mother worked at the Natick Box and Board Company nearby, where her father also labored. Richie got along well with both Nick and Joe, but little Rose, who was always called "Rosie", really thought he was something special. Whenever she had a loose baby tooth, he was the only one she would allow to help pull it out. Rosie was also assigned the role of "chaperone" and often went out for rides around town in the evenings with her sister and her beau. As much as the senior Ortenzi's were happy with Richie dating their daughter, they still felt that having a little pest along on their rides wasn't such a bad idea.

Eventually, to show Lena how much he cared about her, Richie built a beautiful jewelry box for her. He fashioned it from handsomely grained cherry wood and did an exceptional job in all respects. The joints and corners were worthy of a highly skilled cabinet-maker. The hinged top fit perfectly and the lift-out partitioned shelf inside was lined with a silky and puffy material. It had a lock and key and he decorated the top and front side with very nicely done artwork in what appears to be black ink, but giving the illusion of inlay. The design on the cover both impressed and embarrassed Lena. Everyone was quite taken with the fanciful scroll that ran from one corner to another and contained her name and the date, "1932". The keyhole on the front side of the box was centered in a triangle with his initials; "RR". One corner of the cover was illustrated with a silhouette of a man on an old-fashioned large-wheeled bicycle tipping his hat to his lady. The other corner contained the silhouette that caused Lena's embarrassment. It showed a stork in front of a full moon with a "special package" dangling from its bill flying over a sleepy little house. Her reaction to that artwork was along the lines of, "My goodness! What does he have in mind?"

CHAPTER 7

THE WHEAT FIELDS OF FARGO, NORTH DAKOTA
1909

After what must have seemed to Floyd to be "forever" on the uncomfortable freight trains, he arrived in his destination city of Fargo. It was mid summer with the wheat fields nearly ready for the harvest when he found himself in this strange location surrounded by unfamiliar faces but ready to dig right in and be the kind of worker that the boss would give lots of overtime work to. He must have had a good idea of many of the procedures to be used in harvesting the wheat, but was ready to learn whatever tricks would make him extra valuable and dependable. There is no record of just what really happened over the next few days and weeks, but a very likely scenario could have been as follows.

Floyd knew that the wheat fields here in Fargo covered a large area, but he was still surprised to see that no matter in which direction he looked, just about all he could see was this lovely grain softly waving in the summer sun. Here and there were set up tents for the many workers, most of them migrants, like himself. Many of them had been in this area since early May and had done the plowing of the land followed by sowing the seed. Now that it was the middle of August, it would soon be time to do the heavy work of cutting, gathering, and threshing this important product.

Once he had been shown to his cot in one of the worker's tents, told where the nearest outhouse was, and signed the simple forms provided by the field boss, he was eager to begin. A muscular and well tanned young fellow who seemed to be at least ten or more years older than Floyd ambled over to where he was standing. Without fanfare of any kind or even so much as a "Hello", he began to explain that Floyd was assigned to him. How fast he picked up all that was about to be explained would determine what jobs he might be trusted to do. It was also hinted that if Floyd didn't meet this character's standards, he would be told to look for work elsewhere. After a short period of uneasy silence between them, Floyd introduced himself and made it very plain that not only was he strong and fit, but he was motivated to be the best damn wheat field worker they ever saw. And as an added bonus, he was a helluva good cowboy and could not only ride any horse; he could tame a wild one if the need should arise. This display of courage and determination made a hit with the "boss" who for the first time since approaching Floyd, smiled, stuck out his hand and said that his name was Jed.

"Well Floyd", said Jed, "We've got enough damned wheat growing around here to keep you and a hell of a bunch of other men working plenty hard. You ever use a scythe? We keep ours razor sharp. Old Zeke over there, that's one'a his jobs, to keep a edge on them scythes."

Floyd started to reply that he had indeed used a scythe back in Winchester, but Jed cut him off saying,

"Don't matter. I'm gonna show you how I want it done. Tomorrow we'll start working you at that. The wheat ain't quite ready to be harvested just yet, but I 'spect it will be in a few more days. You look like a bright kid and I've got a hunch you're gonna be good at this game.

"I been at this business long enough to know how much we depend on good ol' Mother Nature, or as I've heard some say, "The Gods of the Wheat Fields." You see how the plants are turning yellow? That means they're near ready. Got to keep an eye on the fields. Want to start the harvest after the kernels have fully dried, but don't want to wait no longer than we got to. Be just our damned luck that a big wind, rain, hail or some dam thing comes to wreck it all."

Over the next few days Floyd learned more than he ever expected to learn about the whole business of growing and harvesting wheat, and even thought that maybe he could see himself someday as an owner (a very rich one of course) of hundreds of acres of wheat. But he realized that first he would have to keep hard at work and let his muscles build and strengthen to the point where he could get a good night's sleep without feeling as if he had fallen off a freight train.

Occasionally, Jed would get Floyd to ride horseback over to one of the other wheat fields to deliver or retrieve messages and sometimes to bring a piece of equipment that needed fixing. Having a spirited horse under him again was just the thing to bolster Floyd's spirits. He would often ride a lot faster than was really necessary and would then take a longer route back, just to enjoy the thrill of the ride. He always would see to it that the horse was properly groomed and put away well cared for.

He was surprised at how good the food tasted every day. A "hard-as-nails" looking old lady named Sarah did all the cooking for the whole crew of workers who shared the tents. She managed to cook up some delicious meals: big hearty breakfasts and amazing suppers, at her cook car. She had what was basically a well equipped little kitchen resembling a small house set up on a wagon. She had this pulled right in with the small community of tents and did nothing else but cook and clean up all day. When the whole work party moved between fields to process new areas, she'd have a horse team hitched up and haul her cook car to the new location and set it up again in close proximity to the group of tents. He thought, "If she wasn't so darned old and ugly, I'd ask her to marry me, just so I could have such great food all the time. But then again, maybe sawdust would taste good after the way I've been working."

Floyd rapidly became very proficient at the proper use of the scythe. It was a lot harder than it looked to do this job in a way that would make Jed even a little bit pleased with the result. By not just swinging the scythe, but by simultaneously moving it forward through the wheat, he made it look effortless, even if it wasn't. One of his tricks was that he kept a small whetstone in his back pocket and very frequently would hone the blade to the razor edge it needed. He was able to make great strides through the fields and soon picked up the nickname of "Floyd the Flyer".

Floyd soon learned a technique for tying the cut-down wheat into small bundles, about six inches thick and maybe three or four feet tall, which were called stooks. He thought that was a mighty strange word, "stook", and was told by someone that it was a bastardization of "stock" or maybe even "stack", but out here they just used the word without thinking much about it. The height of each bundle depended on how tall the wheat was before it was cut down. The process was known as "stooking". He learned to use the wheat plant itself to tie the bundle together. He would take a small handful of wheat, wrap the bottom end of the straw into a knot, and then wrap the wheat around the stook and tie the wheat end of the straw into another knot. After he had a few of these bundles made up he would stand them up leaning against each other where they would resemble armless scarecrows and could quickly be gathered up.

When enough groups of these stooks were standing in the newly cut wheat field, they would be gathered and brought in to where they were to be threshed. Floyd also learned to be one of the fastest at the manual threshing task. This looked like fun, but in fact was very tiring and was dangerous to any casual passersby.

Threshing was done with flails that reminded Floyd of something he had read about which seemed to him to have its origins in the Orient, except that these flails were much larger. Later, he would recall reading about a mean-looking weapon used back in feudal Japan. It was known as a nunchaku, and he pronounced it "none-chuck". The wheat threshing flails were king-sized versions of the old nunchaku and were made of two very straight willow branches each about four feet long and about an inch and a half thick. They were connected with a short length of rawhide through holes drilled through their ends. He and other workers would gather up the stooks, and toss them onto a large canvas tarp which was spread on soft ground. Then using these flails, they would beat the daylights out of the bundles of wheat. The technique, which was not easy to master, involved kneeling on the ground along side of the tarp with one of the willow branches and its rawhide connection lying in the bundle of spread-out wheat. The end of the other branch was grasped firmly in both hands, then raised overhead and swung down with a vengeance. This was rapidly repeated until the person doing this chore was ready to collapse. After a short rest, the flailing would continue until the supervisor said it was good enough.

After they had beat most of the wheat out of the straw, they had to pick up the straw and move it off to the side. More than once, some over-eager flailer just had to get in one more whack when someone else was reaching in to start separating out the straw. To prevent this, it was normal procedure for only one person at a time to flail at a tarp full of wheat. They had to be careful not to throw away any heads of wheat while separating out the straw. Floyd came up with a simple coarse sieve to help to get the straw out of the wheat. He was surprised that no one had the brains to have thought of it before, but they all thought he was a genius for thinking it up. He found that there always were a lot of wheat heads that had to go back on the threshing floor and be beat out with the next stook.

Unless a person was in awfully good shape, a few days of this kind of work would be enough to make them want to head for the nearest shade and hide for a day or two. But, usually it seemed that there was no end to the doggone stooks. Then, once a lot of threshing by flailing was done, the next step was to separate the wheat from the chaff. (The chaff is the fibrous outer shell that surrounds each kernel of wheat on the head.) This part of the job seemed even more primitive than the cutting and threshing and, in fact was basically the technique people had been using for thousands of years. It seemed as though the wind in this part of the world never stopped and that free source of power was put to good use now. Handfuls of threshed wheat with chaff were tossed up into the air over a clean tarp. Since the wheat is a lot heavier than the chaff, it falls to the ground first while the chaff is (hopefully) blown away. This process was repeated over and over until the wheat was clean enough.

The owner of the wheat fields where Floyd was laboring was aware that some much more modern equipment was beginning to be put into use by his competitors. He had seen a terrific little invention known as a binder, which would cut the wheat and put it into stooks all by itself. What a great labor saving device that was. He had heard about but had not seen the latest threshing machine into which the stooks were tossed. He heard that this machine always left a huge pile of straw on one side of it and did a great job of threshing. However, he lacked the capital resources to invest in these new machines. He preferred to pay higher wages to a few strong young workers who could do it all and who didn't mind working extra shifts for overtime pay. This suited Floyd just fine, although in his mind he would surely have all the latest machines in his fields if he were ever to become a force in this industry.

The August weather was perfect when he had first arrived on the scene, but now it was beginning to become unbearably hot, cooling off only in the evenings. It was becoming necessary to take more frequent rest breaks and to drink plenty of water. This interfered with Floyd's plan to get a lot done and work extra shifts for the money he could make. In his first two weeks on the job he had sent nearly all of his pay home to his mother by way of Western Union. He wanted and needed to keep this pace. He was really getting the hang of this whole business and, although he surely didn't want to work like this every summer, he felt strong enough and confident enough to not give in to the sweltering heat.

Friday, August 27, 1909 promised to be brutally hot. Floyd was a bit more tired than he cared to admit, but he was in the field shortly after breakfast at sunup. There was no doubt that this was going to be a real scorcher. The high humidity in the morning made it feel even worse, but he figured to pretty much ignore it and do his jobs.

Most of the other workers had really slowed down the previous day and he expected that a lot of the work was going to fall on him today. He was careful to wear light colored, loose fitting clothes with a wide brimmed cowboy hat. He was perspiring heavily by 8:00 AM and stopped to drink a little water from his canteen. He tried his best to ignore the weather, but found that by 10:00 he was wishing that he could call it a day like so many others seemed to be doing. He thought that the boss would really be impressed and would give him a good size bonus if he kept at it.

By noontime, with the temperature in the blazing sun up to 92 degrees and the relative humidity nearly 90%, he noticed that he wasn't sweating anymore. This really surprised him, but he thought that maybe he was getting tougher. When Jed showed up with a horse to ask Floyd to ride an important message to the main boss, he took one look and said, "Hey there Floyd, you look awful! Your face is all red. Your eyes don't look right - - they're too small! And, my God boy, you stink! Let's get you to some shade. You've done enough work for today."

"Aw hell, I'm OK", came out as "Ooww hall ahh oh hay"

With that, Floyd took the package to be delivered, and clumsily swung himself up onto the horse who by now was very used to his every mannerism. He intended to ride the package containing the message to the other boss and thought the wind might cool him off. He suddenly saw his father standing right in front of the horse. "Pa. What are you doin' here?" The apparition vanished as suddenly as it appeared. He thought he could hear Jed talking to him, but his voice was coming from far away, even though he was right next to him. When Floyd kicked his heels back, the horse reluctantly began to trot forward, but was confused about the way the rider was holding the reins and was unsure about what was expected of him.

Floyd began to feel nauseated and was seeing strange visions, when the poor horse reared back causing Floyd to crash to the ground in a heap, with everything going black.

Jed hollered for help, recognizing the signs of heat stroke and worried that the fall from the horse, who was now galloping riderless away, could have done even more damage to an already seriously sick man.

Floyd, still unconscious, was carried into the shade of the nearest tent. Nobody knew just what to do. Several men gathered around, some with flasks of cold water to try to give to the inert form lying in front of them. "Reckon he's dead", said one of them. "Shore looks dead ta me" was the verdict from a few others.

Floyd could hear these idiots! He could actually hear them pronouncing him dead! His anger rose inside him and he tried to shout out that he was not dead - - that he just couldn't move any part of him! They covered him with a sheet not knowing what else to do for a corpse. Sarah left her cook car and came running to where Floyd was stretched out. She lifted the sheet from his face and began to shudder with tears streaming down her face. "He cain't be dead! He's just a kid. He looks like my youngest. Who said he's dead? Where's the doctor?" came tumbling out between sobs. She put her face down close to his and suddenly jumped straight back. "He's alive! I can feel his breath coming out his nose! Get the doctor! Now!"

Floyd, hearing Sarah's exclamations felt as if a great weight was lifted from his chest. He worked as hard as he could to force his eyes open, finally succeeding.

Even with proper medical attention soon provided by the doctor who reached Floyd's side in a matter of minutes, there was only a 50-50 chance that he would survive the night. The severe spinal injury caused by being thrown from the horse combined with the ravages of heat stroke did not make for an optimistic prognosis. The doctor saw to it that everything was done to reduce Floyd's core temperature and to get fluids into him as soon as he was able to open his mouth. He was stripped and sponged with cool water, then lowered into baths of progressively cooler water. Eventually, he was brought to the local hospital by wagon and after a few hours was alert and coherent, but still very weak.

A Western Union telegram was sent to Floyd's mother back in Lampasas informing her of her son's brush with death due to heat stroke and a fall from his horse. She was advised to have someone come to bring him home, since it would be a long time before he would be well enough to work. The main harvesting activity was nearly over and there may not be any work for him by the time he was well.

Shortly after this telegram was received, Benny Haden was on a passenger train headed for Fargo to bring his brother home. He thought it ironic that the only way he could afford the luxury of taking a train over that distance was to use up some of the money that Floyd had practically killed himself to earn.

While recovering in the hospital from the effects of what was believed to be heat stroke and telling himself that working so long in such heat was really just plain stupid, Floyd began to lose the feeling in his legs. Try as he might, he was unable to move them. Soon his arms began showing signs of paralysis, with the left arm totally immobile in a short time. His condition worsened rapidly with headache, fever, and sore throat. He was having trouble swallowing. The alarmed nurses called for the doctors. A quick examination of their patient revealed to the medical staff that they were dealing with something far more sinister than a recovery from heat exhaustion. There was no doubt that Floyd was infected with paralytic poliomyelitis, or simply polio.

This was a devastating turn of events for what had just days ago been a man in his youthful prime. "Polio". Just the mention of its name, sometimes called "infantile paralysis" was cause for serious action. It was not well understood at that time how the disease was spread, nor was there any effective treatment for it. Persons with polio were quarantined or otherwise prevented from coming into contact with others, since it was believed that the disease was spread by contact. Epidemics were feared. From what is now known it is likely that he was exposed to the virus at some time while living at the tent quarters in the wheat fields.

Years later it was understood that poliovirus can be isolated from human feces and sewage. In areas where raw sewage enters a watershed without treatment, polio can be found in rivers, lakes, and streams. The virus can enter a susceptible person's digestive tract by drinking water from one of these sources. After replicating in the person's intestines and bloodstream, it can enter the central nervous system. This often leads to paralysis of one or more limbs, or even death.

A second telegram was sent to Floyd's mother informing her of the terrible news that her son had developed full-blown polio and that the prognosis was not good. His brother, Ben, was already most of the way to the hospital when this second telegram was delivered. He was not prepared for the sight that greeted him when he arrived at his brother's side. Curled under blankets with his legs drawn up and unable to move on his own, he bore no resemblance to the vital young man who just a short while ago set out to earn a little more money for the family. Talking was difficult for Floyd, but Ben felt paralyzed himself, unable to accept what he was seeing. He wanted to hug his brother, to comfort him and reassure him that he'd be up and about in no time. The nurses had instructed him however not to get too close and certainly not touch the patient. Ben was told that if he had any direct contact with Floyd, he too would be confined to the area in quarantine.

In about another week, Floyd had recovered enough to be sent home even though he was nearly totally paralyzed. The hospital was anxious for him to be out of there, but also was obliged to warn any and all persons who may come in contact with him of their belief that he represented a high risk of transmitting polio to others. Feeling terribly depressed and at a loss as to how he could possibly live the rest of his life with no more animation than a bundle of rags, he wanted to ask Ben to take his six-shooter and put him out of his misery. He knew however that it would be terribly unfair to ask his brother to do such a thing and he never actually voiced this wish.

He convinced himself that he would recover and that he would walk and ride horses again and continue with the life he was just maturing into. It was probably his strong feelings of self-reliance and his stubborn refusal to give in to this unwelcome setback that allowed his system to fight back. Whether or not it was true, he actually felt in a few days that he was regaining a bit of movement, especially in his right side and arm. He was now looking forward to returning to Lampasas where he believed that he would have his best chance of recovery. He remembered the mineral springs back there and the miraculous healing that he had heard about but never paid that much attention to before.

Feeling like the lepers of biblical times, sort of "unclean" and kept away from the rest of the populace, Floyd was loaded onto one of the baggage cars of a long train. It was completely up to Ben to make all the arrangements with the railroad lines, pay the fare for the two of them to ride as human baggage, and to tend to all his brother's needs. Ben was instructed by the doctors to avoid direct contact with "the patient", being especially careful in handling his waste products. He was given surgical gloves and masks to help in that regard as well as a letter describing Floyd's condition. He was to show this letter to whatever doctor he might find if he should need to get help on the way home. He was also told that they had wired the officials in the town of Lampasas with the facts, as they understood them so that the good people of that town could decide for themselves what to do to prevent an epidemic of polio in their community.

It was an agonizingly slow and uncomfortable ride home for the two young men. Although Floyd was feeling a little stronger and was perfectly lucid, his dreams frightened him.

Ben pretty much ignored all the advice he had been given about avoiding contact and did his best to see to it that Floyd was made as comfortable as possible and took in as much nourishment as he could manage to force into him. Floyd had never before appreciated the strength his older brother possessed, hardly ever having managed to have gotten the better of him at their spontaneous wrestling matches back home. But now, as Ben hoisted and shifted his dead weight around for him, he was thankful for this young powerhouse who seemed to never require sleep, or to ever lose his good-natured attitude about everything. Ben, who had developed an unusually strong upper torso as a result of working long, hard hours at building railroads, had no real physical problems with providing the lifting power, but found it completely unreal to be doing it. It felt like a bad dream and he prayed that he'd wake up to find that that's all it was - - a dream.

Often, during the otherwise quiet and forlorn hours in the train, Ben would fish out the banjo Floyd had brought along on his journey. With remarkable skill, he would entertain them both with some old tunes that brought back better, carefree days. Floyd would often be surprised at how what he used to think of as happy songs now would cause tears to roll down his cheeks.

CHAPTER 8

BACK IN LAMPASAS - - A BUDDING ARTIST
1909 - 1923

Eventually, the train lumbered into the station in Lampasas, Texas. As Ben began the task of unloading Floyd and his baggage, he was approached by a deputy sheriff who it seemed wanted to help with the unloading, but was hanging back a bit. The deputy told Ben that he was sorry, but he had orders to keep Floyd from returning to his home or to actually enter any part of the town. It was not yet clear whether or not Ben would be allowed to go home or have to stay with Floyd. A tent had been set up a short distance from the depot and this is where Floyd would have to stay until it could be determined just how contagious he might be. There were signs posted at this tent to warn people that a person with polio was living in it and to avoid direct contact. This must have angered both of them and made them feel uneasy at the sideways stares from the travelers and workers at the station. Floyd must have felt that all eyes were on him, but at the same time strangely felt almost invisible.

Soon, Floyd and his few possessions were set up in the tent, which was surprisingly roomy and, with a wooden floor and window flaps was not the worst place he had ever been in. But it was a big disappointment to have to stay there instead of being home, which was so close. Voices outside the tent, at first a jumble of conversations now were becoming clear. Explanations were being given as to the rules that must be followed for those few persons who would be allowed to enter the tent. As he lay immobile on his cot, Floyd suddenly heard his mother's voice and his half-brother, Tom Ivy arguing with the officials. When the entry flap was pushed open and his mother came in, Floyd wanted desperately to get up and run to greet her - - but he could not move more than his right arm in a half-hearted wave of greeting, which simultaneously warned her to not get too close. "Hello, mamma. It's awful good to see you. Guess I got myself into a bit of a fix. But don't you worry none, I'll be up and around before you know it." Molly, crying softly, dropped to her knees next to her son and hugged him, assuring him that all will be O.K. He was nearly home now.

For the next six weeks, Floyd's mother would visit him every day in his special tent, bringing him his meals and fussing over him. She would bring him fresh clothes and take soiled items home to launder on a regular basis. She had the understanding from the officials involved that only she, and no others would be allowed to make these visits and to handle his belongings and to bathe him. She was told that it was highly likely that she was being exposed to the polio virus and that it was possible that she might contract the disease herself. It was also likely that whomever she was in direct contact with was at risk. This naturally included the rest of her children at home. She was told that if she wanted to take these chances of infecting herself or her family, that was her business. But under no circumstances would she be permitted to go anywhere else in the town of Lampasas. She was told that the sheriff and his deputies were carefully monitoring her comings and goings, and if she violated the rules she would be put in jail. This was not something the kindly sheriff wanted to have to do, but an epidemic of this disease must be prevented at all costs. The residents of the town expected no less.

With regular visits during these six weeks from the one doctor in town with an understanding of Floyd's condition and some idea of how to treat it, it was becoming apparent that, with precautions he could be allowed to go home. No one who had been in contact with Floyd had any symptoms to worry about and he seemed to be making some progress even though the paralysis still ruled his legs and his left side. He needed assistance to get up to a sitting position after having been helped to lie down. Once he was sitting upright, he could move himself slightly on his cot with considerable effort by pushing with his right hand. He tired quickly and had no interest in food. But the anxious doctor could see no valid reason to continue to require that he be held there in quarantine.

So, sometime in mid-October, 1909 Floyd Niles Walser was returned to his home. Ben and Tom brought the family wagon with a comfortable mattress and blankets carefully placed inside. They gingerly lifted him from his cot and carried him to his nest in the wagon. Once he was settled, with a half smile, half frown on his face, they placed his belongings around him and worked the horse carefully to try to give him the smoothest ride they could manage over the dirt roads. Shortly, the wagon pulled into the front yard he had left three months and a lifetime ago.

His sisters Erie and Lena had tears streaming down their faces when he came into their sight, even though they had promised themselves that they wouldn't cry when they saw him. His brother Tansey, who was almost 13 years old tried to pretend that nothing was wrong, but knew right away that just wasn't going to work. He presented Floyd with an eagle he had carved for him and worried that it really wasn't very good. Floyd told him it was fine and was a great present. Little nine-year-old Clara gave her brother a big hug and announced to him that she would be seeing to his every need. She promised to read to him every day and would play games with him and sing him her favorite songs.

Floyd's young sister-in-law, Viola (Ben's wife) wanted to welcome him home, but was very concerned about keeping her little 4 year-old old Daniel and baby Agnes protected from any possible contact with the horrible polio virus, so with a tear-stained face, she kept her distance. Ben and Tom had arranged his room for him in a way that they thought would be comfortable for him. They were the ones whose jobs it would be to lift Floyd in and out of bed, to help with his bedpan needs, to bathe him and to help him into a chair where he could sit for his meals and to pass the day. A wheelchair was borrowed and he was often placed into it so he could be wheeled outdoors.

Floyd was determined to help himself as much as he possibly could. It grated on him that he was such a burden to his whole family. He must have experienced overwhelming sadness at his plight, realizing that the paralysis was not going to go away and that for the rest of his life he would be dependent on others for even basic needs. How could he adapt? How could he earn money to pay for at least part of his needs? What could he do with only his right arm and hand functional, and those only to a limited degree? When his brothers propped him up into a sitting position and brought him something to read, he had to wait for them to turn the pages for him. It would be understandable if he had sunken into a deep pit of despair, but with innate courage and determination, and with the support of all those around him, he managed to keep his spirits up, at least for a little while.

Ben and Tom took turns bringing Floyd to the famous mineral springs that were only a few miles away. There had been reports of some remarkable healing having occurred for a few of the visitors to these springs. It was definitely worth a few visits. However, although the waters were soothing to his body, and he wanted to believe that he was getting some real benefit from the springs, not much changed. He exercised his right arm and hand constantly. His brothers helped him to work his legs and his left arm in attempts to keep them supple and prevent them from atrophying, but there simply was no life in them. Someone provided him with heavy metal braces that were clamped painfully to his legs. With one brother on either side of him supporting him plus the awful weight of those braces, he would try his best to walk. It was an impossible task, which was immediately given up, then tried again months later with no better results.

As the winter months rolled into the Texas plains and the skies seemed a constant sullen gray, Floyd's spirits sunk to a level from which he may have thought he would never return. He often thought of his six-shooter and how simple it would be to have an "accident" with it. Every time his thoughts went in that direction, he would get out of it by imagining what a messy job his poor family would have to clean up after such a cowardly act. He knew he'd never do it. As he sat, brooding alone in his room, he heard a soft knock at his door. It was Clara who had come for her daily visit. Frowning, she brought him a picture she had drawn. It was of a horse in a field standing under a tree. "I can't make my tree look like a real tree", she said. "And my horse looks more like a dog than a horse. I wish I knew how to draw." "Hand me your pad of paper and your pencil", drawled Floyd. With his right hand seemingly guided by some unseen agent, Floyd rapidly sketched a horse, and then added a tree in the background while Clara held the paper steady. "Wow!" she exclaimed, definitely impressed with this unexpected display of artistic ability. "How'd you know how to draw like that?" "Don't know. It just sort of was easy to do, but I don't think it's so good, really."

That evening, shortly after his 22nd birthday, Floyd thought seriously about studying art somewhere. Perhaps he could learn enough about drawing so that he could earn a few bucks to help pay for his keep. After scouring several magazines, he found an ad for a correspondence school of art that sounded very intriguing. But then he realized that he still would need many months of learning how to adapt to his paralysis and how to arrange himself within his room in order to make the job of caring for him, which now was a full-time task for his mother, as easy as possible. He tossed the correspondence school ad on the floor with other items he had lost interest in, and put the whole idea of this preposterous notion out of his mind. An artist! Indeed! He could not even sit up for long by himself. And when he was sitting, he couldn't do anything or move more than a few inches to one side or the other by pushing or pulling with his right arm. If he toppled over and happened to get his right arm pinned under him, then he would be stuck since there was no way he could move or use his left arm. He would have to shout for help and wait for someone to rescue him. He hated this useless body of his and could see no purpose in life ahead. He needed someone to help him with his bedpan two or three times a day, and to dress him. Someone was always there to get him settled in his bed for the night and to haul him out of it in the morning, often while he complained bitterly about the fact that they were hurting him, or that they weren't doing the job correctly. He would then apologize for being as he would call himself, "an old fart" and would try his best not to look sullen, if not actually happy while mumbling something about being "not worth a damn by a damn-and-a-half".

It was a long, slow process during which everyone in the Walser household would seem to age at an accelerated rate, for Floyd to gradually come to grips with the terrible blow that had been handed him.

After five years of adapting and learning how to function, he was finally able to accept his condition and had mastered the techniques of taking care of himself as much as possible. The strength in his right arm and hand had increased due in large part to constantly exercising this only part of him that he could move on his own. He was now smiling and outwardly appeared happy, but had yet to find any real meaning to his existence. Gradually, thoughts of learning about art and how to draw sketches began to come back to him. Soon, he was thinking about this all the time. He recalled the gray winter day back in 1910 when he sketched the horse and tree for little Clara. He asked his mother to get him some art supplies, mainly sketch paper and a few good pencils. A board with a clip to hold paper was provided for him to prop in his lap. He began sketching some of the objects that surrounded him in his room. When he would be brought outside he did his best to draw the trees, flowers, and animals that he could see from where he sat.

After a few weeks of working his way through reams of sketch paper and tossing out most of his efforts, he began to feel as though maybe he had some innate talent for drawing. Family members all made many favorable comments on whatever sketches of his that he failed to throw away. But, he figured these folks were not art critics and didn't know good work from mediocre. Not only that but they would most likely encourage anything he did that would get him out of himself. Still he must have thought that perhaps it was time to get some lessons somewhere. He wondered if perhaps he could locate a good correspondence school, remembering that a few years ago he had found an ad but had tossed it away. This time, when he found what appeared to be just what he was looking for, he wrote the school a short letter of introduction along with the modest fee they required for lesson number one. He made no mention of his handicap. This particular remote school was in Kalamazoo, Michigan and was operated by a person known as G. H. Lockwood.

In a few short days, he had received his first packet of material with information and instructions, which he promptly devoured. His first lesson (in pencil sketching) was completed and sent back within two days. He eagerly awaited the response and looked forward to whatever criticism they would send along with lesson two.

When, three weeks later, lavish praise was heaped on him with the receipt of lessons two, three and four all together, he assumed that this was a standard response, guaranteed to keep customers for the school. He had asked his family to pick up some art instruction books at the nearby library for him. He studied every page in these books, quickly absorbing the material and anxious to try his own hand at some of the techniques he read about. When he responded to the latest correspondence school lessons from Kalamazoo, he incorporated some of these techniques along with what the lesson had asked him to do. The response a few weeks later was more than flattering, leading him to believe that he did indeed have a natural talent for art. He was now thirsting for more art instruction in all the ways in which artists worked. He loved watercolors and oil paintings and even charcoal sketches. He opened up to Mr. Lockwood in one of the letters he sent along with a completed lesson and related the particulars of his handicap and how it came to be. He described what it took for him to try to get around and how much it meant to him to be learning a useful skill. He also stressed just how wonderfully supportive his whole family had been right from the start.

On the weekends, Floyd would be carried to the family's horse-drawn wagon and with the borrowed wheelchair tossed in back, he would be transported to the nearby art museum. He would spend the entire day sitting in front of a painting that particularly impressed him, absorbing as much detail as he could and making sketches of what he saw. Whichever brother it was who had taken him to the museum would leave him there, to return many hours later. Occasionally, another visitor would help him position his small wheelchair in front of a different painting. Then upon his return home, he would do his best to imitate what he saw. It was never good enough for him and he would toss out everything he did.

As the next several years rolled by, Floyd learned more and more about how to manage his body to try his best to be as self-reliant as possible. His mother had converted what had been a corncrib a few years back into a small shack, complete with a little wood stove, and had set it up in the backyard. It looked somewhat like a trailer; except that it was not meant to be moved anywhere. Stuffed into this small shack with one window was his bed, a surface that would pass for a desk, and several shelves for the many books he had by now accumulated. This became Floyd's house and he felt less and less like a burden and more like his own man, even if he did require a lot of help.

Either Ben or Tom had rigged up an old upholstered living room chair with large swiveling wheels in place of the legs it used to have. Sitting up in this chair was comfortable for him and allowed him to work at his little desk. He needed help to get into and out of this chair, and then someone to push him outdoors in it when the weather was good. He was determined to be as independent as possible, and eventually taught himself how to get in and out of bed on his own (with great difficulty), to dress himself, and attend to his own personal hygiene. He still never refused meals from his mother, however. And he always enjoyed visits from whichever of his siblings could spare the time to pop in to see him. He especially enjoyed visits from the "baby" of the family, Clara. Her personality and sweet disposition made her his favorite.

He had maintained a fairly steady stream of correspondence with Guy Lockwood of Kalamazoo. Floyd took great interest in his lessons and particularly enjoyed reading the magazine, *Art and Life* published by this teacher whom he had never met, and yet thought of as an old friend. The many letters that Floyd would mail out to him always were upbeat and cheerful and spoke of how busy he was as he learned new skills. He confided his ambitions to his unseen friend and wrote in those letters, things that he would have had a hard time vocalizing to his own family. He made it clear that he fully intended to be able to make his own living in this world and become independent of others. It was important, even vital to him that he have a skill so that he would know that he would never be too much of a burden on his loved ones.

His little house soon filled with an imposing collection of classic books, including most of the works of Shakespeare, Herman Melville, Victor Hugo, Mark Twain, and many others. Art books and art supplies of all kinds began to produce a level of clutter, which could prove both annoying and comforting at the same time. He read with great interest and uninterrupted pleasure, and was able to recall most of what he read. He soon added a good dictionary to his collection of books so that unfamiliar words could be grasped and added to his vocabulary.

His principal interest however, was in eventually mastering all art mediums. While still focusing on drawing and sketching, over the past few years he had taught himself a bit about working with watercolors and manipulating oil paints. Pen and ink sketching was something he was developing, particularly to do likenesses of family and friends. The idea

Above: Floyd at target practice in his mother's backyard, sometime in 1920.

Below: An early Floyd caricature made while studying with Zim. He called it "Jury."

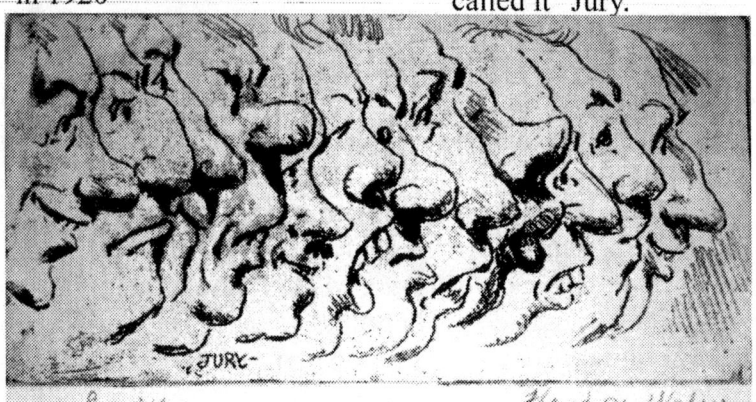

Right:
Tansey and Zepha with Floyd's mother looking over their shoulders. Young Billy doesn't like the sun in his eyes. (1926)

Erie, Lena, and Clara (about 1915)

of cartooning and drawing caricatures began to insert itself into his thoughts of how he might direct his talents. He had seen some really creative cartoons and had heard of caricature artists making good money. He began a deliberate search for a place to study this aspect of the art field. Then, in the summer of 1920 he saw an ad for what looked to him like just the thing to get him going in this new direction. Although he had never heard of this school, the ad caught his attention with its cartoons of farmers, animals and people in ridiculous situations. It was called "Zim's Correspondence School of Cartooning, Comic Art and Caricature" and was evidently run by some character named Zim in the unlikely town of Horseheads, New York. He sent for more information and within a few days received a fully illustrated 24-page booklet generated by the teacher in which many of the attributes of the course and its methods were persuasively presented with many cartoons and sketches. It pointed out that the course was presented in a series of 20 booklets at a cost of $25.00 for the entire course. Those 20 booklets, consisting of 32 pages each, would contain "over 700 sketches and drawings illustrating the matter; also good advice, business pointers, and warnings of the many pitfalls along the way to success which I am sure will prove of inestimable value to you".

With a fair amount of skepticism, he enrolled in this mail order school hoping to learn a few special techniques that might just help him earn a little money. The way Zim presented himself and his correspondence school really must have intrigued Floyd. He certainly sounded like the genuine article. The things he promised in his advertising booklet sounded terrific and if even half the promises were kept it just might be worthwhile. For example, one of the pages in the little booklet carried the following.

> HERE ARE A FEW OF THE THINGS I PROMISE TO DO.
> I will teach you correct drawing and how to caricature it.

How to put the spirit of life into human and animal figures.

How to render your drawings interesting and salable.

How to group figures to have your drawings well balanced.

The proper materials to use.

I will point out your faults clearly and show you how to correct them.

I will do what no other school could afford to do - - that is, give you 40 to 50 pencil, crayon and pen and ink sketches (originals), demonstrating the work from all angles.

Show you how to put "pep" into figures in action.

How to caricature animals.

How to put expression into hands and feet as well as faces.

How to wrinkle garments to render them graceful and artistic.

And a hundred other bits of information that will prove beneficial in your art career.

Floyd wasn't sure if this "Zim" character was on the level, but he must have thought it was worth a try. He couldn't see how a truly comprehensive course could be offered at such a relatively low price. The paragraph that probably convinced him to give Zim a try was this one:

When you have once gone into the work of my Course and see the manner in which I criticize drawings, you will realize that you are getting the Course at a very reasonable figure. I do not send you printed slips with checked off answers upon them, but make you actual lead pencil, pen, crayon and wash sketches demonstrating how I should render the drawings that you have submitted and point out in a comprehensible manner weak points in your technique. I have endeavored to make my twenty books as complete as possible, but if there is anything that you wish to know which you do not find mentioned in them you are at liberty to ask me questions and I shall write you personal letters to set you right in the matter. I am receiving letters every day from successful and satisfied students, some of whom are now in lucrative positions.

When Floyd sent in his enrollment slip, which was inserted in the booklet, he added a brief note explaining that he had the limited use of only his right arm, having been paralyzed 11 years ago. He went on to say that it was his ambition to get out in the town and sketch some comical versions of the people he saw, hoping that they would toss a few coins his way.

Floyd could not have realized at the time that this was the beginning of a truly unique teacher/student relationship. He would soon get the training in cartooning and caricature that he was looking for, but it would develop that Zim, who never used any other name professionally, was much more than advertised. Eugene Zimmerman was a genius in the art world who made his mark by catering to the public's (and his own) love of satire and silliness. The fact that he knew so much more than that, including working in a wide variety of artistic mediums was suppressed so that he could focus on his true love of the comic and absurd. He was a truly talented observer of humanity and seemed to love everyone, especially children. The entire community of Horseheads really loved this unique man who was so generous of himself.

When Zim died in 1935 his townspeople mourned him publicly, closing schools the afternoon of his funeral while many businesses closed for the hour of the of the funeral. The Reverend Mr. Harry E. Malick of the Horseheads Presbyterian Church officiated at the funeral and summed up Zim's life as follows:

> Zim might well be characterized as a lover of God's great outdoors, friend to all mankind, tender hearted as a child; kind beyond expression, generous to a fault, liberal and tolerant in his religion, gentle in spirit, exponent of a simple and homely philosophy of life, a talented artist who

gave freely of his time and service to whomsoever solicited it, famed the world over for his caricatures of humor, entertainment, and satire and yet this man . . . loved modesty and obscurity better than renown and publicity, and thus he almost hid his genius and greatness .

As the summer progressed, Floyd would carefully complete all the assignments sent to him from Zim and mail them back for the critiques. He rapidly learned how to draw cartoons and began developing the techniques of doing caricatures. On a whim, after his second lesson, he sent a sketch of an outdoor scene he had done along with his assignment. The response back from his far away teacher was unexpected. Zim told him that although he could most likely develop his cartooning skills, what should really be done would be to focus on "real art". He encouraged him to get as much training in classical art as he could possibly manage.

Floyd surely must have been a fast learner as is evidenced by the letter he received from Zim dated November 13, 1920. (See facing page.)

By the Spring of 1921 the development of Floyd's artistic skills prompted Ben and Tom to suggest that he could probably make some spare change by getting out into the town and sketching various historical sites, buildings, monuments, and perhaps even people as they sat at tables and benches.

A wide board with small wheels, or casters on its bottom was made up which was strong enough to support Floyd who would sit, strapped down cross-legged on it. This put him right down near the ground and required that he be lifted on and off it by his brothers. Once on this strange vehicle and set in place, surrounded with his sketching materials and a parka to throw on if the weather should turn bad, he was prepared to sketch whatever caught his fancy. As long as the place where he sat was level and hard packed, he was able to move himself and his supplies around to get a different perspective of whatever it was he was sketching.

ZIM'S CORRESPONDENCE SCHOOL OF CARTOONING, COMIC ART AND CARICATURE

HORSEHEADS, N. Y.
November
Thirteenth
1 9 2 0

Dear Mr. Walser:--

    I'll take off my hat to you, old man, for cleverness. You have the boys all cheated and I have a great many very good students. You certainly have improved wonderfully since your first lesson.

    You may pay for this criticism whenever you feel able. No hurry.

    Regarding the color work, you are using too brilliant colors for close-up work. Of course, for stage effects, to be viewed at a distance, it is advisable to slap on vivid colors in bold daubs because distance from stage to audience softens the effect. Flesh tint is obtained by using light vermillion very thin and in the cheeks a bit of carmine. The ears are transparent, hence Indian red will produce that effect. You should also be more positive in shading, leaving bits of white for highlights on the raised parts of the features.

    I cannot tell you anything about pen drawing further than you already know, and your crayon work is O.K., likewise the wash. You ought to draw up some good character heads and put them on display in some show windows of your home town, or in the cities you visit. You have a line that will bring in the dough wherever you go, never fear.

    Now dig in again and study hard this winter.

    With all good wishes, I am

        Cordially yours,

EZ/L   Criticism #3

    Depending on just where he was left on this little platform of his, would determine what he would sketch. At first, simple pencil sketches of the buildings in sight were attempted. As he gained confidence, he would switch to pen and ink sketches and do more complicated subjects. When he had several sketches completed and signed, "F. N. Walser"; he would prop them in front of him with a little hand-made sign offering them for twenty-five cents apiece. Some were offered for a little less if he thought they really weren't so good. The day he sold his first sketches must have been a day to remember for him. Actually getting paid for doing something he loved was no doubt quite a thrill.

Eventually he would ask people if they wanted a likeness of themselves for a quarter. This became a popular item and he was developing a following in town. People would go out in search of "the crippled artist" who would do your portrait for a quarter. For an extra quarter, he would create a caricature in which he exaggerated whichever of your features he thought would make for a humorous picture. It developed that people really loved the caricatures and would often bring him photos of relatives for him to make look goofy. He raised his price to 75 cents for such drawings and could have gone higher. He maintained his correspondence with Zim, who by now felt like an old friend, taking additional lessons and sending him some of his latest more serious work. A letter from Zim dated March 12, 1921 points out the progress Floyd was making. (See facing page.)

After several months of sketching a variety of subjects out in the town, he was approached one day by an attractive young woman who introduced herself as a journalist for a nationwide magazine. She said that she had heard about him and wanted to see for herself what he was all about and that maybe she would do a short write-up about him. She asked a lot of questions about his past, especially about how it came to be that he was crippled and how he got to be so talented.

Embarrassed to tell her he had contracted polio after having suffered heat stroke, he simply told her that he had been thrown by a wild horse. He said his job had been breaking and taming wild horses for use by cowboys when this one particularly ferocious beast just managed to get the best of him after a long and tiring day. He figured that sounded a lot better that what had actually transpired. Actually, he *had* fallen off a horse, hadn't he? And what difference did it make anyway? This woman was never going to

```
Floyd Walser,
Criticism #6,
March 12, 1921
```

Dear Mr. Walser:--

You're getting better every day. I weary of saying merely, "This is a good bunch of stuff". The fact is, I don't see how it could be much better.

You have a wonderful swing to the pen and pencil. I wish you would tell me what sort of a pen you are using. It appears quite elastic and just the thing for vigorous drawing. I have been unable to find any flexible pens unless of the very expensive variety. If you have a supply, please send me one so that I may try it out. Gillott's 303 is a standard pen but too stiff. I like a pen to act similar to a brush, to respond as bristles do to the swing of the hand.

Don't worry about this criticism. Pay when you can.

In your color work, don't use the raw chrome yellow. Subdue it with yellow ochre or umber. The yellow is too virulent and detracts from the other colors or tints.

I'm glad you think so well of my sketches. I don't believe other schools would go to this trouble. Takes too much time to serve big classes in this manner.

Good luck to you.

Sincerely yours,

EZ/L

actually write anything about him, and even if she did, who was going to see it? He explained how he got interested in art more than a dozen years ago as a way to get his mind off himself and to recover a sense of value by earning a small wage as an artist. He explained that he was pretty much self-taught after a few lessons from a correspondence school. He told her that one day he would get into the technique of etching, but currently lacked the money for a press and the copper plates this art form required. She seemed to be genuinely interested in everything he had to say, so he embellished the details a bit. She thanked him for his time and left saying that her article on him would probably appear in her magazine in a few months.

The next year rolled by with further improvements in both Floyd's ability to deal effectively with his handicap and in his artistic skills. He was now fairly proficient in both watercolors and in the use of oils on canvas. He loved to capture the raw beauty in many of the trees he could see both near his home and on the short jaunts his brothers would sometimes help him with. Many of the trees that he found to be compelling subjects for his drawings, had twisted and gnarled branches. Was this a way for him to make some sort of a statement about his own distorted limbs?

On a steamy day in August 1921, Floyd was sitting under the shade trees that surrounded his little house, and studying yet another art book. His sister, Erie, brought him a letter that had just been delivered. It was addressed simply,

> Mr. Floyd Walser
> Lampasas, Texas

The letter inside was from a woman named Madame Edith Noyes Greene who stated that she had come across a most interesting article about him. She went on to say that she was moved to tears reading about his courageous battle with his crippling disability and his wonderful artistic talent. The fact that he was self-taught and was so bravely working to expand his gifts in spite of what she allowed would make other men wallow in a pit of self-despair, had truly touched her heart. She indicated that she and her husband, Roy, were both patrons of the arts and lived on a lakeside estate in a place called Framingham in Massachusetts, surrounded by wonderful musicians. In fact, she wrote that she was a world-famous composer of classical music and had always had an abiding interest in, and love for art. Her main reason for contacting him was to suggest that perhaps he would like to come to live with her and Roy at Harmony Home on Melody Lane, which is what she called her estate. He would be their protégé and they would see to it that his art education would be accelerated by his being able to attend art classes at the Museum of Fine Arts in Boston which was not too far from their home. She stated that she was eagerly awaiting his affirmative reply and she would make all the necessary arrangements for his trip.

Floyd must have thought that by golly, that young lady he met a few months ago must have actually gone off and written her piece. But move to this place called Framingham? How could he possibly leave his family and the security of knowing that by now they really understood all his needs and how to provide for him without suffocating him? He was, under the circumstances pretty happy about his home, family and his ability to get out and sketch whatever he saw. He believed that he could continue to make improvements in his skill level at his own pace and on his own terms. He also loved Texas, and the weather there (most of the time) suited him just fine. It was cold and snowy around Boston in the winter and they didn't have much of a summer lots of the time. He could do without Madame Greene and her high-toned, fancy estate.

He discussed the letter with his mother and the rest of the family. Some of them thought he should really not be so quick to say no, but should explore it a little. It might be good for him. His mother thought it was a bad idea and wanted him to have no part of it. She loved having him around and took great pleasure in watching his artistic skills grow. She was expecting great things some day.

After a short discussion, Floyd knew how he wanted to respond to the letter. He had his mother take a picture of him sitting in his little house, surrounded by his books and art supplies. After it was developed, he wrote the following note on the back of the picture:

Benny Haden Walser and Viola Jennings on their wedding day, August 22, 1903.

Floyd outside his converted corn crib house. Lampasas, Texas - circa 1915

Floyd's 1920 self-portrait published in G. H. Lockwood's magazine "Art and Life."

Photo he had made to send to Madam Greene. He called his place "Home Sweet Home."

work that are published in this issue, the portrait of himself and the pencil drawing of the young lady's head that we are using as a frontice piece.

During these long months of correspondence I have never received a discordant or discouraging letter from him, He always writes in a cheerful vein and shows that he is busy and in spite of his handicap, happy, or at least as happy as anyone could be under like circumstance.

Floyd's ambition is to be able to make his own living in this world and become independent of everyone; that is, to be able to do something so he can feel he is paying his way and hoeing his own row.

I can't tell you all about Floyd Walser, but I've told you enough now so that if you have a real human heart in your bosom you'll want to lend a helping hand in some way, that this real fighter in the world's great battle can have a chance to win, for it is the fighters like Floyd Walser who are worth while.

I am publishing herewith my last letter to Floyd, as in it you can read something of my own feeling towards him, and also of my plans for his future as well as his own.

My Dear Walser:--

Whenever I think of you I feel like kicking myself for ever feeling down in the mouth or the least bit discouraged or cross or ugly.

What excuse have I to ever complain? I have health, the greatest of all blessings; am my own boss; have pleasant work to do in a pleasant environment; can get out and enjoy the world when work is over; have many friends, and, last, but not least, I have recently married the dearest little mate in all the world.

And then I think of you, paralyzed, cooped up most of the time in a little den by yourself, without means, with few friends, for so few have a chance to know you, with only a fighting chance ahead to even make your own living?

And in spite of it all you seem to keep so cheerful and optimistic, and you have really accomplished wonders in your art work, considering the handicap you had to start with, and still have.

Somehow, old boy, I feel you will win.

As you say the commercial game has difficulties for you that are practically insurmountable. I think your chance is to learn to do beautiful head drawings or comic drawings of faces only, or scenes, and sell them direct. I believe your work could sell on its merits, but that many, knowing of your hard battle, would help, as they should, and not only buy, but help you sell.

Talk is cheap - - I'm going to do more than talk, I'm going to put this letter or a part of same in the magazine and publish one of the heads you sent in last and ask our readers to buy a drawing from you.

Fix me up a bunch of samples at once, all on 9 x 12 sheets, a pencil, chalk, and pen and ink if you wish, and let me know about what you think you ought to get for these.

You might sell pictures of prominent men, like Roosevelt, Wilson, Bryan, Harding, Pershing, etc.

But get about 6 fine woman's heads - - the last one sent in is a dandy - - and a few comic character heads such as could be used in chalktalks. You might also work out some chalktalk programs - -??

Try gray paper, black crayons or chalk. Touched up a bit with white - - that is a quick way and gets nice results. If you had about 25 or 20 pictures in all, you could use same layouts over and over - - and get so you could make them very rapidly.

If you get what I think will get by, I'll give you some advertising space and boost like the very dickens for you, and I know we have some big hearted readers who will help muchly, and I also feel that you will do your part and deliver the goods in the form of pictures that will be well worth a frame.

...I wish we had a good picture of you at your drawing board inside your little shack. If you can get a friend to make one, send it in. ...

...Don't give up the fight - - Stick and WIN.

Go on and fix up another bunch of samples and I'll help you make final selections.

Believe me, old boy.

Your friend,
LOCKWOOD

Now, what can you do? Well for one thing, if nothing else, you can write him a cheerful and encouraging, newsy letter. Remember, he is way out in the West, out in the country, shut up in a little shack, and has no chance of knowing of the outside world excepting the word brought in to him, and an occasional trip that he can take away from the shack with some friends, for it is to be understood that Floyd has friends, and deserves to have good friends, and many more, so YOU can be one of them. And don't forget to put in a stamped envelope for reply.

Another thing you can do - - send him a dollar for a picture. Tell him if you want a girl's head, or comic, or scene, or a drawing of yourself, for if you send him a photo he can make that. Floyd is not yet a finished artist, but you will find you will get your dollar's worth just the same. (Even if you don't ask for any picture, bread cast upon the tide will come back. It is the things we do for others that are really the most worth while, and especially is this true when these 'others' are not those near and dear to us, but some one out on life's great road battling against conditions and needing the help of a friendly hand.)

It is a pleasure to print this little article about Floyd, for I feel that many who read it will respond, and I want to thank all who do in advance. Anything you can do for Floyd Walser, I will consider you are also doing for me, for it is one of my ambitions to see Floyd Walser realize his dreams and be able to hoe his own row and feel independent, and I expect he will do this, and that his hard work will bear fruit and his drawings sell purely on their merits, for Floyd, in spite of his handicap, is some day going to be a fine artist, he has already made a good start towards his goal. Let us all wish him well and lend a helping hand."

Madame Greene had evidently been touched not only by the description of Floyd's condition in life, but also by the very noble-minded things that Mr. Lockwood had to say in his article.

So now, Floyd must have been thinking, "Just who are these people in Framingham, and what are they really like?"

CHAPTER 9

MADAME EDITH ROWENA NOYES GREENE AND ROY GREENE
1875 –1923

On the 26th of March 1875, Edith Rowena Noyes was born. Edith's parents, Charles C. Noyes and his wife, Jeannette (Pease) had both descended from wealthy families and were financially reasonably well off. It was Charles, however who provided the main source of income for them. Their home was on Oxford Terrace in Cambridge, Massachusetts in a house next to the home of Henry Wadsworth Longfellow, considered by many to be the greatest American poet. This famous personality, thought of by all who ever met him as uniquely kind and courteous, was 68 when Edith was born and lived another seven years as their neighbor.

Charles and Jeannette must have been thrilled to have a healthy, beautiful baby girl born to them. Her middle name was chosen in memory of Charles' beloved mother who was named Rowena (Cox). The Noyes household was refined and genteel, with classical music frequently played on their grand piano by the young mother. Whenever musically talented guests would attend dinners and teas, it would not have been unusual for them to gather around the piano with their stringed instruments and entertain each other with wonderful chamber music. Jeanette was a very gifted oratorio singer and had been a well-known contralto before meeting Charles Noyes.

When Edith was a little over two years of age, a second daughter, named Lora was born. Both little girls were brought up to be proper young ladies in whom an appreciation of the arts was instilled from the very beginning. It was young Edith, however who showed the most talent for music, teaching herself to make sweet sounds at the piano by age three. This love for music would not only stay with her throughout her life, but would become central to her very being as her gifts for composing and playing would flourish. Sadly, Edith's father contracted tuberculosis and passed away in 1885, when she was barely 10 years of age. He did not live to see his oldest daughter's rise to prominence in the music world. He would have been proud indeed.

It was here in her home in Cambridge that at the age of 7, she composed her first serious work for piano. She had been playing a lovely piece of her own invention, which she called "Whispering Trees" for many months with the music not yet written out. She would carry the piece in her mind for years and even mentally correct it before finally writing the finished work on manuscript paper when she was 14. This same method was used to create other compositions as well. At some point in her early music education she became the protégé of Edward Alexander MacDowell (1861-1908). It must have been through a combination of her own talent for the piano and the fact that her father had been well known in Boston society that she was able to study with such a renowned artist as MacDowell.

MacDowell, born in New York City, studied in the United States, France, and Germany, becoming principal teacher of piano at the conservatory in Darmstadt, Germany in 1881 and 1882. Returning to the U.S. in 1888, he became head of the music department of Columbia University from 1896 to 1904. He was a prolific composer whose works included two piano concertos, one written in 1885, the other in 1890. He also generated a number of other compositions for piano including *Woodland Sketches* (1896) and *Sea Pieces* (1898). His most famous work, *To a Wild Rose* is from *Woodland Sketches*. He loved his home in Peterborough, New Hampshire where he gave lessons to especially gifted students, including Edith Rowena Noyes. Many years later, she would found The MacDowell Club in Boston as a tribute to this great man and to foster the appreciation of classical music. It is not known how long she studied with MacDowell, but even though it couldn't have been an extended period, she increased her musical skills significantly under his tutelage.

At the age of 15, she had an opportunity to use her talent to honor her father. She gave a benefit recital, playing some of her own compositions, some works of MacDowell's, and Beethoven's *Moonlight Sonata*. The appreciative audience must have felt that they were hearing a young genius at work and happily placed a little of their hard-earned money in the basket. When the recital was over, with the piano chords still echoing in her mind, Edith was thrilled to realize that she had raised over 200 dollars. With great pride, she happily gave the entire proceeds to a Boston hospital for tuberculosis. The funds were used to furnish a room in that hospital in memory of Charles C. Noyes.

The passing of her father 5 years previously had now left the once prosperous, well-to-do family in serious financial difficulty. Following is a quote from an interview with her as reported in The Boston Telegram, Thursday, June 21, 1923.

> My whole life has been a struggle against misfortune and ill health. At the age of 16, I was forced to support myself. It was difficult for a girl born with two gold spoons in her mouth to earn the porridge that was to be eaten with one of those spoons.
>
> I trimmed hats, and played [piano] wherever and whenever I had the opportunity, earning, all told about eight dollars a week. Cheese and crackers and prunes for lunch - - and really I've never since had anything that tasted nearly so good. Many times have I peered over the small windows of my room on Oxford Terrace - - my room was always distinguishable from the street by several handkerchiefs carefully pressed against the window panes to dry - - wondering if I should ever become great, if I could do great things. It is strange indeed, that this studio which has been my haven for many years, should be the

very one on which my eyes rested in those days when fortune was less kind to me.

While still in her teens, she had generated 20 compositions; 10 songs, with parts arranged for four voices in each, and 10 piano works. Most of her pieces were of a soothing, gentle style - - almost lullabies. A few works were more robust, but she was developing a style that was peaceful, and even almost religious and sacred in nature. A famous American contralto, Madame Helen Eaton loved Edith's work and while on a concert tour in Great Britain, sang two of her songs for Queen Victoria and her two daughters. The Queen was delighted with the peaceful beauty of these songs and asked about the composer. Her Royal Highness then asked Mme. Eaton what she thought the little American girl would like as a gift so that the she may show her appreciation for this youngster's talent. Edith was overwhelmed to receive a stunning photographic portrait of Queen Victoria beautifully autographed with the Queen's words of praise for her music. Understandably, this was a memento she treasured all her life.

At the age of 16, she wrote a soft and gentle song, which she simply titled *Berceuse*, which is a synonym for lullaby. It was introduced into France by a handsome young man by the name of Baron Dalwyn, one of France's most famous baritone singers at the time. When she was 19, she played some of her compositions at the White House for president and Mrs. Grover Cleveland, a most unusual honor for such a young person. During this same time period she wrote the operetta, *Last Summer,* which she dedicated to her brother and which was produced four times in that season. It was a great success and netted over $4000 for hospitals. (Her mother had remarried a few years after Charles' passing and had a son whose name was Paul Rice. Edith loved him dearly.)

At the age of 23, she composed a violin sonata and dedicated it to Emil Paur, the new director of the New York Philharmonic orchestra. Maestro Paur held this position with this world-renowned group from 1898 to 1902. He then went on to become a conductor of the Boston Symphony Orchestra for nearly two years. He would be important in her life in subsequent years also.

When she was about 27, she composed *The Hymn of Peace*. This song, with its simplicity and beauty became widely known. It was inspired by and dedicated to her mother. The words had been written by John Quincy Adams, who had lived in nearby Quincy during the first half of the 19th century. During both World Wars this hymn was sent to men and women everywhere in the armed forces of the United States. Here is the story of how she came to have it published, told in her own words as reported years later in the official bulletin of the Massachusetts Federation of Woman's Clubs

> In the beginning of 1900, I was possessed by a theme running through my mind. Two years later I went to see my great master, Edward MacDowell at Columbia University to attend a reunion of his pupils. Mrs. MacDowell gave a tea for us. Though late for classes, Mr. MacDowell took time to show us his rare old instruments and the room where he played to his pupils. He invited me to play anything I was composing at the time.
> So I sat down at his grand piano and played the theme, asking if it was anything worth developing. He was very kind, and said, 'A good theme. Make it an anthem for a church', which I did. Returning for an umbrella, for it was pouring outside, I heard the master, alone, playing over my music from memory; a never to be forgotten thrill. I stole away and he never knew I overheard him. The Hymn of Peace was sung on the first Armistice night at Jordan Hall, Boston. [At the New England Conservatory of Music.]
> (From the archives of the Framingham Historical Society and Museum, Framingham, Massachusetts.)

Edith became very well known as an excellent teacher of piano and although she taught pupils of all ages and skill levels, she was especially sought out as a teacher for those who had developed their abilities to a high degree. Sometime in 1908 when Edith was 33, she was pleasantly surprised to greet a handsome young man who had come to her studio in Boston for advanced lessons on the piano. His name was Roy Goddard Green and although he was about 5 years younger, she was impressed with his maturity, serious nature and quick wit. She liked him very much from their first meeting. The fact that he was a skillful musician possessing excellent technical skills at the piano keyboard ensured that he would be her pupil. That he was also gracious, charming and handsome only added to her interest. As she got to know him better she would discover that he was passionate about classical music and had formed his own orchestra. He enjoyed conducting this small ensemble and found that he could get the members of his orchestra to produce very pleasing renditions of many of his favorite works by the masters. Her fascination with him grew and it was obvious to everyone around them that Roy was quite taken with his new teacher for more than her musical talent. The relationship soon turned to love. Edith asked about his background and discovered even more that she liked and it all added to her feelings for him.

She knew that Roy was a remarkably talented musician, and although short of stature, he was quietly self-assured and thought of highly by all who knew him. He had grown up in the town of Harvard, Massachusetts (about 30 miles from Framingham) the son of Warren Wetherbee Green and Mamie Goddard Green. He lived there with a younger sister and brother on their parent's fairly large property. His father's profession was listed as "dancing master", although he spent a considerable amount of his time working the farm on his land. There is little doubt that Roy's own parents were very influential in his upbringing and his belief in a strong work ethic as well as his love for music. But it appears that it was his father's father, Simeon Green who had the most profound impact on the youth.

Simeon Green was born on May 28, 1824 in Townsend, Massachusetts and moved to Harvard about the time he married Susan Elizabeth Wetherbee. He was incredibly well known in Harvard and many surrounding towns not only as a gifted musician, playing the violin, but primarily as the best dancing teacher anywhere. He was a dancing master from whom everyone for miles around wanted their children (or themselves) to learn to dance. He also carried on general farming having many acres of grapes, as well as several large apple orchards. When he was a farm boy he was especially fond of dancing, and as he grew older he became well known as an expert in the graceful art. He was also the organizer of Green's Orchestra of Fitchburg, a small but talented group who played classical music together for many years.

In February, 1894, over 1000 people joined together at the Harvard Town Hall to take part in a testimonial and reception to honor this man for fifty years of teaching dancing to the young people of Harvard and many neighboring towns. Most of them came in horse-drawn sleighs over the snow-covered roads. To say that this very special affair was a tremendous success is understating it considerably. Over 60 people formed the committee for the arrangements, working out the plans for over a year in advance, and representing 22 surrounding towns. The old Town Hall in Harvard, a three-story structure sometimes referred to then as "The Opera House" built many years before this big celebration, was chosen as the setting for this event. The lower hall was totally taken up by the enormous meal being served, a presentation that people today would call a "pot-luck" supper. As reported in The Boston Herald, February 15, 1894, "The supper was served on a sort of cooperative plan. There was no caterer, no colored waiters, but every housewife in Harvard and surrounding towns contributed a large mite…. So the supper was a howling success in every way, and opportunities were offered of sampling the best that the finest cooks in Worcester County could offer." The upper hall was decorated with red and white bunting and banners of all colors. The orchestra, which Mr. Green had formerly led, provided all the music for what turned out to be an all-night celebration, lasting until the wee hours.

It took over three hours for the assembled guests just to shake hands with the old dancing master and to reminisce about how much they had enjoyed his spirited lessons. They were taught such dances as quadrilles, polkas, lancers, waltzes, minuets, galops, schottisches as well as contra dances such as Money Musk, Lady Walpoles, Hull's Victory and the Virginia Reel and many more.

Many of his former pupils were now solid businessmen of Worcester County. Their children and grandchildren also had benefited from the valuable lessons learned at the hands of this fine teacher. Mr. Green not only taught his many charges to dance, but to deport themselves like gentlemen and ladies. Always a gentleman himself, he expected and required the same courtesy from his pupils. Young Roy Goddard Green clearly was the recipient of the same moral value teachings by example, but also was in awe of the wonderful sounds produced by his grandfather's orchestra.

Roy, with all this music in his genetic makeup, became proficient at the piano at a young age and while still in his teens, formed his own small orchestra. He subsequently enjoyed conducting small ensembles. He moved with his parents and siblings from Harvard to South Framingham in the late 1890s where they lived on Hollis Street.

Within two weeks of her 34th birthday, Edith Rowena Noyes became the bride of the handsome and musically gifted 28 year-old Roy Goddard Green. The young musician, who was head-over-heels in love with the beautiful and famous Edith, had no objection to her request that he change the spelling of his last name prior to their wedding. In fact, he agreed that simply adding an "e" to the end of the name did make it look a bit more dignified and not simply "high-toned" as some may have thought.

The wedding of the two lovebirds took place on March 6, 1909 and they moved in with Roy's parents in their home on Hollis Street.

Gifts of money received from their many friends at their wedding were soon converted into real property. Roy had often paddled a rented canoe around the picturesque shores on Framingham's Waushakum Pond which touched Hollis Street a short walk from his parents' and his home. Many times he had thought about someday buying some lakefront property and building a home in the secluded woods that surrounded so much of this lake with the old Indian name. Before their wedding he would take his lovely Edith for a romantic canoe ride around this lake and they both were caught up in the dream.

Now, they put the dream into action and found a small parcel of land for sale which was not only secluded but had frontage on a short stretch of this shore. As they quietly glided westerly by this property in another rented canoe to examine it from the lake, the newlyweds fell in love with everything about it. Just past the western-most part of the property that was for sale, the shoreline wrapped around so that now they were headed almost due north and continued on into a delightful cove that was home to a tiny wooded island. Several birds, including what appeared to be Blue Herons called this island their home. The surface of the water in the cove was heavily covered with pure white pond lilies, their pads of dark green forming small resting-places for frogs as they basked in the sun. Tall pine trees and a variety of oaks and other trees and shrubs gave the entire property a cool and inviting appearance. In short, the small portion of it they could afford was ideal.

This piece of land, measuring about a third of an acre was but a small part of the many acres in the vicinity owned by one Frank H. Gerrish of Framingham who was a farmer and poultry dealer. Although there were no roads that led directly to this property, Mr. Gerrish maintained a right-of-way from nearby Winthrop Street, where he lived. There was little doubt that in a relatively short time, roads would be put in.

The Gerrish property had included two more lakefront lots one on either side of the one the Greenes were interested in as well as much land that went far from the lake out toward Winthrop Street and beyond. It turned out that both of these adjacent pieces of property had been recently sold. The one just to the west of the one the Greenes now wanted would have been their preference had they found it in time. It was the one at the point in the cove and had nearly 300 feet of lake frontage with a view of both the longest part of the lake facing south as well as the more rustic view west towards the island and the water lilies. The people who now owned this property had set up a tent there from time to time and thought that some day they would build a house, but currently lacked the means to do so. Roy and Edith hoped that they could eventually acquire that marvelous lot. But now the available land, small though it was, seemed perfect for them.

Title to this idyllic lakefront lot with 81.5 feet of waterfront, located back 193 feet from what would later become Lake Avenue, was deeded to the Greenes on April 13, 1909. In addition to the very detailed surveyor's language that described the exact boundaries there was a stipulation written into the deed which controlled any future building's use. "…Said parcel is conveyed subject to the restriction that no building shall ever be erected thereon by the grantee, their heirs and assigns except as a dwelling house or private camp, and after the same be erected, it shall not be occupied for the purpose of carrying on any business, trade or avocation whatsoever…"

With the land now purchased and with thoughts of soon acquiring the adjacent lots, Roy and Edith set off for their honeymoon and began planning the design and construction of their home. It would take nearly 4 years for it to be ready for them to move in. In the meantime, they lived in rented houses in the vicinity of Hollis Street very near the home where Roy's parents and his brother, Clifton, were living.

As a part of their honeymoon, the newlyweds sailed to Europe in the summer of 1909 on a grand concert tour. The details of that trip, including just where they went and for whom they performed are lost. However, it is known that they did spend several days with Emil Paur who sponsored them in several concerts throughout Europe and who was very kind and helpful to them. Maestro Paur was touched by the fact that the bright young Edith Noyes had, about 11 years previously dedicated her violin sonata to him just because she was so taken with the fact that he had just become the director of the world famous New York Philharmonic Orchestra. He had maintained his friendship with the lovely young composer and now was thrilled to be of help to her and her new husband, with whom he was also very impressed.

Upon the Greene's return home to Framingham, they continued a very active lifestyle with their days and nights fully occupied with all aspects of music. This included teaching, composing, and performing classical music as well as being socially active in their town. But there is little doubt that much of their time was taken up with monitoring the design and construction of their lakefront home. What they came up with was unique for the time. It did not copy any existing houses and was sited far back from where a street would one day be. It was as far towards the lake as the contour of the land would permit. The lot was nearly flat and level for a distance of about 160 feet, then dropped sharply down to the lake whose surface was about 20 feet lower than the rest of the lot. The south side of the house, facing the lake was where their spacious living room was located. It measured 28 feet long by about 16 feet wide and had exposed wooden beams in the plastered ceiling. The 4 large windows they installed close together in the center of the lake-facing wall allowed an unobstructed view of the pond below. On the west wall of the living room a rectangular glass window that measured about 2 feet high and 5 feet long was installed about 5 feet above the floor. It was a custom designed window and was quite beautiful with its wooden divisions that created a pattern of 10 vertical rectangles and 10 diamond shapes above. It was against this wall and under the unique window that Edith's upright piano would be placed. This beautiful old instrument had been exceptionally well crafted and had full, rich tone with crisp high notes that had always pleased them both very much.

Along the easterly side of the house and reaching to the south-facing rear, they built a screened veranda accessible directly from the living room. It provided additional views of the lake as well as glimpses of sunrises. A large brick fireplace was built against the interior back wall of the living room near the veranda.

The first floor had, in addition to the large picturesque living room and veranda, a neat, well-equipped kitchen next to a large dining room. The dining room, with windows on the west wall of the house, connected directly to the living room through an 8-foot wide opening. Upstairs there were four bedrooms, with the master bedroom, the largest of the 4, having 2 windows in a dormer that faced east and one facing south, overlooking the lake. All in all, it was a lovely house that drank in the beauty of its location. Since Roy and Edith expected that the house would be nearly constantly full of music, Edith suggested that they call their place "Harmony Home". To add to its charming name, since there was no named street anywhere near it when it was first built, she amplified it with "On Melody Lane". Roy and Edith moved into their new place in the spring of 1913. They both truly loved the place and Roy would delight in telling his friends that every window in his new home had a view of the lake, a feature made possible by its location close to the cove. They felt the special, almost therapeutic feeling that being within sight of a body of water would bring. The midday light show that always was provided at no charge on sunny days when their living room ceiling would fairly sparkle with the reflections of the sun off a choppy lake surface, was something they never tired of seeing.

Shortly after they were settled in and for years to come, many evenings, especially during the spring and summertime, "Harmony Home on Melody Lane" would come alive with the beautiful sounds of string quartets and a variety of other talented musicians. Edith and Roy both loved to entertain at their lovely home and enjoyed making music with their friends and colleagues. The screened-in veranda was the part of the house that was favored for many of these impromptu musical gatherings. Sometimes, on warm summer evenings the musicians would look out onto a full moon over the lake and see a collection of canoes drifting lazily just off the shore, their occupants, usually romantic couples, enjoying the free concert.

In time, Edith founded the MacDowell Club in honor of her famous teacher who had passed away at the age of 47 in January 1908. She also founded the Music Lover's Club of Boston in 1912 and was its president for 20 years. Not busy enough with all of this, she was also a charter member of the Professional Women's Club as well as the Chromatic Club of Boston.

Edith was the first American woman to compose light opera, writing the score for the Indian opera *Osseo*. She worked on this over a period of several years beginning sometime around 1915. Her collaborator and librettist in this work was a dear friend and fellow patroness of the arts, Lillie Fuller Merriam, an extremely talented and energetic woman. Mrs. Merriam was one of those people who seemed to never require sleep. She wrote stage plays, poetry, books on a variety of subjects, and composed her own music and was thrilled to create the libretto for her good friend. Both she and Edith felt that their collaboration was smooth and natural with their combined talents improving the opera more than either one could do alone.

While still not completely finished, the opera *Osseo* was performed on May 9, 1922 in Jordan Hall at the New England Conservatory of Music in Boston. This was a production with three acts and had four characters at this point. In other configurations there were 8 characters and a large supporting cast of dancers and singers. It had been presented at various times previously to such audiences as the Framingham Women's Club as well as the Professional Women's Club, at the Copley Plaza Hotel. At this performance in Jordan Hall, only four instruments: a violin, cello, organ and a piano that was played by Edith, provided the music. The role of the reader was filled by the librettist, Mrs. Merriam.

An overview of this unfinished work can be derived from the foreword printed in the program.

> The story groups itself about the ancient Indian village of Waushakum, of the authentic Massachusetts tribe of the Nipnets [a variant of Nipmuc] before the advent of the white man, and embraces those phases of life common to all human experiences regardless of time or race; misunderstanding, treachery, loyalty, love of man and maiden, forgiveness and restored harmony. (From the archives of the Framingham Historical Society and Museum, Framingham, Massachusetts.)

A partial quote from a local newspaper of May 11, 1922 gives an appreciation of how this version of the opera was received.

> ...All are artists in their individual lines and gave perfect interpretations of the parts. In quartet, the blending of the voices and the volume of tone achieved was pronounced by many in the large and discriminating audience as truly remarkable. An audience numbering nearly 1100 listened to the program with many expressions of pleasure and appreciation. Among those prominent musically and otherwise were noticed: Pierre Montaux, M. LeVin, Conductor Mason, John Orr, J. Albert Baumgartner, Mrs. William Arms Fisher, Mrs. Wendell Luce, Mrs. Sarah Fisher Wellington, Mr. Burger from the Symphony Orchestra, and several others from the Orchestra, Mr. Tillotson, pianist, Margaret Ruthven, Gertrude Sands of the MacDowell Club, Prof. Smith of Wellsely College, and many others.
>
> A real ovation was given Mrs. Greene by the club, who presented her with flowers and other more substantial

tokens of appreciation. Mrs. Merriam also received a beautiful sheaf of roses from the club, and such appreciation for the delicate conceits and graceful wording of the libretto, which she read with a mellow, full and sympathetic vocalization that brought out every shade of thought and feeling.

(The above is from the archives of the Framingham Historical Society and Museum, Framingham, Massachusetts.)

While Edith was keeping busy with her many clubs and her composing, her husband was also fully involved with his musical career. He taught piano to many of the young people, as well as some of the adults in the Framingham area. Many days of the week would find a steady stream of pupils making their way to Harmony Home for their private piano lessons. Until Cove Avenue was built in 1915, the only road that led to this charming place was a right-of-way through woods and farms. Roy had maintained his interest in orchestras and bands, after starting up his own small band as a youth in Harvard. Shortly after he was married he formed the Framingham Band in which he directed up to 45 energetic and enthusiastic performers. He then founded the Framingham School of Music and did all the day-to-day work of running it. He gathered up the best of this school's pupils and formed a junior orchestra whose many performances enthralled their parents and friends.

He was continually meeting talented young musicians now and felt that it was time for the town of Framingham to have a high quality classical orchestra. In 1925 he founded the Civic League Orchestra with a membership that numbered around 30 to 40 highly motivated and skilled instrumentalists. Neither he nor any of the members of this group received any pay whatsoever from the Civic League. They worked diligently, rehearsing together at least weekly and practicing daily at their homes. Roy worked extra hard at keeping the Civic League Orchestra going in the right direction and constantly finding and booking famous guest artists

Civic League Orchestra, Roy G. Greene Conductor, circa 1928.

to perform, heightening the public's interest in the group. The fact that he was so personable and friendly and had such an obvious love for good music were qualities that endeared him to many and, no doubt helped him to succeed.

Sometime around 1916 or so, the land on either side of the Greenes became available for purchase. Once they had acquired those 2 very special lots, they owned an additional acre. Harmony Home on Melody Lane was now safely surrounded by wooded tranquillity and they both often enjoyed quiet walks and even a picnic now and then in this area with the aroma of pine trees in the air.

It was at the height of all the activity going on in and around Harmony Home in 1922 that Edith first read about the crippled young man out in Texas who so bravely was working at developing his artistic abilities. When she read the article by G. H. Lockwood in the magazine *Art and Life* about the young polio victim, she was moved to tears. She immediately thought of her mother, Jeannette Noyes who had recently passed away. That compassionate woman had, her entire life been keenly interested in aiding crippled persons and had for years been connected with the Peabody Crippled Children's Home in Boston. The more she thought about this fine young gentleman, the more the idea of bringing him out to Harmony Home as her protégé appealed to her. She had no concept of what it would take to properly care for someone who had such limited use of his body. She simply did not give that aspect of her plan any real consideration. The high and noble thought of providing a way for this fellow to advance his artistic abilities by studying in Boston at the School of the Museum of Fine Arts was just too strong to let go. She would care for him in memory of her mother.

So she wrote him a letter describing her home briefly and suggesting that he come to live with her and Roy and become their protégé, allowing them to look after him and to further his art training. She pointed out that she and Roy had no children so there would be no distractions caused by a rowdy family around him. He would be able to concentrate on developing his artistic abilities.

She was unhappy with his response to her letter, in which he basically said, "Thanks, but no thanks." She wrote a second letter in which she emphasized the advantages he would realize if only he would come and spend a few years at their lovely estate. When his second letter to her contained the message that, yes, he would come, but probably would spend no more than a year or two, she was thrilled. She immediately sent him money for his train fare from Lampasas to Framingham plus a little for incidental expenses. To what extent Roy was aware of this plan is not clear.

CHAPTER 10

FLOYD COMES TO FRAMINGHAM - - .
THE ARTIST FULFILLED
1923 - 1932

The information that is in print in the archival material, mostly newspaper clippings, forming background for this true story describes a situation very different from that actually related to me by Floyd. All the written accounts suggest that both Edith and Roy were involved in the plan to bring the crippled artist into their home. The details vary, but in essence they suggest that they both became aware of him and his plight, and took an immediate interest in having him as their houseguest and protégé. One version is that they were on a concert tour through Texas when they first became aware of him. Other accounts have them reading about him in a variety of publications. In any event, the "official" versions of the way in which Floyd came to reside at the shore of Lake Waushakum with the Greenes are that they sent for him, or that they actually went out to Texas and brought him back with them. Sounds nice and neat and may even be factual. However, years later when Floyd was living with my mother and father and me, the story he told us of his arrival in Framingham is quite different. For what it's worth, and perhaps it's only an interesting variant on the truth but fascinating none the less, this is what "really" happened as related to us by Floyd.

After reading and re-reading Madame Greene's second letter and discussing the implications of it with his family, Floyd came to a conclusion. He figured that if these people, who must be wealthy and probably well-connected, really wanted to help him out as they described, then why not take them up on it, if only for a short time - - maybe a year or two at most. It certainly sounded from her letters that she and her husband had a good understanding of the amount of care he would require and were prepared to handle all that it would entail. He wrote back to say that he was very moved by their compassionate offer and would pack up only his essential belongings and art material and would have his brother bring him to the Lampasas train station. He would ride in the baggage car along with his luggage and supplies, since he couldn't see how he could manage in a regular Pullman compartment. He had talked to the railroad officials who confirmed that, in spite of it being unorthodox it would be all right with them if he wanted to travel that way. They would see to it that he would be looked after a couple of times a day during his trip. He explained to them that he really didn't require much food, but that he would need someone to empty and clean his bedpan and to bring him fresh water to drink. If they could help him to get sitting up each morning, that would be a real plus.

So, in the spring of 1923, Floyd Niles Walser found himself once again riding the rails. This time, however he was no hobo and was riding in relative comfort. Fourteen years had elapsed since his ride home in a combination freight and baggage car with his brother Ben at his side. That was an extremely difficult time for him, feeling totally convinced that life was over for him and that he would never enjoy anything again. Now, emotionally fully recovered, he was on his way to what appeared to be the beginning of a new chapter in his life. A life he had come to feel very grateful to still have.

The day his train pulled in to the depot in downtown Framingham was cold and overcast with a chilling mist falling from the clouds. He had made good friends with the various train personnel who had been more than helpful to him along the way. They carefully helped him out of the baggage car and retrieved all his belongings. After setting him down on the floor inside the depot, with his trunk stuffed with clothes and boxes full of his art supplies surrounding him, they wished him good luck in his artistic endeavors and continued on their way.

Back at Harmony Home on this same day, Edith sweetly asked Roy to kindly do her a favor. She asked him to please drive down to the train depot and pick up Floyd. His response was along the lines of, "Who the heck is Floyd?" She replied with something like, "Oh, he'll be staying with us for a while. I'm sure you'll like him. He is an artist and wants to study at the School of the Museum of Fine Arts. I thought we'd help him get started there." She failed to mention that he was also crippled and unable to walk or that her plan was to have him live with them for an indefinite period.

Roy hopped into his relatively new 1920 Ford Model T roadster and after cleaning out most of the accumulated junk in the back seat so that it would look presentable, drove off to the depot, which was only about a mile and a half distant. Roy's spirits were good in spite of the miserable weather with the wind driving the cold mist right into his bones. As he drove he was probably thinking about all his commitments with his various orchestras and piano pupils. He may have thought that in spite of the fact that he and Edith had very limited incomes and really not much in the way of financial security other than the house and their beautiful lakefront property, they were fortunate to have the life they had. They were both in good health, although Edith was occasionally not well, and they were doing what they wanted, enjoying it all.

Once he had parked next to the uncrowded train station, he dashed in to meet this stranger, Floyd. He had forgotten to ask Edith how he would recognize him, but felt that would not be a problem. As he entered the waiting area he saw a stern-faced creature, who seemed to have no legs, sitting on the floor partially covered with a poncho and surrounded by a ragtag collection of dilapidated old boxes and a trunk that looked like an antique. He must have felt a wave of compassion for this poor creature and wondered where in the world he had come from and where he was going. But, he felt that did not concern him. He was there to pick up this fellow he knew only as Floyd Walter, or Waltzer, or something like that. Seeing no one who appeared to be waiting to be met, he inquired at the desk if a Floyd "whatever" had come in. He was told that the gentleman sitting on the floor over there was Floyd Walser who had arrived from Texas in a baggage car.

As he approached the strange apparition huddled on the floor, he tried not to let the expression on his face mirror his shock at finding that his charge was in such a condition. He greeted the stranger with, "Hi. I'm Roy Greene. You must be Floyd. I'm pleased to make your acquaintance." He awkwardly extended his right hand down to where Floyd could grasp it. "Howdy", replied the stranger. "It's good to finally meet you. Is Edith with you?" After Roy explained that Edith was waiting for them at their home, he began to figure out how he was going to get this person into his car and bring him and his belongings to the house. Then what in the world would he do about providing an appropriate place in his home? He thought he was there to pick up a young man who would spend a few weeks in the spare bedroom upstairs and who could easily trot up and down the stairs, to and from the kitchen and be mostly on his own. He even had thought that the young fellow could help him around the house with a variety of chores that never seemed to get attended to.

Floyd quickly saw through the mask that Roy had put up and indicated that he figured that Edith hadn't told him the whole story. He suddenly felt betrayed and disillusioned and was determined to not be a burden on this good man who obviously had no idea of what lay in store for him. He went so far as to suggest that perhaps he should just get on the next train headed for Texas, and forget the whole idea. Roy could simply tell his wife that he had changed his mind and not come out after all. He would return her money. He surely did not want to cause any problems for them, and suddenly realizing that Roy was simply not prepared for the significant amount of work he could require, he wanted no part of the deal.

One of Roy's endearing traits was his belief in the goodness of people - - all people. He was more than a little disappointed that Edith had misled him about what this boarder would require in terms of special equipment and how much effort it would be for them. Perhaps she didn't realize the full extent of this man's handicap herself. But whether she did or not, Roy had already formed a strong feeling for this strong-willed Texan who had trusted that he would be taken care of. Roy was determined to make this a positive experience for all concerned. He quickly assured Floyd that he had a plan in mind for equipping his house with a special room that would be his own studio apartment. It was just going to take a while before he could get started on it. He expressed the thought that he hoped that Floyd would be patient with him and that he was sure that he would be comfortable in the room that temporarily would be his quarters. He did not confide that of course this was not the upstairs room that he had planned on allowing the young man to use for what he had understood to be a short visit. He was so calm about the whole idea and so convincing that all of this was what he really wanted to do that Floyd soon agreed to stop talking about returning to Texas on the next train. This was the start of a close friendship between these two very different men. A friendship that would last for years.

Roy easily persuaded a couple of strong young fellows who were standing around in the waiting area to help him load his friend into his auto. With this accomplished, he squeezed in as much of the baggage as he could into the unused areas in the car and left the rest to be picked up later. There was little concern that anyone would steal what was temporarily left behind. There was more of a chance that someone would think it was all junk and toss it out, so Roy planned to come right back for it. Before they drove away from the depot, Roy called his brother, Clifford and asked him to meet him at his house to help unload Floyd. He said he would explain later. Roy was not a big man, and his brother was even shorter. But both of them were strong and would have no difficulty lifting Floyd out of the car and carrying him into the house.

When they arrived at the Greene's home, Roy went in to explain to Edith what she already pretty much knew. He most likely did not scold her or in any way show that he was upset with her lack of complete truthfulness about the situation. She came out to greet the new arrival and made a big show of concern for his well being, suggesting that he must be exhausted from his long trip. She surprised both men when she candidly admitted that poor Roy had not been consulted prior to her invitation for Floyd to come stay with them. She allowed that she had been afraid that if he had known in advance, he might have not agreed with her plan, and she really wanted a protégé. She said that she felt a bit ashamed of herself, since now there was no fully equipped place for him to be as comfortable as he should be, but they would soon do something about that. Just what that "something" was, she wasn't sure, but Roy would come up with a plan no doubt.

And Roy did indeed have a plan in mind. Only a couple of years previously they had taken a second mortgage on the house to help buy a car and to make some planned improvements to their home. The improvements had not been started, and the auto didn't cost as much as they had estimated. So there were some available funds with which they could add a small room on to the front of the house. However, until they better understood Floyd and his requirements, he would be located in what had been the dining room. There was access into the living room through the kitchen, so Roy's and Edith's piano pupils would not have to in any way disturb Floyd by going through his "room" to get to the piano. Roy planned to place a beautiful oriental folding screen as a privacy barrier in what was the wide opening between the dining room and the living room.

Once the bewildered Clifford had helped his brother carry the surprise houseguest from the car into the house and place him on the floor of the living room, both men began the task of removing the dining room furniture. The large table was dismantled and carried to the low-ceilinged, dirt-floored cellar. Chairs were brought upstairs and/or into the living room. The China cupboard and serving sideboard were moved up against the wall to a location which they judged to be most out of the way for now. The bed was brought down from the room that was planned to be the visitor's quarters. The old trunk and the boxes that were still in Roy's auto were brought in and Clifford drove out to the depot to retrieve the rest of the boxes. After a couple of hours, Floyd's temporary room was ready for him.

While all this muscle work was going on, Edith had been chatting away with her new friend and beginning to try to understand his life story. She also was trying to understand the full extent of the work it was going to be to provide all that he would require. She may have had some reservations about the wisdom of her emotional plan to have brought him there, but she never let those feelings show.

Floyd must have felt more than a little uncomfortable at first, knowing what an unplanned pile of trouble he suddenly was in Roy Greene's life. But Roy seemed to be having no problems tipping his house upside down to accommodate him, and he actually believed that Roy, more than Edith, was looking forward to having him as part of the family. The more Roy found out about Floyd's artistic abilities, the more he seemed to brighten. Also, from their first meeting a few hours ago at the depot, there was an easy camaraderie between the two men. And Roy very quickly demonstrated that, in spite of being short and not looking very muscular, he had the strength to lift Floyd whenever it was necessary. Also, he did not seem to be the least put off by Floyd's physical limitations, just naturally dealing with him, man to man.

Within a matter of a few days, Roy had pretty much seen to all of the things that made all three of them comfortable with Floyd living right there in what had been their dining room. He quickly learned that he would be the sole caretaker of Floyd's bedpan. Edith could not deal with that at all. Roy would tug Floyd up to a sitting position each morning, but had no choice but to leave him propped up in his bed for the day. Floyd described the old overstuffed living room easy chair that he had been using back home. It had been rigged up by one of his brothers, with casters in place of what had been short legs. It was comfortable for him to sit in all day, so long as he was on a level surface. He could even manage to propel himself around a little bit by thrusting his upper body forward, causing the chair to move forward slightly. By pushing against the floor with his cane, he sometimes got a bit of an advantage over his inertia and might be able to move a little better. He had an old wide belt that had been cut in two, fastened to this chair in order to keep him securely anchored in place. He would thrust and push his way up to or away from his bed each day. He suggested that he send for this clumsy-looking but valuable old chair at the first opportunity.

From time to time, Roy would carry Floyd out into the veranda where he could get a good view of the lake through the large screened windows. He enjoyed sitting out there for hours at a time. It is possible that he may have actually been set up out there during the first summer in what was a temporary studio apartment.

Discussions soon focused on adding a complete and private room with a platform just outside its door. Another high priority item was the plan to get their charge in to the School at the Museum of Fine Arts. All of this attention had by now convinced the Texan that he perhaps had made the right decision in coming to this strange place. He sent for the rest of his personal items, still back in Lampasas. Included in the next shipment from home, along with the caster-bottomed chair was his old collapsible wheelchair. This portable chair would be vital if he were to go to such places as the art school. Roy would easily be able to carry it in the back seat of his car whenever he ferried the new student for his lessons. But now that he had his familiar old living room easy chair with its casters, he had some small degree of mobility around the inside of his new home.

Regardless of the circumstances surrounding his arrival in Framingham with Roy and Edith, there is no doubt of the fact that he was taken into their hearts as well as their home and was treated especially kindly. There is no record of how long it took to build Floyd's studio apartment onto the house, or how much of it was actually crafted by Roy himself. It is most likely that the musician, although talented in many things and not afraid to tackle anything, had the bulk of the framing and roofing done by hired carpenters. However, over the next few months, the special place for the visiting artist was built. The room was attached to the front of the existing structure, off to the right of the front entry that led into the kitchen and was now the first thing seen by a visitor coming in the driveway from the street. Floyd thought it looked pretty nice. Inside, it measured approximately 12 feet by 18 feet and had a good-size skylight built into the roof in such a way as to allow north light to enter; a nice touch for an artist who planned to do portraits and basically dedicate himself to constant artistic growth.

A doorway was cut into the dining room wall in such a location that it opened into a hallway, which ran along the width of the addition out towards the street. At the end of this hallway were two doors, one to the left, opened into Floyd's room, the other across from it, opened to the outdoors. With this arrangement, Floyd could receive visitors directly without them having to go into the main part of the house and also the Greenes could access his room through the connecting hallway. A small raised wooden platform was built just outside the new exterior door, and a couple of stairs led down to the cinder driveway. Eventually, a long sloping ramp would be added to make it relatively easy for Floyd to be pushed in his old chair out to ground level.

The floor of the studio room was made of wide pine flooring boards, but was less than perfectly flat and even, and although he never complained, this unevenness caused a bit of difficulty for Floyd in his caster-bottomed chair. Three casement windows were incorporated, two in the front or north-facing wall and one in the opposite wall, right at the end of the room. This part of the addition extended out past the house by about 6 feet, so that looking out that window, one could see the sun glinting off Lake Waushakum, visible between the heavy growth of trees. This part of the room was where Floyd's bed was installed, right up against the window and in the corner.

The windowsill was a few inches above the top surface of the mattress. Right outside this window, Roy had dug, by hand, a small cesspool with a stovepipe leading up from it and angling against the outside of the windowsill. The stovepipe was closed off with an old porcelain saucepan that fit nicely into it. In this manner, Floyd was able to, completely on his own, take care of his bedpan waste. He had to be sitting up in bed in order to use the bedpan daily. Then he would open the window, reach out to grasp the saucepan's handle and lift it into his room. After dumping the waste down the chute formed by the stovepipe, he would replace the saucepan and go on about his business. About once a week or so, he would toss a cupful of lye down into the small cesspool as a means of controlling it.

In lieu of a sink, a rather primitive set-up was provided near his bed. A galvanized steel bucket, such as what might be used in the garden, had a small hole drilled in its bottom. A small diameter copper pipe was brazed into the hole so that it was level with the inside of the bucket and protruded out the bottom about 4 inches. A cold water pipe was run under the floor and then came up through a hole and terminated, about 2 feet above the floor in a faucet of the style that one would find on the outside of a house. A small hole was drilled into the floor in front of this faucet and the bucket was placed there, with its pipe sticking down into the hole in the floor. This would pass for a sink. A rubber stopper could be used to hold the cold water in the pail if wanted, and then pulled out to let it all run out under the room and eventually seep into the ground. There was no hot water supply. An electric hot plate with two burners was placed on a handy nearby surface to be used to heat food or water. A steam radiator, connected to the main house's steam heating system, provided a comfortable level of heat for the cold New England winters to come.

Floyd loved his new home. He sent for all the rest of his belongings in a letter to his mother back in Lampasas in which he detailed his good fortune at having met such fine and caring people as the Greenes. His studio room was wonderful. He would be able to study and paint and he had plenty of privacy, but was still close enough so that Roy could look in on him several times a day and provide a bit of help if he should need it. He was determined to be of as little bother to his benefactors as possible.

By the end of the fall of 1923, Floyd was pretty well set in his new studio room. As the last shipments of his belongings arrived by train from Texas, there seemed to be far more material to be stuffed into the 200 square feet of floor space than could possibly be made to fit. Old chests and traveling trunks were piled one on top of another and along with musty-smelling boxes and crates, filled most of the space from floor to ceiling. A narrow passageway was left from the door to the "kitchen" and sleeping area, with a little space left over for an easel to be set up under the skylight. Door handles, or what he referred to as "hand holds" were attached to most available solid surfaces so that Floyd could grasp them with his right hand to help him to move himself in his chair around the narrow spaces.

True to their word, arrangements were soon made by the Greenes for Floyd to study at the renowned School of the Museum of Fine Arts in Boston. This was perhaps the most exciting aspect of the whole new adventure. To be able to learn from the exceptional staff at such a prestigious institution was more than he had ever hoped for. His old collapsible wheelchair, which had arrived from Lampasas, was tucked into the back of Roy's roadster whenever the hour-long trip to Huntington Avenue was to take place. The physically fit young musician soon learned how to manage to lift Floyd from his caster-bottomed chair into his car without help. Then, upon arriving in Boston at the school, he likewise was able to haul his friend out of the car and into the portable wheelchair unassisted.

Whether it was due to his handicap or had more to do with the artistic talent he quickly displayed, Floyd soon became well known to the faculty and other students. People were fascinated at his technique and tried not to stare. He would work with only his right hand nimbly guiding his pencil, pen, or brush at his easel, while his basically useless left hand was plunked down next to him and acted as a sort of vise with an assortment of art tools clamped tightly in it. This was like nothing they had ever seen before.

Roy would drop him off in the morning once each week for what was to become several years of study, and then pick him up again late in the afternoon. His interests were in all aspects of art including using oils and watercolors, but he had become especially interested in the art and science of etching. He had seen what he thought of as truly marvelous works of art produced through the etching process by such masters as Rembrandt, Jacques Callot, James McNeill Whistler, and others and had a burning desire to learn the technique. That it might be particularly difficult for him to do all that would be required, including the acid etching and then printing, never seemed to even enter his mind. The works of the local and contemporary noted etcher Frank W. Benson, who had been a student at the museum school in 1882 and then an instructor there from 1889 to 1913, inspired him even further.

He was fortunate to have the opportunity to study under Philip Leslie Hale, one of the most respected members of the faculty of the museum school at that time, who taught him anatomy and drawing from the human figure. Floyd's portrait work, which had previously been one of his many strengths improved dramatically with the guidance provided by this gifted teacher. Hale (1865-1931) had also studied at the Boston Museum School and was a classmate of another local, famous impressionist, Edmund Tarbell who was born in West Groton, Massachusetts. In 1887 Hale had traveled to Paris where as an art critic he made regular visits to the home of Claude Monet and the art colony of Giverny. By the mid-

1890s, Hale was turning out dazzling neo-impressionist scenes, typically of women and flowers bathed in golden light. However, since the press at that time was rooted in conservatism, they were generally not supportive of his visionary efforts. That criticism combined with the constraints of teaching at such a strongly academic institution as the Boston Museum School, led to his return to a more academic form of Impressionism.

Floyd was perhaps one of the most serious minded and dedicated students to have entered this famed art school in some time. As soon as Roy would get him back to his lakeside room, he would practice the special techniques he had just been shown. He would very often get up early and after a small breakfast would set to work with his art material, sketching or painting but always progressing. It was not unusual for him to work without a break for most of the day, then after a short rest and a little food, continue with his passionate commitment to his objective of constant improvement.

Floyd's first winter in Framingham was a particularly cold and snowy one. Lake Waushakum was quickly frozen solid and to the Texan who was not at all used to seeing snow, the vistas in all directions were spectacular. He had Roy take some photographs of the house so that he could send them home to his mother to see what a strange and lovely winter wonderland he was now living in. On the back of the photo that Roy took of the house from about 50 feet out on the snow-covered surface of the frozen lake he wrote, "Our place looking north. Boat house at shoreline at right. Big ice storage Co. house at left in distance. Ice on lake is 20 inches thick. Floyd" In the margin on the front of the picture he penciled, "To Mamma".

Within a few years of his arrival in Framingham he had done so many drawings of old houses and interesting trees in the surrounding towns where Roy would drive him that he started to become well known. People couldn't help but notice him when he would be set up outdoors somewhere in his old wheelchair working with only his right arm, but turning out beautiful renditions of what he saw. He particularly enjoyed watercolors and used a free, impressionistic style. Some days he would focus entirely on creating an oil painting and would stay at it for so long that the natural lighting on his subject would completely change so that he would be painting the effects of light and shade from memory.

He was more than a little surprised when Roy showed up one fine morning in a light duty truck that he called a "commercial canopy express". It was of 1920 vintage and was fitted with large windows in its boxy and spacious body. It had 2 full-length doors that swung out in back. Roy pushed "Tex" out in his trusty old chair onto the platform just outside the door to his room and explained what he had in mind. He thought that perhaps this would make a fine vehicle for getting out to sketch the scenery in the surrounding towns. When he backed this truck, which Floyd always would refer to as a car, up against the platform, it was as though it was made especially for them. The back doors swung out clearing the platform by a few inches. The cavernous interior fairly called out for Floyd to be wheeled right in.

Roy quickly placed a couple of boards to form a short ramp and easily pushed Floyd right on in. There was plenty of headroom and ample space surrounding the artist in which he would be able to locate a nice assortment of his painting supplies and equipment, as well as his old folding wheelchair. Roy pointed out that he needed to incorporate a way to firmly anchor Floyd in his chair so that he wouldn't roll around when the "car" was in motion. Roy was excited with the thought that with this vehicle all rigged up, they would be able to drive their protégé out to any reasonable location in any kind of weather. He'd be able to paint whatever caught his interest, rain or shine, wherever that may be; so long as Roy could park near enough for Floyd to get the view he wanted. Roy's excitement was more than shared by the artist, who was so thrilled with this new development that he for a

Above: "Harmony Home" from the frozen surface of the lake -1923.

Edith reviewing one of her compositions - 1925.

Floyd did this pen and ink sketch of "Harmony Home" in 1936.

Floyd's sketching car -1925.

moment forgot that Roy had other things going on in his life, and began listing all the places he wanted to go during the next few weeks. He was also planning all the places where Roy could drive him where he would ask to be placed into his old wheelchair and positioned outdoors when the weather permitted. The fact that Roy would not only be his chauffeur for the whole day, but would be lugging him into and out of his wheelchair, in and out of the back of the truck, and carting his art supplies here and there did not even enter his mind. At first.

Once the initial excitement had worn down a bit, Roy allowed that with this new rig, the 3 of them, Floyd, Roy and Edith could have some enjoyable weekends in the country. They would pack a light lunch with some beverages and they would all enjoy their outings to interesting places.

After a few more years, Floyd began giving art lessons himself. Many townsfolk brought their youngsters to the Greene's home so that they could study the techniques that he was just mastering. He was a firm believer in the thought that the best way to really learn a subject is to teach it to someone. The mental discipline required to effectively teach any subject forced the teacher to truly grasp the concepts involved. He had had such an interesting life that his pupils and their parents would enjoy hearing all about the "Wild West" and some of his particularly exciting adventures, even if he had to make them up. He did have an impressive collection of about 100 or more, old Indian arrowheads. He told the fascinated audiences that he had found most of them himself as a youngster roaming around the Texas plains. He enjoyed being called by one of his favorite nicknames: "Tex". He appreciated the few extra dollars he derived from his art students. Adding that small amount to the meager disability pension he was receiving helped him to pay for his art supplies and other incidentals. The Greenes would not allow him to pay them any rent, since he was there at their invitation, but he tried to provide for his own expenses as much as he could.

He was truly engrossed in the study of preparing etchings and was determined to master all that it would take to become a noted etcher. At his lessons in Boston there were plenty of people around to help him with some of the difficult and potentially dangerous aspects of the process, particularly the nitric acid bath. But back in his studio he was on his own and didn't want to bother Roy or Edith for any help. He had accumulated a supply of rectangular copper plates that measured about 8 by 10 inches or so, as well as a nice assortment of sharp tools known as etching needles in a variety of sizes. He had no press at first with which to make the actual prints, preferring to avoid the expense of such a device until he had convinced himself that he would really be able to scratch out copper in an acceptable manner. He also wanted to avoid the use of acid in his room until he was sure of what he was doing and had the proper equipment for dealing with and properly disposing of the corrosive and dangerous fluid. His thought was to simply take his completed plates to school and use their facilities or more likely, have someone there do it for him.

He soon learned to apply the correct amount of the acid resisting material the artists called the "ground" to the copper plate. He was especially pleased with the results he got when the ground he used was a special mixture of beeswax, bitumen and resin. It took many hours of practice for him to master the technique of using the etching needles. He had to find just the right amount of pressure for each unique tool and for each effect he was trying to create. Too much pressure and the cut in the copper plate would go too deep. Too little and the line may not be as strong as he wanted; that is, assuming he wanted a strong line. There was a lot of technique to be mastered in order to achieve the artistic result he could see in his mind. He also found that when he blackened the ground by holding the coated plate over a burning candle, the copper lines he had cut would gleam and showed up very nicely.

Floyd self-portrait. "Tex."

Etching by Floyd. "Texas Ranch House"

He sometimes worked from photographs he had asked Roy to take of the scenes he wanted as his subjects. Most often he would create a sketch himself and work from that back in his studio. He kept the first attempts relatively simple, using trees and straightforward structures as his inspiration. When he was convinced that he had scratched just the correct amount and strength of lines into his copper plate, he would apply what he referred to as a "stopper" varnish to the back surface. This was to prevent it from dissolving away in the forthcoming bath in nitric acid. Then he would carefully wrap up his masterpiece to be brought to Boston. There he would get the help and instruction he needed in order to effectively deal with the actual acid bath etching of the copper plate. He paid close attention to each seemingly minor detail including just how long to leave the copper immersed and how to know for sure that it was time to remove all the ground to reveal an acceptable, if not perfect master.

His first few attempts most likely were disappointments, but his resolve or some might say stubbornness, kept him at it until he started to get the results he wanted. He was reminded that the great etching master, Frank W. Benson abandoned etching for 30 years after the first one he produced in 1882, *Salem Harbor*, dissatisfied him so much.

The teaching staff as well as the other students, were impressed with his rapid progress. It was unusual for someone to be able to spend essentially every waking moment (and some dreaming ones as well, no doubt) working at developing his skills. With no distractions of family or job or any of the many other things that so often could get in the way, Floyd's dedication to his chosen field was legendary.

Before very long he was turning out some very acceptable etchings. Spurred on to do even more, he purchased a press for making his own prints and had Roy set up an area in his room where he could safely use and dispose of the required acid. Between using burning candles to blacken the ground, sharp etching needles to scratch out the copper, and vials of nitric acid poured into and out of porcelain dishes, all being done with one hand, it is surprising that no disaster ever occurred.

When he wasn't actually working at creating art in the many forms he chose to develop, he was studying every art-related book he could get his hands on. When he studied the career of Frank W. Benson who was in his early sixties then and still creating, his interest was heightened, since that genius was working in all the artistic mediums that interested him as well. The fact that he had been so closely connected with the Museum School only increased his fascination with the man. He knew he would never even approach the level of perfection and fame achieved by that great artist, but what a role model! A much-publicized quotation of Benson's became one of Floyd's deep convictions and he would try to convey the thought to his best pupils.

> The more a painter knows about his subject, the more he studies and understands it, the more the true nature of it is perceived by whoever looks at it, even though it is extremely subtle and not easy to see or understand. A painter must search deeply into the aspects of a subject, must know and understand it thoroughly before he can represent it well.

He maintained quite a bit of correspondence with his old remote tutor, Zim who had provided him with inspiration and encouragement when he was just beginning to stretch his artistic wings back in Texas. Now he wrote to his friend in New York to tell him of his good fortune in having moved near Boston and his studies at the Museum School. He described his new studio apartment and how wonderful Mr. and Mrs. Greene had been to him. He also sent several drawings to him for comment and critique. This is from a letter back to him from Zim, dated November 28, 1925.

Mr. Floyd Walser
Framingham, Mass.

Dear Walser:
I am pleased to get your letter and bunch of drawings. The pastels show a keen sense of color. There is splendid harmony in them. I am not doing much watercolor work lately; haven't the time to fuss with it.

Regarding wash, it is simple enough when you understand lights and shadows. These crude demonstrations may serve to start you in on the rudiments, showing great contrasts in light and shade effects. I handled these in a very broad sense with a quarter inch brush, black sable. For wash, use lamp black or sepia and a red sable brush No. 6, to get the best results.

The description of your new studio amuses me. It must look swell. One can work so much easier in such inspiring surroundings. I don't know of anyone having a bigger collection of my sketches than you, so you may safely lay claim to such distinction. Thanks for the honor. I am sure they will be appreciated always by you and your friends.
I trust this finds you in good spirits.
Sincerely yours,
(signed) ZIM

Floyd truly flourished in his new home and loved every minute of his busy life. He and Roy had become very good friends and they both enjoyed spending whatever free time Roy could squeeze out of his hectic schedule, chatting about all sorts of things. Sometimes when Roy would have a particularly difficult personal issue with one or more of his students or orchestra members, he would find that the wisdom and careful thought that "Tex" could bring to the problem was a real plus. Roy discovered that Floyd was a very astute observer of the human condition and that the many books he had read, combined with his innate appreciation of ordinary folks made him a great sounding board.

The Greenes also took great pleasure in bringing their hard-working and superbly talented protégé out for fun adventures whenever they could. All three of them particularly relished their trips to the ocean at Cape Cod. Just the ride there and back must have been great fun for Floyd as well as providing a diversion from his unrelenting efforts to master all aspects of art. But he couldn't get enough of the ocean water. How he loved being totally immersed in the buoyant, cool salty waters of those beaches, with not much more than his nose and mouth exposed to the air. The Greenes always chose beaches where there were essentially no waves when they wanted Floyd to actually get in the ocean, but would later drive to other locations where the pounding surf was great fun to watch.

Roy put together a sheet of leather fastened to a couple of old wheelbarrow handles. He would place this on the sandy beach, lift Floyd onto the leather seat and drag him into the ocean. In short order, Floyd would be in water that came up to Roy's knees and then Floyd could simply lie back and float. He asked Edith to snap a few pictures so that he could show his mother and the family back in Texas how he swam. On the back of one of these photos he wrote, "This is the way Roy carried me into water deep enough for me to swim in. I swam 75 yards on my back at the time. It was fine exercise for me." On the back of a picture showing him happily floating with little but his face and arms above water he wrote, "Did you know I could swim on my back alone? It was easy, 'tho of course Edith and Roy watched me constantly. F.W."

When the Greene's hectic schedule permitted them a weekend or perhaps even longer to get away to the Cape, they would often stay in tents that Roy would set up in various campgrounds close to the ocean. One of those tents was the cook tent in which Roy was happy to do all the cooking. The fresh ocean air did wonders for their spirits as well as their appetites. No matter that they were "roughing it", Roy

Edith, Floyd and Roy at their campsite at Cape Cod. Roy was well-dressed even in a tent.

The picture Floyd sent to his mother to show that he could swim on his back.

The technique Roy used to get Floyd into water deep enough for him to float on his back.

Edith and Floyd getting some sun on a Cape Cod beach.

would feel incomplete without his bow tie, so he wore it most of the time or at least until he changed into his bathing suit.

The number and quality of Floyd's drawings and paintings soon began to overwhelm his little studio room. The Greenes were proud to display his latest work on the walls of their rooms where their many knowledgeable visitors would not only be impressed, but also ask for similar renditions for their own collections. Floyd was never sure what price he should ask for any particular painting commissioned by the friends of his benefactors. He always kept it low, since he knew that he was only a beginner and still had a lot to learn. But the enthusiastic praise always lavished upon him whenever he would present his latest finished work, gave him far more than any monetary reward ever could.

There was no question that the Greenes were more than pleased with how well he was doing and that they were very proud to be the recipients of so much of his work. But Edith would always cherish the very first sketch that her new protégé had presented her as a surprise gift to show his appreciation for her kindness in initiating the plan to bring him into their home. She had told him of how much she had always been impressed with the works of the great, Hungarian-born pianist, Franz Liszt. She told him how when she was only eleven years old she found her mother sobbing because the greatest pianist and composer who ever lived had just passed away. The impressionable young Edith knew then that if only she could have been born 60 years earlier, she would have been madly in love with this god. She would talk to Floyd at length about how Liszt had turned out more than 300 compositions and also had transcribed much of the work of other famous composers. Now that she had become a composer herself, she understood the dedication and denial of other worldly pursuits that was required. She was also in awe of the fact that he had taken the time to impart some of his great talent to over 400 advanced pupils from all over the world. She had given piano lessons to a fair number of students herself, but she had to admit that many of them would have rather been out playing baseball or some such activity. And on and on she would go. Somewhere Floyd came across a photograph of Edith's idol and without her knowing about it, he set to work to produce a remarkably life-like charcoal sketch of the great Franz Liszt. Edith was moved to tears with this well-chosen and superbly well-crafted gift and kept it on her piano sheet music rack for all to see and admire for years to come.

Floyd studied hard and worked at his art constantly, with a single-mindedness that most people would be hard pressed to match. To the casual observer watching him work, he looked more than serious; he appeared to be angry with his paint brushes or his pen or etching needles. But nothing could have been further from the truth. He loved what he was doing passionately and felt deeply that he was always meant to be doing this. He was so focused on what was on his easel or sketchpad or coated copper plate, that it was not unusual for him to lose all sense of time. He would often completely forget about eating or stopping for any kind of a break for hours.

Edith's many friends in the various clubs she was so closely aligned with would frequently sit for their portrait. It usually took Floyd most of one afternoon to rough out the basic image then complete the work on a subsequent day. There were several of these sketches that cried out for caricature the way Zim would have done them, but he held back, not wishing to offend anyone. Several of Edith's acquaintances were artists themselves, or knew of established painters and etchers. Floyd would often find himself in the company of accomplished art experts and took great pleasure in hearing their praises for his efforts. He needed to be sure that they later didn't temper their enthusiasm as they walked away by saying something to the effect of "Not bad for a guy with such a handicap." It was important to him that the praise he was constantly receiving was unconditional. Eventually he became convinced that that was indeed true.

Starting sometime in 1930, Floyd began to paint what was to become one of his favorite motifs. In about a half-hour's drive from Harmony Home, he would be in the charming New England town of Sudbury. There, near the Old Boston Post Road could be found Longfellow's Wayside Inn and its associated buildings. This very well known property, a National Historic Site, was originally called How's Tavern, or the Red Horse Tavern and was built between 1702 and 1707 as a 2-room house for David How and his wife. They operated it as a tavern starting in 1716. It grew in size and fame over the years and was a popular accommodation for traveling colonial patriots. Henry Wadsworth Longfellow was captivated by the inn and in 1863 wrote his famous *Tales of a Wayside Inn* giving the place its popular name from that time on.

Henry Ford owned the Wayside Inn from 1923 until 1946. Mr. Ford's genius was not limited to building automobiles and after he learned about the gristmill that David How operated in the early 1740s, he was fascinated with the topic. In 1929 he constructed a fully operational water-powered gristmill as an educational replica of the original a short distance downstream from where How's mill had been located. It began operation on this picturesque site, grinding its first corn on Thanksgiving Day, 1929. It has continued ever since to grind grains for use and sale at the Wayside Inn. Often referred to as "Ford's Grist Mill", it has become one of the most-photographed mills in America.

Floyd was immediately captivated by the artistic nature of the gristmill, its stonework, its huge water wheel and the stream. He studied it from every angle and in all times of day with natural illumination highlighting various portions of the structure. He captured it in pastels, watercolor, and oil paint in his own style creating truly sought-after renditions. He visited the area around that site several times over the next 10 or more years, never tiring of its beauty.

There must have been at least one time during Floyd's many sketching visits to the "old mill" where he most probably would have seen Richie. The two men did not know each other at that time, and Richie was fascinated with the mill for very different reasons than the artist was. Richie loved to go right into the mill proper and talk to the miller who enjoyed explaining how it all worked. Richie was enthralled with the huge quartzite millstones slowly turning and grinding. He learned that these unique objects, weighing about a ton each had been specially shipped to this location from France for Mr. Ford. The whole idea of capturing the quiet power of naturally falling water in a slowly rotating 18 foot diameter wheel and then using that energy through huge shafts and gears to produce a useful product had an almost magnetic attraction for the young man and he visited there frequently. All of it appealed to his mechanically creative mind, while he was only marginally impressed by the artistic beauty of the place.

One of Floyd's oil paintings of the Grist Mill.

In the spring of 1931 Floyd's skill as an etcher was spotlighted by the prestigious International Competitive Print Exhibition sponsored by the Print Club of Cleveland, Ohio. This exhibition took place at the Cleveland Museum of Art from March 18 through April 15, 1931. He had submitted a couple of prints of what he thought were his best etchings, and when one was accepted he was stunned by the magnitude of the honor bestowed upon him. He knew that from the many superb etchings that were submitted by the great artists throughout the world, only the best works, in the eyes of the club, were chosen for the exhibition.

This was truly an international competition with works of a total of 184 artists from 12 countries on display. The styles of prints on display were mainly from etchings, although other graphic arts techniques were involved, such as lithograph, woodcut, drypoint, linoleum cut, colored aquatint and wood engraving. There were also 2 prints from chiaroscuros, a 16th century technique involving the use of several blocks to print different tones of the same color.

Floyd was one of 78 artists representing the United States in this exhibition. Page 12 of the 25-page catalog describing the artwork lists item number 118 by Walser, Floyd "Tex". Its title is given as *Where Dad was Born* and is shown as "etching" with a price of $15.00. Many years later when I came across a copy of this print I was surprised to see that his creative title, suggesting that his father was born in the building shown, was a bit misleading. The house is a very famous place in Framingham and is situated just behind the even more famous elm tree known as the Gates Street Elm. Floyd captured that tree, as well as the house, many times from all angles in all mediums over the years.

The record does not show whether or not the print from his etching was sold. Although he won no monetary prize, the prestige associated with simply being chosen to be included was reward enough. A top prize of $1000 went to an American artist named Louis Lozowick for his lithograph titled *City on a Rock*. A second-place prize of $100 and a 3rd of $50 was also given.

In early spring of 1932 Floyd was invited by the Society of American Etchers, Inc., formerly known as the Brooklyn Society of Etchers, to submit a print from one of his etchings to be included in the seventeenth annual exhibition of the National Arts Club. The show was to be held in November and December of that year in New York City in the club's headquarters at 15 Gramercy Park South. Floyd selected what he thought of as one of his best etchings. It was of an old white house in Framingham Centre that he titled, *For Rent* and he sent it to the Jury of Selection. He was very impressed with the credentials of this particular organization since he knew that its honorary president was none other than Frank W. Benson whom he respected so much. Floyd's submission was accepted for inclusion in the exhibition.

"For Rent." The etching Floyd entered in the 1932 Annual Exhibition of the Society of American Etchers in New York.

In spite of all the accolades received and remarkable progress made, Floyd for some time now had been feeling more than a little homesick. Maybe he felt this way precisely because of all he had achieved in the past 9 years while living with the Greenes and the fact that he had no real way to share it with the folks he left in Texas. "Shucks a-mighty", as he would have said, he wanted to show off. He was surprised at how much he missed his family. Occasional letters to and from home were no substitute for actually seeing the folks who had helped him through the toughest, darkest days of his life. It sure would be nice if he could visit them now and show them how well he was doing. He could not see a way that such a thing could be worked out.

But Roy and Edith had a plan. Roy had been talking to a local auto mechanic about the possibility of getting a car rigged up in such a way that Floyd would be able to drive it. This seemed like such a far-fetched idea that Floyd put it out of his mind. At least for a little while. But within a day or two of Roy's first mention of the idea, he became nearly obsessed with the thoughts of such a bold plan. It clearly couldn't be an ordinary passenger car, but something more along the lines of a small, enclosed truck of some type. It could be something similar to the windowed truck he had used a few years previously for his sketching excursions. That darned machine had been unreliable from the beginning and had been sold.

There would have to be room for him to actually sleep in it as well as enough space for him to carry along much of his art equipment. If this could actually be accomplished, he would be able to get himself back out to Texas for a good long visit, during which time he could show his family how far he had progressed. He had always wanted to paint the glorious scenery all around his home state. This was too good to be true.

Roy brought Floyd some articles he had seen in magazines that catered to people with disabilities of all kinds. Some of these described modifications that had been incorporated into a variety of autos that ostensibly allowed the vehicles to be driven by folks who had some pretty severe limitations due to paralysis, amputation, or other crippling handicaps. Many of these people were veterans of the World War and the effort to modify cars for them was not only a fascinating task, it was downright patriotic.

Once the seed of the idea was firmly planted in Floyd's mind, all of his energies flowed to it. Art and its study were temporarily forgotten as Floyd imagined what the inside of a specially configured car might look like. Roy and his brother, Cliff, were both gifted musicians but had only a passable working knowledge of the mechanical aspects of automobiles. But they had located a nearby garage that specialized in retrofitting cars for use by people with similar limitations. It would not be cheap, or easy to do, but they all agreed it was something they must try. Roy and Edith took a second mortgage on their property, obtaining $2100 in this manner. This was judged to be enough to purchase a used, but good car and get the required modifications incorporated. Floyd committed himself to earning enough money from the sale of the drawings he would make once he got back to Texas, to pay a significant part of this new debt the Greene's had incurred. He promised to send them money on a regular basis to help meet the monthly mortgage payments. Characteristically, both Roy and Edith must have insisted that he needn't concern himself with such thoughts, but realistically must have hoped for as much help as he could provide, since they really didn't have very deep pockets at all.

The next thing Floyd knew, a slightly used 1930 Chevrolet delivery wagon that had seen very little use was parked right next to Roy's trusty old Model "T" roadster. It looked like the perfect machine for him and when Floyd gazed upon it he could actually picture himself behind the wheel, chugging along the dusty roads towards Texas. Roy told him that when new, the car sold for $595, but he had been able to get a pretty good deal on it considering that it was only 2 years old, and hadn't actually accumulated very many miles. Roy wanted his young friend to get a good look at the vehicle, inside and out before he drove it out to the garage where the special, very unique modifications would be developed and incorporated. Roy also had agreed with the people who would transform it into practically an extension of Floyd's personality that it would be a good idea for him to bring the eager Mr. Walser out to their shop. Then they could better understand his limitations and figure out what types of things they could "borrow" from other machines they had rigged up and where they would be breaking new ground for this particular operator.

Now, in 1932 after nearly nine years of frequent, often once-a-week trips into the museum school, Floyd had made truly remarkable progress. But it was now time to end this specialized and very valuable schooling. And also it was time for the accomplished and gifted artist to travel back home for a visit. A special tribute was arranged by the Greenes for the determined young Texan who had overcome so much and had shown such promise. In the late spring, this tribute was written up in a local newspaper. Excerpts from that story follow.

CRIPPLED ARTIST WINS HIGH COMMENDATION

Walser Gives Exhibition in Brookline

Few artists have been accorded such a reception as Floyd N. Walser of Texas got yesterday afternoon from some 400 prominent people as he sat in his wheel chair in the large hall of Longwood Towers, Brookline, where an exhibition of his paintings and etchings was held. There were more than 200 on the list of patrons and patronesses, including representatives of most of the women's clubs in and around Boston.

It was in a sense a sort of crowning testimonial given an artist who had triumphed over what at one time seemed [an] insurmountable handicap and won a distinguished place in the art world. And there on the walls were 50 or more etchings and paintings as visible testimony of his triumph. ...

...A number of Boston artists went out on invitation of Mr. and Mrs. Greene to see Floyd Walser at their home and to help a little in his education.

The result of it all has been that his young man in the wheel chair has become a rather fine etcher, watercolor painter and pastel artist. Some of his etchings from nature are remarkable and have been accepted in the big exhibitions.

The last fine act of Mr. and Mrs. Greene for their protégé was the designing and building of a special automobile in which he will be able to travel and go back to his native Texas to show the people of that state - - and other states - - what he can do.

It was to celebrate the completion of his education that this reception and exhibition were given in the Longwood Towers yesterday afternoon. There were music and singing and readings and speaking – and tea- and Floyd N. Walser said it was the happiest day of his life.

The fine, noble thing which Mr. and Mrs. Greene have done was not forgotten by the guests who were present. Floyd Walser expects to start for Texas the latter part of June.

(The above is from the archives of the Framingham Historical Society and Museum, Framingham, Massachusetts.)

There was some other excitement in Floyd's life at around the time of this reception. On the night of April 6, 1932 a spectacular blaze consumed the Cove Ice Company's icehouse. This structure was only a few hundred feet away from Floyd's studio apartment attached to the front of the Greene's home. Floyd called out to Roy and Edith shortly after 9:00 PM when he could see through his street-facing windows, that the night sky was all-aglow. The three of them watched in horror as the flames from that inferno leapt skyward, and glowing embers began falling closer and closer to their house. Floyd must have been glad to realize that his precious car was not out in any danger from this inferno since it was still at the garage being modified for him. Within a few minutes the entire fire-fighting team of men

Floyd's 1924 pencil sketch of a young Edith Noyes, from an early photograph.

Floyd's 1924 pencil sketch of Edith at the Piano.

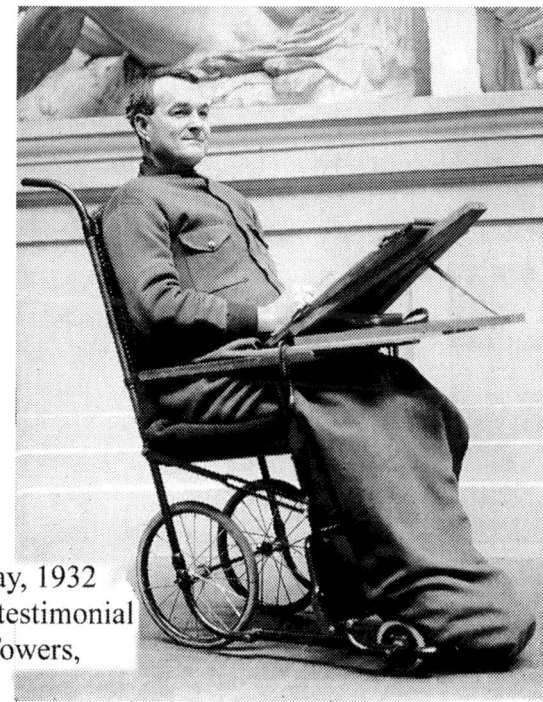

Floyd at his May, 1932 exhibition and testimonial at Longwood Towers, Brookline.

and equipment from the town of Framingham was at the scene. As soon as the fire chief arrived at the blaze, he ordered an emergency alarm to bring in an off-duty platoon and asked for, and received assistance from Natick and Ashland.

With fire shooting through every section of the huge wooden structure, and the front already collapsed, there was no chance of saving any of the building. Dwellings within an area of at least a half-mile radius were in serious danger. The Greene's property was one of the closest. It was fortunate for them that the strong wind that was blowing that night was carrying most of the fiery embers to the West, out over the cove. In fact, Monkey Island soon had all its trees ablaze.

The firemen laid lines of hose from the hydrants on both Cove Avenue and Lake Avenue and they set all three pumps at the hydrants to give as much pressure as possible to the streams. They battled not only the principle inferno, but worked hard to prevent brush fires from enlarging and to keep nearby homes safe. Even the trees and brush on the property at the Bethany Convent, about a quarter of a mile away on the other side of the cove caught fire, requiring several of the Ashland firemen to work at keeping it under control and eventually subdued. A crowd estimated at more than 3000 people had gathered on the grounds of Anna Murphy playground, which was located right across Cove Avenue from the spectacle. The police managed to keep automobile traffic from clogging the nearby streets. (It is highly likely that Richie and many of his relatives were anxiously watching the whole conflagration, since their homes were on the next street over, behind the playground and fortunately for them, on the upwind side.)

Frank Fair lived near his father, James, who owned the Fair Ice Company, located on Nipmuc Road just off Dow Street. Frank hurried to the scene and helped out by taking the horses from their barn to remove them from danger. By the time the blaze was finally put down sometime after midnight, the property that had been the Cove Ice Company was totally destroyed, with the loss estimated at more than $20,000.

Two weeks to the day later, Fair's icehouse on Nipmuc Road went up in flames and was totally consumed. The five-alarm blaze began shortly after 7:30 the evening of April 20, 1932 with the loss on the uninsured building estimated at over $15,000 by the owners. As the firemen rushed to the call and sped along Hollis Street, they saw clouds of black smoke soaring from the icehouse. As they approached the fire from Wood Avenue, flames burst out and the entire roof crashed in. With nearly a quarter of a mile of hose laid from the hydrant at the corner of Nipmuc Road and Wood Avenue and with no chance of saving any of the main structure, the firemen worked to protect the sheds adjoining the ice house as well as the nearby homes. Within a few minutes, five lines of hoses were in play and the fire was confined to the icehouse, with all other nearby property saved.

Just prior to the arrival of the fire trucks, James Fair and his sons rescued two horses from an adjoining barn. They were also able to get two trucks and some other equipment out of the danger zone. Investigations later caused the fire chief to express the belief that someone loitering around the icehouse caused the fire. He also felt sure that if those who discovered the fire had sounded the alarm a few minutes sooner, it was possible that at least some of the building may have been saved. The ice company was soon rebuilt on the same location, only to burn to the ground again about twelve years later, ending its existence for good. (This was the inferno I watched from my front porch on the second floor of my home on Dow Street when I was about 9 years of age.)

Within six weeks of the Cove Ice Company fire, a total of five icehouses in the vicinity of Framingham, Natick, and Ashland met an identical fate. It was the opinion of the State Fire Inspector that a "fire bug" was operating in the area and was causing these spectacular blazes, but no one was ever caught.

CHAPTER 11

RICHIE, LENA AND DICKIE
(And the Trailer)
1933 - 1937

On a glorious Saturday morning, June 24, 1933 at Saint Tarcisius Roman Catholic Church on Waverly Street in Framingham, Lena Ortenzi became the bride of Richard Charles Rotelli. Her father had very willingly signed the required paperwork to allow his daughter, who was three weeks shy of her 18th birthday to marry this great young man who was highly thought of by the whole Ortenzi family. She wanted to be a June bride and there was no reason to postpone the wedding only to avoid a little paperwork.

Lena's maid of honor was Richie's sister, Selma while Nick, Lena's older brother was proud to be the best man. This foursome had spent a whole day in Boston shopping for their special wedding attire. Lena's bridal gown was lovely, and Selma looked radiant in her outfit. Richie and Nick both cut a handsome figure, looking just about as sharp as the law allows. The much-admired pastor, Father Maschi solemnly officiated at the wedding mass, giving an impassioned sermon on how to stay happily married, while the assembled relatives and guests occasionally dabbed a teary eye. One of the guests did more than brush away a tear of happiness. Little sister Rose sobbed out loud as she realized that even though she adored Richie, her big sister, who was much like a mother to her, was about to move away.

A reception for these close family members and special friends was held at Lena's home. Her mother had done all the cooking and baking and had transformed her modest home and yard into a lovely and festive site. Several of Richie's relatives from Dow Street, including his Aunts and Uncles and their oldest children were delighted to be among the few guests, forming what would be long-lasting friendships with Lena's family. All had much in common, with backgrounds of humble yet proud Italian heritage

June 24, 1933 The happy wedding party.

The newlyweds in the Ortenzi backyard.

as well as the desire to succeed in their new roles as American citizens.

A friend of the Ortenzis who was an accomplished accordion player sat out on the back porch and provided a constant background of lighthearted music. His repertoire included many old Italian songs as well as some of the more contemporary fun stuff from the roaring '20s. Lena's mother's cooking, which included all the courses from antipasto, anolini, beautifully roasted chicken and deserts such as the deep-fried tubes of pastry filled with sweetened and flavored ricotta cheese, known as cannoli, made a hit with everyone. By the time her wedding cake was ceremoniously cut all the guests were having a wonderful time. To what extent the exuberance was enhanced by the homemade wine Lena's father and grandfather generously poured out for all to consume is not recorded.

After a 10-day honeymoon in the White Mountains of New Hampshire, as well as parts of Maine, where they stayed with well-to-do relatives, the newlyweds settled into their own place, the second floor of the house at 43 Dow Street in Framingham. This was the place built about 12 years earlier by Richie's father, Luigi and his relatives. It was perfectly suited to the young couple and considering that they were allowed to live there rent-free until Richie found a steady job, it was ideal. Like so many other young men and women of that depressed era, Richie was unemployed. The fact that he had no job was in no way a deterrent to his getting married since everyone assumed that with all his skills and previous excellent work record with a variety of employers, he would not be unemployed for long. That optimistic forecast proved to be right on the money, since it was only a matter of a couple of weeks before he started what was to become more than 40 years of steady employment with the Dennison Manufacturing Company in downtown Framingham. He began as an apprentice and it wouldn't be long before he was in demand by many of the supervisors as a top-notch machinist.

Richie and Lena were happy in their apartment, with Lena developing her cooking skills to satisfy her husband's seemingly unending appetite. She had learned a lot about how to prepare really tasty meals of all kinds from her mother. In the 8 or 9 months since her wedding day, she had also taught herself some new ways to prepare some of her husband's favorite meals. She soon found that he loved to eat and enjoyed everything she prepared. Her mother-in-law, living right downstairs had always been the one to keep Richie happily fed. Now she was finding it a bit hard to think that this little kid upstairs was probably doing her best, but poor Richie looked to her like he was losing weight. She just couldn't let too many days in a row go by without putting a steaming casserole of Richie's favorite food on her table and asking her son to come in for a minute. "Mangia, Riccardo, mangia", she would implore him as he stood with obvious interest in the meal in front of him. He didn't want to hurt her feelings, so the dutiful son would take a few bites and before long she would be placing all sorts of other good stuff in front of him, including freshly baked bread. Richie was pretty hungry having just finished shoveling the latest February snowstorm off the steps and digging a path to the garage.

By the time the now stuffed husband went upstairs to supper that evening, he would realize that he had a bit of a problem. When he picked at the meal that Lena had prepared for him she might have thought that he didn't like her cooking. She knew better. Somehow, she knew what he had been up to downstairs and calmly asked him to simply let her know which meals he preferred to take with his mother, so she wouldn't have to cook on those days. Once he got over his embarrassment at trying to be both a good son and a loving, caring husband by being a human eating-machine, he assured his wife that he would greatly prefer to have all their meals together; just the two of them. They both agreed that once in a while, a Sunday dinner could be a group affair either downstairs or up in their apartment.

But when Lena coyly said that no matter how hard they might try, it was not going to be possible much longer for the newly-weds to have their meals with just the two of them, Richie was a bit confused. Then it hit him. She was trying to tell him that they were going to have a baby. Soon, everyone on Dow Street knew the good news.

So on Wednesday, September 12, 1934 I was born in a Framingham hospital. The total costs to my parents for the doctor's efforts as well as the hospital's role in this activity amounted to less than $50.00. My middle name, Louis, was chosen in honor of Richie's father, Luigi who was pleased with the selection. The small family on the second floor at 43 Dow Street, now with a baby boy would continue at this total size. Fate was not to bring me any siblings. In later years, I would tell people that once my mother took one look at me, she figured that she had achieved perfection; no point in having any more.

Richie's enthusiasm for designing and building things did not diminish just because he was now a married man and a father. One of the thoughts that he had been a bit preoccupied with for several months was how much fun it would be to develop a design for, and actually build a house trailer. He had been thinking about not just a "seen one- seen 'em all" kind of trailer, but a streamlined, modern one that would catch everyone's eye. He also thought it could be great fun to actually travel around on the weekends, towing such a unique little home and spend overnights at many popular tourist destinations. He had planned right from the start, that he could sell such an attractive and unique product and no doubt make a handsome profit.

He subscribed to a couple of magazines that featured all types of mechanical "goodies" and found some interesting articles on how to build your own house trailer. He studied these references very carefully and concluded that there was no doubt that he could design and build a better product than any he had read about. He would incorporate his own unique features, making it truly streamlined and not boxy like the ones in the magazines, and have a lot of fun doing it.

The brick two-car garage with its handsome hip roof, topped by a large galloping-horse copper weather vane, was just the place to assemble the trailer. This garage nestled under large, sprawling cherry trees was several feet from the back door of the house and had plenty of space, so long as the cars were left outside. It also had an excellent sturdy workbench that had been put together a few years previously by one, or possibly both of the master craftsman uncles. All sorts of hand tools hung from their storage hooks on the walls, and shelves and drawers were loaded with neatly assorted hardware and more tools. There was also plenty of light where it was needed. In short, he couldn't have asked for a better place in which to fabricate his dream trailer.

Of course, there were plenty of interruptions in his attempts to make rapid headway on his portable house. But between working at his job at Dennison, including extra shifts whenever he could get them, helping his father who lived in the downstairs part of the house at the time, with all sorts of chores and tending to the family garden, he managed to get his pet project assembled to the point where you could tell what it was going to be. And it was going to be something special. Everyone who saw it taking shape, even if it was only a skeleton at the time, was impressed with its clean lines and how roomy it looked to be inside.

By the time I was nearly three years old, the house trailer was basically completed. Richie had done every bit of the work right from the basic design through the fabrication of the chassis with its rubber tire automobile wheels, the cutting and assembling of the framework and the completion of all the interior finish. He had purchased the upholstered items including the seats and beds, but other than that he built everything himself. He wired it so that it could have all (or almost all) the conveniences of home once it had been docked at the few trailer parks that were becoming popular. Although it was not especially large by today's standards, it could sleep up to 6 persons in relative comfort.

Richie's homemade trailer.

A view of the inside of Richie's trailer.

So now with his beautiful, streamlined, one-of-a-kind house trailer ready for use and enjoyment, Richie planned a trip to the quaint New England town of Plymouth, Massachusetts. The first thing to do was to pull the new marvel out of its hangar where it had been born over the past year or so. As the trailer was slowly pulled toward the open door of the garage, a strange feeling of déjà vu came over the builder. He was remembering the episode of the iceboat and how he couldn't get it out of his Uncle's cellar until he and his co-conspirator, Mario, took it apart. Could it be that he had failed to double-check the size of the doorway opening compared to his pride and joy? (It is very likely that I was his pride and joy, but we are referring here to the one with wheels.)

Sure enough, the roof of the trailer was a few inches higher than the clear opening. The exact wording of just what might have been uttered at that embarrassing moment of truth is lost to history. Exactly how the dilemma was resolved is likewise not known for certainty. Either it was as simple as letting enough air out of the tires to allow the trailer to just squeak through, or a more ambitious effort was required. It may have been necessary to jack it up, remove the wheels completely, lower it down onto rollers and then slowly work it into the fresh air outside where it was cooler (or maybe just seemed so). In any event, with a crowd of relatives and other neighbors looking on (with some of them no doubt cheering Richie's efforts) the modern house trailer was soon ready to make its maiden run.

Sometime in the summer of 1937, on a Saturday, the trailer was loaded with provisions and hooked up to the hitch on the rear bumper of my father's car. With Richie at the wheel and my mother, my Aunt Selma and me as excited passengers, the trailer followed us smoothly all the way to Plymouth; practically to Cape Cod. Richie spent a lot of his driving time watching the hulking load behind us, silently praying that the hitch would stay put and that the trip would be uneventful. He had practiced hauling his invention all around town and perfected the technique of backing up with a minimum of back and forth moves. He continued to remind my mother of his proficiency towing this new load since she spent most of the trip looking back to be sure everything was all right.

Once we arrived at our site and had parked on nice level ground, the car was unhooked and the electrical connection to the receptacle in the side of the trailer was made. This was to be home to us for the next week. At least it was to be the base for all of us except my dad, who had to drive back home after only one night so that he could get to his job the next Monday morning. When we had set out on our little adventure, the weather looked pretty nice. But soon after arriving at our destination, ominous black clouds with occasional rumbles of thunder rolled across the sky.

The actual torrential rain held off until right after Richie left for home. So here we were, my mother, my aunt and me cooped up in this little place in what turned out to be one solid week of nearly steady rain. It didn't take long for the rain to find the few places in the roof where the caulking was incomplete. My mother placed saucepans and other containers under where most of it was coming in, but it soon seemed that it was going to be difficult to catch it all.

To add to the misery, I was frightened out of my wits by the chemical toilet my dad had installed, and refused to have any part of it. My mother had suggested that we bring my potty-chair along just in case, but for some reason it remained back at Dow Street. When the rain let up for a bit, my aunt dashed out, purchased a couple of umbrellas somewhere and found a telephone. She called her brother and pleaded with him to come right down and "for heaven's sake bring Dickie's potty-chair".

So it was that Richie was back with us on Monday evening with my all-important portable throne. Of course by the time he arrived, the sky had brightened, the birds were chirping and people were strolling around the damp grounds everywhere with water dripping from tree branches. If I had been of the age of reason at that time, I would have concluded that it was Richie's aura or something that controlled the weather. When he was around, the sun was out.

He was more than a bit dismayed to find out that so many pots and pans had been needed to keep our cabin relatively dry. He knew that he could fix all the leaks easily, but it would have to wait until the trailer was back home. He expressed the thought that the worst of the rainy weather was over and that the rest of the week should be nice. Soon after that cheerful forecast, he was gone so that he could be at work the next day.

The rains continued the rest of the week until (of course) my dad showed up early Saturday morning, when the birds were once again twittering happily in the sunshine.

In spite of the poor weather most of that week, the unusual trailer attracted a lot of interest. One young family who loved spending time in Plymouth and parts of the Cape in their tent had come to visit us at the trailer. They made no bones about the fact that they really wanted to buy it. They were not concerned about what it may cost, nor did the leaky roof upset them, since they were used to sleeping in a soggy tent. Richie agreed to sell it to them, but insisted on fixing the roof first. By my third birthday, the trailer was history. Its proud new owners happily towed it from our driveway and we never heard from them or saw the trailer again.

CHAPTER 12

FLOYD'S TRAVELS IN HIS CAR
1932 - 1933

When, in the spring of 1932 word got around to the various people who had visited with Floyd, either as students, as models for him to practice his portrait skills upon, just friends, or a combination of all of these, no one could believe what they were told about the car. They probably thought that the Greene's as well as Floyd had taken leave of their senses. No matter that cars had been rigged up in all kinds of ingenious ways for folks with various handicaps, the thought of this man, who just managed to get himself around his little room by shaking his torso while strapped into his old living room chair, now driving across the country was just too much. But the Greenes, including Roy's brother Clifford and especially Floyd himself had very few doubts.

The design for the modifications of the 1930 Chevy Commercial Body was essentially separated into two major areas. One was the engine/drivetrain and the driver's controls; the other dealt with the interior of this roomy vehicle. The Greenes had made a wise choice in the selection of this particular automobile from many points of view. Chevrolet had a solid reputation for reliability, having produced its 7-millionth vehicle of all styles in 1930 and cranking out its 500,000th commercial vehicle in 1929. The in-line, 6-cylinder overhead valve engine in this car had been introduced in 1929, developed nearly 50 horsepower and was offered at "the price of a four". Chevrolet promotional material called it the "Cast Iron Wonder". The body style was perfectly suited to the unorthodox requirements its unique driver would demand. It was originally built to be a delivery wagon or panel truck, and was advertised as a "sedan delivery". It was now going to be used to "deliver" its operator home. The space behind the driver's seat in the cargo area was six feet long, almost four feet wide and just over four feet in height. This space was easily loaded by means of two full-height doors which when hinged all the way open, allowed unobstructed access.

While Floyd had absolutely no experience with automobile engines or really what it took to drive a car, he did have a very good idea of how the inside of the "cargo" space should be set up for him. He set out to sketch how the interior could be fitted with drawers and cabinets for all the art material he would be bringing on his trip home. He also knew that he would need to provide a place for a cot for him to sleep on as well as storage space for his clothes. His main interest was in providing adequate secure space for his art supplies and perhaps even his etching press as well as some of his recent best work to show off. While he was sketching and planning the design for the space behind the driver's seat, Roy and Cliff worked closely with the mechanic they had hired to do the very critical and complex modifications to the driving controls.

When this truly collaborative effort was finally complete, the overall result was nothing short of amazing. There was little doubt that this was the most unusual vehicle anyone had ever seen. It is also highly likely that most people who examined the finished product were more than a little skeptical of anything other than a disastrous finish to the start of the planned journey by the talented, but seriously disabled driver.

The driver's seat was partially rebuilt to suit Floyd's unusual shape and a special strap was installed to hold him securely in place. The brake pedal had been reworked to incorporate a metal "shoe" into which he was able to insert his right foot. Although there was absolutely no way he could get his legs to move on their own, he could reach down with a modified cane and place and then clamp his foot into the "shoe". In theory at least, he could apply the brake by thrusting his body forward and release it by leaning back again. The brakes on his car were strictly mechanical, and although they worked on all four wheels, it took a significant amount of pressure on the brake pedal to bring the vehicle to a stop. Of course there was a floor-mounted "emergency brake", which was really only to be used when the car was to be parked. Floyd must have thought that it surely would be one hell of an emergency if he had to pull back on that lever with the car in motion.

Vacuum assisting technology had been in use for handicapped-equipped cars for a few years and a very clever adaptation of this technique was incorporated. A button or knob was added to the end of the gearshift lever, which protruded up through the floor. When this knob was depressed, it caused the vacuum system to activate, operating the clutch and allowing the driver to shift gears. The throttle was connected to a lever mounted on the steering wheel reminiscent of the arrangement on the old Model "T" Ford. The plan was that with Floyd strapped safely in his specially configured seat, and with his right foot strapped into the boot on the brake pedal, he would actually be able to drive.

But he had no actual driving experience of any kind to draw upon. By the time that Floyd was dreaming of driving his own car, the American public was very fascinated with all aspects of automobiles. Most people of his age then and many even younger were comfortable behind the wheel and had learned to drive in a variety of ever improving machines. But back in 1909, when Floyd was still an able-bodied young man, he probably hadn't even seen an automobile, much less driven one. He had always been comfortable with horses as the principle way to get somewhere in a hurry. At the turn of the century, "motoring" as it was then called, was the sport of a few rich eccentrics. He had had a good laugh when he was still in grade school over the reports that in England at that time there was a law on the books that required that the driver of a "horseless carriage" must have a man swinging a lantern walk ahead of the car. He was even further amused at the excitement that prevailed when that law was repealed and the speed limit for cars was raised to 12 miles an hour. Just about the time when Floyd set off stealing freight train rides to the wheat fields, Henry Ford was captivating everyone's imagination with his Model "T". That car soon became so popular that the inventive Mr. Ford was led to develop the car industry's first moving production line in order to build enough cars to satisfy demand.

There is no doubt that the inexperienced Texas cowboy/artist would require a considerable amount of trial and error practice, with probably many errors, before he could be entrusted with his own and other people's lives by driving on the open road. How in the world was he to steer his vehicle using only his good right arm and hand while still managing to shift gears and work the accelerator? But, by golly he did it! He found that he could place his useless left arm on top of the steering wheel in order to hold it in position (but not steer it) while he deftly operated the vacuum assist button and the throttle as he shifted gears. He would then use his right hand to knock his left arm off the steering wheel, causing it to fall limply onto his lap until he needed it again. He could then grab enough of the steering wheel with forefinger and thumb of his right hand to effectively steer while operating the throttle control.

Of course whenever he wanted to make a turn at an intersection, it would be up to other drivers to try to figure out his intentions. He could not simply stick his left arm out the window and produce a hand signal, and of course his car was not equipped with any kind of turn signal indicator, so it must have been a bit confusing, even dangerous at times for him to deal with traffic at intersections.

He did have a single windshield wiper mounted in the center of the windshield. The only problem was that it was operated manually and so if he were ever caught in much of a downpour by himself, he would have no choice but to pull over and wait for the skies to clear before proceeding. A choice between steering, shifting and using the accelerator versus operating the windshield wiper was no choice at all. One of the things he particularly liked was that the windshield could be opened a bit. It was pivoted at its top on a piano hinge so he could get a bit of a breeze on a hot day.

The array of circular gauges on his dash included an electric gasoline gauge, new for 1930. It is not known if he had the optional illuminated dash, or cigarette lighter but he

Floyd in the back of his 1930 Chevrolet with Roy.
June 1932.

Edith with Floyd in his car.

Floyd in his car at unknown Indian village.

did have the front bumper, which oddly enough was listed as an option. He also had an externally mounted rearview mirror; another item which, unbelievably was listed as optional equipment even for the sedan delivery model. With this large mirror he could see some of what was behind him when he had to back up, but it must have been every man for himself whenever Floyd put his machine into reverse.

Roy must have spent many hours teaching and coaching his friend how to manage all that had to be done so that he could safely operate this very unique machine. He had to carefully explain and reinforce the rules of the road, a task he may have found difficult since his pupil had no prior experience behind the wheel of a car. There must have been many hours spent with Roy in the driver's seat and Floyd as his passenger watching his every move. Roy would try to operate the controls as if he had the same limitations as the new driver, but felt more secure if he occasionally used both hands and feet. He wondered if it may have been a little too much of a challenge; too daunting a task for a person with Floyd's limited use of his body to embark on such an adventure as they had planned.

There is no record of how long it took for the artist to master the controls or how many hours he spent with the basics of starting the engine, slowly driving forward, shifting gears, steering around obstacles in the yard and smoothly bringing the car to a stop without stalling. After an undetermined number of days bumping into trees and getting stuck in odd predicaments on the Greene's property, it must have been a scary sight when Floyd first took to the roads around the neighborhood. (If Richie ever saw him go chugging slowly up and down Dow Street, he paid no attention. Floyd was not known to Richie at that time. Although only a short distance separated their homes, they were worlds apart in many ways.)

It is clear that the Greenes as well as Floyd recognized that it would be in his best interests to have a traveling companion along with him for as much of his trip as possible. Simply having someone to help him to get from the driver's seat to his cot and back, as well as to empty his bedpan as needed and to run into a market along the way to get some food and water would be vital. Finding a reliable and trustworthy aide to perform these tasks could easily have been a significant challenge. However, it appears that just such a person was located without a lot of effort. It developed that a young fellow named Jimmy, who was nearly 14 years of age and whose cousin had been a pupil of Edith's a few years earlier, was anxious to return home to his family in Texarkana, Texas.

Jimmy had been sent to live for a while with relatives in the Boston area when his mother had taken sick and his father was working at two jobs to help keep the rest of their little family together. Now that his mother had recovered, he was looking forward to getting back home. Being Floyd's helper in the special car was the perfect opportunity to get there at no cost. He was bright, physically fit and would be good company as well as an indispensable resource in the ambitious plan for Floyd to go west; even if he had never driven an automobile. He knew how to read a map and could keep a sharp eye on the road ahead, helping with the navigation.

So, at the end of June 1932, the car was fully packed with as much of the 44-year-old Texan's art supplies and equipment as could possibly be stuffed into the cargo area along with his sleeping cot. The cabinets that he had designed for holding and arranging his important art material were fastened to interior walls and worked out just fine. With his portable wheelchair stuffed in, a few of his clothes and enough cash to meet his expenses along the way, as well as a couple of changes of clothes for Jimmy, it was time for Floyd and his young helper to head off "into the sunset". It must have been a heart-wrenching scene when Floyd slowly drove out of the Greene's driveway and out onto Cove avenue, with Jimmy waving goodbye for both of them while Floyd concentrated on handling the controls. He wanted to be sure that at least while he was still in sight of his great friends and benefactors he made no driving errors of any kind. Edith surely had tears in her eyes and Roy most likely would have a hard time saying anything at all for several minutes. The look that probably passed between the two of them as their young protégé drove out of sight would have said it all. They must have had some serious thoughts about just how dangerous and difficult a situation it was that they had helped put him in. When they walked back into their house they couldn't have helped looking into Floyd's studio room. His trusty old caster-bottomed chair was empty, sitting there silently waiting for the artist to return. They were surely going to miss not having him around until his planned return in a year or so.

Floyd also had given a bit of thought to the amount of danger he and his young companion could be in until he was finally settled at his Texas destination. His "insurance policy" was to surreptitiously include his trusty old six-shooter and a few extra rounds in his personal belongings. At their first planned stop on their journey, he asked Jimmy to fetch it out of its hiding place and bring it to him so that he could keep it within easy reach. He carefully explained the dangerous nature of the old Colt as well as the safety features he took great care to follow. Jimmy, who had never seen anything like this gun was surprised at its heft and was not at all sure that he would be safer with it in the hands of this one-armed artist.

Floyd's main ambition was to get back to see his dear mother, whom he always referred to as "Mama" in his correspondence with her. He had mailed her a small photograph Roy had taken the day his car first showed up, showing him in the back of it with Edith standing next to him. He wrote a short note on the back of this snapshot telling her that he would take her for a ride in a year or so. He was equally as determined to get to see the brothers and sisters he had left nearly a decade ago. They would have all changed so much in those few years. He was proud of his own development in these intervening years and was anxious for all of them to see just how well he had progressed. He remembered marvelous vistas in close proximity to his old home and further out to the Southwest. There were many scenes in his memory, some of them a bit fuzzy now, that he was eager to paint. Old houses, trees, valleys, plains - - so many things for him to capture in his own unique style. He would work in watercolors, pastels, and oils and of course he would produce some exciting etchings. The more he had thought about all this while the plans were being developed for getting a car made up for him, the more eager he became. Now that he was at last actually underway, he didn't want to stop until he was home. He was about to apply the single-mindedness of purpose that he had shown while studying art, to the task at hand, namely getting to Texas - -now!

He knew that the home in Lampasas that he had left to come to the Greene's wonderful place was not where he was headed. His mother had sold that place just a couple of years ago and was now spending up to six months or so each year living in Austin at Benny Haden's household (Floyd's older brother) along with Ben's wife, Viola (Jennings) and the youngest of their children who were still living at home at the time. She would then travel off to spend some time with other of her children and their families as well as some dear friends who lived in a little town named Muldoon, just South of Winchester, Fayette County where she had spent her early days of married life.

But now at the end of June 1932 Floyd knew his mother, who he was so anxious to see again would be with Ben and his family, or at least those who were not married and off on their own. He was truly excited about seeing Ben once again, the brother who had risked being infected with polio when he had come to bring him home all those years ago. He felt a great debt of gratitude toward Ben for the courage and love he had shown then and for the many ways he had helped him to keep his spirits up when life at times looked so useless. He was particularly anxious for Ben to see for himself just how accomplished he had become in the 9 years he had been away, for he remembered Ben's constant encouragement in his early attempts at learning to draw.

Then his thoughts must have gone to his dear sisters, Erie, Lena, and Clara all married now with young families. And his half brother Tom Ivy who had also been such a supportive source of encouragement when he needed it the most. And of course, he was anxious to hear his youngest brother, Tansey play that fantastic fiddle of his once again.

But now it was time to concentrate on driving and also to remember to enjoy the sights along the way. Floyd had several maps marked to show the route he planned to follow. He made sure Jimmy had a good grasp of the notations he had made on these maps and that he could rely on him to point out key landmarks and intersections.

The roadways in 1932 were vastly different than the superhighways that began to come into place after World War II and which expanded and grew to the point where driving practically anywhere in the continental United States became a relatively straightforward matter. What Floyd and his pal were driving on was a combination of dirt or gravel roads much of the time and a fair amount of "improved" or paved roads. Few of these streets were very wide and sometimes on little offshoots he would have to pull way over to the side to make room for an approaching vehicle to pass. None of this in any way bothered the determined Texans. They were "hell bent for home" and the adventure all this provided seemed to energize them both.

There is no detailed record of the exact routes they traveled or where they stopped to rest for the night, but what follows is very highly probable based upon careful scrutiny of road maps that existed in 1932 and a knowledge of their plans. When they eventually arrived in Texarkana, Texas it was reported in a newspaper that they had made the trip of nearly 2,000 miles in one week and that Floyd did all of the driving, not being assisted in that task by his youthful traveling companion.

Shortly after leaving Harmony Home, Floyd pulled onto Route 20, and continued southwesterly half the way across Massachusetts to Springfield. Here he drove South on Route 5 midway across Connecticut to Hartford. He then turned West onto Route 3 heading for his planned crossing of the Hudson River. He wanted to cross the Hudson above the congestion of New York City and his studies of possible routes led him to realize that crossing over the impressive Bear Mountain Bridge, just past Peekskill, New York would be a smart way to go.

They stopped for the night at a filling station somewhere in the vicinity of the entrance to the bridge, perhaps in the town of Cortlandt, which is where the tollhouse for the bridge was located, and planned to drive across this marvelous structure first thing the next morning. This would have been about 220 miles from their starting point and a good distance to have traveled on their first day as Floyd became better adjusted to his machine. He no doubt was feeling more confident about the tricky maneuvers he had to execute to keep the car from stalling or otherwise reacting unfavorably. The record does not indicate how young Jimmy took to what must have been strange antics, complete with grunts, groans and an occasional outburst of salty language coming from the straining driver.

While Floyd may at first have thought that Jimmy was a shy and quiet youngster, once they were rolling along with the familiar sights fading away behind them and exciting new views popping up all around, the kid found his voice. He was in awe of each new thing he saw and commented intelligently about it. Floyd must have enjoyed having an interesting and interested person along with him. It wasn't long before the talk between them centered on one of their mutual interests, baseball. Back when Floyd was a teenager he had wanted to play in the Texas League teams that were popping up all around him. He loved the game and tried his best to play every position, but seemed to find himself playing outfield most of the time and being a good utility hitter. But Floyd's heavy workload around his home back then really prevented him from spending as much time as he might have liked at what some may have called "a child's game".

Jimmy knew all the statistics about the major league teams and was a die-hard New York Yankees fan. Floyd had really not paid anyway near as much attention to baseball in the 30's as Jimmy had, and really was not particularly wrapped up in any of the teams. He did enjoy following the stumbling progress of the Boston Red Sox, who had finished in 6th place in the American League in 1931, 45 games behind the Athletics. (At this time he had no way of knowing that the Red Sox would sink all the way to the bottom of their league at the end of the 1932 season finishing 64 games behind the World Series champion Yankees.) He really couldn't help but admire the Yankees' gifted athletes and their hot bats. It looked like Babe Ruth and Lou Gehrig were going to lead the Yankees to the World Series this year, after finishing the '31 season in second place behind the Athletics.

The miles and the hours rolled by quickly as the conversation became more and more animated about all the great things Jimmy's beloved Yankees had done and were about to do. Batting averages, number of home runs hit, number of strike outs, walks, errors, earned run averages of their pitchers - - all sorts of statistics came pouring out of Jimmy. The kid was an encyclopedia of knowledge about his favorite team in his favorite sport. There may have been a few wrong turns made by the driver when the navigator was so engrossed in all his baseball trivia that he failed to pay attention to the road.

If the roadways the excited duo were traveling were vastly different than those that were to come along in future years, the filling stations at that time were even more different than their modern day counterparts. For one thing, they truly were "service stations". You could actually get service for your car and be treated politely and with what appeared to be genuine concern for your well being. This fact was of enormous importance to Floyd in case, for whatever reason, he might have to spend some of his drive alone. If Jimmy should get sick, or if he simply decided he just wanted to quit somewhere along the way, Floyd would be on his own. Even though those events were judged by Floyd to be highly unlikely, he still was going to have a good long drive by himself after Jimmy got to Texarkana. Also, he had no plan at all for having anybody help him on his drive back to Framingham in about a year. So being able to depend upon a helping hand at filling stations along the route may become very important. It might not be in everyone's idea of part of their job description as an attendant to empty and clean his bedpan for him, but without a "Jimmy" at his side he would have to depend on the good will of others. He must have decided not to worry about that aspect of the adventure at all, but just deal with it if and when it might arise.

It is most likely that the strange duo would have parked the car for the night in an out of the way area of one of these friendly filling stations, with the owner's OK. Jimmy would have scurried around and located some kind of supper for the two of them. The next task would have been for them to try their best to get a good night's sleep, so that they could be on their way at the crack of dawn. Jimmy would have to drag Floyd out of the driver's seat and get him onto his cot where he would get himself ready for some much needed shut-eye. Before poor Jimmy could consider trying to make himself comfortable for the night sprawled across the passenger seat with as much of him as would fit into the vacated driver's seat, he had to tend to the unsavory job of emptying and cleaning Floyd's steel bedpan. He must have left all the windows open in the car while he was in the service station's Men's Room taking care of that and his own personal hygiene as well.

As they settled in for their first night's rest Floyd told Jimmy all about some of the excitement in store for them the next day. He made it plain that not only would crossing the Bear Mountain Bridge be quite a treat, they had to be sure to get a good view when they passed New York City, of the two magnificent skyscrapers they had both only read about until now. Floyd explained to Jimmy, in an amazing amount of detail what he had read about the competition between two millionaires to see who could build the tallest building in the world. Walter Chrysler, head of the Chrysler Corporation and an equally gregarious, extremely wealthy man named John Jacob Raskob, who was one of the creators of General Motors, poured their millions and their hearts and souls into the creation of buildings that would "scrape the sky".

Floyd said that the Chrysler Building was built as a commercial office tower at 405 Lexington Avenue in the 2 years between 1928 and 1930. It was in what has been called an "Art Deco" style with its metal clad steel frame topped by a very unusual pinnacle. The architect, William Van Alen understood that Mr. Chrysler wanted a provocative building and really let his creative juices flow. He incorporated never-before-seen features in an American building of this type. As the building rose above the street, at each setback he incorporated story-high basket-weave designs, radiator cap gargoyles, and a band of abstract automobiles. His lobby was stunning, being composed of African marble and chrome steel.

But perhaps the item that would be talked about for years, Floyd went on, was the building's crowning peak. It was as much how it came into place as how beautiful it was. Architect Van Alen's dramatic revelation of this seven-story tall pinnacle, with its graceful, sweeping arches, was unprecedented. That entire structure, complete with its steel facing, had been assembled inside the building. When it was ready, it was worked into position up through an opening in the roof and fastened in place. It only took an hour and a half for this amazing building to suddenly have a top that seemed to pierce the sky. Having a total of 77 floors, and reaching 1048 feet to the top of its spire, it was the tallest building in the world. But not for long. Within a year or so of its completion, the Empire State Building was finished.

Located not far from Chrysler's colossus, just a few blocks downtown on Fifth Avenue, the lights of the 1454-foot tall Empire State Building were first illuminated on May 1, 1931 just a little over a year ago. It had 25 more floors than its rival did and, even though it was still considered Art Deco, it was thought of as modernistic.

As Floyd continued with what he thought should be highly educational and useful background material about its dirigible mast and other worthwhile facts, he soon heard soft snoring sounds coming from the front of the car. He figured that the kid was smart enough to know that the important thing now was to get some sleep. He'd fill him in on the story of the bridge they would cross in the morning as they approached it.

Before setting out on their way each morning they would most likely have the gas tank filled with a good grade of gasoline, which cost the princely sum of 18 cents for a gallon of regular, had the attendant check the engine oil, adding some if it measured a bit low, check the radiator, fully examine all belts, pulleys, hoses, and anything else that they could think of. The tires would be inspected thoroughly and the air pressure measured, with air being added as needed. The windshield would have been washed until it looked like it wasn't there. It's a fair bet that these two would be seen off by the filling station owner who would have enthusiastically and heartily wished them well on their journey. Such was Floyd's personal magnetism that once he met a person, that individual just couldn't seem to do enough to be of help. This may have been true because he always tried to do so much for himself and in his good ol' Texas drawl with a pleasant approach, could charm even the hardest hearted of them.

With the early morning fog slowly lifting to hint at the promise of another fine day, and after a small breakfast, with the driver having been hauled back into his seat and the navigator being mostly awake, the machine chugged to life and day two began.

In what must have seemed like practically no time at all, Floyd was handing the outrageous sum of 75 cents for the one-way toll to the collector at the quaint Tudor-style building that was the toll house of the Bear Mountain Bridge. At a time when you could buy a new tire for your car, guaranteed for almost 30,000 miles, for $3.83; get an engine tune-up for a buck and a quarter and buy a nice juicy steak for about 9 cents a pound, this toll must have seemed like highway robbery. The toll collector wasn't even wearing a mask.

Floyd's car was no doubt the most unusual of the nearly 5,000 vehicles to have crossed this beautiful bridge that day and Jimmy spent most of the time in it watching closely to be sure it was being operated with all due caution. He may have had a hard time convincing himself that this was really not much different than driving on roads on solid ground, but it looked so narrow and seemed to be a mile above the water. In fact, as Floyd insisted on pointing out to him as they drove along, it was only 135 feet over the river at its highest point and the 4 lanes of traffic fit very nicely into the 40 feet of width of the roadway. Jimmy was told that the bridge was just a little over a quarter of a mile long and then they'd be back on the regular roads again, zipping along and soon would be trying to sight the famous skyscrapers. Cars had been safely streaming across this engineering marvel for nearly 8 years now, with many folks making this route a high point of their trip. On its opening day in November 1924, about 400 cars followed the West Point Band as they led the way from Peekskill.

Jimmy was fascinated when Floyd told him that this bridge was erected at the very same location in the Hudson where back in 1778, Colonial Americans had strung their first huge iron chain-link barrier right across the river to keep the hated British ships from advancing.

With the excitement of crossing the Hudson behind them, the two travelers were soon heading South on Route 9W and in about 2 hours found themselves constantly scanning the view to their left looking for a glimpse of the famous New York skyline and finally spotting those fantastic skyscrapers. They soon picked up Route 1 South, which would be the only number Jimmy had to remember now until they got down into the middle of Georgia. Jimmy voiced the thought that it sure would be a fine thing to do if they could only stop in to see the Yankees play a game in their fabulous stadium. The response was along the lines of, "Next time we come this way, we just might stop in and see 'em."

They pressed on, making good time in the steady, but light traffic with Floyd now handling the car as though he had been driving it all his life. They stopped for a lunch break somewhere around Trenton, New Jersey. Jimmy had been complaining about the fact that he was starting to get a bit cramped up and needed to get out and stretch his legs. Practically as soon as the words had left his mouth, he felt a flush of embarrassment and anger at himself. Of course whenever the car stopped, he could get out, jump up and down, do a jig or run around the block, but Mr. Walser - -. He mumbled an apology, but Floyd immediately put him at ease in that way he had of making light of his own problems.

They whistled through Philadelphia, wishing they could play the tourists and go see the Liberty Bell that was located just outside Independence Hall and see other famous landmarks, but pressed on – eager to get to their destination. By the end of the second day, after watching Baltimore, Maryland go by, they stopped for the night in the vicinity of our nation's capitol in Washington, DC.

There was simply no way they could possibly drive through this part of our land without stopping to gawk at the buildings and monuments fairly dripping with historical and contemporary significance. Route 1 became Maryland Avenue and sliced right through the heart of this famous place. So by simply staying on Route1 South they couldn't help but drive through the center of all that history and vitality. But it was late in the day. They both must have been tired and hungry and in need of rest.

But there was something else that made Floyd want to stop and rest up before actually entering the heart of the District of Columbia. That something else was the information he had read in many newspaper accounts shortly before leaving Framingham, about the huge crowd of veterans of The Great War who were by now assembled in and around the main streets. The depression had been awfully hard on a large segment of the population of the United States. Definitely not immune from the economic calamity were the many veterans of the war. As it did to so many others, the crash of 1929 had wiped out many of their jobs as well as whatever savings they may have had. Many of them had been forced out onto the streets. At the end of the war, the federal government had passed legislation that would provide the payment of cash bonuses to war veterans. These bonuses were to be adjusted for individual length of service and would certainly be a welcome benefit. However, the payouts were not set to materialize by this plan until 1945.

In the spring of 1932 a group of about 300 vets in Portland, Oregon got together and began to trek across the country to Washington to personally lobby the government to pay out the cash bonuses immediately. They called themselves the "Bonus Expeditionary Force", or "Bonus Army" for short. By the end of May this rag-tag group had increased in numbers and over 3,000 veterans and their families had made their way to the capitol. And their numbers were still increasing rapidly. Their living conditions were terrible. Most of them set up shacks and tents on the mud flats along the banks of the Anacostia River just outside the city limits. This river flowed into the Potomac just South of the capitol. The summer was becoming oppressively hot and humid and the crowds of vets and their wives and children were not enjoying this camping experience one bit.

Shortly before Floyd and Jimmy left Massachusetts, at the end of June, the Patman Bonus Bill, proposing immediate payout of the veterans' cash bonuses, was debated in Congress. Even though President Hoover's administration was adamant about maintaining a balanced budget, and this would go hard against that with an estimated cost of over $2 billion, it passed in the House of Representatives on June 15th. The thousands of veterans parked practically under the noses of the congressmen must have been jubilant. But, two days later, the Senate overwhelmingly defeated the bill. The response was strong and unmistakable and caused government officials serious concern. A mob of nearly 20,000 hot, sweaty and angry veterans slowly shuffled peacefully up and down Pennsylvania Avenue for 3 days. Local newspapers dubbed this sorry spectacle, the "Death March".

When the travelers from Massachusetts arrived just to the North of the capitol, the situation was still unresolved, with thousands of protesters still crowding the streets, but traffic moved pretty much unimpeded. The population of what was referred to as a "Hooverville" ghetto to the Southeast along the muddy banks of the Anacostia River was still increasing.

It is fairly certain that at the break of dawn, or soon thereafter on the beginning of day 3 of their journey, in the last week of June, Floyd and Jimmy found themselves slowly patrolling the famous streets of our nation's capitol, and stopping to let the significance of just where they now were, slowly sink in.

It was very hot and humid as Floyd carefully made his way along Maryland Avenue and turned Northwest onto Pennsylvania Avenue. He must have stopped and talked at length with the many tired and frustrated young men milling about. He no doubt must have had strong feelings of sympathy for their cause and when a few of them became aware of his handicap and his courageous plan to drive himself home, he soon had a large crowd following along with him for a while, shouting words of encouragement to him. He probably felt quite strange about their wishes of good luck for him when they were the ones who had suffered in so many ways, first on foreign battlefields, fighting for their country and now here, fighting for what they believed to be their due.

Eventually, after he had slowly driven past the White House, he turned south so he could drive down by the reflecting pool to pause and admire both the Lincoln Memorial and the Washington Monument. The Lincoln Memorial was only 10 years old at the time and he had read quite a bit about the extremely talented artist who had created it. Floyd knew that he was a gifted sculptor by the name of Daniel Chester French who had studied anatomy and drawing in Boston. French, who had been encouraged to pursue a career as an artist by Louisa May Alcott, had died just the year before at the age of 82. Jimmy did not seem to appreciate the scope of what was right in front of him. Floyd parked as close as he could get to the building and ordered the youngster to scramble on up the wide steps and get right in there and look with not only his eyes, but his head and most of all, his heart. There is no doubt that Floyd would have loved to have had the chance to have been carried on up into that marvelous place. He instructed the semi-interested youth to walk around inside to the north wall and read Lincoln's inaugural address, and then to scamper over to the south wall and read the Gettysburg Address. He told him to see for himself if the great president's eyes didn't seem to follow him as he moved in front of the statue. When Jimmy got back into the car after several very memorable minutes, Floyd asked him to count the number of Doric columns lining the outside of the building. Jimmy reported that there were 36 of them. His history teacher asked him then if he had any idea why there would be that number. After careful deliberation and as they were pulling away to get back to their trip, Jimmy said something to the effect that 36 columns just seemed to fit in there just right. After a short while, during which time Floyd hoped that Jimmy was still thinking about the question, Floyd pointed out that at the time of Lincoln's death there were 36 states in the union. Jimmy was duly impressed.

In no time at all they were back on Route 1 again, headed home. The images of what Floyd had seen that day of monuments and famous buildings stayed in his mind. But what must have lingered even longer and reached him at an even deeper level was the determination and strength of purpose those ordinary citizens, those brave veterans had so clearly displayed. He must have realized that if fate hadn't intervened that terrible day years ago in North Dakota, he could very well have been one of them.

(As it turned out, Floyd was very fortunate in the timing of his arrival in Washington. If he had come a couple of weeks sooner, he could have had his path blocked for 3 days by the "Death March". But if he had tried to drive through that area 3 weeks later in July, it would have been worse for him. Congress adjourned in mid July with the bill voted down. Many of the marchers left the city after that, but at least 10,000 remained, causing President Hoover to express serious concern about the possibility of civil disorder and perhaps even violence. There had been scuffles with police and some Senator's cars were stoned by angry crowds of veterans. On July 28th, in a riot that broke out at the bottom of Capitol Hill, two veterans were shot and killed by panicked policemen. The president told the Secretary of War, Patrick Hurley, to tell the Army Chief of Staff, General Douglas McArthur, that he wanted the marchers evicted from the city.

Troops were ordered in to remove the bonus marchers by force. A battalion from the 12th Infantry Regiment and 2 squadrons of the 3rd Cavalry Regiment, commanded by Major George S. Patton, massed near the White House. In the late afternoon, the infantrymen put on gas masks and fixed bayonets. The cavalry drew sabers, and several light tanks led the whole force down Pennsylvania Avenue, clearing it of people.

President Hoover had specifically ordered McArthur to clear Pennsylvania Avenue only, but the insubordinate and manipulative General cleared all of downtown Washington, herding the Marchers out and setting fire to their huts and tents. By 8:00 PM, the downtown area was cleared, with the bridge leading across the Anacostia River to where most of the Marchers lived blocked by several tanks. Although a lot of tear gas was sprayed around and several bricks were thrown in defiance, no shots were fired.

Hoover gave duplicate orders to McArthur forbidding him to cross the river to clear the camp, but these orders were flatly ignored. He crossed the Anacostia at 11:00 that night, routed the Marchers along with 600 of their wives and children out of their camp, and burned it to the ground. The last of the beaten Bonus Army Marchers left Washington by the end of the following day. Although no shots had been fired by the military, four people were killed; the two demonstrators shot by the police and two infants asphyxiated by tear gas. The whole event turned public opinion heavily against Hoover who was defeated in the upcoming election by Franklin Roosevelt.)

Jimmy was glad to finally be moving along at a speed that at least made the hot outside air blow through the front of their car. It didn't seem to lower the temperature, but at least there was a breeze. He was back to navigating and watching carefully to be sure they stayed on good old Route 1 headed south. They needed to make up for lost time, having spent longer than anticipated in Washington but they were both moved at the sights and sounds of that exciting place and felt proud to be Americans.

They had traveled not much more than 5 miles when another, much newer monument was in view. About ¾ of a mile to their west stood the impressive George Washington Masonic National Memorial in Alexandria, Virginia. It had just been dedicated about 6 weeks ago on May 12, 1932 after 10 years of construction. It stood proudly at the top of a small hill just off to their right. Floyd slowed the car as they drove past so that Jimmy could get a good view of the 333-foot tall structure. Floyd maneuvered the car around the nearby streets so that he could get a good look at it himself. Jimmy had never heard of this particular Memorial and, after seeing so much marvelous architecture in the heart of the District of Columbia, was only marginally impressed. Floyd had read about the construction and the plans for its dedication and surely was pleased to be so close to it and no doubt wished that they could take the time to examine it thoroughly. The thought must have crossed his mind that it would surely be possible for him to persuade one of the guides on duty to haul him out of his car and into his portable wheelchair. It would be something to tell the folks all about if he could get up to the observation deck and view the surrounding landscape for miles in all directions. But, the need to get to their destination sooner rather than later scuttled the thoughts.

Their plan was to keep going until they got to Raleigh, North Carolina where they could stop for the night. If they could get south of that city before stopping, so much the better. They pulled over for their lunch break somewhere in the vicinity of Richmond, Virginia, where they certainly showed signs of tiring of the hot, dusty ride but lost none of their resolve to press on.

At the end of the next day, the determined duo, continuing on trusty old Route 1 and headed south, found themselves holed up for the night in Augusta, Georgia. They had been on the go now for 4 solid days and had seen things they had not expected. By now, they were used to the routine and both had a good feeling for when it was getting close to the time that Floyd needed to pull over and rest a while. Fortunately, the weather held with no rain in sight and in spite of the hot summer, they both were enjoying the adventure. Jimmy surely must have been looking forward to sleeping in a bed and getting some good home-cooked meals, but never complained.

The next morning after not much more than a couple of hours of steady driving, it was time to leave the familiar Route 1 and head west on Route 80 at Swainsboro, Georgia. They stopped for lunch just outside Macon and spent their 5th night sleeping tucked safely away in a filling station parking lot in Tuskegee Alabama.

The next day they drove across Alabama and into Mississippi, continuing west on route 80. They had to pull over in Montgomery, Alabama while a heavy, but brief rainstorm passed through. Jimmy worked the windshield wiper blade back and forth as efficiently as he could, but they figured they'd just stop a while and let Mother Nature blow on by. With the air freshened a bit by the storm, but soon as stifling as ever, they continued to their home for the night in the vicinity of Jackson. Jimmy was excited about driving over the mighty Mississippi River the next morning and couldn't help but try to sing the great show tune, *Ol' Man River*. After singing the only parts of this song that he could remember, about "keeps on rollin'" over and over again, Floyd was happy when the kid finally settled back and gave up the attempt.

The morning of their seventh day, Sunday July 3, 1932 was hot and bright as they chugged away from their service station near Jackson, Mississippi. The car had held up beautifully to the strain of nearly steady driving. Floyd most likely planned to send a letter to the Chevrolet people telling them what a great vehicle they had built and would no doubt include a mild admonishment to the effect that he sure hoped they didn't make too many changes to what looked to him to be a nearly perfect machine. He took great pride in seeing to it that he always used the best grade of gasoline and was careful to keep the radiator coolant and engine oil levels where they should be. He did not skimp on the quality of oil he used, being convinced that if you treat your "horse" properly, it will serve you well for a long time.

He was helped greatly in his maintenance efforts by the wonderfully supportive folks at the gasoline stations along the way. Not only were these places safe and friendly areas for him to park for the night, but the attendants were terrific. Most of them wore a uniform of one sort or the other. For many, this included a military-style cap, jacket and matching Jodhpur trousers and leather shoes shined to perfection. A long-sleeve shirt with matching bow tie completed the outfit. The company's insignia was proudly worn on both the jacket breast pocket and the cap. This was particularly true of the Shell Oil Company's top personnel. Others went for a more casual style and wore a jumpsuit, usually white with a soft cap of the same white fabric. Again the company logo was carried on the jumpsuit and cap. A classic bow tie was usually worn as part of this "uniform" as well. Both of these styles of dress for service station attendants were carefully chosen by the parent oil company to instill a sense of quality and service in the minds of the motoring public. With more than 170,000 gasoline stations in operation in the United States at that time, and the number of persons owning automobiles increasing daily, it was only good business to have the attendants dress for success in such a competitive arena.

The travelers enjoyed seeing the variety of oil company slogans and catch phrases, but couldn't have helped wondering if there was really any difference from one brand to another. It seemed as though everywhere they looked they would see "The Sign of the Flying Red Horse" at the Mobilgas Socony Vacuum stations. Floyd may have been partial to Gulf's product mostly because their No-Nox gasoline was always referred to as "That good Gulf Gasoline". But then the slogan promoting Atlantic Refining Company's Polarine, "Puts pep in your motor—Keeps upkeep down" surely sounded good too.

But for sheer beauty of appearance and "at home" feelings, none of them could match the neat little houses that had become the trademark of the Pure Oil Company. In the mid 20s, this innovative company had made a corporate decision to revitalize its filling station structures. Practically any business or store along any roadway at that time could set out a couple of pumps with underground storage tanks and sell gasoline to the drivers of thirsty autos that rumbled up to them. Pure Oil Company leadership looked for a distinctive new building style that the motoring public would readily associate with their brand known as Purol gasoline. The architect they hired came up with an easy to build, inexpensive English-cottage-style house. Blue tiles were affixed to its high-pitched gable roof, all its exterior woodwork was painted white, while window shutters and moldings matched the roof. Two tall chimneys, one located at each end of the house had blue chimney pots with red-faced brick trimming the top. The letter "P" in elongated Old English lettering was cut out of metal and fastened to the exterior of each chimney flue. With the standard tall gasoline pumps and their clock-dial-indicator faces out in front, this design was loved by the public. The neat little roadside houses made drivers feel comfortable and sure that they were in a friendly place. Several models of the basic design were built over the years, some with only an office and a toilet, while others were equipped with dual greasing bays housed under their own angular roofs to provide "full service". This innovative, highly successful marketing approach set the pace for the design of many other houses for hundreds of roadside businesses and gasoline stations that followed.

As they drove into the historic city of Vicksburg, Mississippi which had been so devastated by the Civil War nearly 70 years earlier, the bridge over the river loomed ahead. Almost before they knew it, they were into Louisiana and Jimmy began to picture himself home at long last. He babbled on about the familiar places he would see once again and the old friends and family he would be reunited with. He didn't want to admit how much he had missed his family, but his feelings surely weren't lost on Floyd who shared Jimmy's thoughts and emotions. Floyd found himself driving a little faster and concentrating a little harder on the roads ahead as they neared Texarkana. Both of them were anxious to get there before sundown.

When they got to Shreveport, Louisiana they turned off Route 80 and proceeded north on 71 where they soon found themselves on a winding gravel road. Jimmy's excitement increased by leaps and bounds as familiar landmarks came into view. Even though it was past the time they normally would have stopped somewhere for supper, Floyd pressed on, determined to get to Jimmy's home before dark.

Then, they were there. It was shortly after 6:00 PM when Jimmy leaped out of the car and ran to the house. Soon, people came streaming out and rushing up to meet the crippled artist and to see for themselves if it was possible that he could really have been the driver. Jimmy's letters said that he would be riding along with "Tex" Walser from Lampasas who had the use of only his right arm and hand, but would be doing all the driving anyway. With genuine Texarkana hospitality and a good strong love for their fellow man, Jimmy's folks insisted on rustling up a real meal for both the weary travelers. They wanted Floyd to stay several days to rest up and allow them to do his laundry, air out his cot and haul him on out of the steel box he had been living in for the past week. Over very minimal objections, Floyd was carried from his car into their house by two husky young men and carefully placed in a comfortable upholstered chair. They all fussed over him so much that he was beginning to think they were more interested in him than in Jimmy. But the youngster didn't mind at all as he related all the exciting things that they had seen in the past 7 days. Floyd didn't mind the attention either.

He must have really appreciated the comfort of once again being in a real house with interesting people who knew how to prepare food the way he liked it. He agreed to spend 2 full days with Jimmy's family during which time he was able to rest better than he had in the back of the car and regained his full strength as well as his determination to drive to Austin with no further delay.

His route from where he now was to his destination was the subject of spirited discussion. He allowed that he really wanted to make it there in one day of driving. If he drove back on down to route 80 and headed west all the way past Dallas to Fort Worth and then went south on 81 to Austin it would be a distance of about 520 miles. But it would be on paved roads all the way. Getting through Dallas and Fort Worth would surely slow him down. He figured he'd be lucky to make it to Austin in 15 or 16 hours of steady driving. He knew that would not be possible without taking too big a risk of falling asleep at the wheel. Everyone agreed that he'd be better off taking a more direct route, even if it meant he'd be on gravel or even dirt roads most of the time. Traffic on those roads was not too heavy and as long as he paid attention and didn't get lost he figured he could average about 30 miles an hour over the 380 or so miles. This meant that, with a couple of rest/lunch stops he could expect to arrive in Austin by 7:00 or 8:00 in the evening if he were underway by 6:00 AM.

When, early Wednesday morning he was carried to his car, he was eager to continue, but a bit sorry to have to leave such nice folks so soon. They loaded him up with plenty of jugs of water, delicious-smelling sandwiches and a box of home made cookies. They had laundered everything they could get their hands on for him. They wanted to do more for him and constantly expressed their gratitude for having brought their Jimmy home to them, safe and sound. As Floyd drove away in a cloud of dust, Jimmy wasn't the only one who had to wipe away a tear.

Floyd was on his own now, without his helper and companion. He had come to really like the boy and was sure that he'd grow into a fine young man. But now he had to concentrate on getting to Austin and pay attention to the navigation. He really didn't want to have to spend the night in the car. Without a helper to haul him into and out of his cot, he'd have to stay in the driver's seat, so he might just as well keep on driving. He'd stop to eat some of the great food lying right there next to him and drink some water when he needed it, but otherwise, he'd just keep driving. He was sure that if needed, he would be able to rely upon someone to help out at any of the service stations he would be sure to come across along the way. He made sure that his six-gun was within easy reach, but may very well have wondered if he was kidding himself about any protection it might afford. Still he must have felt somehow a sense of security just knowing that it was nearby.

It was shortly after 5:30 that morning, Wednesday July 6th, that the strange sedan delivery and its even stranger cargo began the drive headed south on Route 43 out of Texarkana headed for Atlanta, Texas and then Jefferson. It was not quite 8:00 when he crossed Route 80 at Marshall headed for Henderson on a glorious, sunny day that was already getting hot. The road from Jefferson to Marshall was nicely paved and he had made good time. He knew that except for a few short stretches, the roads now until almost to Austin would be poor, at best. He felt no reason to stop and kept rolling right along, but wished he had someone to talk to.

He barreled through Henderson and pulled up at a filling station in Jacksonville where he ate a few cookies and drank a little water while his car was being attended to. Shortly after 10:30 he was kicking up dust as he motored on through the town of Palestine and finally stopped in Oakwood for some lunch and a bit of a rest at about 12:30. The sandwiches Jimmy's folks had prepared for him were so good that it made him realize just how hungry he was. All this solo driving was hard work. It was awfully hot while he was parked, even in the shade and he wanted to be moving again if for no other reason than to have some breeze.

By 1:00 PM the impatient Mr. Walser was bouncing along the gravel road on his way to Buffalo which he drove through by 1:30 and pressed on, jouncing and bumping 'til he got to Hearn at 3:00. He didn't stop, but continued to Rockdale through Cameron, a distance of about 35 miles that somehow seemed to drag slowly by. It was now about a quarter past 4 o'clock and he felt tired, so in spite of an inner voice urging him to keep going, he knew that it was in his best interests to take a break. The heat and the strain of pretty steady driving were wearing him down a bit. He reckoned that he was about 70 or so miles from Austin at this point and although he was anxious to get there, he didn't want to look all tuckered out when he arrived. He wanted everyone to see him at his best and not to be worried that he might collapse at any moment. So - - he rested. He nibbled at the remains of his sandwich and wolfed down more cookies, washing it all down with slow gulps of warm water.

By quarter of five he was moving again on his way to the town of Round Rock, about 50 miles west, where he would pick up the paved highway of Route 81 that would take him south into Austin, Texas. Before he left Rockdale, he pulled into another neat and friendly filling station where he had his gas tank filled up, the windshield washed and the engine oil checked. He asked the attendant to carefully examine everything under the hood and to also check the pressure in his tires. He wanted no mechanical problems to suddenly surface when he was showing off in his new car when he got to where he was going.

The 20 or so miles on the smoothly paved Route 81 were a joy to travel and his speed increased with his anticipation of seeing his family once again. But then, once he was actually in Austin, he had to slow down, carefully check out various landmarks and look for certain street signs. He didn't want to ask a stranger on the street how to find the place he was looking for, but he found himself doing just that. At just about 7:00 PM, he was honking his horn in front of his brother Ben's house.

Although he must have been exhausted from the efforts of the last leg of his trip, Floyd most likely would have appeared in remarkably good shape and probably glowed with the radiance of pride in his accomplishment. It must have been a very emotional reunion for Floyd, his Mamma, Ben and Viola and their kids the first moments of which everybody was talking at once with joyful tears staining a few faces. He looked great. They nearly all looked healthy, with most of the younger Walsers now grown to adulthood and with a few "younguns" he had never seen before.

Floyd's nieces, Agnes Ruth and Tessie Mae, now 24 and 22 had both been married for 6 years and had some little ones of their own. Agnes Ruth was now Mrs. Marvin Chapman of Austin and had 4 year-old Marvin Herbert racing around the place. Tessie Mae had married John Franklin Friday and they had produced 2 children, 5 ½-year old Joe Haden (who would later be killed in the service of his country at Iwo Jima in 1945) and a 2 year-old, Betty June. Fiery-tempered Daniel Abishia, who had been 4 years old when Floyd returned to Lampasas suffering from the effects of his crippling trauma and polio, was now 27 and had been in the Navy for nearly 9 years now and managed to get leave so he could come visit. Ben's second oldest son, Benjamin Herbert at the age of 20 now, resembled his dad, was strong and capable and was in the Texas National Guard. The youngest girl, Frances Eudora who was not quite 9 the last time her talented uncle had seen her before he left for Framingham, was now an attractive young lady of 18.

The only one of the bunch of Ben and Viola's children who happened to be sick at the time Uncle Floyd arrived was their youngest, 14 year-old Gordon Allen. He had been bed-ridden for a couple of weeks with high fever, alternating with body shaking chills and heavy perspiration. His mysterious illness would continue for a total of nearly 6 weeks, at the end of which he would be weak as a kitten and several pounds lighter. He recovered fully, never had a recurrence and continued in good health. But, because he was so ill at the time, he has very few memories of what transpired with their special houseguest.

Floyd's mother no doubt hovered over him and expressed her concern about how tired he must be and that he should get some rest after having a good home-cooked meal of his favorite vittles. She probably alternated between wanting to discover all the interesting things he had been up to in the 9 years he had been away, and suggesting that he take a nap and rest up. She no doubt also was eager to take him up on the promise he had made to her in a letter in which he said he would take her for a ride in his car when he got to Austin.

In short order Ben had his kid brother hauled out of the car and into the house while everyone pitched in to unload what they thought should be brought in. Floyd had to slow them down in their eager attempts to take everything out of the car. He wanted much of his art supplies to be left in their specially configured cabinets attached to the interior of the delivery wagon where they would stay until he was ready for them.

There is no record of just what happened over the next year or so while Floyd was in Texas and surrounding locales. From the information that is available combined with some reasonable speculation, what follows may be a fairly accurate description of his visit.

He surely would have spent several days, probably weeks, at Ben's house during which time he would have done a lot of talking to his mother and anyone else who would listen, about the Greenes and how wonderful they had been to him. He would have described their home at the edge of Lake Waushakum with his comfortable studio apartment Roy had built just for him as well as the many trips to Boston to the museum school and the many accolades he had received. He surely brought along some of his best work to not only impress the folks with how good he had become, but also to give them as special gifts from him.

It must have been difficult for anyone to believe that he could actually drive any car, no matter how skillfully it may have been retrofitted for his unique needs. It is likely that the men spent a fair amount of time carefully studying just how those modifications were incorporated. They must have been impressed with the fact that he had done all the driving of nearly 2000 miles. They had forgotten how determined he could be and how much he could accomplish when he set his mind to it. He must have beamed with joy at their expressions of wonderment and praise for his skill in piloting his vehicle as well as his physical strength in making the journey.

He most definitely would have spent a fair amount of time with each of his sisters, Erie, Lena, and Clara and their families, none of whom lived near Austin, but were within a day's spirited drive. Erie's husband Eddie Ross had died of yellow fever or some other mysterious illness back in 1918 leaving her a young widow with a 7 year-old son, Frank, to raise by herself. She was now Mrs. Lloyd Voss Risinger whom she married in the fall of 1920. They were now living in Lubbock and had 2 children; a very tall nearly 11 year-old boy named Lloyd Voss, Jr. who was always known simply as "LV", and a daughter, the very pretty Ouida who was almost 7. Erie's son Frank Ross was now 21 and was an independent young adult with his own agenda.

Lena, a telephone chief operator was Mrs. Nabours, married to a serious-minded young man. Baby sister Clara was happily married to John Wesley (Jack) Thurman and had one daughter, Jacalyn Fay who was now 10. She would tell Floyd that she did not like her given name, since it sounded too much like an animal - - a jackal. She much preferred to be called Jacquie. Floyd always remembered to honor her request.

He also spent a lot of time with his youngest brother, Tansey his wife, Zepha Ophelia and their 2 boys, Billy James and Kelly who lived quite a distance from Austin in the town of Abernathy, just north of Lubbock. Floyd had been distressed to learn by a letter to him in 1926, that Tansey's son Ray Edward had died 2 days short of his second birthday. It may have been that Floyd spent the winter months at Tansey's place in Abernathy, although he may have alternated those colder months with other relatives.

It is very highly probable that some quality time was spent visiting with Tom Ivy, Floyd's half brother and about 10 years his senior. Tom and his wife Nettie lived in South San Antonio where Tom was employed in government civil service. In years past, Floyd and Tom had always been close, with the young Floyd looking up to the more mature big brother who was always thought of by everyone as "a good man". Nettie was an accomplished sculptor and artist and

Floyd always enjoyed exchanging thoughts on artistic technique with her.

It is certain that Floyd got out to paint much of the landscape for miles around the homes where he stayed. Just what vistas captured his interest and how much artwork he created or in which mediums he worked are all unknown. What became of the scenes he developed is likewise a bit of a mystery. It is reasonable to assume that he gave much of what he did to his family and also sold quite a bit of it to local folk who had heard of the visiting artist. He may have done portrait work as well as many landscapes, and may even have done a bit of caricature work to show that he hadn't forgotten what Zim had taught him.

It is possible that he may have driven himself around to the various members of his family and may have slept in his car at some locations or may have had a room in the house he visited. He wanted to not be a drain on anybody and was fiercely independent and resolved to do as much for himself as possible. He probably tried to do even more than he was really up to actually doing, to prove to all that he was getting along exceptionally well. It is equally likely that each member of his family did as much as they could to make him comfortable and welcome in their homes. It would be difficult to keep a "normal" household however with such a special guest and there may well have been times when he may have felt he was beginning to outwear his welcome. He was very sensitive to any sign of being a nuisance and surely would have taken special pains to be as little bother as possible.

It is fairly certain that Floyd spent about one year in and around the state of Texas. He loved his home state and was proud to be called "Tex" by some of the Massachusetts people who had gotten to know him. He must have especially enjoyed painting outdoors, working on capturing the rugged beauty of many of the places he had known as a boy when his life was carefree and there seemed to be no limit to what he may eventually do or to where he might travel.

It is very possible that he managed to get as far west in Texas as El Paso. He may also have driven, or been driven into Arizona and/or New Mexico. Just how he got around to these places and others, and who may have accompanied him is not recorded, but it is known that he really wanted Ben to simply drop everything - - family and job responsibilities - - and travel all over the country with him for months. There was simply no way Ben could comply with such a request from his brother, but he may well have driven him around on weekends.

Eventually, after what surely had been a satisfying year in Texas, painting copiously and visiting with his dear family, it would have been time for him to head back to the shores of Lake Waushakum. His mother must have wished that he could just stay put and let her look after him, although they both knew that would not be realistic. She was now 72 and in reasonably good health, but clearly not up to the strain of caring for her talented son on a daily basis. It was difficult for the two of them to say their good-byes, since they must have known that they would probably not meet again in this world.

It is not known how Floyd's return trip to Framingham was arranged. Someone must have located a person who was willing, if not eager to be his companion and helper on the long trip back. In any event, sometime in the middle of 1933, the specially equipped and very unique auto was headed north. It carried not only its unusual owner, his belongings and his helper but also the many prayers and wishes from his family for Floyd's continued good health and a safe journey.

CHAPTER 13

THE ARTIST RETURNS
(At least for a while)
1933 - 1943

Roy and Edith were thrilled to have their long-lost protégé home with them again, after nearly a year's absence. They were relieved to hear that his travels had gone so well. They had really appreciated the many letters he had written them in which he related all his positive experiences. They were touched by his admission of the fact that after he had been in Texas for a few months he was feeling homesick for them and was looking forward to returning. Everything had changed in the 9 years he had been living with them. Not only had he developed into a respected artist, who still was growing and improving, but his family had also changed and all were very much into their own families and careers. He confided to the Greenes that he had been a bit disappointed that his brother, Ben had not taken very kindly to his strong urging to take off together in his specially rigged car. He wanted Ben to simply drop everything and spend several weeks or maybe even months, driving all around the country with him so that he could paint whatever caught his interest. He told them that after he had made the suggestion to Ben for what must have been the 4th or 5th time, his brother made it painfully obvious that there was simply no way he was about to leave his responsibilities to his job and his family to go cavorting around the countryside like a free spirit. Some of the words exchanged by the brothers seemed a little harsh to Floyd. This was particularly true of the statement Ben had made to the effect that, "it's not all about you anymore, Floyd." Once he had related that little exchange to his old benefactors, he could see the truth and obvious clarity of the situation. It was indeed true that his family had made it "all about" him when he needed that kind of support years ago. But now, he appeared to them to be pretty independent and had found good, caring people who could look after him.

One episode that Floyd casually related to Roy and Edith after he had been back with them for a while had them reliving their early worries for his safety. By the time he had finished his little narration, they were all smiles and realized once again just what a special person he really was. He told them that on his return trip to Framingham he was without a helper for a couple of days and had been pushing himself perhaps a bit too hard. The fellow who had been riding along to help out, lost interest in the job at about the Mississippi/Alabama state line and simply disappeared. There was nothing for him but to press on hoping that he could pick up a new helper along the homeward route. Somewhere east of Macon, Georgia in the early evening with the sun just about ready to set behind him he felt extra tired, but had not located a good stopping place. He suddenly saw what looked like a promising spot on a road to his left and up a steep grade. But he hadn't reacted quickly enough so that when he turned the steering wheel too sharply and at the same time failed to execute a proper gear change, he stalled the car. What's more, the sudden turn to his left combined with his overwhelming tiredness caused him to topple to his right in his seat. His belt had not been snugged up as tightly as it should have. The result was that he was suddenly laying over on his side, with his good arm pinned under him, his right foot out of the special shoe on the brake pedal, the car stalled and out of gear and rapidly gaining speed as it rolled back down the hill. He could do absolutely nothing about it other than to shout "Whoa, whoa!"

He had gotten a glimpse to his right before he had made his bad turn, of an old farmhouse set back from the road about 100 feet. He remembered that a little old man was sitting out on the front porch lazily rocking in his chair, probably enjoying a bit of a rest after dinner and a long, hard day's work. Now, he felt himself being bounced up and down and jostled from side to side as he raced blindly backwards right off the road he had been on and continued into the front yard of that house. Fortunately, there were no trees, fences or large rocks in his unplanned path, and the front yard gradually sloped up toward the house. Suddenly, he stopped with a jolt. He had no choice but to wait for help to get him sitting up again so he could see just what in the world he had done. After a few minutes, which must have seemed like forever, he heard a man's voice at his window. "Howdy", said the voice. Floyd, feeling more than a little foolish and embarrassed responded with a polite, "Howdy", right back.

"Thought ya'd drop in for a visit did ya?" continued the still unseen man, who certainly sounded friendly enough and didn't seem the least bit perturbed by this uninvited stranger. Floyd tried to quickly explain his predicament. The man caught on immediately, opened the driver's door and putting a strong arm around Floyd's shoulder, effortlessly had him righted in no time. The man, whose name turned out to be John, was fascinated by the special controls the car was equipped with and even more taken with the person behind the wheel. He also made no comment about the Colt .45 now exposed on the passenger seat. In a few minutes Floyd's basic story had been told and John, who turned out to be not an old man at all, as Floyd had first assumed, called out for his wife, Maggie, to come meet their new guest.

The unplanned backwards jaunt across John's and Maggie's front yard turned out to be one of the best parts of Floyd's journey back to Massachusetts. Neither his car nor their front porch were any the worse for having made such sudden contact. In fact, to a casual observer it would have appeared that the car was purposely backed right up against the front porch, with its rear doors just clearing the floorboards.

Floyd spent the next two full days with this accommodating couple. John carried the visiting Texan into his home, where he made him comfortable in a chair in the front parlor, while Maggie quickly rustled up a plate of her best home cookin'. Floyd was a lot hungrier than he had realized and the food was beyond delicious. He was also much more tired than he had realized and welcomed the kind offer of a soft bed in a room of his own.

They spent pretty much the entire next day getting to know each other, or more accurately, them getting to hear all about Floyd's travels, his unique training in art, his Framingham benefactors, and how he came to be paralyzed. He played down the roles of heat stroke and polio in his paralysis, leaving them with the belief that a rogue wild horse he was taming had thrown and trampled him. They were in awe of his artwork and remarked at the beauty of some of what he had created just a few weeks ago in Texas. He tried to give them one of his watercolors that they seemed to be especially taken with, but they stubbornly refused to accept. So while they made him a guest in their home for 2 days, feeding him, washing his clothes and bed sheets and John helping Floyd into and out of their bathtub for a much needed bath, he did what he could for them. He asked the strong homeowner to carry him out into the front yard and set him up in his portable wheelchair with his easel and paints. Within a few hours he had captured the beauty of their home and yard in a stunning watercolor, with "F N Walser" printed in his unique style in the lower right corner. They accepted it with great pride and indicated the exact spot on the parlor wall they would hang it once they had it framed.

If all the food, rest and companionship of those 2 days weren't enough, it developed that John's cousin, Harry who lived nearby, had a hankerin' to get himself up to Boston to try to hook up with an old girlfriend of his. He quickly agreed to become Floyd's helper for the rest of the way to Massachusetts. However, once he saw how difficult it really was for Floyd to work all the special controls in his car, even though he could see that the Texan could actually do it, he insisted on being the driver as well as the helper. Once underway, they made good time to their destination.

Now in the summer of 1933 Floyd was eager to pick up where he had left off with respect to his calling. It was so wonderful that he still had his fully equipped studio with its skylight to bring in the cool and steady north light to enhance his efforts at portrait work. He quickly settled into his place, and after a few weeks, if it hadn't been for catching a glimpse now and then of his special car parked out next to the barn, he may have found it hard to believe that he had been away at all.

Roy showed Floyd the little 26-page booklet from the Society of American Etchers 17th annual exhibition that had taken place at the National Arts Club in New York City last November and December while he was off on his adventures in Texas. There on page 22 was shown entry number 347, *For Rent* with the artist listed as Floyd T. Walser and the price given as $5. Although Floyd was very pleased to be shown in the same exhibition with the likes of Frank W. Benson, he was a little miffed about the incorrect middle initial they had given him. He grumpily commented something to the effect that they didn't list Benson as Frank N. or any other such goof. Once Roy pointed out that the good folks who put together the catalog must have thought his middle name was Tex, he felt a little better about it.

Floyd was captivated by the impressive beauty of the old warship, the U.S.S. *Constitution*, nicknamed "Old Ironsides". Anchored at the Charlestown Navy Yard in Boston, she always had fascinated him from the first time Roy had driven him to that mooring place. In the fall of 1934, shortly after school children all over the country had raised money to help defray the costs of re-rigging this wonderful old ship, he produced a superb drawing of her. From that drawing he had created one of his finest etchings with the masts and all the rigging shown in detail, and yet rendered in a most artistic style.

Floyd continued his drawing of the many buildings and historic places in and around Framingham and the Boston area. For all the grandeur and eye-popping spectacle of the buildings in New York City and Washington, DC, he was never moved to want to capture any of them as his subjects.

In 1935, yet another high honor was bestowed upon ol' "Tex". The Second International Competitive Print Exhibition sponsored by the Print Club of Cleveland was about to be held. His *Where Dad Was Born* had been shown in 1931 and the officers and judges of the Print Club were impressed enough with that early work of his to invite him to submit up to 3 prints for possible inclusion in the 1935 exhibition. He was flabbergasted to be told that all 3 of his prints were being hung. Roy and Edith excitedly told everyone they knew about the superb compliment to his artistic talent that this selection demonstrated.

The prints in this competition were: *Old Whaling Ship*, which was Colonel Green's boat at South Dartmouth, Massachusetts, "Old New England Home", a rendition of the Fay place in nearby Sherborn, and "Framingham Elm", his old favorite famous giant elm tree, which was located on Gates Street in Framingham Centre. This old tree had been planted before the American Revolution and had been viewed with great interest by generations of people ever since.

Floyd was one of 163 artists with a total of 370 prints entered in the competition. There does not seem to have been any monetary prizes awarded at this event, but a wood engraving entitled *Corsican Washerwomen* by one Clare Leighton received the popular vote of the members of the club. Once again, Floyd was not the least bit upset at not having won anything more than the honor of having his work included.

In the middle of the 1930s Floyd was employed by one of the biggest programs of President Franklin Delano Roosevelt's "New Deal". As a way to fight off the lingering economic hardships brought about by the Great Depression of 1929, President Roosevelt introduced the Works Progress Administration, simply called the WPA, in May of 1933. Its name was changed in 1939 to Work Projects Administration, but was still known as the WPA. While initially, most of the work created by this organization was in construction, such as roads, bridges, and other structures, it expanded into several branches and at its peak it provided jobs for close to 1/3 of the nation's 10,000,000 unemployed. It typically paid its workers about $50.00 per month.

By March of 1936 the Federal Art Project, as a part of the WPA, was going strong, employing about 6,000 people across the country. Fifty percent of them were directly engaged in creating works of art, while 10% to 25% worked in art education. Floyd was one of those teachers and was dedicated to the task. All during the summer months when school was out, he taught classes made up of large groups of youngsters, many of them elementary grade pupils, some even younger. Several times a week, on warm sunny days, these occasionally serious-minded youngsters would sit out under the trees in front of Harmony Home and do their best to put on paper some of the ideas he was trying to teach them. It must have been tough on both teacher and student with the distractions of the Anna Murphy Playground right across the street acting to remind them all of just how much fun they could be having over there. Many of his young students would, in their adult years, look back fondly on Mr. Walser and his art classes, remembering his gentle encouragement at even a hint of something done right.

Floyd teaching some of the town's youngsters for the WPA.

In December 1937 Floyd received a penny post card from the firm of M. Grumbacher of New York. It notified him that one of his paintings, which was made using their Schmincke artist-grade water color paints was then being exhibited in what was referred to as an "Aqua-Chromatic Exhibition of Watercolors" at the State Teacher's College of Fitchburg, Mass. This was just one more of dozens of places all around the country where people could see and enjoy his best works.

He was quite pleased and proud to be listed in the 1938 edition of *Who's Who In Massachusetts*. This catalog of notable persons had him listed along with U. S. senators, judges, attorneys, architects, professors, and economists as "artist and etcher". The brief biographical account really didn't do him justice, but he was thrilled to be listed among others who had accomplished much in their lives.

Floyd wasn't the only one keeping busy. Edith had many piano pupils coming in for advanced lessons on a regular basis and was still very active with her many clubs and organizations, although her health was deteriorating. It was becoming difficult for her to get through her busy day without stopping to rest frequently. But she continued to enjoy all aspects of classical music, especially teaching and playing. Roy was busier than ever with the Civic League Orchestra as well as his own students. Edith often performed at concerts given by Roy's constantly improving and immensely popular orchestra.

But on December 12, 1939 Edith enjoyed what had to have been the highlight of her career. She was honored at a testimonial dinner in the ballroom of the elegant Hotel Pioneer in Boston. This was to celebrate her 50th anniversary as composer, teacher and pianist. It was quite a tribute for someone at the age of 64 to be feted for 50 years of noteworthy musical contributions and was very appropriate since her first composition had been published in 1889 when she was but 14 years old.

With several of her pupils as ushers, hundreds of very well known people representing the local music world as well as officers and dignitaries from the many professional clubs in the Boston and Framingham area were delighted to be in attendance. There were at least a dozen speakers who extolled the merits of Madame Greene's distinguished career. Included among them were former Mayor Malcom E. Nichols and Mrs. Nichols of Boston, Mrs. Jessie Eldridge Southwick of Emerson College, and Miss Elsie Winsor Bird, a Boston singing teacher.

Six of Edith's songs were sung, being performed beautifully by a contralto and a soprano, both of whom were great friends of hers and who were no strangers to lovers of fine music. They were accompanied by a highly skilled violinist and a pianist. For some of the songs, Edith was persuaded to sit at the grand piano and be the star accompanist. She demurred at first, but thrilled everyone with her special piano technique. After the violinist played the guest of honor's very popular *Romance for Violin*, the audience broke into sustained, heartfelt applause to show their appreciation for Madame Greene's versatility as a composer.

Edith received many letters and telegrams of congratulations from distant friends who were unable to attend in person. A beautiful bouquet of flowers was presented to her by her friend, Serge Koussevitzky of the Boston Symphony Orchestra. Only 4 years before this special evening, he had established the Berkshire Music Center, which soon became known as Tanglewood, to train the most promising young composers, conductors, and instrumentalists. Just one year previously, in August, 1938, the "Shed", the structure that partially enclosed the musicians, was completed and named for him. It must have been a special honor for the Greene's to simply be among the people who knew this great man, but to be presented with flowers by him had to have been truly special.

At the end of the evening, a purse of money from her many friends and admirers was presented to Edith. It was an evening she would remember fondly for the rest of her life.

Shortly after Edith's special tribute at the Hotel Pioneer, she and Roy were visited one evening by Dr. Koussevitsky who brought along Lenny, one of his latest and, according to him, his most gifted student. The handsome 21-year old, who had been born in Lawrence, Massachusetts had recently graduated cum laude in music from Harvard University and was looking forward to assisting Dr. Koussevitsky at Tanglewood the following summer. Edith and Roy both maintained a special interest in the meteoric rise of their new acquaintance - -Leonard Bernstein.

Just before Christmas 1939, Floyd got a most unusual letter from his sister, Erie. It had been several months since her last long letter to him in which she told of what was to him, marginally interesting tid-bits about various family members and their comings and goings. Before he opened this new letter from her he must have assumed it to contain more of the same. By the time he had finished reading this one he was chuckling heartily and called for Edith and Roy so he could relate its contents to them. Before he read the story to the Greenes he must have thought very carefully about whether or not it was a strange joke of some sort, but convinced himself that Erie surely wouldn't have gone to the trouble of making up anything as outlandish as this.

The letter told how Erie's and her husband Lloyd's son, LV Risinger who was now a freshman at John Tarleton Agricultural College in Stephenville, Texas had been involved in a bit of mischief, but was paraded around the campus as a hero for doing it. It seemed that the annual Homecoming and its traditional football game were about to take place at the end of November. The rivalry between the 2 colleges that would square off at this most auspicious and important football game had been bubbling for decades. JTAC, as LV's school was referred to, could have a successful football season if they lost every other game but beat the stuffin' out of nearby North Texas Agricultural College (NTAC) located in Arlington.

LV made the football squad almost as soon as the coach had spotted him during freshman orientation week. His size, 6 foot 6 inches tall when he slouched and his body mass, which tipped the scales at nearly 300 pounds as well as his intimidating appearance, had the coach determined that he would be on the team in both the offensive and defensive lines. The fact that LV had no particular interest in the sport or desire to work out at it made no difference to the coaching staff. He started every game and his sheer size and bulk, if not his speed and talent, were instrumental in JTAC victories over hapless opponents. But it was not a football game Erie wrote about. It was what would in later years in the JTAC newspaper be referred to as "The Airplane Incident."

Both rival colleges maintained an almost sacred tradition for the Homecoming Weekend every year by setting up and then torching a huge bonfire the night before the big game. It was always a spectacle to behold, and returning alumni took great pride in watching the night sky lit up even more brightly than they had caused it to be when they were undergrads. They had learned, by painful experience, to guard the stack of wood and rubbish against "premature conflagration" caused by spirited and sneaky rivals from NTAC raiding the campus.

On the evening of November 29, 1939, two days before the Homecoming football game, LV and a large gang of JTAC students were gathered in the vicinity of the completed stack that would become what they thought would be the best bonfire yet. They were congratulating themselves on the previous night's raid on the NTAC campus under cover of darkness during which they had managed to torch their adversary's very impressive stack of combustible material. They fully expected a retaliatory strike from the "Grubs" as they called their opponents, and to let everyone know of their vigilance, they began what was planned to be an all-night beating of drums. When they heard the sound of a small open-cockpit airplane approaching at a very low altitude, they knew this could be a threat to their bonfire. Sure enough, it could be seen that while the pilot was guiding the plane on a low and direct path, which would soon have it right over the stack, his accomplice was preparing to drop a phosphorus bomb on it. As LV and his pals watched in anguish, a small package containing white phosphorus was dropped but landed harmlessly a few feet from the target. It was quickly buried and nothing came of it.

Excited defenders grabbed what little they could get their hands on and threw various objects up at the plane with everything missing the target. LV searched for something to throw and picked up the only thing he could find. It turned out to be the cut-off end of a 2 x 4. He judged it to be heavy enough for his intended purpose. He figured that if he could somehow disable the bomber, it could land on the nearby field. He waited until the plane was nearly over his head, and at just the right moment hurled it up with mighty force. To everyone's amazement, just as the wooden missile reached its highest point in the air and was about to fall back to earth, the plane flew into it and its propeller whacked it. The engine sputtered and with the airplane now disabled, the pilot had no choice but to continue his present course, unable to steer right or left. A second phosphorus bomb fell far from its intended target causing little damage.

The airplane meanwhile was on a direct path which looked for all the world as though it would surely crash into the home of the Dean of Students. In the ensuing seconds, LV's heart was in his mouth while he prayed that no horrible tragedy was about to occur. Much to his relief, the wheels of the attacking airplane cleared the roof of the Dean's house, although it was only by a scant 3 feet. It crash-landed harmlessly in a clump of trees. Its occupants were not injured in the unplanned landing, but were swarmed over by JTAC students who, once they were convinced that the enemy aviators were OK, ganged up on them to drag them out and tie them up.

While the airplane distracted most of the defenders, 3 truckloads of NTAC students had been attempting to invade the campus by land. Outnumbered and overwhelmed by the superior force, they were all captured, had the hair on their heads shaved into block "Ts" and after considerable heckling, were sent on their way to relate their sad tale of humbling defeat.

LV was the hero of the evening and took enormous pride in his fame, which would endure for many years. The fact that Tarleton beat the Grubs in the ensuing football game by a score of 6 to nothing only added to the glow.

When Floyd finished reading the account of this event to Edith and Roy, they probably had mixed feelings about what could have been an occasion of serious injury, but an event none the less that demonstrated a strong college spirit. They were all laughing over the part of the story in which Erie related what Walter Winchell had said on the air just 2 nights after the episode. That famous radio personality had made the point that perhaps the English military should call LV to come over. He could probably knock down attacking German aircraft a lot more economically than they were doing.

When the Greenes asked how in the world LV could have tossed a board high enough to damage the propeller, Floyd responded with something along the lines of, "Aw heck, he's so damn big he could'a probably just reached up and grabbed ahold of one of the wheels and just pulled it down."

Floyd would remember the "airplane incident" for many years with pride in a Walser relative who had demonstrated more than a little toughness. (He would have been proud to know that many years later, after LV had passed away in 1993, that Tarleton College would continue to commemorate that infamous night back in 1939. The traditional bonfire is now known as "The L.V. Risinger Memorial Bonfire".)

Sometime in late 1940 or early in 1941 Floyd put together a typewritten summary discussing the background of 8 of his prints and offered them for sale. Although it included two ships and a gristmill, the list carried the title, "OLD FRAMINGHAM HOUSES".

The noble Elm on Gates Street is 90 feet high, has limb spread of 165 feet, is 12 feet through the trunk, and is said to be near 400 years old. The tree is owned by Mr. and Mrs. W.E. Dumont who live in the fine old house at right. The drawing was done with lead pencil.

The town library building was finished in 1873. The drawing was done with lithographic pencil.

Pen sketch - - Plymouth Church, which was built in 1830. The tower and spire were added in 1848.

The old Nixon place on Edmonds Road is now owned by Mr. and Mrs. Sohier Welch. Drawing done with ink and wash.

The Foster house on Grove Street was built by Jonathan Pike in 1693-4. Miss Foster told me that she finds it difficult to get modern paints to match the old paint on the house. Charcoal and chalk drawing.

The mill is owned by Henry Ford and is located near Wayside Inn. Drawing done in watercolor.

I went to South Dartmouth to draw Colonel Green's old whaling ship. A duplicate of this dry-point Etching was in the International Print Exhibition at the Cleveland Museum of Art in 1935.

The drawing for the Etching of the *Constitution* was done at the Charlestown Navy Yard, Boston, in 1934, soon after the nation's school children raised money to re-rig the old ship.

The set of eight prints, described above, will be sent anywhere in the United States by insured mail upon receipt of one dollar. Address: F. N. Walser, 70 Lake Avenue, Framingham, Massachusetts.

Note: I have 40 original (signed) etchings of the old Badger place, size 6 x 7 inches. A duplicate of these was in the Society of American Etchers, New York exhibition in 1932, and sold there for $5.00. I will sell these original etchings at $1.00 each. Etching and set of eight prints both for $1.75.

(The above is from the archives of the Framingham Historical Society and Museum - -Framingham, Massachusetts.)

By early spring, 1943 Floyd was once again feeling the powerful urge to get back in his special auto and head out west again. He had been deeply saddened to learn in April 1941 that his dear Mamma had passed away at his brother Ben's home where she had been staying. She was almost 80 when she died and had been in failing health for a while. Floyd was troubled at the thought of not being out there with her in her final days, but knew that it would have been nearly impossible. He was satisfied that when he did visit with her in 1932 that they had had good, happy times together. But he still felt her loss very strongly and recalled the good, strong and caring woman who had not only given him life, but perhaps more than anyone else, saw to it that he never lost his will to fight on and to overcome the devastating effects of polio.

Old Nixon Place

The Constitution

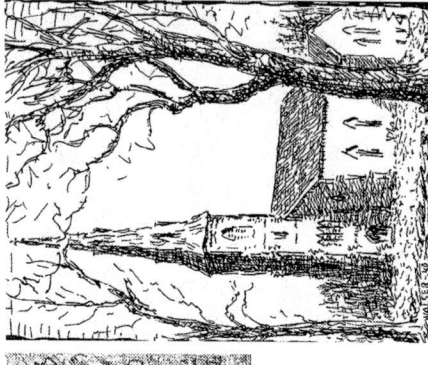
Plymouth Church

Ford's Mill

Town Library

Col Greene's Old Whaling Ship

Noble Elm on Gates Street

Floyd offered, in 1941, to send this set of prints anywhere in the United States by insured mail, upon receipt of one dollar.

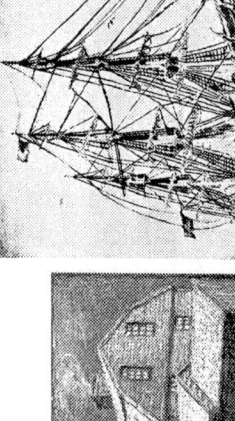

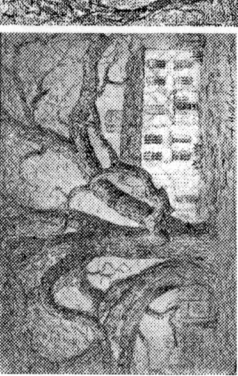
Foster House

Now he put together a plan to get out to Texas again and this time to see even more of the country. He really wanted to get out to Oregon and spend some time with his sister Clara and her family who had moved out there. There was a practically limitless supply of incredibly beautiful country that he was just itchin' to paint.

But he knew that in the 11 years that had elapsed since his first daring dash to Austin, a lot had happened to make this journey much more of a challenge. For one thing, he was that much older and although he didn't feel the least bit less capable, even if he was now 55, he was reminded of his age by both Roy and Edith as they expressed concern about such a trip. Other factors that did give him pause, at least for a while, were that the number of vehicles on the roads had increased dramatically and the roadways themselves were more complicated and allowed for higher speeds as well. Also, his old 1930 Chevy had been sitting idle in Roy's barn for the past 10 years and would need to be gone over with a fine-tooth comb before anyone would even begin to feel that it would be safe to operate.

He figured that he'd need to hire a driver, at least for that part of the trip that would get him to Texas. Perhaps from there on up to Oregon and points in between, he could manage on his own, so long as he could find someone to help him the way his young friend Jimmy had done. His optimistic nature, or as Edith may have felt, his stubborn streak, allowed him to feel not the least concerned about having this all work out just fine - - somehow.

For the past several weeks he had been helped quite a bit by a youngster who lived down off Nipmuc Road, not far from the beach of Lake Waushakum and within easy walking distance of Harmony Home. Fourteen-year-old Skippy Carlson would come into Floyd's apartment each morning and help him to get sitting up, do a few quick errands, then be on his way to school. Floyd recognized that this kid was brighter than the average teen-ager he had met and was sure that he would mature into a fine young man with a promising career.

He reminded Floyd of Jimmy, but really had more on the ball.

The few men that responded to Floyd's call for a hired driver had let it be known that they were not the least bit interested in being asked to empty his bedpan and perform what they may have thought of as nursing duties. His thought was that if he could find a man that he could hire as just his driver, he might have Skippy ride along as his helper, even if it would be a little crowded in the car. When he brought up the idea to Skippy, the youngster was immediately excited about the chance to see the sights on the way to Texas and to spend a little time in that exciting state. Floyd told him that once the 3 of them had arrived at his brother Tansey's home in Abernathy, he would be welcome to stay as long as he wanted and then Floyd would provide money for him and the driver to return home by train.

The Greenes probably thought that there was simply no way the boy's parents would allow him to be part of such a harebrained scheme. Roy and Edith were not much in favor of this second trip which would take their old pal away from them for another year or so and secretly hoped that Skippy's sensible parents would veto his request. Such was not the case, however since his mom and dad had great faith in their son's good sense and his mature attitude about life in general and this chance-of-a-lifetime experience in particular. Feeling strongly that Mr. Walser was a fine person and that the trip would be educational for their young son now that school was out for the summer, they gave their OK.

Floyd had exchanged several letters with Tansey and determined that he would be more than welcome to stay there with him in Abernathy as long as he wanted. Both Tansey and his wife were still grieving over the sudden passing of their son, Kelly who had died at the age of 18, leaving them with only Billy, who was now all the more precious to them. Floyd also wrote to Clara who lived in Shady Cove, Oregon with her barnstorming flyer husband Jack Thurman and their young daughter, Jacalyn (Jacquie) who was then about 21.

He told Clara that he wasn't at all sure of just when he might actually show up at her place, but if all went well, he'd be there. It might not be until the following spring, assuming he wintered with Tansey. He really wanted to see as much as possible of the beauty of the western states and Oregon in particular. Also, he was looking forward to seeing her again after all the years apart.

And so it came to pass that in the early summer of 1943, with our country embroiled in WWII, and things very much not normal because of everything a wartime economy entailed, the cowboy artist was ready once again to head west. He had in some way managed to either store up extra gasoline rationing coupons or in some other creative way was able to be not terribly affected by the fact that the ordinary citizen was only able to get enough coupons for about 5 gallons a week.

He had hired a driver somehow. Practically nothing is known of who he was or of just how he came to sign up with Floyd and Skippy for the journey, but it is clear that his only interest was in driving and definitely not in providing any help for Floyd. He wanted the contraptions that had been installed to allow Floyd to operate the car to be removed so that he wouldn't have to contend with their strangeness. Floyd would not hear of such a plan, since he fully expected to be driving himself for a considerable part of the trip around Oregon whenever he could manage to get out that way. The driver would just have to put up with the special levers and controls. He was allowed to remove the special boot on the brake pedal, stowing it away under the seat, since it had been designed to allow easy attachment and removal for just such future use.

It must have been crowded and somewhat uncomfortable for Skippy who no doubt rode somewhere behind the front seats, with Floyd riding as front passenger, acting as navigator and captain of his "ship". It is possible that there was a fair amount of tension or perhaps even friction between the independent-minded driver, who will simply be called Joe, and Floyd who was very much in charge of all aspects of the trip.

It is known that Joe enjoyed whiskey, although Floyd was not aware of that fact until they were underway. At every opportunity, when they pulled into a service station for fuel and various maintenance checks, Joe would hop out and inquire as to where the nearest barroom was located. He would work up some pretext or other to permit the car to pull up near a bar and run in for a quick one. When they had settled down for the night, wherever that may be, the driver would be gone for hours, finally returning to sleep off the effects of too much liquor and not enough food. Floyd was very upset with this behavior and told him that if he didn't straighten out he would not be allowed to continue to drive. Joe laughed at the rebuke, feeling that he was a vital link in the plan to get Floyd to Texas.

Joe's love affair with the bottle became critical when they were somewhere in North Carolina. Floyd and Skippy were settled in for the night, but Joe was nowhere to be found. When he stumbled into the truck sometime after midnight, so drunk he could not utter a coherent sentence, Floyd had had enough. He let the bum sleep it off and then at first light he and Skippy made preparations to continue the journey. Joe was still immobile and practically unconscious. Skippy must have wondered what the seriously annoyed Mr. Walser had in mind. With a stronger voice and even stronger language than the youngster had ever heard Floyd use, Joe was roughly roused from his deep sleep, his heavy-lidded eyes nearly unable to blink open, and his numbed brain not understanding what was happening. Once he was standing outside, partially supported by the front fender, he began to realize that he had just been fired. Floyd saw to it that Joe got the money he had earned to this point and made it abundantly clear to him that his services were no longer needed and that what he did from that point on was completely up to him.

Skippy, still not understanding how they would continue was surprised to hear Floyd tell him, "OK, Skippy. You drive." The kid had just turned 14 and was still a couple of years away from being old enough to get a driver's license. He had fooled around with his older brother's car from time to time and did have a good idea of how to drive. He was thrilled with the new plan. He'd be the driver <u>and</u> the helper. He figured that if he had too much trouble, he could haul Mr. Walser into the driver's seat and let him drive, like the good man had done 10 years previously. But he knew that wouldn't be necessary. He had been paying close attention to the way Joe handled the controls and was confident of his abilities.

As they pulled away from their parking place, with Skippy trying not to stall too many times, they couldn't help but feel a little bit bad at the pitiful sight of the still confused ex-driver standing out there scratching his head and wondering what the hell just happened. Floyd knew that they were much better off without the poor old drunk as part of their team. He later confided that he had strong guilt feelings about leaving the guy the way he did, but felt he had no choice for safety sake.

Several days later, with Skippy handling the car like an old pro, they were at Tansey's farm in Abernathy, being warmly greeted by Tansey and his wife, Zepha Ophelia, who soon prepared what she knew to be one of her brother-in-law's favorite meals, which included pickled pig's feet. Their son, Billy was very close in age to Floyd's new driver/helper and was amazed to find that the kid had actually driven a good part of the way to their home. He immediately began campaigning to be allowed to drive the vehicle around the yard, something Floyd was not interested in having him do.

In short order, Tansey had Floyd all set up in the room he had prepared for him. Skippy slept in the extra bed in Billy's room and the two teenagers got along like long lost pals. After about a week in the hot, noisy old car, it must have been like heaven for the two travelers to be in a real house again with good food and comfortable beds.

Floyd was looked after constantly by both Tansey and Zepha. They took turns fussing over him and seeing to it that he was comfortable and that he was able to catch up on a little rest after his trip. Within a few days, the novelty of having the new visitors had worn off and the household returned to near normalcy. Skippy was quick to learn all the chores that were needed to be done on the good-sized farm he was now living at. Billy thought it was great fun to have a kid his own age who hadn't worked on a farm before to good-naturedly boss around. Skippy was a fast learner and it wasn't long before he was pointing out labor-saving shortcuts to his mentor, so they'd have more time to goof off.

A job Skippy particularly did not like to help with was killing chickens. Years later he would still recall the unnatural and to him, gruesome way it was done. He would tell his family, "They would actually grab the poor chicken by the head and swing it around off to one side a couple a times until its neck snapped. - - Ugh!"

After a month living at the Walser household/farm, it was time for Skippy to head back home. Floyd had given him money for train fare and a little extra for food and whatnot, telling him that he wished he could stay with him as his helper for all the rest of his adventures. Skippy surely would have enjoyed spending the next year or so "bumming around" with Mr. Walser, but he had promised his folks he'd be back in plenty of time to enjoy the last of the summer with them and to be ready for the start of school in September.

The train Skippy found himself on headed home was loaded with U. S. Army soldiers on their way to another training camp. He soon became their "mascot" and was looked after by them for the duration of the trip that they were together. This episode was one more high point in his whole adventure. He had lots of good true stories to tell everybody once he got back to Framingham.

From the few clues that can be found, it appears that Floyd spent most of his time at Tansey's home and probably spent the winter there with his younger brother's small family. A notice in an Abernathy newspaper dated November, 1943 appeared as follows:

SEE MY ORIGINAL
Paintings & Etchings
At My Art Shop in Abernathy,
South of Zeman Auto Co.
MODERATE PRICES
I Can Put Your Ideas Into Picture
Form in Any Medium You Like.
HAVE TIME FOR A FEW
TALENTED PUPILS.
Paintings and Etchings Make
Splendid Christmas Gifts.
FLOYD WALSER
- Abernathy-

So it appears that Tansey must have set up his big brother with an art shop as well as providing a home for him. It is also highly likely that Floyd may have tried to persuade Tansey to "run off with him" as he had pestered Benny Haden to do 10 years previously, and with the same negative result.

In early spring 1944 Floyd, with all his art supplies stashed away neatly in their special storage spaces in the back of his car, somehow managed to get all the way into Oregon to spend time with Clara and her small family. He must have had a helper/driver along for most, if not all of this leg of his trip. It was a journey of over 2000 miles from the familiar sights of Abernathy, Texas to his destination of Shady Cove, Oregon, about 20 miles north of Medford. On the way he would have encountered many spectacular views as he made his way through New Mexico, Arizona and California. It is hard to imagine that he wouldn't have taken the time to have his traveling companion set him up at various places along the way so that he could paint some of these vistas which surely ignited his artistic passion. When he finally arrived at Clara's place, he must have been thoroughly exhausted and ready to be catered to as he knew his "little" sister would do.

Clara and her stunt-flier husband John Wesley Thurman, who was always called Jack, welcomed him with open arms and made him as comfortable as possible, with Clara fussing over him just as Floyd knew she'd do. The years had been kind to Clara and she still looked the pretty young lady her traveling brother had remembered.

The Thurman's young daughter, Jacalyn was now in college at Texas Tech, but was thrilled to come home during one of her breaks to visit with her dear Uncle Floyd. She was in awe of his superb talent as an artist, but was even more impressed by his exceptional strength of character and practically unbelievable resolve to live his life to the fullest in spite of his disability. She was also very pleased that he always called her by the name she preferred - - Jacquie. She felt that she had a fair amount of artistic talent that had shown itself in many of the sketches and paintings she had done and listened carefully to whatever he had to say about the subject. He was impressed with the work she showed him and suggested to her that if she truly wished to be a complete artist it would have to be a life's calling. His view was that one had to commit oneself totally to one's art in an almost monk-like resolve to eliminate worldly distractions. Uncle Floyd lectured her about how difficult such a true calling could be if she determined to make a successful career at it. No family issues would interfere, since it would be best to remain single. Any jobs that she might hold in order to pay her way in what were sure to be lean years at first, would always have to take a back seat to the priorities of constant study and practice. She was not really sure if he was pulling her leg, but he surely looked serious all through his discourse and kept a straight face the whole time.

In her one visit with her Uncle, Jacquie asked for some suggestions on how best to render a tree in a painting she was working on while still wondering if she ever could live up to his views on full commitment. She was surprised at his first words on the subject, having expected a technical description of how to hold and use her brushes and how to apply the paint. Instead, he began by telling her that if she wanted to draw a tree then she needed to understand a bit about what it feels like to be a tree. She should spend several days closely observing how trees respond to the changing sunlight and the variety of weather they are exposed to. Again, she was not sure if perhaps he was just teasing her, but in later years she would take this portion of his lecture to heart, even if her level of commitment was not up to his single-minded dedication.

He also spent some time discussing how notoriously difficult it was to work in watercolors since so much depended on directness and speed, and having a clearly made-up mind of how to proceed. He pointed out to her that the artist could not be tentative or use fumbling touches since they would be nearly impossible to obliterate. He stressed with her that a rough pencil sketch of the subject would be far more valuable than a snapshot for the serious watercolor landscape painter, another thought that ran counter to her intuition.

In college, Jacquie learned fencing and was good at it. Somewhere along the way she happened to notice that the textbook that was used in her fencing class was another link to her remarkable uncle. This book, aptly named *The Book of Fencing* by the leading female exponent of fencing at the time, Elanor Baldwin Cass was heralded as "…the most complete, most authentic, and without exception the most entertaining book ever written upon any sport." Jacquie was proud to discover that the several instructive illustrations of fencing positions were all signed "F. N. Walser".

The scenery in all directions from Clara's place was breathtaking. Due east about 24 miles was the 9495 foot tall peak of Mt. McLoughlin, which Floyd sometimes called Mt. Pitt. This is one of the major volcanic cones in the Cascades of Oregon and was a frequent subject of the artist's work. He rendered it in watercolors, pastels and oils and tried to capture it from several angles and at various times of day as well as showing its different moods as the sky changed from clear and sunny to bleak and stormy.

Crater Lake, situated about 40 miles northeast of Shady Cove was another place where Floyd would have been set up to paint the panoramic views and to do his best to capture the unbelievably deep blue color of the water. Equally impressive to him was the Rogue River, which emerges from the western slope of the Cascade Mountains and Crater Lake, flowing over 200 miles, winding across farmlands and orchards and then wilderness before it empties into the Pacific. He was mesmerized by the wide forests of Douglas fir, ponderosa pine and other conifers as well as the peaceful meadows and wandering streams, and the occasional narrow canyons and high, steep ridges. He wanted to paint all of this country and did his best to do just that in the time he spent in Oregon.

But there was one particular tree that caught his attention more than any other. It was situated near the Rogue River and he spent many hours studying it carefully, absorbing the personal message he felt it conveyed directly to him. What captivated him so much about this particular tree was that one half of it stood tall and proud and flourished, its branches reaching skyward with good, vital foliage. The other half was dead, its branches gnarled and twisted and completely devoid of leaves. Other people, perhaps even other artists may have only seen a half-alive tree, but to Floyd, it was a metaphor for his own body. He rendered it in pastels, watercolors and oils and produced a number of pencil sketches as studies. In addition to the paintings he did of that special tree while he was in Oregon, he would in future years find great comfort in recreating it, again in a variety of mediums.

Floyd's Oregon tree

Clara was in awe of the professional quality of each landscape her brother would generate, but the work he did that made the longest-lasting impression on her was the large and very flattering portrait he did of her as a gift. She would treasure that painting her entire life.

By late summer of 1944 he realized that it truly was time for him to head back to his home with his benefactors in Framingham. Although he would miss this glorious country in Oregon and, for that matter just about all of the West and Texas, he knew he would miss his family the most, especially Clara. But the reality of it all was that he was comfortable with Roy and Edith, he was getting a bit older and did find it more challenging to get himself around, and knew that he would be better off back at Harmony Home.

It is not known if his trip back east was made in his car, with helpers of course, or if perhaps he sold the special machine in Oregon and made the long cross-country journey in the baggage compartments of railroad trains. Either scenario is possible, but since no one now remembers seeing the car parked in Roy's yard after 1943, it is likely that he rode the rails once again, but this time in as much comfort as the train personnel could provide to their uniquely needy passenger.

Once again the Greenes were thrilled to have him back with them and this time he assured them that he was there to stay.

CHAPTER 14

LUCKY POINT
1945 - 1949

All through the winter of 1944, and on through the first half of 1945, the talk around our kitchen table seemed to me to be always either about the progress of the war, or of us building a house. My dad was really almost obsessed with the house-building idea and I could tell that my mother was picking up on his enthusiasm for such a project. I would often hear them discussing this long after I had gone to bed and I began to realize that, by golly we were going to be house-builders. An additional exciting part for me was that the place they were talking about to build this house was the woods right next to where Mr. Walser lived with the Greenes - - the very place I had "discovered" just the previous summer.

World War II was nearing its end with victory in Europe having just been declared on President Truman's 61st birthday on May 8th, 1945. There still were a lot of horrible things happening throughout the South Pacific and the Japanese showed a resolve to continue to battle at all costs. It seemed obvious to all the adults I came in contact with that the war would soon end, so in spite of the fact that a wartime economy was still in effect, things were looking brighter.

It was in this spirit of a forthcoming rebirth of freedoms that planning to build a house was so exciting. For several weeks, my dad had been talking seriously to Mr. Greene about buying a major chunk of his property. The land that Richie wanted to buy was right at the corner where Lake Ave. and Cove Ave. met. It was so densely wooded that most people who passed by never realized how much potential for a house lot it had. However, the intrinsic beauty of this portion of the Greene's land was not missed by Richie, who had always been blessed with an uncanny ability to envision solutions to problems that others were hardly aware of. He had often walked through this property with Mr. Greene, bending to duck under thick, low branches, and slowly working his way between majestic pine trees and towering oaks, down to the edge of Lake Waushakum.

The lake came around on two sides of this land so that if you faced South you would be looking out towards Ashland, across one of the longest portions of the pond. If you walked around the shore a bit to your right, you would be facing West into the small cove. Monkey Island, which was about 50 feet long and 30 feet wide, was 200 feet or so off shore in this cove. We would soon refer to this geography as "the point".

The land was basically level from the street back in quite a way, but then rapidly dropped off to meet the edge of the lake on two sides. This natural arrangement of the land inspired Richie to plan his house to take advantage of these slopes. He would design his home to have its basement walls fully exposed on both the South and West-facing sides. There would be no need for a bulkhead to gain access to the basement, but a direct, walkout door could be provided. This raised the idea that it would be possible to build a house there in stages, living in the "basement" while completing the main portions. This approach would help to conserve the available funds for such an undertaking while still allowing our little family to have a new home in a beautiful location.

Then, on a crystal clear day in July 1945, the deal was made. Roy Greene agreed to sell this magical property to my mom and dad. I had never seen my father and mother and their parents so happily excited about anything before. Some of us wanted to camp out in the woods there, or at least spend all day roaming around between all kinds of trees and shrubs. We found a bunch of blueberry bushes on our new land and my mother made the best tasting muffins and pies from them. I must admit that I was not really much help in picking these berries, since I was more interested in exploring the long shoreline, picking up flat stones and skimming them across the water. While selecting just the right item for best surface skimming, I came across an area loaded with small white, sparkly stones. I had always called these "lucky stones" whenever I would find one or two. But here was the motherlode of lucky stones. The clear, shallow water, softly lapping over these beautiful rocks illuminated by the warm sunlight made them appear to me as gemstones.

That evening at supper, after showing my small collection of a few of those wonderful stones to my folks, I made the suggestion that we call our new piece of property "Lucky Point". The nickname stuck, at least for a while. Years later, in looking back fondly at the home on the lake, we would occasionally refer to it as Lucky Point. In so many ways it truly was a lucky place and time for us.

With the land now purchased, it became a priority to get the detailed design of the house worked out in order to obtain a building permit. Equally pressing, at least to Richie, if not to me, was the very laborious task of clearing out the heavy undergrowth and chopping down whichever of the many trees would be in the way. Of course, until some reasonable idea was determined of just what the house would look like and how it would be situated on the lot, it was not all that obvious which trees must go and which should be left standing. My grandfather was very eager to help his son with all the physical work involved in clearing out as much of the area as would be necessary. Now at the age of 62 he was, or at least seemed to be, as strong as ever and was no stranger to hard work. For a while, it seemed as though if he were left unchecked, the place would soon resemble a desert more than anything else.

That was the summer that I learned what a grub-hoe is and how to use it. I can still remember the sweet smell of the cut-up branches and the good, rich earth as we worked in this hot and humid jungle. I was almost eleven and thought I had good muscles, but I was no match for Richie and his father, and their non-stop chopping, cutting, digging, and hauling. As the heavily overgrown woods on our land gave way to our manual labors, passing neighbors would often stop to see what was going on. More than once I heard my dad refuse a pretty good cash offer to buy the land from someone who now could see what they never noticed in all the times they had passed there before. This was a beautiful piece of lakefront property.

Occasionally, especially when the heat and humidity started to overpower my enthusiasm for tearing into the scrub brush, I would suggest to my dad that I should walk over to see if Mr. Walser needed anything. My dad hopefully would think that I was just being concerned about the welfare of this poor old guy and would allow, if not encourage me to take a little time off from helping clear out the woods to attend to whatever tasks might be waiting for me next door. Much to my relief, usually when I showed up at Mr. Walser's door, he really didn't need me to do any particularly difficult chores. Often, he would ask if I wanted to take a few practice target shots outdoors with his B-B gun. After taking a few quick shots and occasionally hitting the target, my conscience would get the best of me and I'd scurry back to help my dad. He never really minded my short diversions and probably welcomed a chance to work without having to explain every step to this easily distracted kid.

Each night that summer, my mom and dad would huddle over the house design drawings Richie was developing at the kitchen table. They really collaborated on this design, both trying to be sure to include features that would make the house special and attractive. They wanted to have large picture windows for unobstructed views of the lake. They both knew that they wanted the house to be of brick construction, but Richie knew there was no way it could be solid brick, and would have to be veneer. He was concerned about the high cost of purchasing all those bricks, even if the plan didn't call for them to be put on for a few years. His idea was to use the bricks in an unorthodox way; a method he had seen used only once. Instead of stacking them in the usual manner, the way the brick manufacturers expected them to be used and the way 99.99 percent of all brick construction is done, he planned to put them on edge, thereby requiring approximately half the bricks he would otherwise need.

The whole design was based upon the idea of having us live in two rooms in the basement once the entire house was framed and roofed. With many full-length basement windows to let in lots of light and a door that let us step right out to the back yard, it was felt that this arrangement should be very comfortable for as long as it would take us to get the upstairs livable. This was indeed the case and it worked out very well.

At about the same time that the house plans were drawn up with enough details so that Richie could apply for a building permit, the war was over. An atomic bomb had been dropped on Hiroshima on August 6th, and three days later, one was dropped on Nagasaki. Japan surrendered on August 14, 1945. Although the official surrender did not take place until September 2 aboard the USS Missouri anchored in Tokyo Bay, peace had returned. A sense of normalcy with high expectations for a healthy economy prevailed. It had been impossible to get building permits by the ordinary citizen while the war raged on, but now, things were getting back to normal. The plans that Richie presented were most likely a little short on detail and probably not as complete as those a trained architect would have generated. He was still carrying a lot of the details in his head. However, his conviction that he was building a beautiful home for his family, along with his serious no-nonsense approach, convinced the official that he should indeed be given a permit which, at that time cost $5.00. As if to show that it wasn't going to be quite that easy, he was asked if he planned to sell this house to a veteran. If he were building the place to sell to a vet, there would be absolutely no problem. Richie quickly answered that yes, he would plan to (someday) sell it to a veteran. He came home that day with his permit. As it would turn out years later when it was time to sell this dream home, the fellow who bought it, was a veteran.

Now, with a good set of plans in hand it was very clear just which trees had to be removed. Roy Greene would often walk over to where we were chopping and sawing at what, until recently, had been his favorite area for solitude on his property. If he felt badly about seeing this area opened up, he never showed it. Sensing his feelings, Richie promised him that the only trees that would come down would be the ones where the house itself, or the driveway would be located. As it turned out, the largest and most majestic oak tree in the entire plot was situated smack in the middle of where our driveway had to go. It was to be a long driveway, curving around in front of the house and then down around back to where the garage was to be located in the basement. We could see no way at all to save that old tree, whose trunk easily measured three feet across. Roy watched with a combination of fascination and despair as the tree was felled.

We did as much land clearing and general clean up of the property as we could through the Fall, but then pretty much abandoned the area for the winter while the design plans were fleshed out in more detail. When the winter days were relatively mild we continued with what seemed to me to be a task that would never end. All the trees that had been downed had to be cut into fireplace lengths, split lengthwise and stacked into neat piles for our future use. My grandfather was great at this job. I was not. It was far more fun to visit this future site of our new home during the winter and bring my pals over to my very own ice skating place. My mother's two brothers, my uncles Nick and Joe both loved to fish, and they often would get out on the ice from our new yard and set out their traps. As they pitched in with the log cutting and splitting chores they would keep an eye on their traps for a tipped flag indicating a possible catch. When a red flag was spotted, they would both run out onto the ice, trying not to lose too much traction on the slippery surface. Whichever one got there first would own the fish, regardless of whose trap was involved. I never could prove it, but I would swear that they sometimes ran like people possessed to traps whose flags were still neatly tucked under, just to get a break from the log piles. They very rarely left there without some nice fish.

Shortly after New Year's Day in 1946 we got the shocking news that Mr. Greene had passed away. He had gallstone surgery just before Christmas and was sent home 8 days later on December 30, 1945. Four days later he died suddenly at Harmony Home with his beloved Edith by his side. The cause of death was a heart attack, possibly brought on by a post-surgical blood clot. Mrs. Greene, overwhelmed with grief, called one of the nearby persons who had been especially good to her the past few years. She called our downstairs neighbor, Rica Bortolussi for support.

Immediately, Rica and her young son Freddie drove around the corner and did their best to console the distraught widow. They stayed at her home that night and looked after her needs and did their best to help her grieve. Rica had gotten to know Edith very well as a result of having helped to clean her house for a few years. Mrs. Greene was always more than pleased to receive the beautiful fresh flowers that Rica would so often pick from her productive garden. Edith had come to think of herself as "Aunt Edith" to the Bortolussi family and was truly grateful for the many kindnesses shown to her by Rica and her husband, Fred.

We were all shocked to hear of Mr. Greene's sudden passing. Always a youthful-acting person, now not quite 66, he seemed way too young to die. And such a kind, soft-hearted man he was. Many of our neighbors had gotten to know him, mainly through Mr. Walser who had given art lessons to so many of the area children. Many expressions of concern were voiced about how poor Mrs. Greene would handle the loss of her dear husband who, in the last several years had taken such loving care of his dear wife. Her frequent illnesses had progressed to the point where she was now an invalid. Who could possibly look after her needs the way he did? And what about Mr. Walser? What was to become of him now that this small but strong provider of much-needed help was gone?

Many of the neighbors, in addition to Rica and Fred would make frequent trips in the next few days and weeks to visit Mrs. Greene and Mr. Walser. They brought their genuine expressions of concern, but more importantly, to them at least, they brought good nutritious food for them both. As the days wore on through the cold, gray winter months, my mother would do her best to continue to try to help out these two poor souls. After all, we were soon going to be neighbors, and good neighbors looked after each other's needs. There were many other people, a combination of friends of the Greenes and social welfare agency personnel who were constantly coming and going at the Greene residence. My mother did what she could to help out by preparing some homemade meals that we would bring over for both Mrs. Greene and for Mr. Walser. My mother and I would carry these meals, usually enough to last for several days, through the often snow-covered Dow Street and around onto Lake Avenue 'til we came to their house. We would see to it that used dishes were washed and put away and that soiled bedclothes and articles of clothing were laundered.

Mrs. Greene, bed-ridden most of the time, tried her best at first to not be too much of a bother, but with her frail constitution and generally weakened body, she needed a fair amount of assistance. She was able to get out of bed on her own to attend to her personal hygiene needs, but preferred help. In fact it seemed that the more we would do, the more she would seem to need. Mr. Walser, in his attached studio/bedroom was also very appreciative of the delicious food my mother made and our efforts to provide whatever assistance he needed. I would often run errands for him, dashing off to the nearby grocery market to purchase his favorite items, or when I could get someone to drive me, to the Post Office for "stamped envelopes, size 13"

We soon began addressing Mr. Walser as Floyd, which is what he preferred and it seemed very natural and easy now. We were really getting to know each other a lot better than we would have if Roy Greene were still there to keep all his needs met. We found that he was remarkably resilient and amazingly self-sufficient considering his handicap. His spirits had quickly rebounded and he always would do his level best to let us know that he was really O.K. and that we need not be so concerned.

The members of the Framingham Civic League Orchestra however, had a very hard time adjusting at first to the sudden and unexpected loss of their leader and founder, Roy Goddard Greene. A new conductor was named and he (Fred W. Pope) and several orchestra members, aided by Mrs. Greene, conceived of a very fitting tribute to the man they knew so well and loved so much. On Sunday, March 10, 1946 at 3:30 P.M., a memorial concert was performed in his honor at the E. W. Dennison Memorial Hall by 30 of the most talented members of the Civic League Orchestra. One of the three extraordinarily gifted French Horn players at this tribute was Roy's brother Clifton Greene.

The guest artist at this moving performance was the brilliant young pianist Kurt Paur, a long time friend of the Greenes. He was the son of Emil Paur who had conducted the New York Philharmonic Orchestra and then the Boston Symphony Orchestra back at the turn of the century, and to whom Mrs. Greene had dedicated her violin sonata, written when she was 23. Emil Paur sponsored Roy and Edith in several concerts while they were making a tour of Europe in 1909 shortly after they were married. Maestro Paur had been more than a sponsor to the young musicians; he had taken them "under his wing" and looked after their well being. His son, an extremely gifted pianist performed flawlessly at this memorial concert as an expression of personal tribute to Mr. and Mrs. Greene.

The program that was so thoughtfully arranged and rehearsed so thoroughly included well known works by nine famous composers plus a special arrangement of the Berceuse composed many years previously by Mrs. Greene.

At the start of the memorial program, the capacity audience as well as the orchestra stood in respectful silence while from offstage one of Roy Greene's favorite hymns, *The Evening Hymn* by E. J. Hopkins was solemnly played by a muted brass section.

Included in the tribute that followed and performed by the whole orchestra was the march, *Semper Fidelis* by Sousa, Suppé's *Light Cavalry Overture* and the waltz, *Espana* by Waldteufel, as well as a selection from Victor Herbert's *The Red Mill*. The second part of the program included the entire orchestra's performance of *Prelude and Intermezzo* from *Cavalleria Rusticana* by Mascagni and *Marche Lorraine* by Ganne. In both portions of the performance, guest artist Kurt Paur's piano solos were brilliant. In part one he played 3 pieces by Chopin; the *Funeral March* and *Presto* from the *Sonata in B Flat Minor* and *Fantasie Opus 49*. After the intermission, during which a silver collection was taken up, he performed Brahms' *Capriccio Opus 76, Nos. 1 and 2*, *Rhapsody in C Minor* by Dohnanyi, and a heart-felt rendition of Edith's sweet and wistful *Berceuse*, so appropriate to the occasion. As an encore, the guest artist played a delightful *Intermezzo* composed by his noted father, Emil Paur.

In order to capture the depth of respect for Mr. Greene that was felt by the members of the Civic League Orchestra and many others, the heart-felt testimonial to him printed in that afternoon's concert program is quoted here in its entirety.

A TRIBUTE

Roy Goddard Greene was born on January 25, 1880 and died on January 3, 1946. He came of a musical family, and with such a heritage his lifelong interest in music was a natural one, his chosen instrument being the piano. As a boy he formed an orchestra and later conducted small ensembles. For years he was director of the Framingham Band, with a membership of 45, which became extremely well known and gave numerous concerts throughout New England. He founded the Framingham School of Music and was its head for 36 years. From its pupils he formed a junior orchestra and in 1925, the Civic League Orchestra.

In all this he was given the loyal help of his former teacher and wife, Mme. Edith Noyes Greene, whom he married in 1909. Both extremely talented pianists, they played many concerts together here and abroad, where they met the famous father of today's guest artist, who showed them many kindnesses.

Today's concert is held in Mr. Greene's memory. He above all others was responsible for the growth and development of the Orchestra. Its members, some of whom have been in it since the beginning, have served as he did without remuneration. They have attended hundreds of weekly rehearsals. Noted guest artists have graciously given their services at the public performances of the orchestra. Why? The reason is not hard to find for those who knew him.

Roy Goddard Greene was a friendly man who inspired loyalty and, yes, devotion. He, himself, was a modest man, who at all times placed the success of the Orchestra above personal success. He loved good music and wanted others to have the opportunity to play it and listen to it. He had a vision and was willing to make many personal sacrifices of time and effort to cause it to become a reality. He gave more than he ever asked of others. He was ready with his praise of work well done. He was kindly in his criticism and corrections. He desired perfection of performance, but was never impatient.

It is hoped that for many years to come, the Civic League Orchestra will continue to serve as a living memorial to the man and the musician - - Roy Goddard Greene.

* * * * *

The snow and slush of winter finally melted away and the ground once again became soft and pliable, with the smell of Spring in the air. The excitement of actually beginning to build our lakeside house was nearly overpowering. All through the bleak winter months, the detailed plans for the house were reviewed and modified to incorporate new ideas, and to further delineate the actual dimensions and specifications of all the critical parts and pieces. Cost estimates for the lumber needed for each stage were obtained, and the cost of getting a foundation poured was determined. Figures for bulldozer work to push away the huge stumps of the trees we had felled a few months earlier as well as to actually excavate the area for the foundation were in hand.

In early April, 1946, Richie hired an experienced bulldozer operator, someone he had known casually from somewhere. For a grand total of $75.00, this highly skilled operator and his oversize machine dislodged all the tree stumps (about 10 or 15 of them) and pushed them completely out of the way, then dug the cellar hole. In fact, the tree stumps wound up completely off our property onto what was in actuality an unusable extension of Lake Avenue where this "road" dove down abruptly to meet the water. Some of the stumps actually were shoved into the lake a bit at this location, providing in future years a great little place for various fishermen to stand and cast for whatever fish they could find as well as a home for all sorts of wildlife.

With the stumps out of the way, and after careful review of Richie's blueprints, the earth was pushed away to form the opening for our foundation. When completed, the excavation resembled more of a chopping away of the slope of the land rather than a pit, since the plan called for two sides of the foundation to be exposed.

The first of many loads of lumber was delivered to the site and was carefully sorted and stacked. With the rich, sweet smell of the newly disturbed earth still hanging in the air, wooden forms were assembled and leveled to create the footing for the foundation. As soon as possible, after double checking to be sure these forms were laid out exactly according to the plan, a "ready-mix" concrete truck from New England Sand and Gravel was brought in to pour the footing. Most house builders would then have the foundation walls poured into forms, known as cribbings, which are put up by specialty contractors. (Whenever I heard this word it was always pronounced "cribbins", and for many years believed that to be the proper term.) These forms would be taken down and removed by the contractor once the concrete had been poured and allowed to set up for a few days. The contractor would then reuse many of the forms for other foundations, adding whatever special requirements each new job required. This approach was too costly for Richie. He built his own "cribbins" very carefully and assembled them on top of the cured footing, incorporating window and door openings exactly as his drawings called for them. Each evening after a quick supper he would be hard at work building, assembling, and bracing his special forms. Each weekend of course would be totally devoted to this construction project. Richie had no power tools to make this formidable task any easier. All work was done by hand, and my role always was "gopher-in-charge", often supplemented by performing extraordinarily well at holding the end of a long board being cut. I would try to not let my attention wander from the task at hand, but with the various distractions our lakefront world so often seductively presented, was frequently reminded to pay attention. Fortunately, my grandfather continued to take enormous pleasure in whatever physical work his son needed help with, so there were almost always at least two good dependable laborers on the job. This small crew was often supplemented with help from various of the uncles and/or cousins, most of whom were experienced in carpentry and were no strangers to hard work.

In March, on his 36th birthday, Richie's parents and sister had presented him with perhaps the best gift he had ever received; two handsaws and a perfectly balanced hammer. The saws, one crosscut, the other for ripping, as well as the hammer, were of top quality and were carefully selected to withstand the heavy use they were expected to be subjected to. These tools lasted for many years past the completion of the house.

Richie was a natural left-hander, although he could use both a hammer and a saw equally well with either hand. However, when given his choice it was always the left hand that guided the saw for precision cuts or swung the hammer with incredible accuracy. Observers, and often during the course of the house construction there were plenty of them around, would watch in awe as he would nonchalantly switch to use whichever hand best suited the situation at the time. There was never a need to lose valuable time in getting off and relocating a ladder, or switching sawhorses around to get a preferred working hand in position.

With the foundation forms fully assembled on the footings and reinforced, braced and double-checked for accuracy it was time again to call in the concrete mixer trucks. This time, trucks from the Ashland Sand and Gravel Co. lined up to deliver their specialized load of fully mixed, wet concrete. With the truck's chutes positioned over the tops of the forms, the drivers started the concrete flowing. I think Richie silently prayed that the homemade cribbings would not burst apart under the strain of the heavy load being slowly poured into them. As the concrete trucks filled in the forms, we diligently ensured that the spaces under the window openings were solidly packed with concrete, with no voids or air inclusions. Several people helped with this part of the job; everyone manning long narrow boards to force the heavy and slow-flowing concrete to pack well under the seven window frame forms within the forms. The "cribbins" held. Just as Richie knew they would.

With this major accomplishment behind us, it seemed as though it may be time for a few days rest while the concrete set up enough to remove the forms. No such luck. There still were more trees and their branches to deal with. Also, the dirt floor which was now enclosed by the concrete slowly curing in the forms, needed to be leveled out and graded.

About a week after the concrete trucks had left, Richie judged that it was OK now to start removing the forms. This was slow, deliberate work and as each section was removed, revealing a perfectly cast wall, I was entrusted with two new, important jobs. These were to carefully straighten out each and every nail that was pulled out of the boards that had just been liberated from being part of the cribbings, and then to scrape off the dried concrete from the boards. All these critical materials were about to be reused in the rough framing of the house. It was important to get off as much of the dried concrete as possible, so that the saws would not be dulled too quickly. It was equally important that the nails be as straight as possible to reduce the chances of them bending under the forthcoming blows of Richie's unrelenting hammer. As the cribbing boards and the used nails became available, along with fresh new lumber and nails, the rough framing of our new abode rapidly developed. In a few weekends supplemented by workday evenings until dark, the first floor was completed. (I'm sure I got most of the dried concrete off the endless succession of ex-cribbing boards, but I recall that many evenings as I headed off to bed, Richie would be busily sharpening his saws. I swear he enjoyed this late evening task, planning the next day's assault on the lumber and nails while getting his saws back to their required sharpness.)

The rest of the framing of the house with both exterior and interior walls taking shape went along without a hitch. If Richie was getting overtired by the constant physical and mental demands of this job after working a full shift each day at "The Dennison", he surely didn't show it. In fact, he seemed to flourish with each challenge of practically single-handedly building his dream house. Friends and relatives who helped out with the construction whenever they could were amazed at the quality and detail of his house plans. He had no training in architectural or engineering drawing, and yet the blueprints he had generated over the previous few months left very little to the imagination. This is not to say that occasional adjustments were not needed from time to time to make everything go together properly when real-world tolerances on precise dimensions caused a minor discrepancy or two. The ability to rapidly and effectively deal with these little setbacks was just one more very natural strength this amazing man possessed.

This enthusiasm for and obvious enjoyment Richie had for carpentry was not missed by Floyd. Several times he would ask me to position his chair out alongside his room where he could get a good view of the whole project. He told me, "I really enjoy watching your father work. He almost never stops. It sure looks like he knows what he's doing." I would assure Floyd that indeed he truly did know what he was doing and that he possessed some amazing skills and talents. Once in a while, Richie would stroll over to where Floyd was parked in his old chair and spend a few minutes catching his breath while both men started to get to know one another a bit. Right from their first meeting there was an easy camaraderie between the two of them, with Richie learning a little about Floyd's past and Floyd being filled in on some of the fun things Richie had done. But with so much construction still to be done, these visits never lasted very long. Often at the supper table on a day when one of these impromptu get-togethers had occurred, the conversation would center on what an amazing person this Floyd Walser was and what an interesting life he had. We at that time had only a tiny fraction of a portion of understanding of just how fascinating and really unbelievable Floyd's life had been.

By the end of July of '46, the house actually looked like a house. It was fully framed and had its roof in place and shingled. All of the window and door openings were wide open and you could easily tell how the finished house was going to look. But within a month or two, those indicators of the finished appearance of the house began to disappear as these openings were boarded up, causing those not "in the know" to wonder if the builder was suddenly going a little strange. Since our plan, right from the beginning, was to get the main structure up and live in the basement while we finished the main part of the house, this all seemed to us a perfectly natural course of events. It was months later, after the heavy tarpaper fully covered every square inch of vertical exterior surface of the house in a swirling green "camouflage", leaving no clue as to where windows or doors might go, that even we had to agree that the place looked sort of weird. But doing this allowed the upstairs to be fully insulated from the coming winter cold.

My grandfather, Luigi, contributed an impressive amount of manual labor combined with real skill in helping get this entire act together. He single-handedly dug a trench for the water pipe all the way from the foundation of the house through the toughest soil you can imagine right out to the street. The trench ran a distance of at least 150 feet at an average depth of four feet through roots and rocks that would have made a backhoe slow down. He used a pick, shovel, grubhoe, and a long heavy iron bar. He worked, often in the blazing sun at this task every day, unless the weather interfered, for many days, never complaining, constantly chewing on his usually unlit stogie. When these things were lit up, when he sat back to enjoy a smoke, we normally gave him plenty of space since the acrid aroma of those little Parodi cigars must have been an acquired taste. Many of us never did manage to grow to appreciate the odor at that time. But years later, whenever I would get wind of someone's smelly little stogie, good memories of my grandfather would come flooding back.
Luigi was also instrumental in building the chimneys. There were to be two important fireplaces in our new home, an exciting thought since we had never had even one such romantic item before. The one in the basement was to be our main source of heat during the two winters it was planned to take us to get the upstairs done. The fireplace in the main house's livingroom, to be located just above the basement one, was to be both functional and decorative. Both were to be constructed around a metal housing produced by a company known as Heatilator, a firm who had been in business since 1927 and is still one of the leading fireplace suppliers. The Heatilator's unique metal frame had chambers built-in along the sides with a grate at the base and at the top of each side. The idea was that as the fire heated the metal frame, cold room air would be drawn in at the bottom grates and

warm, heated air would rise in these chambers and naturally exit the top grates. This would provide even more heat than what would come directly out the main fireplace opening. It really did work. Luigi's job was to lay the bricks around the flues to form the basic chimney, for both fireplaces, from the top of the foundation where it jutted out for the fireplaces, all the way up along the outside of the rough-framed house, to the roof. Somewhere along during his hard-working past, he had learned to mix mortar and lay brick. Richie made a framework to control the exact shape and size of the chimney. While he was at his day job at Dennison, his father would happily build the rough chimney, stacking the flue pipes, laying the bricks, and gradually progressing higher and higher. When the chimney was finished, it was hard to tell who was more proud of the completed project, Richie or his dad. In subsequent years when it came time to put the brick veneer on the entire house, it was with some sadness that Richie covered over his father's handy-work with the new brick placed edgewise.

    Luigi, with some help from Richie, also built the other chimney for the house. This one was located inside the house and would be used later on for the oil-fired furnace which would be added after we moved out of the basement so that we could enjoy a more dependable and controllable source of heat. This chimney, with only one flue, was of a simple square cross-section and was not much of a challenge for Luigi compared to the large exterior one for the fireplaces.

    I was always impressed at how much work my grandfather could do, even though I thought of him as an old man. Not only did he not mind the heavy digging, chopping, mixing and rough brick laying, but he was always cheerful, if not actually smiling. He did not smile easily, probably because his serious hearing loss caused him to miss what was said a lot of the time. He had a "laid-back" style and it seemed nothing bothered him. An example of his casual attitude toward what others might think of as a reason to panic was the "Great Dane Episode". A couple of years back, the folks who lived directly across Dow Street from Henry and Sonny, and therefore very close to our house as well, had a full grown, mean-looking Great Dane. He was called a "pup" by his owners and perhaps he was only playful, but my pals and I were quite frightened of him and his drooling, vicious jaws. It didn't make him seem any less scary when a tall chain-link fence was erected in his owner's front yard to keep him from roaming the neighborhood. Whenever we walked by that yard we kept to our side of the street and never teased or tormented the animal. One particularly hot and steamy August afternoon, my grandfather was taking a little nap, fully reclined in his favorite wooden outdoor chair in the shade of one of his large cherry trees. Henry, Sonny, Freddie and I were not doing much of anything. It was too darn hot. Suddenly, Henry's faithful mutt, Major, flew past us with his tail between his legs and he disappeared somewhere. The Great Dane was out! He had tunneled under his fence and gotten free. Galloping between our houses like the horse he seemed to be, it looked for all the world as though he was searching for a nice tender kid to devour. I don't recall where my pals vanished to, but I climbed up the nearest tree faster than I could have fallen out of one. The marauding beast quickly circled the base of my escape tree and soon was on his hind legs with his snout reaching up toward my feet, which I rapidly pulled up. I was safe. But suddenly I looked through the leafy branches to see my Nonno, still sound asleep with his hat tipped forward over his eyes, blissfully unaware of any danger. The dog trotted over to stand right next to this dozing person and stood there panting heavily, with his huge mouth open and his tongue, dripping saliva, dangling out. Deep, menacing growls came from somewhere down in that huge body. Slowly, my grandfather tipped his hat back from his eyes to find himself face to face with that frightening apparition. I was sure he would not survive the encounter. The dog stood there, growling and panting. Luigi calmly reached out one hand and did what I could not believe anyone could do. He grabbed the dog's enormous tongue firmly and gave it a strong yank. The Great Dane immediately curled his tail between his legs, broke free from his captor's grip and ran, yelping and crying back to his safe caged-in yard. Luigi wiped his hand on his trousers and went back to his nap. The dog lost his reputation while my grandfather now seemed larger than life.

It was amazing how rapidly the house-building project progressed. Even more amazing was the fact that Richie basically did it all, or at least 90 percent of it. With some help from a plumber friend he installed all the basement plumbing, doing nearly all of the detailed work himself. Having an acquaintance who was a licensed electrician was all Richie needed to accomplish the formidable task of getting the downstairs portion of the house wired properly per code. The "real" electrician did the hook-up to the town electrical supply at the street and inspected Richie's work with the BX cable and all his connections.

The basement was divided into two long rooms, with the walls and ceilings paneled with four-foot by eight-foot sheets of an inexpensive material known as "Homosote". This material, a super-compacted felt-type composite board, was very easy to cut and was lightweight, making it easy for one person to install it to ceilings and walls. It also provided a fair amount of insulation from cold foundation walls. After it was painted a nice light color, it looked OK.

One of the two rooms was to be our main living area. At one end of this room was the kitchen sink, counter top, refrigerator and cabinets. A small, but well-made table saw was purchased from Sears and Roebuck to help Richie with the building of the kitchen cabinets. This handy little machine, with its unusual tilting table was the only power tool to be on hand for the entire house-building project. The corner of the other end of our living room housed the door which opened out directly to ground level facing the south end of the lake, which was about 50 feet away. Built into the opposite corner of this end of the room at a 45-degree angle, was our workhorse Heatilator fireplace. It had a handsome brick front with a built-in brick mantel, all fully designed and built by Richie.

Back past the kitchen end of this room, was a small bathroom in which every fixture; sink, toilet and claw-footed bathtub, had been obtained from old houses being renovated. Even the door to this private place was from an old house somewhere. There were five windows along the west-facing wall of this room, three full-length and two half-length, including the one in the bathroom. This area was always cheerfully bright with natural light during sunny days.

At the opposite corner of this room, across from the kitchen area was a kerosene-burning stove and heater. This, combined with the skillfully designed and built fireplace at the other end of the room, would provide all the heat needed for even the coldest winters. It was also the stove my mother used every day to cook our meals.

The other long room, accessible through a door a couple of feet from the fireplace, was to be a single bedroom to be shared by my parents and me. My bed would be right up against the outside wall. A large cedar-lined armoire, which had been built several years earlier by Uncle Angelo, one of my grandmother's brothers, would be placed next to the pillow end of my bed to provide some small degree of privacy for my parents.

With the main part of the house finished, complete with its total wrap of heavy tarpaper, insulation stuffed between all the exterior wall 2 x 4s, and the roof fully shingled; all effort was concentrated on completing the downstairs apartment. On Saturday, October 26, 1946 we moved into our new home. Richie was in the process of installing wooden baseboards in the bedroom when the mover's truck pulled onto our property after having driven around the corner from Dow Street. It didn't take very long to get all our stuff carried in and set up since we had previously carried in whatever we could fit into our car.

We quickly settled in, with Richie very happy that now that we actually lived right on site, he could get to work on the many tasks that remained with no lost time driving back and forth from Dow Street. Even though the total driving time had been only about two minutes, this little bonus was appreciated as if it were a major breakthrough. Now, every day, rain or shine, day or night, Richie was able to spend every free minute, once his shift at Dennison was over, working at whatever priority bubbled to the top of the list. A fair amount of time was spent cutting up the many felled trees into fireplace lengths and splitting them lengthwise. Winter was coming soon, and it promised to be a cold one. Living practically at the edge of the lake, nestled in next to an interesting assortment of small animals gave us many opportunities to witness nature in ways we had never enjoyed before. The thought of frigid winds whipping off the long frozen surface of Lake Waushakum, trying to find its way into our basement home gave added impetus to the firewood preparation job.

I started to spend more time visiting with Floyd now that we were right next door. It was always fun to pop in on him and help out with little chores and then listen to his many stories about what it was like growing up in the "Wild West". Occasionally he would be working on a sketch of the trees and the lake just outside his studio room. I continued to be amazed at his strength of character and his determination to do whatever he wanted without complaining or dwelling on how tough it was to get around, or what a rotten break it was that he was in such a "fix". One Saturday morning when I knocked on his door and then let myself in after hearing a soft response, I found that he was still in bed. This was unusual for him, to be in bed after 10 AM. He was struggling with a group of pillows and his cane as he did every day in order to get sitting up. He was turned away from me, half way to being vertical and obviously having a difficult time of it. With his voice slightly muffled by the pillow which was jammed into his face at the moment, he said that if I felt strong that morning, maybe I could give him a hand. I was a little afraid of hurting him, worried that I might break off one of his limbs if I pulled the wrong way, but I quickly did what I could to force his dead weight up to a sitting position. With a big smile, he acknowledged my help and said that I had done well. Now, all I needed to do was to pull him around and help him back into his chair. He said he was already dressed and had been in those clothes for a few days. He figured that since he didn't "go rolling around in the mud" and had no plans to do so, his clothes never got dirty. I grabbed hold of his belt and partly lifted, but mostly dragged him from the bed into his chair. Once he was satisfied that his torso was stuffed just so into the special nest-like base of his chair, he fastened the strap to securely hold him in place. He said he'd need a couple of minutes to catch his breath, but in no time he was chatting about what the weather looked like and asked what had I planned to do that day. I had no specific plans, but was fascinated by the effort it took this man to simply get out of bed in the morning; something that I never even thought about. When I asked if he had gotten stuck that morning trying to get up, he laughed and said that was what he had to do every time he wanted to get from laying down to sitting up if there was no one around to help him. He said that a few years ago he had hired a young boy who lived a few streets away to come there in the mornings, whenever he could and help him to get up and into his chair. That kid was now off to college somewhere and was no longer available to do the morning get-ups. He told me he had worked out his specialized solo get-up procedure many years ago, back in Texas. It had always taken him about a half an hour, sometimes more, to accomplish the task, forcing a succession of pillows under his back while using his cane to grab a "handhold" to pull himself up enough to jam in another pillow. If he rushed, he always ran the risk of toppling over onto his right side. This was a serious problem for him, since with his right arm buried under him, he would be stuck with no easy way to correct. But, most days he took his time and got himself up on his own. Now of course, with Roy Greene gone, Floyd had no one to call to for help if he should run into a similar problem. I offered my services to him for his morning get-ups whenever I could, and he thought that just might be a good idea.

He had a few adult students coming in for their weekly lesson that afternoon, so he had some material to prepare for them. He was teaching them the basics of etching and he confided to me that one of them showed a little talent, but all were paying customers to be served. I helped him open a can of chili con carne for his lunch, which I guessed was also his breakfast, and left him to prepare for his afternoon class. I could not imagine having a breakfast of chili under any circumstances and was happy that I looked forward to my daily Wheaties, banana and milk.

By the time the cold weather arrived in earnest, we had a pretty good stack of firewood ready. After a few smoky trials, we soon learned how to get a good fire burning in the corner fireplace in our basement's main room. It was unbelievably hypnotizing to sit and stare at the leaping flames and listen to the hiss and pop of the split oak and pine logs. More than once we had to open a few windows to cool the place down.

The following year, Richie managed to obtain a large supply of old railroad ties to burn in our fireplace. He was concerned that we might use up all the firewood we had been cutting and splitting, although we never even came close to finding the bottom of the pile. I think the real reason for him getting the railroad ties was that he was told that they were a far more efficient fuel than wet oak and pine logs. But he never worried about the fact that they were soaked with creosote. This flammable oily liquid which consists mainly of aromatic hydrocarbons and is made by the distillation of coal tar, was used as a preservative for the ties since they normally would be imbedded in the ground to support the railroad tracks. It was no small job for me to try to handle my end of the two-man saw my dad and I used to cut those heavy old beams into fireplace lengths. Once we had a few of those monsters cut to length, we would try to split them lengthwise, but that was not so easy. The first time we placed one of the full size chunks into the fireplace, on top of what was already a pretty good fire, our reaction went from pleasure at how rapidly it "caught" to downright terror at the roar and unbelievable size of the flames. The entire metal chamber of our Heatilator fireplace was full of fire. The sound, which had previously been those comforting hisses and pops, was now the roar of a freight train. The amount of heat being belched into our little room was way beyond what was needed for comfort, and Richie began to worry that the flue might crack from the unusual heat. My mother was not too pleased with the strong smell this inferno was creating. (My dad and I were too concerned about the size of the fire to notice the odor until later.) I went outside and was surprised to see flames shooting out the top of the chimney! It turned out that the previous winter's burning of "normal" firewood had left a small coating of creosote deposited within the chimney flue. The flames and heat from our creosote-maddened tie managed to ignite some of the deposits inside the chimney. Just as we were about to call the fire department, the flames emanating from the chimney disappeared and the fireplace settled down to become almost normal appearing. This exciting experience with burning railroad ties in our fireplace did not prevent us from using the balance of the supply of old ties. We split them each at least once lengthwise and often split those pieces again, and were careful not to pile more than two quarter-split pieces into the fireplace at any one time.

    Our first winter living so close to a large lake provided a little entertainment that really took us by surprise. As the surface of the pond went from very cold liquid to expanses of ice, we enjoyed the new calmness that seemed to descend. Then, as day after day of below freezing temperatures thickened the ice, we were wakened from our sleep one night by deep, loud sounds we had never heard before. In the middle of a cold, moonlit night, we heard what sounded like cannon shots going off immediately followed by snapping sounds. First one loud bang-snap, then after a few minutes one or two more reports would be heard coming from all round the cove and out towards the deep part of the lake. Of course, we knew these were not cannons being fired and soon realized that Mother Nature was providing us an up close and personal chance to *hear* the process of a large lake freezing up. As the ice got progressively thicker, and continued to freeze, the expansion that went along with the process would create long cracks, which would be announced by those loud bangs and grinding snaps. Once we got used to this phenomenon, we could sleep right through the explosions and enjoyed the signals that the lake was becoming a good place to skate and go ice fishing.

It took longer to complete the upstairs of the house than originally anticipated. While the downstairs where we were living was cozy and comfortable, it was a lot more rustic than we wanted for our "real" house. So for the next two and a half years, while Richie worked full time at Dennison Mfg. Co., often working extra shifts, he continued to slug away in his "spare" time at all the many tasks of getting this place finished. This included the many finishing details in our basement apartment, but principally centered on the upstairs. He soon realized that the work would probably never be really finished, since there would always seem to be something else to do. He also very often would work at extra jobs to earn a few more bucks to help pay for this project.

One of these extra jobs was as a bartender at his cousin's restaurant/nightclub, known as The 126 Club. This little place in Ashland, a short drive from our Lake Avenue home, was a secondary establishment for Pietro (Peter) Rotelli, Richie's first cousin. It was a short distance from Peter's main reason for living, Marconi's Restaurant, which was famous for miles around as about the very best Italian restaurant outside of The North End (of Boston). The 126 Club was a bit of a diversion for Peter and a way for him to expand his business. It in no way competed with Marconi's for business, catering to a different clientele with more of a "singles bar" flavor. It had a good size dance floor surrounded by booths with a classic jukebox in one corner in a room separate from the bar.

Luigi continues to do his share of the manual labor while Richie is at his job at Dennison Mfg. Company.

Below: Our house as seen from the frozen lake our first winter at Lucky Point.

Angela talking things over with Spots.

Richie in a rare quiet moment listening to both sides of the story from Spots and "Mr. Murphy."

Richie had absolutely no training as a bartender or for that matter, any experience in mixing drinks. He would have an occasional beer when hot and thirsty, but was not a "drinker". That he was very sociable and outgoing and willing to learn a new trade, combined with his complete honesty was all Peter needed to hire him to tend bar on Saturday nights. The last time he had done anything even remotely like bartending was about 23 years earlier when he was a short order cook at Gibbon's Lunch. The first 2 or 3 times he was behind the bar, he managed to avoid having to do anything more complicated than pouring beers and making "highballs", or measuring out an occasional shot of whiskey. But he was studying all kinds of special drink preparation, just in case some customers happened to be a bit sophisticated or perhaps even a little daring. It wasn't long before he was asked for a Zombie. Never having made one before, and trying not to let this fact show, he quickly mixed together the ingredients he thought he remembered from the little book he had studied. He knew it called for several kinds of rum, some liqueurs, and special fruit juices, but he couldn't remember too many details. Using a tall glass, with a little crushed ice and pouring some of the proper items, but not in their correct order, and adding his own ideas, he produced his "Zombie" with a flourish and a smile in front of the confused customer. Richie had no idea if this concoction of his would taste anything like it should and was relieved when, after the first tentative sip it was declared to be the "best damned Zombie I ever had - - anywhere!" Requests for Zombies at Richie's bar became quite numerous after that. His only problem was trying to remember just what the heck he put into the first invention. He must have done it well, since no one ever complained. However, he noticed the effect his tall drinks had on most people, so he made it a rule to try to limit each customer to one such drink to protect them from looking and acting like the creature the drink was named for. He was to learn sometime later that there are several "official" variations on this drink, including Acapulco, Canadian, Jamaican and others. He called his The 126 Zombie, for the club not the 151 proof rum, and was careful to add his chosen liquors and fruit juices in the proper sequence for the best looking result.

He soon learned to put together popular cocktails such as Martinis, Manhattans, Ward Eights, Brandy Alexanders, Pink Ladys, and many others. All were quickly prepared with his unique left-handed style, and always presented as though they were works of art. He also found that he really enjoyed talking on any subject with his regular customers and soon discovered that they enjoyed some of his jokes and the little "magic tricks" he would perform when things got a little slow. Peter was delighted at the growing crowd of customers when Richie was tending bar, and they often showed their appreciation by leaving substantial tips. By the time he got home after closing at 1:00 AM, he was dog tired and smelled strongly of cigarette smoke, but felt that he had had a fun night out and earned some extra cash at the same time. Judging by the amount of house building work he was able to accomplish every Sunday, it would have seemed as though he must have spent the previous Saturday resting up. Somehow, tending bar must have recharged his batteries.

Shortly after we had settled into our lakeside home, we added a new family member. An old friend of my dad's had driven to Framingham from his home in New York City to visit relatives. The day he was heading back home he drove into our as yet unpaved driveway for a short visit. While this person, a complete stranger to me, was talking to my dad and trying to figure out why our house had no windows and was completely camouflaged with thick sandy tarpaper, I was admiring his big black Cadillac. As I stood at the rear of this marvelous automobile peering through the back window and picturing myself behind the wheel, I heard a whimpering sound in the trunk. I listened more carefully and heard the sorrowful cry again. I rushed over to where Richie and his visitor were talking and interrupted them to tell them what I heard. The Cadillac owner said, "Oh that's just my stupid dog. He's been a royal pain in the ass today, so I tossed him in the trunk again to shut him up." When I expressed the thought that it seemed awfully cruel to treat a dog like that and that the poor thing could suffocate in there, he laughed and said that if I wanted the damn dog I could have him. I didn't even know what kind of a dog it was in there but Richie picked up on my concern and asked that the dog be let out. The dog hater opened the trunk to reveal a beautiful, fully grown but young Dalmatian who was trembling with fear, curled into a ball and sniffing at the fresh air, but afraid to move. When I reached in to lift him out the poor animal must have sensed that I meant him no harm so he scrambled into my arms and allowed me to hold him like a baby. I carefully placed him on the ground and he stood there looking at me with pleading eyes, begging me to rescue him from this monster. I asked the man what the dog's name was and he said that he called him the first thing that popped into his mind when he got him - - "Spots".

    I didn't even have to ask my dad if we could keep him. He felt as strongly about this abused animal as I did and suggested to his friend that having a handsome dog like that around our new property would be just the thing for us. Without a look back at his old master, Spots walked along with me down around to our basement door, keeping very close to me the whole way. I heard the big car start up and drive away as I opened the door and introduced our new dog to my Mom. She was quite surprised to say the least to suddenly and with no previous discussion, have a pet. She and Richie almost always talked important things over in advance, so when he came in he immediately explained the situation. This dog needed love and affection. The poor thing also looked like he could use a good meal and a bath, but his soulful eyes did magic on us all. We were hooked. Spots was in. He never fully overcame his timidity, but Spots proved to be a lovable and loving pet. It didn't take him long at all to show in many ways that he was *my* dog, but he always knew that my mother was the one who usually got him his food. He did his best to spread his affections to the three of us equally.

Through the winter of '46 and '47, we continued to look in on our strange next door neighbors occasionally, to be sure that they were getting along OK and that they had plenty of heat and food. It turned out that several of Mrs. Greene's friends were calling on her quite frequently as well, and in addition to their social calls to cheer her up reminiscing about times past, they also worried after her welfare. Floyd was not excluded in their visits, but confided to me that he would just as soon be ignored by those women who really had no idea of what he was all about and who seemed somehow frightened by him. He took to chewing tobacco, a messy habit he had outgrown years previously, in order to encourage these "do-gooders" to keep their distance. When they saw his chipmunk-like cheeks, his jaw slowly churning and a river of brown tobacco juice trickling down one corner of his chin, they respected his wish to be left alone. But it was good for Mrs. Greene that she had these close friends, people she had met years earlier through the various clubs and associations she had either formed or had been deeply involved with. The Boston Music Lover's Club, The MacDowell Club, The Professional Women's Club, The Chromatic Club, and The Framingham Women's Club each now were showing their concern for a famous sister in need by helping to look after her. Two or three of her closest friends were instrumental in helping her with her finances and saw to it that her few bills were paid on time. Her financial resources, never more than slightly adequate to meet current needs, were no doubt lacking in any depth. The small life insurance policy on Roy barely covered his final expenses. Now, in failing health and becoming intellectually less able to cope with her daily needs, she had to rely more and more on a few trusted associates and friends. Fortunately they were honest and caring people who compassionately looked after her.

One of the things they had her do was to rent out the upstairs part of her home. There were four good-sized rooms and a bathroom up there as well as a small kitchenette, providing a very nice little apartment for the right persons. Unfortunately there was no separate entrance to these accommodations, so future tenants would have to always go right through the first floor kitchen to get in and out. Mrs. Greene was hardly ever in her kitchen at this point, spending nearly all her time in bed in what used to be the living room of her beloved "Harmony Home".

It was nearly impossible to walk though this old living room, now bedroom or for that matter, what had been the dining room either. Both of these rooms, with a musty, museum-like odor were stuffed with furniture, odds-and-ends, trinkets, vases, overflowing bookcases, clocks, some ticking and nearly working - - others silent, as well as newspapers and magazines scattered about. Every available wall surface was covered with paintings and photographs. Much of this artwork was of Floyd's creation. There was a stunning oil portrait of a very young and beautiful Edith Rowena Noyes in which she wore a diamond tiara, an expensive looking necklace and a high collared but low-cut white dress. In this painting, she sat holding long gloves near a tiny waist. I do not know who created that masterpiece, but with its large, thick gold-colored frame it captured the essence of a time long gone.

Her upright piano, which she kept tuned to perfect pitch was totally buried under an assortment of photographs and drawings of famous people, including Roy Greene, several packets of sheet music, many of which were autographed by the composers, books, clocks, vases, and trinkets of all sorts as well as a fairly thick layer of dust. When she wished to play this piano, which she occasionally did, it took several minutes to transfer a collection of old tea cups, pewter dishes and various other precious gifts from dear old friends to any available space just so she could lift the cover to get to the piano keys. One of the most fascinating items on this piano was a beautifully sculptured life-size rendition of the hands of the young Edith Rowena Noyes. It was a stunning white sculpture in what looked like marble, and must have been done by someone famous; perhaps given to her as a gift. If it faithfully rendered her hands, she had been blessed with the most delicate, perfectly shaped fingers; a real asset to a talented pianist.

When she did manage to get to the keyboard and seat herself in front of the piano to play for us, we were always amazed and moved by the beauty and charm of her performance. Her fingers hardly seemed to touch the piano keys. She sat up straight and while she played, it seemed as though she somehow went back in time, even to the extent of appearing almost youthful. She would play her *Berceuse* and *Hymn of Peace* both composed by her so many years ago. Often when she would complete a little impromptu concert for us, there would be a tear slowly rolling down her cheek and, as she would settle back into her bed, she would seem somehow older than her 72 years.

Floyd continued in his remarkably self-reliant ways, determined to not be a burden on anybody. (Mrs. Greene thought he was stubborn.) He prepared his own meals, took good care of his own health and personal hygiene and most days when we would drop in to check on him he would be in good spirits. He had a small income from his welfare disability check, occasionally supplemented by a few dollars from various art students. Carlo Belloli and a few other men from the neighborhood visited him frequently and were instrumental in keeping him out of trouble, his groceries stocked and his spirits up.

In January 1947 Floyd turned 59. He had been crippled for nearly 38 years and had learned to deal with his fate many years ago. He still had a wonderful sense of humor and a twinkle in his eye, although he was beginning to tire out more easily than before. One of his favorite sayings was, "The first hundred years is the toughest!" As we got to know him better over the next several months however, it would seem to us that he was beginning to feel the strain of getting older and really being the one on a daily, 24 hour-a-day basis, to listen for any signs of trouble from the frail and sickly Madame Greene.

His studio room was separated from the main house by two doors and a short hallway, the floor of which sloped back towards his room. He was still using the old caster-bottomed easy chair that he had sent out from Texas 25 years ago. Getting around in this overstuffed old chair was very difficult on a level surface, but navigating the connecting hallway with its uneven sloping floor was a real challenge. On the rare days that no one showed up to see Edith, which was how he always addressed her, she would sometimes feel a bit frightened and confused and begin calling out. He would shout back from his room asking if she were OK. If she continued to call to him, he would force his chair to carry him across his room and into the connecting hallway. From there, he would try to communicate enough with her to hopefully settle her down. If she still seemed upset and troubled, he would strain to force his chair against gravity and eventually work his way the 7 or 8 feet to the door that opened into what had been the dining room. The slope of the hallway floor was really quite gentle and would not be noticed by most people. But Floyd had to work hard to pull himself along by grabbing the railing Roy had attached to the wall for just this purpose, with either his cane or his right hand. As he would inch forward he would thrust his upper body sideways enough to make the chair jam against the wall to prevent it from rolling back. This journey of a few feet could sometimes take him nearly a half-hour. Once inside the main portion of the house, there was really no way he could get through the clutter of the first room to get closer to Edith in the old living room, so he would do his best to talk with her in his soothing old Texas drawl and assure her that everything was all right. More than once, after completing this difficult passage, and before he said a word, he would hear her peacefully snoring.

Getting back to his room was a far easier adventure during which he had only to worry about rolling a little too fast. Since the floor leveled out in front of his door, he never really had a problem with the return trip. Of course, if Edith's calls of distress happened to come at night when Floyd was in bed, there was just no way for him to try to comfort her, since it would take over an hour for him to get close enough to talk to her. At times such as those, there was nothing he could do but feel heartbroken at her pain, and remember how much she and Roy had done for him in the last quarter century. The emotional and physical strain he felt was beginning to wear him down. Fortunately, there were many days when the various combinations of visitors and helpers made things quite comfortable for Edith. But he surely must have had troubling thoughts about what must lie ahead in the months and years to come.

    Back at "Lucky Point", we were enjoying the experiences our new place provided. Work on the upstairs continued with most of the electrical wiring being installed by Richie, with help from me. A licensed electrician had obtained the proper electrical permit and checked up on Richie's work. I felt that my role in this part of the project was minor and sometimes had trouble keeping focused. But I realized years later that simply having someone around to fetch tools and equipment and to hold a stubborn length of BX cable while it was being cut was an important, albeit lowly job. Of course along the way, I also managed to acquire a pretty good education in all aspects of house building. Not such a bad deal.

    When spring came, and we could work outside as well as inside I thought seriously about running away to someplace where there was nothing to do, but I didn't know of such a place. I was almost fourteen and had lots of schoolwork to do and friends to be with and really always had a good time, in spite of grousing about having too much work to do.

    As soon as the ground was workable, I watched my father turn over an area of rich topsoil for a vegetable garden right alongside the part of the upstairs of the house where our kitchen eventually would be built. This was a nice level plot and by the time he stopped digging and turning the soil with his long-handled shovel, he had defined an area that looked pretty big to me. Memories of plucking out weeds in the scorching sun back in my grandparents enormous garden on Dow Street came flooding back to me as I thought, "Oh no!

He's making a torture chamber for me!" As it turned out, the tasks that needed to be done as this excellent little garden went progressively through the natural phases of growth never overpowered me. I actually enjoyed the cultivating, weeding, and watering. It really helped that Richie used natural compost around his excellent tomato plants and actually did most of the work. As the seasons sailed by, it was always pleasant for my mother to simply walk over to this productive locale and harvest whatever was ready for her to cook up into healthful meals for us.

In early summer, 1947 one of my pals who lived not too far from The Memorial Junior High where we both went, showed up at our house with a small cardboard box in his hand and a goofy look on his face. The fact that he looked goofy most of the time really didn't matter. I knew he had something strange planned. In the box, which couldn't have been more than 6 by 6 by 8 inches, he had a new kitten. It could easily fit in one hand and was awfully cute. All black, with a little tuft of white on its chest, it mewed up at me from the bottom of its temporary home and seemed hungry - - no, starving.

Spots must have smelled the poor thing and although as far as I knew he had never even seen a cat, he was after all, a dog. Dogs chase cats. He quivered with excitement and possibly fear while trying to get his nose into the box. I tied him to a tree to keep him out of the way and he responded by barking and pretending to want to be free. I think he was relieved to be away from any danger.

I put a small saucer of milk in the box with the cat and was surprised to find that, after a few tentative laps, it continued to cry with its mouth wide open showing sharp little teeth. It was telling me that it needed more substantial food. I immediately thought "fish!" and quickly scurried down to the newly built pier my dad had just completed; my fishing pole and bait in hand. I figured such a small cat would probably not be able to handle anything too large, so I peered into the shallow water looking for just the right little fish. In no time at all I had hooked a red perch about four inches long and quickly carried it back to the cat in the box. I had folded the top flaps of the box over to prevent the cat from getting out and becoming food for the many creatures which roamed our lakefront abode. I lifted one of the flaps and tossed the live perch, flapping and twitching for all its might into the box and quickly closed up the flaps to prevent it from jumping out. The box flopped from side to side and nearly tipped over while the strangest sounds I ever heard were coming from inside. Then there was a sharp "crunch" followed by several crunches and the box no longer shook. In a couple of minutes I carefully opened the top of the box and at first thought that somehow the fish had managed to escape. Upon closer examination, I saw that the cat's belly was about three times its normal size, and the bottom of the box was covered with fish scales. This wild little animal had eaten the whole fish in nothing flat. The cat was lying in there and purring contentedly. I gave him (or at this point I should say "it", since we didn't know if it was male or female) about a half an hour to digest this fresh meal and then reached in and carried it out. It was lethargic and sleepy-eyed, but still purring happily.

    Spots continued to show his displeasure at being kept out of this whole business and was tugging eagerly at his restraints. I thought it was time for these two animals, natural enemies by birthright or some such pre-ordained agreement, to meet and to try to get along with one another. Even though my parents had yet to see the cat, I knew they would have no objection to us having it for a pet. At least I tried to convince myself of that fact. I kept the dog tied to the tree and brought the fish-stuffed kitty over to meet him in my bare hands. The cat never stiffened or showed any concern whatsoever when it saw this beast who was many times its size and whose jaws could easily dispatch it with one bite. Spots, on the other hand, was a mess. He couldn't figure out what he should do. On some level, his instincts must have been pushing him to kill it, but he could see that I obviously thought it was something special. I knelt down a few feet from my dog, holding a very calm little cat and placed it gently on the ground. No reaction from the cat. Poor Spots looked like a statue. He was at the end of the restraining rope, leaning as far forward toward the cat as he could get, his whole body rigid, his nose inches from the ground, and his tail curled down between his hind legs. He looked up at me with a totally baffled expression as if to ask what in the world he was supposed to do. The little fish lover must have quickly sensed that this dog was a big sissy and that he needed to be shown who was boss. It walked right up to him, lowered its head in front of the big fake's jaws and head-butted him right in the nose. Spots reacted by jerking his head back away from this strange little creature and looking up at me with a puzzled expression. He had always been able to convey his feelings with his expressive face. From that moment on, these two understood each other and would grow to be the best of pals. The cat, as we soon learned was a male, and had a natural hunting instinct. He never outgrew his love for freshly caught live fish.

Eventually, in April of 1949 the upstairs of the house was completed enough for all of us to move up. I was the first one to be installed in the upstairs. Back in September of 1948 on my 14th birthday I moved up. As soon as the plastering was done and before it was even fully dry, with its unique aroma lingering in the air, my bed and dresser were moved up to my real bedroom. The oak flooring had yet to be installed and there was a lot of building material all over the place, but I was thrilled to be the sole occupant of this great place. I'm pretty sure my folks were also happy to finally have some privacy with a bedroom all to themselves as well.

Over the next five or six months the upstairs was practically completed. Kitchen cabinets and counter tops, designed and built by Richie with an assist from his Uncle Angelo who was a master cabinet-maker, were installed. Richie also did all the upstairs plumbing with help from a plumber friend whom he had known for years. The upstairs fireplace was finished off nicely with a handsome brick front and mantle.

Again the design and construction were done by this energetic homeowner.

When it came time to install the oak flooring which was to cover every room except the kitchen and bathroom, it came as no surprise that the guy who had shown that he could do anything, did that job too. I helped out there by selecting the flooring boards and lining them up on the rough floor ahead of my dad, who did all the nailing. I made sure that the ends of the oak boards never lined up with the ones already nailed and saw to it that Richie always had a good supply of the special flooring nails at the ready. I begged him to let me do some nailing. He made it look so easy and I really thought I had developed enough to be able to handle such a task. He did not pre-drill the boards to be nailed but simply held a cut nail at the proper angle on the "tongue" and, ensuring that there were no gaps to the previous board, guided his hammer to a perfect result. He must have had a temporary loss of his normal good sense when he agreed to let me nail. We were in the master bedroom and I think he assumed that their bed would be over the spot where we now stood, so that if I messed up it wouldn't show.

I started out just fine and felt really good about what I was doing. I couldn't have been more focused and in more control with my hammer. It was going perfectly. The nail was about a half-inch from where I would stop hammering and then would switch to hold another nail against it to sink it under flush. Then it happened. I couldn't believe it. I missed the nail and left a hammer-shaped dent in the edge of my board. I was mortified and dumbfounded. I suggested that we rip that board up and replace it with a fresh one. However, since it was a long one and had already had about six other nails driven all the way (perfectly of course) it was decided to leave it and try to minimize the dent with the finish sanding to be done. As it turned out, not only did the sanding fail to remove the damage, but the bed did not cover my handiwork. A scatter rug later did that. Richie did all the remaining nailing but never made a big deal out of my "contribution".

The only part of the entire house-building project that Richie did not actually do himself was the plastering of the walls and ceilings. Our neighbor on Cove Avenue, Jim Antonioli, was an experienced plasterer by trade and he agreed that he would do most of the plastering if Richie would build new kitchen cabinets for him in exchange. Eddie Belloli, who at that time was a novice plasterer, was eager to lend a helping hand. The walls and ceilings came out beautifully. It was a very long time before Richie would even think about driving as much as a little nail into any of that plaster to hang anything on those perfect walls.

Now in the spring of 1949 we were fully moved in, finally, to our real home. Now that the downstairs was emptied of furniture, Richie's priority was to install in the basement, an oil-fired furnace and the hot water heating system which would keep our place warm next winter. He used black iron pipe to bring the heated water from the furnace, which he located in what had been the bedroom, around to all the baseboard radiators that were strategically located in each upstairs room. He also included the entire basement in the allocation for radiators with the idea that this area really should be heated too, on its own zone of course, in case we ever needed it for more than simply a basement. He borrowed special pipe-cutting equipment, including tools to cut threads onto the ends of what seemed to me to be miles of the pipe that he cut to length, and a free-standing vise to clamp the pipes as he worked on them. This was another job that he did completely on his own, with help from me of course. I enjoyed working with my father and learning so many "tricks of the trade", although I was still mainly his chief gopher. I recall that he needed to install special down-flow valves at the downstream end of each radiator to ensure that an adequate amount of heated water would flow through them instead of simply bypassing them. I was fascinated by the concept, and read about Venturi valves and how they worked to create a suction. When I told my dad that these special valves were named after an Italian physicist who had discovered the principle back in the 1800's, he thought that was really good to know.

Our visits next door to check up on both Mrs. Greene and Floyd had become more frequent over the past several months. We had seen earlier that Floyd was having more and more difficulty dealing with Edith whose health was deteriorating. He was actually now quite frequently making her meals for her in his poorly equipped room. Friends of hers had seen to it that her sickbed was moved from the living room into the old dining room so that she would not be so far from Floyd. How he was managing to deliver her food to her two or three times a day was a complete mystery. Knowing how difficult it was for him to get around in his old chair by thrusting his upper torso in the direction he wanted to go, left us puzzled as to why all the food wasn't spilled everywhere. I discovered later that he would open cans of soups and vegetables and after heating them on his small electric 2-burner hot plate he would transfer their contents into jars with screw-on tops. He would heat water and pour it into a small thermos. Then he would stuff his prepared meal along with the thermos and some tea bags into pockets that he had somehow managed to attach to the sides of his chair.

His delivery of his "meals on wheels" was still a tortuous and tiring effort requiring about an hour for the round trip. He would get his chair up as close as he could to Edith's bed where she would be waiting, often asleep or quietly listening to her radio. He would remind her why he was there with her food and once she had managed to get herself sitting up and turned to face her bedside table, he would transfer the contents of his jars onto her dishes. He would place a tea bag into her favorite cup and pour the hot water from the thermos. Doing all of this with only the limited use of his right arm must have been extraordinarily difficult for him. But by this time, Edith no longer fully realized the extent of his handicap, and would ask him to do things that there was no way he could do. Usually when he was presented with such a request he would simply quietly agree and then forget about it, as he knew she would too.

He kept a supply of napkins and silverware near her bed. He would wait patiently, often in silence, while she slowly ate whatever of his prepared food she wanted. He always tried to remember to bring her favorite cakes or cookies for her dessert, but often had to scold her to not eat those items first. On Edith's good days they would chat about her beloved Arthur Godfrey and his radio program, *Arthur Godfrey and His Friends* which she (and about 40 million other fans across the country) enjoyed so much. Floyd couldn't stand Godfrey, but he pretended for his mentor's sake. On her not so good days, Edith would refuse to eat or drink anything he had prepared, and was not easy for him to deal with. This behavior was far from the loving, thoughtful and considerate person she had been for so many years. Floyd felt a debt of gratitude toward her and to the memory of her departed husband, Roy for all they had done on his behalf. He had grown to respect and admire the diminutive Roy Greene, and from the time of their first meeting 26 years previously felt a close bond of friendship and loyalty. So it was with feelings of love and duty that he did his best to care for this woman whose quality of life was diminishing so rapidly.

Fortunately, there still were several people who came to help Mrs. Greene with her personal hygiene and to launder her sheets and bedclothes, as well as to provide food and see to it that she took her medicines. For the past few years, Edith would give her helpers small tokens of her esteem in lieu of any other form of payment for their support. These were often items she had been keeping around for years. Many were treasured mementos from well-known people in the classical music world. Sometimes these little gifts would be signed copies of her original published sheet music, or pictures of herself as a young woman, and occasionally she would give away beautiful pewter dishes or bowls. She had been in the habit of acknowledging various persons who had done even small tasks to help her, by mailing them personally written thank you notes.

Floyd, with a heavy sense of responsibility to the woman who, more than anyone else, had been his benefactor, now drove himself to wait on her and watch over her. It was really taking a toll on him however, both physically and emotionally. We could see the effect it was having on him, noting that he rarely smiled and seemed to be losing weight. That he was also losing interest in life was not so obvious, but in a rare unguarded moment during a visit to him by my father and me, he talked of his feelings of despair. He went so far as to mention that he had been cleaning his old six-shooter and thought that he just might use it on himself. He immediately tried to cover that comment with assurances that he'd never do anything like that because he was afraid that it would probably fall to us to clean up the mess and we had enough to do already. We were very much disturbed by what we heard and saw and now that we had come to know this fine Texas gentleman, we felt strongly about his welfare and wanted his remaining years to be carefree and productive.

Mrs. Greene's good friends from the various clubs had arrived at the realization that it had come to the point where she needed more care than could be provided in her home by any combination of caretakers, including of course, Floyd. They discussed moving her to a nearby nursing home or perhaps even in to the home of one of her closest friends so that she could be properly cared for. With Edith's permission, they indicated that "Harmony Home" would soon be up for sale. The proceeds from the sale of this wonderful old place with such an amazing history would be needed to cover her expenses. But what was to become of Floyd?

My mother and father had a serious discussion one evening shortly after the current situation next door was understood for what it was. The thought was that now that we were living upstairs in the main part of the house, we had what amounted to a nice apartment in the basement where we had lived for the past 2 and a half years. Why not have Floyd move in there? He could have the room we had used as our living room and kitchen. The other room now had the furnace and other items taking up space, but the main room would be more than adequate for everything he had managed to stuff into the little studio Roy Greene had built for him many years ago. Of course he would no longer have the nice roof window with its north light, but he wasn't doing much painting these days anyway. The linoleum-covered concrete floor was flat and level, which would make it easier for him to get around in his old chair. The doorway to outside opened onto a concrete slab only slightly lower than the floor in what would now be his room. This would make it very easy for us to push him, in his chair over the threshold to get outdoors on good days. He had always been pretty self-reliant and without the worry and strain of having to care for Mrs. Greene, who would be moving to a nursing home soon, perhaps he'd do OK down there.

The full-length windows along the cove side of the basement were coincidentally the same height from the floor as was the current window next to his bed. This was important so that we could incorporate an arrangement identical to what he now had for disposing of his bedpan waste. Richie would be able to dig a pit right outside one of these windows, just as Roy Greene had done years ago, and place Floyd's bed next to that window. It had worked perfectly for all those years next door, why not here?

My mother thought that it would not be much trouble to prepare a little extra food each day when making meals for us. I indicated that I'd enjoy delivering Floyd's meals to him by just dashing down the stairs. Overall, we thought that this might be a solution to Floyd's current dilemma. We decided to present him with this plan that evening.

When the three of us showed up in his room after supper that night, he somehow sensed that we had something in mind. Maybe it was my silly grin of anticipation or just some sixth sense of his, but he could tell that something was up. Richie, who Floyd always called Richard, dropped the bomb on him, asking if he would like to come live with us in his own room down closer to the lake. Floyd was stunned and for a few seconds I thought he didn't understand what had just been offered. Then in his soft Texas drawl he said, "I think that might be nice. Are you sure you wouldn't mind?" We assured him that we had it pretty much all worked out, but suggested that he might like to come over and check out the place for himself, in case he should get a better offer, or didn't like what he would see. Richie dug out Floyd's rickety old collapsible wheel chair, dusted it off and helped Floyd into it. It was a warm and clear evening, so with my dad and I on each side of his chair, we simply lifted him up and carried him around to our downstairs back door. When our confused Dalmatian, Spots, saw us carrying our unusual load, he went a bit nuts, barking at what he saw, running up to us and just as quickly dashing away to a safe place, then barking and shivering and wondering what in the world we were bringing into his yard.

We had cleaned the room out completely, washed all the windows, and had washed and waxed the floor. The place sparkled in the glow of the overhead fluorescent lights. We placed Floyd and his wheelchair on the floor just inside the door. The look on his face said it all. It was love at first sight. We all started talking at once, with Richie pointing out how he figured he would arrange Floyd's bed against the second window in from the door. I wheeled Floyd in his chair all around the room so he could see it from every angle. My mother was concerned that I was making him dizzy with my rapid moves, but he was enjoying every minute. He soon began identifying the places he would locate the chests and boxes that held his clothes, and just where he would put his art supplies and other important items. Suddenly, he stopped talking and looked down. He was quiet for several seconds and we wondered what had happened. When he looked up, a tear was glistening in his eye and he did his best to try to say what a wonderful thing we were about to do for him. Even though he was overcome with emotion and his words did not come out coherently, we got the message none the less that he was about as happy as he'd been in a long, long time.

On the spur of the moment, my dad trotted up the stairs and was back in a few minutes with 4 glasses and a bottle of wine. We all drank a toast to Floyd and his new apartment.

CHAPTER 15

FLOYD'S NEW BASEMENT APARTMENT
1949 - 1950

If Richie had entertained any thoughts of slowing down a little or relaxing for a while now that the house had progressed to its current state of being nearly complete, he shelved them. He began the task of digging the sewage pit that Floyd would use daily. It was located right up against the foundation at the second window in from the door to what was soon to become Floyd's new home. He constructed this to be a small, but adequate cesspool, patterned after the king-size one that had been in use at the two-family house on Dow Street for many years. Richie assumed that the one that Roy Greene had provided for Floyd's use and which had also worked well for a quarter of a century, must have been of similar construction. This new one, like its predecessors, was never a source of any problems.

On Labor Day weekend in 1949, several friends and relatives from the Dow Street neighborhood helped my dad and me move Floyd Niles Walser and all his worldly possessions out of the studio room that Roy Greene had built for him in 1923. He was as excited as a kid on Christmas morning, trying his best to be patient with this rag-tag group of furniture movers and at the same time seeing to it that none of his specialized collection of art material or his many unique and highly personal items were in any way damaged. It seemed that no matter where we located him in his old chair he was either in the way or else unable to supervise the event. He wanted desperately to be directing the show, but finally had to settle for the role of an interested observer. He agreed with my parents that he would pay them rent of a dollar a day. That seemed fair to everyone, even if it barely covered actual expenses. My folks were definitely not in this for money.

Mrs. Greene had been moved a few days earlier to a local nursing home and was being watched over very thoughtfully by several of her closest friends. Edith and Floyd had said goodbye to each other as she was being prepared to be placed into an ambulance for her ride to her new home. Edith was so emotionally distraught, that genuine concern was expressed that she might not survive this day. Having to leave the place that had meant so very much to her for the past 40 years and was so packed with wonderful memories was almost too much to endure. She reminded Floyd of how much she loved him and begged her "brother" to please stay healthy and to come visit her, or at least write or phone her regularly. Floyd sat stoically in the chair that by now was part of him, and tried his best to control his emotions. They both must have known that they most probably would never see each other again. He knew that if it hadn't been for this compassionate woman's intervention, his life would have been very different. She and her husband Roy had taken him, a stranger and unknown entity, into their home and their hearts. They had provided him with more than could reasonably be expected in fostering his art studies and encouraging his efforts. To him, they were practically surrogate parents while at the same time being wonderful friends.

With most of its furniture having been disposed of in one way or another, and at this point, empty except for scraps of packing material and clusters of dust, Harmony Home now echoed with the footsteps of the helpers and with the banging of doors being closed. Where once it had echoed and reverberated with the sounds of string quartets, brass ensembles, mixed voices and brilliant piano, it now was silent.

* * * * * *

Over the course of the past couple of years, Richie had managed to cover quite a bit of the surface around our house with asphalt, or as we called it "hot-top". He had paid the going rate for enough of this black surfacing material to be delivered to cover all of the driveway from the street down around back and up to the garage door. The actual spreading and rolling of this hot asphalt was accomplished by none other than Richie with assists from his father, whichever cousins or friends were handy and, of course, me. We prepared old shoes with flat wooden boards attached to their soles so we could walk on the hot and steamy new surface without marring it or getting too much of a hot-foot in the process of raking and rolling it to shape.

Now that Floyd was part of our household, Richie wanted to cover more of the yard down around the garage with additional paving. He also thought it would be a good idea to pave a path or two to the edge of the lake and up to the piers he was always building. This way it would be easy for us to push Floyd in his caster-bottomed chair all around the back yard and down to the lake. He talked to Jim Antonioli the next door neighbor and plasterer whose son-in-law was in the business of delivering hot top. It was agreed that whenever his drivers had some left over material at the end of their route and so long as it was still hot enough to be usable, they would deliver their load to our place at no charge. That meant that there always had to be a prepared area that was leveled or at least partially ready to accept a load of free asphalt. More than once, Richie would be part way through his supper when a loud blast from a truck horn would signal the arrival of an undetermined amount of hot top. We would scramble out with spreading tools and shoes and do our best to pave another bit of ground. This process continued for a couple of years with a total of four or five free loads being delivered at mostly random times, until we called off the deal. Richie figured that the 3 or 4 paved walkways leading to the lake were enough. One of his relatives jokingly commented that he thought the small airplanes he would often see circling overhead might think our back yard was a suitable landing strip if we continued to add more hot top.

A few days after Floyd was settled into what had been our basement apartment, Richie explained to him that for quite some time now the thoughts of how difficult it was for Floyd to get sitting up in bed had really bothered him. Richie had been mulling over an idea for how to greatly simplify the process. After all, there were bound to be days when none of us would be around at the time he wanted to get into a sitting position on his bed in the morning. I didn't mind helping to get Floyd upright (as long as it wasn't too early). When Floyd heard Richie's plan, he very enthusiastically agreed that it sounded wonderful and gave his whole-hearted support to the thought. In a matter of a day or two, the idea became a reality. A small, but powerful electric motor was equipped with a large special pulley on its shaft. Wound around the pulley and affixed to it, was a length of nylon cord with a cloth strap shaped into a loop attached to the free end. At the foot of Floyd's bed, stood an old roll-top desk with its back against the bed. The motor/pulley was bolted to the top of this desk, which was about three feet higher than the bed. The electrical cord from the motor had an on/off switch wired into it so that when it was plugged into the nearby electrical outlet, the switch could easily be reached by Floyd if he was in bed. In order to use this new device, Floyd had to learn a few new tricks, which he did in no time. Each night, after he had gotten himself into his bed, he had to be sure that the nylon cord and its attached loop strap was unwound from the pulley and was placed along his right side against the wall. He also had to be sure that the line cord with its on/off switch was positioned in the bed so that it was near his right hand. He also needed his cane to be within easy reach. Then when he wanted to sit up, all he had to do was to loop the cord's strap around the back of his head, close to his neck, and with his right thumb flick the switch to the "on" position. He would then stiffen his neck muscles, strengthened by years of his old technique for sitting up. The motor would slowly rotate the pulley, reeling up the cord and lifting him up and forward to a sitting position. Once he was fully up, he had only to tip his head forward to allow the cord to slip off and then to switch off the motor. At his point he would be sitting facing the motor/pulley and he would use his cane to slide the pulley on its shaft so that he could unwind the cord. He would then place the cord and its loop along the edge of the bed with the loop end in the proper position for the next use. Then he would use his cane to slide the pulley back towards the motor on its shaft so that it would be ready to wind up the cord. He was now ready to push himself around on his bed and back into his chair. The process, which for years had taken him up to 45 minutes by himself, was now accomplished in something like 45 seconds. What a breakthrough!

The mechanization of Floyd's get-up procedure was just the beginning of things Richie had in mind. It was painfully obvious that the way Floyd got himself around in his old chair was terribly inefficient and tiring. Of course now that he had a flat and level linoleum-covered concrete floor under his casters, his upper body forward thrusts usually resulted in forward progress. This was already an improvement from the uneven wooden floor in the studio room he had just recently left. He was very happy getting around in his old tried and true method. Whenever the weather was the least bit good, one of us (usually me) would push him in his chair out onto the concrete slab just outside his door. From there, the lake beckoned with a smooth, asphalt paved path leading down to a wooden pier jutting out several feet over the water. There was no way he could manage to travel to the pier, or "run" as we usually called it, on his own. The downward slope toward the lake would have resulted in him rolling downhill out of control and probably flying right off the end of the run and into the lake. Not a good idea.

It was very therapeutic for him to be outdoors as much as possible. Basking in the sun, especially with it reflected off the lake down on the pier, was something he loved. I would roll him, facing backwards, down the long paved path and out onto the run whenever I could. The first time I tried this he was a bit apprehensive about my ability to control the rate at which he and his old chair would travel. Of course he couldn't see where he was going, and could feel his chair sloping back away from him as I confidently walked backwards, my hands firmly grasping the top back of his chair. I would lean towards him and let gravity do the work. I only had to be sure to not let my cargo accelerate and to keep myself solidly behind him until we reached the run where the surface finally was nice and level. The first time we tried this maneuver, he coached me the whole way to the lake, constantly saying. "Easy now! Slow! Hang on! Not so fast!" Then finally, "Good job. I knew we could do it!"

He did not seem to be the least bit concerned about making it back up the slope later to go back in, but I had serious doubts about my ability to push him back up. I figured that if it proved to be too much for me, we could just wait until my dad got home and we could easily accomplish the job. As it turned out, I was able to make the return trip with a minimum of grunting by getting a good running start. Floyd did not like my running start. Although his speed dropped down to a slow crawl as soon as we encountered the real slope, this was as fast as he had ever traveled on those wobbly old casters.

The entire time Floyd and I were out on this first adventure to the edge of the lake, my faithful pup, Spots, worried and fussed around the chair. He indicated his concern about what was happening by constantly running around in circles, occasionally nearly tripping me up. It was amazing to me to see how quickly Spots felt so protective about Floyd. He must have sensed that this person just might need extra help and attention. Of course, the first few days with Floyd in our house, the dog was a bit fearful of this human who didn't walk around like the rest of the species, but was closer to the ground and had wheels on his bottom. The special bonding that occurred between Floyd and "his" dog after a few days became a heart-warming sight.

Our cat, on the other hand, being solidly possessed of feline independence and general disdain for people (unless he was hungry) pretty much ignored Floyd. It just didn't matter to him if this person rolled around in a chair, or even whether or not he lived there. Floyd was interested in where we got the name for this handsome cat, who was now nearly 3 years old and fully developed. We called him Murphy, which was short for his "real" name of Mister Murphy. The name was a direct result of my grandfather's good-natured sense of humor. Shortly after this cat arrived on the scene with us and was still unnamed, my grandfather was in the process of doing some heavy digging in the ground of our yard not far from the Greene's property when little Ronnie came to visit.

Living in the upstairs apartment of Mrs. Greene's house at that time, were a single mom and her young son, who was about 4 or 5 years old. His name was Ronnie and we enjoyed his impromptu visits to our yard when we were doing chores. As he came to know us better, he would often pop in to visit us in our basement home, timing his visits to ensure that we had almost finished our dinner. He was always welcomed to sit by the table and tell us about his day. He was very polite and although he really wanted some dessert, he would never come right out and ask for it. We always had every intention of offering him something sweet as soon as we would finish our meal. He would become silent, and gaze wistfully at our plate of cookies. Then with a smile he would tell us to "Say, 'Do you want a cookie?'" It always worked.

Ronnie had not seen my grandfather up close before, always somehow being spooked by the sight of what no doubt seemed to him to be a gruff and scary old man. In fact, my Nonno was a very kindly person who loved talking with little kids and was very gentle with them. But on this day, Ronnie got the courage to get within 10 feet of where Luigi was excavating and stood there watching him work. I was nearby and watched to see what would happen. After a few minutes, my grandfather, stopping to rest on his long-handled shovel, spotted the timid kid peering at him from his safe position next to a large bush. In what must have sounded to Ronnie like a major league challenge, Luigi, in his broken-English deep voice looked over at him and said, "What's a you name?" No response from the kid. Just stealthy movement closer to the bush. Luigi repeated his question, this time a bit louder in case the little guy was slightly deaf. "What's a you name?" In a shaky little voice came a response, "Ronnie."

I'm sure my grandfather really didn't hear him, but at the same time decided to have a little fun and leaned toward the frightened boy and gruffly said, "Huh? What you say?" Ronnie drew back a little further and trying to summon his courage, practically shouted, "Ronnie!" "Oh, Murphy. Nice to meet you Mr. Murphy", came the reply. With tears in his eyes, Ronnie shouted out, "No! My name is <u>Ronnie.</u> Not Murphy!" Keeping the game going Luigi responded with, "Good. Murphy. I like that name, Mister Murphy." (Except when my grandfather said it, it sounded more like "Moofy - - Meester Moofy.")

This little game went on for a few days with Ronnie dashing away from similar confrontations before he finally caught on to it and eventually learned that my grandfather was not to be feared and was having fun at his expense. Then they would call each other Mr. Murphy and both laugh about it. So, when it came time to name our wild little kitty, it seemed somehow right to honor him with the title of Mr. Murphy.

By the end of September, Harmony Home had found its buyers. A nice young couple from Grafton, a few towns away, and their little daughter, fell in love with the charming old place. Everything about it appealed to them. Although they had no idea of the rich history of music and art that this house had known over the years, they found it perfect for their needs and met the asking price with very little negotiating. Friends of Mrs. Greene's who were knowledgeable in such matters had been working with the realtor on her behalf to help get the house sold. These same friends had now taken her into their home in the town of Maynard to care for her, after seeing how poorly she was faring in the nursing home environment.

On October 7th, 1949 the official Commonwealth of Massachusetts paperwork was brought to Mrs. Greene. On that day, in a shaky, but surprisingly strong hand, the signature of Edith Noyes Greene was affixed to the deed, transferring her wonderful old home to these strangers. She said that she prayed that they would love Harmony Home as much as she had.

There were some beautiful and warm days in the fall of 1949. As soon as I would get home from school, I'd help Floyd to get out and down to the run to enjoy being out there. I had a couple of fishing rods and reels and a pretty good assortment of artificial lures in my tackle box. Fishing just seemed the natural thing to do, living practically at the water's edge, and I enjoyed the sport. Floyd had not done any fishing since he was a kid in Texas and suggested to me that I was rather mean to use plugs and spoons instead of worms or other live bait, such as crawfish the way he had done so many years ago. His feeling was that at least when a person used live bait, the poor fish had an opportunity to have a little food. If it happened to get caught in the bargain, well - - -"He had no business being a fish in the first place." But he thought that it was downright unfair to make a fish take after a piece of plastic or metal with ganged hooks on it.

One particularly pleasant fall afternoon while we were enjoying sitting out on the run, Floyd suggested to me that he was eager to do a little fishing for himself. I rigged up one of my casting rods with hook, sinker and bobber for him, put a fresh worm on the hook and cast the bait out a short distance from where he sat. I placed the handle of the fishing rod in his lap and made sure his good right hand had a firm grip. He was concentrating on what was in his hand and wondering how he could work the reel and hold the rod at the same time with only his one functioning hand. He started to ask me to place the handle of the rod into his left hand, which he would then force to clamp down on the handle. Then he might be able to use his right hand to turn the reel crank to bring in the hook with, hopefully, a fish on it. Before he could finish the thought, I yelled at him that his bobber was being yanked under water and popping up again, only to disappear again. We both got so excited that we didn't know exactly what to do. I wanted him to catch this fish, but unless I took the rod myself and set the hook, whatever was messing with his worm would probably get away. I reached down, grabbed the fishing rod and his hand together and like might be done for a little kid, controlled his movements. The bobber stayed pretty much submerged. The fish, whatever it was, was hooked and it felt like a big one. He was too excited to properly turn the handle on the reel to haul in the catch, so I took over. He was whooping and hollering and shouting, "Get 'im Dickie, get 'im!"

Suddenly, our fish was on the deck of the pier, flopping for all its might. It was a bluegill, which I always called a "kivver", and only about 5 inches long although it had a thick body. A kivver? What a fight he had put up! I always thought of these as junk fish. I wanted a bass or a pickerel. I'd even settle for a nice yellow perch, although the red perch were no better than the darned kivvers. I had to admit though, that using the rig I had placed into the lake for Floyd was almost guaranteed to result in such a catch versus anything really good. We used those "trash" fish for fertilizer. That is if we could keep Mr. Murphy away from them. But Floyd couldn't have been happier if he had landed a prize bass. This was the first fish he had caught (even if I did most of the job) in a long time. He wanted to have it for supper, but I convinced him that even though this type of fish is also called a pan fish, and many people loved them fried, it was not such a great idea. He asked me to put it back in the water so that he might catch it again some other day.

From that late fall day on, fishing in Waushakum Pond became a major passion in this man's life. He asked me to buy him some fishing oriented magazines, such as *Outdoor Life*, *Field and Stream* and *Sports Afield*. He would spend hours studying all the ads and would read most of the articles as well. It was beginning to get a little too cold and blustery to enjoy being out at the water's edge, but plans were being made for next year.

Richie had been thinking a lot lately about doing something to motorize Floyd's chair. He didn't want to mention his rough thoughts to Floyd until he had formulated a design in his mind that he thought had a chance of working safely. He had talked about this idea with my mother and me at our meal times. It was becoming apparent that Richie was going to build a motor-driven chair for Floyd. There was just no way that he could allow our new household member to have to work so hard to get around in his room. Besides that, he felt that Floyd should be able to get out onto our paved back yard and down to the lake without help.

My dad had not seen any motorized wheelchairs to try to mimic; there just weren't any of them around, at least that he knew about, in the late fall of 1949. He knew that Floyd would require a sturdy chair whose seat had to be custom tailored to his unique body shape. Richie knew that he could work that aspect of the requirements into whatever he came up with and concentrated on various electric motors and gearboxes. An automobile starter motor seemed to him to be a very logical device, and the thought that he could rig up two of these, one for forward; the other for reverse made sense. A car battery would, of course be needed and he expected that it would require very frequent recharging; perhaps daily. The more he thought about putting together something special like this, the more he was captivated with the thought.

Soon Richie discussed the idea with Floyd, who initially was a bit skeptical and voiced concern about how he would control such a contraption. As the discussion went on, with Richie's enthusiasm and excitement for the project building the more he talked it out with the potential user, Floyd began to see the possibilities. The freedom a motorized chair would provide was a powerful incentive for him to have confidence in this young man who had constantly demonstrated his ingenuity and, it seemed, could build just about anything. Floyd was soon totally engrossed with the idea of zipping around both indoors and out around the yard, possibly even down to the run. The more he thought about it, the more he loved the idea. But then came the terrible thought that, what if this marvelous concept just couldn't be made to work? What if it went too fast, or couldn't be steered dependably? Or if the battery couldn't supply energy long enough to really get him very far and he got stuck somewhere? How in the world would he be able to get in and out of the powered chair from his bed if it had a steering mechanism in the way? Could his inventive friend work all these, and more, issues out successfully? Richie had no doubts about any of those minor problems and was totally convinced that he could build a chair that would be safe, dependable, and fun to drive.

Floyd provided a few dollars from his limited income to help obtain the raw material and components that were needed. He was in the unique position of being customer and end user of what seemed to be a life-altering product, but without a clear idea of what it would look like when built. His confidence in Richie's ability to pull this off without a hitch increased daily. Whether this was due to his observation of how quickly it was taking shape, or had more to do with the thought of how crushed he would feel if Richie failed and had to give up, he never lost faith in the engineer.

Floyd reminded himself of his adventures driving across the country in the car that the Greene's so generously had specially outfitted for him 17 years ago. If he could operate that vehicle successfully, with all its attendant dangers and perils, surely an electrically powered wheelchair should be a snap to handle. Although he had been a bit younger then, he was still in remarkably good condition. He was still mentally sharp as a tack and his good right arm was strong, as was his upper body. He never wore glasses and still had nearly all of his teeth, with nothing artificial in his mouth. It had been a long time since he had so much as a cold, or runny nose. He attributed his continued good health to his habit of eating raw garlic on a regular basis. Whether this was a health boost or simply kept people who might be carrying cold germs from approaching too closely, it seemed to work for him. He was becoming emotionally attached to the prospects of gaining more independence and getting about with far less effort as a result of having this new chair. If only Richie could really do it. A space in the furnace room was cleared out to be the assembly area for this exciting project; a place Floyd could keep an eye on each day. Cutting strong angle-irons to length and drilling holes for the bolts that would be used to join them into the basic framework was done by Richie at his workbench in the garage. I do not recall seeing any drawings or plans for the cutting, drilling and assembly of these components. Perhaps my dad had sketched out some basic ideas with dimensions, but it seemed to me that in short order, a framework was bolted together almost as if by magic. Plywood was cut to shape and bolted to this frame, forming a strong base for the whole chair. A rear axle with large rubber wheels and good ball bearings was attached. These were to be the powered wheels. There was one smaller, swivel-mounted front wheel that Floyd would use to steer, attached to the other end where the plywood and steel base came almost to a point. The linkage that would control the movement of this wheel was the wooden handle cut off a short shovel, or spade. It was to be mounted in such a way that the driver could reach down and easily disconnect it from the wheel to get it out of the way when needed. This would be important when the chair would be pulled right up against the bed so Floyd could then slide himself forward and onto his bed.

At this point the "chair" looked like an oversized, three-wheeled skateboard with a shovel handle attached to the front wheel. The plywood base was about 18 inches wide across the back where the 2 wheels were, and about 3 feet long. I thought it was fun to ride it around the basement like a scooter, steering with the shovel handle and giving Floyd a few laughs each time I nearly fell off or came close to crashing into something.

I didn't have many days to ride around on the platform, since Richie was very soon in the process of mounting a gearbox and chain drive to the rear axle. Two automobile starter motors with solenoids were mounted and connected to the gearbox in such a way that one motor would drive one of the wheels forward, while the other motor would be used to back up. Richie wasn't at all sure about the proper gear ratio to couple the motors to the drive wheels. He wanted just the right forward speed; not too fast and not too slow. It was more guesswork than science. The particular gearbox that conveniently became available as surplus and unneeded equipment at Dennison was quite heavy and very well built, and may have been overkill for this project, but the price was right and it surely could be made to work. He thought it was a lucky break that it had two input shafts so that he could use one for forward and the other for reverse. It took Richie a few days to figure out the best way to mount the motors and to couple them to the input shafts of the gearbox. He tried belts and pulleys as well as sprockets and chains, and soon found the best combination that seemed as though it would reliably transfer the motor torque to the gearbox. The part he was least sure of was the actual gear ratio all the way from the output shaft of the starter motors, through their coupling to the gearbox and finally to the wheels. How all this would relate to the speed of his machine with Floyd's weight on it was a bit of a mystery.

A new 6-volt car battery was purchased from Sears and Roebuck along with the appropriate heavy cables to connect the battery to each motor-mounted solenoid. The electrical connections for the motor controls were made with smaller wire through two round pushbuttons attached to the shovel handle. They were mounted in such a way that Floyd would be able to activate them with his index finger when he was sitting in the seat with his right hand firmly grasping the steering handle. As long as he kept a button pushed, its corresponding motor would be activated. He would be able to control his direction with the front wheel by moving the shovel handle from side to side, turning the wheel. The seat of course, at this time was nowhere to be seen, with Richie fully aware of the general requirements for it, but concentrating on the basic mechanization of this little vehicle.

Shortly after Thanksgiving Day 1949, all of the parts were assembled to the point that, even without its chair attached, the strange looking contraption was ready for a trial run by its inventor. With Floyd looking on, parked in his old chair in the doorway between his room and the furnace room, Richie sat on an old Moxie box he had fastened to the plywood platform about where the seat would be added. He placed his feet at the forward-most part of the platform, grasped the shovel handle with his right hand and pressed the button for forward. Richie shot forward, his head snapped back and he nearly toppled over. This was far too abrupt and sudden a start! And his forward speed was too fast also. After traveling about 4 feet, he took his finger off the button and stopped just as violently as he started, nearly flying off the seat over the handle. Floyd looked devastated. This did not seem to him to be a good beginning. He tried to mask his feelings of disappointment, but failed. He was surprised when Richie confidently announced, "It works! All it needs are a few little changes and it'll be perfect!"

The next several days found Richie making a series of modifications to the power train of his strange looking three-wheeler. Eventually, he was satisfied that the reaction that would follow pushing the buttons on the shovel handle would be acceptable and was something that Floyd would be able to control. He was pretty sure that a fair amount of practice would be needed before the new driver would feel comfortable, or for that matter, before any of us would feel confident that no serious bodily harm or property damage would ensue.

Now it was time to build the part of the machine where Floyd would sit. This would turn out to be a significant challenge since comfort and safety were primary requirements. Having grown so accustomed over the years to his old caster-bottomed chair, Floyd's first thought was to somehow bolt it right onto the framework. Both men knew this was not a workable plan, so with the artist defining all his needs, the inventor proceeded to turn those needs into reality. It was not as straightforward a task as might be envisioned. Floyd's upper torso required a significant amount of padding under him on his left side, with not so much elsewhere, for him to sit up straight and comfortably. There needed to be room for him to cross and fold his legs in front of him and to be able to strap them in place so they would not fall forward and down. He would also need a strong strap to fasten around his waist to anchor him firmly, especially if jolting starts and stops were going to be standard operating procedure. This part of the project moved along smoothly, but frustratingly slowly. Floyd wanted to be in his new powered chair right away. When Richie came down with the flu and had to suspend work on this for several days while he regained his strength, all Floyd could do each day was to gaze at his almost-ready liberator and dream of what lay ahead. In the meantime, Richie's fevered brain continued to evolve plans for completing his invention and upholstering it in grand style.

Just before Christmas, my dad was back at the task and had completed enough of the vehicle's chair for us to lift Floyd out of his well-used old one and into the new. A specially shaped wooden box-like structure was planned to be attached as a cover to the back part of the platform where the motors, battery and gearing were mounted. This would provide protection from weather as well as keep items from getting caught up in the works. It also would give a finished appearance to the product. But there was no patience for taking the time to make such a cover now. It was not needed for the test flight. Nor was the padding exactly right or upholstery by any means finished. None of us could wait any longer to give this thing its first real test.

With Floyd firmly strapped in place, and with his legs folded and tucked under each other, just the way he wanted them, he was more than ready to travel. The look of determination on his face, complete with his no-nonsense attitude was probably similar to how the Wright brothers looked at Kitty Hawk. Richie coached him on how best to position his hand on the steering handle so that his finger could press and hold a button while he maintained a firm grip so he could steer. I pushed the empty old chair as far away in the room as I could get it. We had previously moved anything that could be moved out of the way to try to clear a reasonable length path in both directions from where man and machine now sat. Floyd looked up at my mother, father and me and grinned with anticipation.

Suddenly, and with no warning, he was going backwards and in seconds slammed into the kitchen cabinets while he kept a tight grip on the handle and hollered, "Whoa!" The wheel continued to spin on the linoleum, trying to dig into the cabinets. Richie was shouting at him to get his finger off the button, but it took a few more seconds before he responded. Feeling more than a little embarrassed, and shaken by this first uncontrolled trip of about ten feet across the room, he sheepishly allowed that he knew what he had done wrong. He had grasped the handle firmly as instructed, but failed to realize that he was also clamping down on the button that activated the motor for reverse. So when the machine responded to his input by doing just what it was designed to do, he was not ready for it, and reflexively tightened his grip. While he was going on about how he understood what had just happened, and how he was sure that he could safely operate his new high tech chair, Richie was planning to relocate both motor buttons. He could see that what had just occurred could easily happen again unless the buttons were positioned a little differently.

Floyd was now fully recovered from his initial mistake and with a look of sheer determination, announced to the three of us, "OK now. Here I go." With a slight jolt, snapping his head back just a bit, the chair moved forward a few feet and stopped abruptly, causing him to pitch forward somewhat. He then backed up a couple of feet, stopped, and went forward turning to aim toward his bed. Then he shouted "Whoa, whoa" and slammed headlong into the wooden side of the bed. Once again, he had forgotten to take his finger off the button. We all had a good laugh at the thought that maybe if he yelled "whoa" sooner, he might avoid ramming his furniture.

We lifted him out of the unfinished machine and stuffed him back into his old, familiar chair. We knew he would be very anxious to be done with the old chair for good, but there was still a lot of work to be done to fine tune the controls and to properly upholster the seat and generally complete the job.

This had been enough of a trial run for Richie to see that some slight modifications were needed. It was also enough for my mother to feel that her husband was putting Floyd's life in danger, or at the very least, it was the beginning of the end for much of the furnishings and cabinetry in his room. At supper that night she strongly suggested that this powered chair idea should be scrapped before something really bad happened, like him getting his legs squashed against something. In his usual good-natured style, my dad pointed out that a few little changes were all that were needed and Floyd would be able to get around smoothly and reliably. This was something the poor guy hadn't been able to do on his own since he was 21. Now, after more than 40 years, here was a chance for him, at least partially, to regain his mobility and independence. Richie firmly believed that the strong-willed Texas artist, who had by now become a real part of our family, deserved his best inventive efforts. The get-up assisting motor/pulley he had rigged up for him so soon after his arrival was something Floyd never tired of praising Richie for. Even though there were many unfinished projects all around the house crying out for his time, my dad felt that the priority now was completing Floyd's new chair.

Shortly after the beginning of the new year, Floyd's old chair was relegated to the scrap heap. We thought it prudent to not actually toss it out until all the bugs were worked out of the new one, just in case. Floyd was thrilled with every aspect of his new "horse" as he sometimes called it. The final upholstering job came out looking pretty sharp, in a burgundy colored leather-like material known as "Naugahide". Plenty of padding was provided and shaped into place to Floyd's demanding specifications until it fit him just the way he needed it. An outside pocket was provided all along the right side of the chair into which the driver could easily reach to place or retrieve useful items. Hooks were attached at the front sides of the chair to securely fasten it to the bed to ensure that it would not slide away as he would drag himself into or out of it. His old pals who had gotten used to visiting him on a regular basis were in awe of the fantastic job that had been done to "give him legs" as one of them put it. When one of my father's cousins told other friends that Richie had given Floyd the "electric chair", it became the talk of the neighborhood. Soon, everybody who knew either my dad or Floyd, or both, just had to come over to see this marvelous thing in action. One of the relatives, who had known my dad for many years was so impressed with his inventiveness, not only for the chair, but the motor/pulley assist, as well as how the house had come out, that he made the comment that, "If Richie had gone to college, we'd have to genuflect in front of him!"

In spite of how well the chair worked, Richie still knew that there were things about it that should be improved. For one thing, he knew from the beginning that automobile starter motors were simply not designed to be used this way. They were meant to operate only for a few seconds at a time to turn over a car's engine, and then not run again until the next start. They were not meant for continuous, or steady running. They also drew a lot of "juice" from a battery. Mounted right next to Floyd's bed was a newly purchased battery charger, which was used every night to replenish the battery's energy. A special recharging jack was built into the chair's rear compartment on the right side where he could reach it. Each evening when Floyd parked his chair against his bed, the first thing he would do would be to plug the charger into its special chair-mounted receptacle and switch it on. By morning, if all went well, the battery would be fully recharged and ready to be drained once again by this wheelchair cowboy.

It was too bad that there was so much snow and ice outdoors. Floyd really wanted to drive around out there since he felt that he had pretty much mastered the controls. He would be constantly zipping around; back and forth from his bed to the sink, to the refrigerator, to the bed again and back to the sink. From there he would drive up to the door to look out, then back to the sink, refrigerator, bed, sink, door and on and on. Often, by the end of a day of traveling around his room this way, his speed would slowly diminish, as the battery would gradually run down. He was always able to make it back to his bed and the recharging station, however.

The first few days and evenings that he was down there on his own with his new vehicle, we would hear the rhythm of his newfound independence. The buzzing of the motor, although not at all an annoying sound, could be heard from our living room. Very often what we would hear would be, Buzz, buzz, buzz, BANG - -"WHOA!" This would often be repeated frequently until the final, bang - -"whoa" would announce that he was parked at his bed for the night. He was learning. Slowly. (I couldn't help jokingly suggest to him that perhaps if he yelled "whoa" early enough, there wouldn't be a "bang". He was not amused.)

I had read somewhere that when an automobile battery is being charged, it is possible that hydrogen gas may be liberated in the process. Was this a safety issue? Did we have to worry about an explosion of volatile gas blowing up our house? We decided not to worry about this hopefully minor, non-issue.

As the winter months slowly melted into the spring of 1950, Floyd really mastered everything about his "electric horse", getting around in his room with hardly an unplanned bump. Getting outdoors with his new wheels was a real treat, although he had a tendency to drive around so much that more than once, someone had to push him and his chair back inside to recharge the battery. Evidently the cold temperature and the extra distance traveled drained the system a little too quickly. But the pink flush in his cheeks and the general look of contentment about him after a day of zipping around our yard and down to one of the piers, spoke volumes.

He asked Richie to rig up a board connected to the shovel handle steering control so that he could do some drawing and sketching from his chair. It had been quite a while since he had had any interest in creating any art. Now, he felt so revitalized by the machines Richie worked out for him that he wanted to paint again. Getting out of bed no longer tired him out. Getting around the room was not only no work, but was fun as well. His whole appearance and attitude reflected his good fortune at having found his new home and having an energetic inventor friend like Richie.

Of course, my mother's excellent cooking also went a long way towards keeping him happy as well. She had always been a very good cook and learned early in her marriage that her husband loved to eat. And she always loved to cook for my dad, preparing his favorite meals done to mouth-watering perfection. Richie could always eat more than any two people could at any one sitting, and yet never seemed to gain an extra ounce of fat. He remained trim and slim and bounced from one project to another while still putting in a full day's work, adjusting the high-speed tag machines at Dennison for maximum performance. Naturally, when my mom would prepare our meals each day, she would make an extra serving for Floyd. Usually, I would trot down the stairs with a tray of food, rap on Floyd's door, and without waiting for a response from him, would barge right in with his meal. Somehow he never minded my lack of manners about entering without waiting for him to acknowledge my bang on his door. By now, he felt more like a close relative to me than a mere acquaintance. I would also see to it that his refrigerator was well stocked with all his favorite items, including his beloved garlic cloves as well as pickled pig's feet, a "delicacy" he had enjoyed for years. We kept all the low drawers and cabinets in his room filled with a variety of "goodies" and necessities for him where he could get at them at will. He was also able to utilize the sink, which was built into the counter, even though it was a bit of a reach for him. My dad rigged up a way for him to activate the faucet easily. He was very pleased to find hot water there whenever he wanted it, unlike the single faucet cold water supply he had been used to previously.

Although just about everyone who knew my dad called him "Richie", or "Rich", Floyd had, from their very first meeting, always referred to him as "Richard". Likewise, although my mother had been known as "Lena" from the time she was a little girl, Floyd, from the first time they met, always called her "Angela". Her given name was "Angelina", and it was easy for her siblings to simply call her "Lena" for short. Floyd always insisted upon using the more angelic version. Perhaps he thought of her as his real-life angel. So from this point on, my mother would basically have 2 names. Everyone in her family and her circle of friends would always continue to address her or refer to her as they always had, as Lena. Floyd consistently called her Angela, the name she really preferred. She would continue to use that version in legal documents and when meeting new people and now thinks of herself only as Angela, even if her close relatives still call her Lena. I was always called "Dickie" by Floyd, and I believed that no matter how much older or grown up I might get, I was stuck with that nickname from him forever.

One of the first drawings he produced from his new chair, was a charcoal sketch of my mother in profile. Richie made a frame for it and proudly hung it on a wall in our dining room, overcoming his reluctance to drive a nail into those beautiful plaster walls. After whipping out two or three pastels of views around the edge of the lake, Floyd once again became more interested in fishing and in getting ready for the season. He may have felt that now that he could pretty much come and go as he pleased, he'd concentrate on other things than art for a while. Then, when the mood might strike him, he could always get back to it. He still did have one or two students coming in for lessons in the fine points of producing captivating etchings. And there were a small number of other art students who still sought his experience. So he really did keep his mind on art to some degree, but there was no doubt that fishing was becoming far more interesting to him.

Right: Dickie looking over Floyd's shoulder while he tries to concentrate on his latest sketch. (1950)

Above: Richie discussing driving technique with Floyd anxious to drive out onto the pier. (1950)

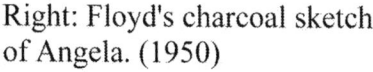

Right: Floyd's charcoal sketch of Angela. (1950)

He told me that the independence that my dad had provided for him was such a wonderful gift, that he sometimes wondered if this was all a dream. He pointed out that Teddy Roosevelt was the president of the United States, and electricity was a novelty the last time he was able to get around on his own, indoors and out. He took for granted, back then as a youngster, that he would always be able to walk and go places without needing help. Now, after 40 years of being heavily dependent on others in order to get very far from his small home base, and at the age of 61, he was finally able to get up and about with relative ease. He still couldn't travel very far on his own, being limited by the amount of paved surfaces available in our yard, and by the durability of the battery that supplied the energy for his motors. He thought it would be one hell of an adventure to drive right up our driveway, into the street and go downtown! He assured me that he would never actually try such a "damn fool thing as that", but wouldn't that be something? He knew that his battery would get him about as far as our mailbox before it tuckered out. But he had dreamed it! He was quite a sight, driving right down the middle of the streets, with cars swerving all around him and people gawking at his marvelous three-wheeled motorized chair. In his dream the cops that came up to him in downtown Framingham, were so impressed with his new chair that they didn't even give him a ticket for driving without a license or holding up traffic by moving so slowly. But then, in this wonderful dream, he would get up out of his chair and walk into a "saloon" for a shot of whiskey. He said that when he woke from that crazy dream, the only thing he was worried about at first, was that maybe everything, including the reality of his new chair, was fiction. He was greatly relieved to see it right there hooked to the edge of the bed, its battery charger doing its thing, and to see the motor/pulley arrangement sitting up there just waiting to quickly and easily pull him up. What a stroke of good fortune!

Of course, his experiences of driving in his car all over the country in 1932 and again in 1943 were pretty special, and wonderfully liberating, but even then, he had to rely on others most of the time. He said that it was now actually hard to believe that he had really managed to travel all those miles, out to Texas and Oregon and back, without getting himself, or anyone else, killed. Yes, he had done a lot of the driving himself, with all the special gadgets that the Greenes had had rigged up for him. A good portion of those trips, however did involve other people to either drive, or in other ways tend to his many needs. He allowed that he felt now, there was just no way he would be able to ever repeat those adventures, even if another car were made up special for him like that one was. Too much had changed. Cars were much faster now, and his reflexes were a lot slower. He had gotten the desire to travel back home, out of his system back then. He no longer felt that pull. Now, all he wanted to do was to get out and fish as often as possible, right in his own "private lake", which was how he thought of the area in our back yard. He was very content in his new home.

Shortly after he had moved in with us, Floyd asked me if I thought I could cut his hair for him. He had a nice set of stainless steel barber's clippers that worked as you squeezed the handles open and closed. I had never done anything like that before, but he said that what he wanted was a "baldy", and figured that I would have no trouble with that. I agreed, and as he sat up straight in his chair (it was the old one back then) I covered all but his head with a sheet and proceeded to clip away, tentatively at first. It was easy. He had a very nice, full head of gray hair and was used to keeping it very short. I called this hairstyle a "Butch". My pals and I used to have our hair cut that way when we were in grade school. At least most of us did. I couldn't seem to manage it for some reason. But here was Floyd wanting me to clip it all off, right down to his scalp, leaving only a short fuzz all over. When I finished, and shook out the sheet, he leaned far over on his side and asked me to pour about a tablespoonful of Witch Hazel into his cupped palm. He rubbed that vigorously into his scalp, complaining all the while that it burned. This got to be a regular monthly event. I would be the barber, clipping away a nice head of hair and he would then slather his scalp with Witch Hazel.

Floyd's interest in getting out to fish as soon as the weather and ice would permit, built up over the winter to the point where most of our conversations dealt with all aspects of the sport. His faithful old friends from our Dow Street area, many of whom were my father's cousins and their pals, began dropping in to visit with him on a fairly regular basis. They all loved to fish and spent many an evening with him talking it up, building his enthusiasm. They told him about the variety of fish he could expect to catch in the pond in his back yard. They pointed out that, although there were no trout in that body of water, there were some mighty fine bass in there, both the large-mouth and small-mouth variety, and what was known as a calico bass. It was harder to catch the calicos, because their soft mouths often resulted in your hook ripping right out before you had them out of the water. There also were several large pickerel, and those guys could put up a hell of a fight, especially the old timers who were known to get up to nearly 2 feet long. They also described the local catfish, which nobody called by that name; they were "hornpout", sometimes simply called 'pout. Those black-skinned, ugly bastards had some fierce points sticking out of their bodies and could inflict a little payback on an unwary fisherman. They made a nice dinner if you cooked them right. You didn't scale them because they had no scales, but you had to peel off the black skin before you cooked them. The hornpout liked really stinky bait; worms dipped in pork fat or some such gunk. Of course there were always the kivvers and the perch. More than one bass or pickerel fisherman would sometimes bring home a stringer loaded with these lowly creatures, but he would have to admit that the darn things put up enough of a fight to be interesting; especially on the days when the "game" fish were on vacation or something. Although none of his tutors in the fine art of fishing this pond had actually caught one, they had heard about other folks latching on to an eel from time to time. Because they twisted their snake-like bodies violently when hooked, they could be tough to land, and made the surprised angler think he might have a prize winning bass on his lure.

With his interest in stalking such quarry inflamed greatly by all this talk, Floyd ordered a variety of fishing gear from mail order catalogs, his favorite being Herter's. He often was a bit like a little kid expecting a new toy. When I got home from school he would ask if the mailman had come yet, hoping that this would be another day for more fishing stuff. Little by little, his room began to fill with rods, reels, lures, monofilament line in a bewildering assortment of strengths, a gaff, a net, a bait bucket, hooks, bobbers, sinkers, tackle boxes, and more. He subscribed to every magazine that had anything to do with fishing, and read every page.

Of all of the old Dow Street gang, the one who visited most frequently was Richie's first cousin, Carlo Belloli, the oldest brother of my close pals, Henry and Sonny. Occasionally, his brothers Tony or Eddie would come over with him or by themselves, but Carlo visited most frequently, sometimes accompanied by his good friend and neighbor, Augie Agostino. They all enjoyed talking with him about fishing, hunting, and baseball. Carlo had known Floyd for many years, having been enthralled by "Tex", as he called him. Carlo and one or two of his friends, sometimes his brothers, back when they were teenagers in the late1930s, used to visit Tex Walser at his studio with the Greenes. They would do odd jobs for him and the Greenes, listen to his stories about the "Wild West" and occasionally take art lessons. Sometimes when Tony or Carlo would do a few hours work for Mr. or Mrs. Greene, they would be paid a dime plus a beautiful pewter pot or dish. These choice pieces of pewter may have been given to the Greenes over the years by any number of famous or, if not famous, at least talented musicians from all over the world. Most of these special items found good use in the boys' father's basement as very convenient holders for screws, bolts, washers and nuts.

The youngsters, back in those days loved to examine Floyd's collection of Indian arrowheads; most of which he had found himself, or so he said. Whenever he would allow them to actually see, if not hold, his unloaded six-shooter, they could picture themselves as lawless gunmen, running out of a bank with a sack of money. Floyd would often elaborate on gunslinger stories, sometimes to the point of totally fabricating them. Once, when he was asked if he had ever met Jesse James, he responded with a straight face, "Hell, did I know him? We were related! He taught me how to shoot!" The fact that this notorious outlaw was shot and killed nearly 6 years before Floyd was born, was something that these kids simply didn't need to know. His audience was usually rendered wide-eyed and open-mouthed speechless by his yarns. They would then repeat these tales to their pals, amplifying and elaborating further, until any shred of reality was nonexistent. Good, clean fun.

One of the things Carlo had particularly enjoyed doing for Floyd in the hot summers back then, was to take him swimming in Lake Waushakum. It always took at least two strong young guys to pull this off. They would push Floyd in his chair, out of his room as far as a paved surface could get them. Then they would lift him out of his chair and carry him down the steep hill, which was covered with slippery pine needles, to the edge of the water, dodging the thick underbrush the whole way, trying not to fall or to drop him. Once they had arrived at a clearing between the bushes where they had good access into the lake, they would place him on the ground. Then they would take the long rope that one of them had carried along, and tie one end of it to Floyd's belt around his waist. The other end of the rope was tied to a nearby tree. Then they would pick him up again, and carry him out into the lake, stepping on rocks, muscle shells and other sharp submerged items, until they were about waist deep. Then they would slowly release their grip on him as he floated like a cork in the cold water. Floyd loved it. This was as close to having a bath as he ever got. Sometimes he even brought out a bar of soap. The boys would swim all around him, keeping a close eye on him to be sure their "cork" wasn't suddenly floating upside down. With only his smiling face visible, he was a sight to behold. The only time he got a bit concerned about his safety was when a small motor boat might come chugging along. If his guardians happened to be distracted, as young kids can easily be, and he heard a motor, he would start to shout and holler. No boat ever came close to ramming him, although a few boat operators looked puzzled as they navigated past this shouting apparition. Usually Carlo and his pals would tire of being in the water before the human float would. Once they hauled him back onto the pine needle covered bank, with their fingers shriveled like prunes, they had to inspect him for leaches. The "blood suckers" as they called them, would very often be lodged between a couple of his toes, and were hard to remove. Floyd never minded these bloodthirsty creatures latching on to him. He pretended that he thought it was good for him to be bled once in a while. Getting him back up the steep slope was always a tough job for the youngsters, tired out from their swim and working against gravity on the slippery surface. But they always managed it, and never tired of doing it again when they could.

Near the end of February 1950, Floyd purchased a Zenith console television set for his room. This was really something special, not only for him, but for my folks and me as well, since we did not as yet have one of these great new entertainment devices. TV was pretty new at that time, even though it had been around since a little before the war. Now though, the number of broadcasting stations was increasing and the broadcast hours, as well as the number of programs, were beginning to take off. Color TV of course, was still several years away from being technically or commercially viable.

It was a couple of years previously that I had actually seen a TV set at Framingham's first TV dealer. My pals and I used to stand out in front of the DeCollibus radio and TV shop on Hollis Street on our way home from a movie or from being downtown for some other reason. We would stare at the test pattern displayed on the sets in the window, being amazed at how nicely everything lined up most of the time. Sometimes there would actually be a program flickering away, and looking at that was even more fun than gazing at the test pattern. We even stood enthralled, looking at a commercial for Bulova watches. You could actually see the second hand sweeping across the face of the watch! We all wanted one of these new sets in our own homes, but the cost of ownership was just a little out of reach for our families at that time. My folks said that they thought it would be a good idea to have the television industry get the bugs out of the technology before investing in one for our home. I couldn't wait. So when Floyd got his handsome set, it was pretty exciting.

Richie mounted an antenna (which he insisted on calling an aerial) up on our chimney, routing the twin lead-in wire down and into the room. He wasn't sure if it should be grounded or not, but thought it would be a good idea, and did so. The design of the television set was reminiscent of the old console radio we had. The small screen (I think it was about 9 or 10 inches) had a fancy bezel around it and handsome knobs to tune in the channel and to adjust all sorts of things, like vertical and horizontal, and brightness and contrast, and more. It had a good size speaker mounted behind fancy grille cloth in the bottom part of the console. Peeking into the actual guts of the set through the back was frowned upon. What a fascinating array of vacuum tubes, transformers, and metal boxes was in there. You could tell this was a quality product because it was heavy and had a nicely finished cabinet.

It had a place of honor in Floyd's room, being located against the wall directly across from his bed, where there was room to put a few extra chairs for visitors to use. He would drive right up to it, never even coming close to ramming into it, and turn it on. The first few times, he needed us to adjust the many controls to keep the picture from rolling up or down, or tearing sideways. We always tuned in a test pattern and adjusted everything for maximum clarity. Then we found that a perfect test pattern on one of the broadcast channels would not necessarily result in other stations looking so hot. It was great fun nonetheless.

Floyd seemed to love just about every program he tuned into. The *Texaco Star Theater* with Milton Berle (Mr. Television and Uncle Miltie as he was known) was one of his favorites. He had never seen anything like what Berle would do, and he would hoot and holler at his antics. He particularly enjoyed watching men tap dancing on the many variety shows he would find. When the camera would zoom close-up on the dancer's feet, he would not miss a trick. It had been a very long time since his own feet could move like that. Dramatic programs, such as The *Kraft Television Theater*, and *Studio One* would occasionally hold his interest. Usually when the program was over he'd make a comment such as, "That was a dumb story." But he continued to watch, hoping for a good one, I guess. Whenever a boxing match was broadcast, he tried not to miss it. When springtime came, he loved to watch The Boston Red Sox, who often played in the daytime back then. This was a sport that he had played as a youngster back in Texas; watching the pros play it on TV must have brought back some good old memories.

We all helped him watch his shows in the evenings when we could. It was easier for us to change channels and adjust the picture when needed than it was for him to do so. (At least that's what I told my folks was the reason I should be spending so much time down there "helping" Floyd.) In the years to follow, as TV sets were made more compact and table models were popular, Floyd got one of those and had it mounted next to his bed where it could be watched after he had left his chair for the day. Remote controls were not generally available then, so Richie made up a special tool attached to the end of an old wooden cane. With this, Floyd was able to turn his set on or off as well as change channels while still being about four feet away.

CHAPTER 16

FISHING IN WAUSHAKUM POND
1950- 1959

By the start of the fishing season in April 1950, Floyd was more than ready to do some serious angling. He had me buy him a fishing license, which at that time cost $3.25. He pinned it right to the visored cap he always wore outdoors so he would not forget it. He wasn't sure his battery would be up to more than one round trip to the fishing run, so he didn't want to have to go back for it. He had agreed to wait for my dad or me before venturing out the first time on his own for a trip down to the lake, just in case there were any troubles with his powered chair. He also knew that he'd need a little help in the actual attempts to catch a fish.

He was a sight to behold on his first outing to the lake. It was quite chilly, with a brisk wind, causing the surface of the water to be very choppy. Of course the cold breeze blew directly in towards the end of the run, so his casts were going to be right into the wind. He was dressed warmly with his corduroy baseball cap pulled snugly on, the license proudly attached. The look of determination etched onto his face spoke of a man on a mission. A man, setting out to do a man's work. He was also planning that a fish fry would soon be taking place in his room, or at least the tasty result of having Angela cook up a mess of newly caught fish.

He steadfastly steered his machine along the hot top and down the gentle incline right to the start of the run. It seemed to me that he was gripping the old shovel handle harder than was necessary. I think he was trying to hold the chair back from accelerating down the slope. Richie had designed this machine so that that should not be a problem. It should run at the same speed on level ground, or down the inclines. Running up hill, of course would always put more of a strain on the system, slowing it down, but the way it was geared and chained, it should not accelerate too much going downhill; he hoped. Floyd drove himself very nicely, right out on to the run and slowly out to within a few inches from the end.

The first several times he put a hook in the water, he had me help him quite a bit. I had carried his rod and reel, tackle box and a long-handled net to the end of the run. What an optimist! He made sure I brought the net so we could safely land all the fish he was sure he would catch. I would set up for him whatever he wanted to use as bait, or if he decided to use a plug or spoon or other artificial lure, I'd attach that for him. I also helped him to cast whatever was on the end of his line out to the spot where he figured a nice bass was just waiting to be caught. More than once I had to remind myself who it was that was supposed to be doing the fishing here and stop myself from casting and retrieving.

His own first few casts resulted in snarling backlashes, with the lure sometimes snapping back almost onto the run where we had located ourselves. It took several minutes to untangle the bird's nest mess in the reel after each such mishap. I found that patience, at least under these circumstances, was not his long suit. We changed lures, at his insistence, about every second or third cast. After less than half an hour we had managed to wet at least a half dozen plugs and several spoons. No fish. He said that he was sure that if we used a good ol' worm on a hook suspended by a bobber, our luck would change. The only problem was that the ground at this time of year was not quite ready to offer up such sure-fire bait.

After a couple of hours of flailing about, with him almost tossing the fishing rod out into the water by accident a few times as he learned to cast, and getting chilled to the bone, we both agreed to call it a day. At first, I thought he would feel discouraged by his discovery of just how difficult it was going to be for him to be able to manipulate his fishing gear. Having only one functioning arm and hand to use to attach sharply pointed lures to the ends of his lines, and then casting and retrieving them with any smoothness or semblance of control, seemed to me almost too much of a handicap. I guess I really didn't know this man as well as I had thought.

I helped him navigate off the run to the flat hot top area at its base. He had to back up the entire 15-foot length of this wooden pier. Although Richie had fastened strong two by sixes on edge along both sides and the end of the run, to form walls, it was still a bit spooky to think of this new chair being backed up and possibly coming awfully close to the edges. He did just fine, with me worrying the whole way for nothing. I must admit though that thoughts that had crossed my mind were, what if his chair ran away with him? What if his motor-activating button should seize up? Or what if the drive linkage came apart on his way down the slope and he found himself freewheeling down towards the lake? There was no emergency brake. What if, what if, what if? Best not to worry about such things. My dad knew how to build stuff that worked.

When we got back into his room, with his battery holding up just fine, he told me that he had some things to discuss with Richard. He had envisioned several additions he wanted my father to add to the end of the run and a couple of minor attachments to the side of his chair. These new "do-dads" would help him with his attempts at proper form for casting, as well as to help him land the big ones. Far from being discouraged or downhearted at the degree of difficulty he faced in order to become proficient as an angler, he was convinced that he would soon be performing like an old hand. Of course, as his experience had shown, there was no doubt that anything he asked Richard to implement, would be translated into something even better than what he had hoped for.

Carlo Belloli and sometimes his younger brother, Eddie spent many an evening after work, visiting with Floyd and encouraging his grand schemes to attack the bass and pickerel in our lake. They talked at length about the various lures they had used and what time of the day they thought best for maximum results. They were partial to early mornings and evenings, when the water was still and the sun low. They offered the thought that even if you caught nothing but a cold, just being at the edge of a lake at those times and tossing out whatever lures or bait you felt like trying, simply couldn't be beat. The sense of peacefulness and the natural beauty all around, combined to rejuvenate one's spirits. Of course, if you happened to catch a few nice-sized fish, so much the better. Carlo pointed out that there were basically two kinds of fishermen. There was the guy who fished to take home his supper, and there was the sportsman who carefully returned to the lake nearly every fish he caught. This latter type would keep only trophy-size fish. Floyd figured that he was the type that would thoroughly love being out at the edge of the water, at any time of day or night. He was the type that would be thrilled to pieces if he could actually manage to cast and retrieve a variety of baits and lures. And he was the type that would then be overjoyed and probably overwhelmed if he could hook and land any good size fish, let alone a trophy.

As the days rolled by, Floyd's single-minded determination and constant focus on learning his specialized techniques resulted in remarkable progress of his fishing skills. Richie had indeed implemented at the end of the run, the "do-dads" Floyd had dreamed up, as well as special holders affixed to one side of his chair so he could transport his fishing rods down to the lake. By summer, he was able to rig up the outfit he wanted to use, cast pretty much in the general direction he intended to, and reel in a lure. That was the tough part; reeling in the lure. Once he had made his cast, he had to quickly jamb the handle of the fishing rod into his left hand, previously pried open by him, and then use his right hand to clamp the left firmly around the handle. Then he would turn the crank on the reel a few turns with his right hand, and work the tip of the rod by pivoting his wrist upward. Whenever he was lucky enough to get a strike by his prey, it was very difficult for him to set the hook and for days he would complain about "the one that got away". Whenever he switched to using worms lazily twisting on a hook suspended by a bobber, he would usually wind up with a fish, since it often swallowed the hook and simply couldn't get free.

A lot of his learning experiences took place while I was at school and Richie was at work. Many times the first thing I would do after returning home from school, was to head down to where he would be parked at the end of the run, usually in trouble with some aspect of his experiments. I helped the budding "Isaac Walton" to rig up an assortment of wire leaders with swivel clasps at both ends. We connected his favorite plugs and spoons onto one end of each of these leaders, so that he wouldn't have to deal with that little complication down at the run. This way all he would have to do at water's edge was to connect the leader attached to whatever lure or hook he wanted to try, to a swivel clasp attached to the end of the line in his fishing rod. All set up in this manner were at least the following lures: *Jitterbug* (4 different colors), *Hula-Popper*, *Flatfish* (4 different colors), red and white spoons (3 or 4 sizes), and an assortment of different size bait hooks with sinkers crimped onto their leaders. A variety of red and white bobbers with spring-loaded attachment clips, were also available to use with the bait hooks. Each of these pre-assembled leader-and-lure combos was individually and carefully packaged into a plastic bag in such a way that it wouldn't tangle; at least not right away.

I was charged with the task of digging up some fresh worms for those times when it seemed as though worms were the only things the fish wanted. Those times became more and more frequent and usually resulted in Floyd actually catching something. Even if these "somethings" were kivvers and red perch, they always put up a good fight and he really enjoyed catching them. Mr. Murphy (our cat) always seemed to know when this strange creature who noisily rolled around our yard, had switched to fishing with worms. He would appear out of nowhere and trot out on to the run almost as soon as a bobber could be seen floating a short distance out. In short order, Floyd would be reeling in a meal for the cat. Poor Murphy had to wait, sometimes several minutes while the fisherman worked at getting the flopping food to where he could get the hook out. Doing that job with one hand took a lot of practice and patience, combined with the use of one or more of those special aids Richie had made. To make the task even more difficult, Floyd had to constantly push the cat's face out of his way until the hook was safely removed from the quarry. No one could believe how many kivvers or perch that cat could put away. There were days when Floyd would set out to the end of the run with one purpose in mind; to catch supper for "the damned cat."

Although I did provide quite a bit of help in the initial episodes of rigging up a variety of lures, there was one area where Floyd excelled while I was all thumbs. That was the whole business of tying knots. With only his one functioning hand, aided a bit by the vise-like clamp of his left hand, he could manage to tie a wide variety of knots, many of which I had never even heard of, much less knew how to tie. He explained that growing up in Texas he had learned knot tying as a critical component of life on a ranching farm. He insisted that I should learn to do more than tie the clumsy old knot I relied on for every occasion. He talked about and did his best to demonstrate a bunch of different knots, explaining the advantages of each and which one to use for which particular purpose. One of his favorites was the half hitch, which could be used in various combinations for tying a line on to something else. After watching how he tied it, I did my best to duplicate it, but only earned his good-natured ribbing about the result; "Looks more like a half-assed knot than a half hitch to me."

Very often, when he would be parked out at the end of the run and concentrating on improving his casting technique while trying to land whatever might take his lure, he would be accompanied by his faithful pal, Spots. Basking in the sun while stretched out next to Floyd's chair was something our pooch was particularly fond of. Whether he felt that he was in some way protecting Floyd from whatever dangers lurked so close to the pond, or if dozing in the direct sun out there was the main attraction, if Floyd was there, Spots would be there. When the spirit moved him, Mr. Murphy would saunter out occasionally to join these two.

One particularly fine, warm fall day in 1950, I witnessed an event involving the cat and the dog that brought laughter to us for years whenever it would be recalled. I had just come home from high school for the day and walked down to where Floyd and his animal friends were stationed in the hot sun at the end of the run. Spots was stretched out, sound asleep on his side next to the left side of the chair, his paws twitching in response to whatever he was chasing in his dreams. Murphy was also sound asleep, but he was positioned right at the very end of the run, facing out toward deep water. Other than the fact that he was asleep, one would have thought that he was in a hunting crouch and about to pounce upon some unsuspecting prey. As I approached the back of Floyd's chair and asked if he had any luck, he replied that the fish were not being very cooperative that day and was about to change to a different lure. As I stood there behind him, he reeled in his line and then pushed the handle end of the rod down under his left arm so that he could reach the lure dangling from the tip. The rod handle got stuck a little on the left side of the chair, so he gave it a good solid shove downwards. The dreaming dog, with his tongue hanging out of his mouth, was struck smartly in his rib cage by the fishing rod handle. His reaction was immediate and predictable. He let out a howl of pain, a combination bark and cry, and rapidly scrambled to his feet. The soundly sleeping Mr. Murphy's reaction was pure instinct and no thought. He took off in an instant, leaping out in a high arc and splashing about six feet out from the end of the run. At the height of his jump, he actually tried to run in mid-air like a cartoon cat might do, but of course to no avail. His belly flop resulted in his disappearance from sight. Meanwhile, poor Spots was standing there, blinking the sleep from his eyes and trying to figure out what had happened to him. Suddenly, the cat's head came popping up out of the water and he swam for the run. When the bewildered dog saw this ugly black creature heading for us, he immediately went into "attack mode", forgetting completely who it was that had been sleeping there right next to him. He barked and growled and snapped his teeth in a very convincing imitation of a mean machine. I tried my best to convince him that it was his pal, Murphy, out there just trying to swim to the shore and to somehow regain his lost dignity. This was not an attacking creature from the black lagoon that we needed to be protected from. Spots would not be persuaded, even as I physically restrained him as much as I could and yelled at him that, "It's Murphy! It's only Murphy! Leave him alone." The cat's original plan of trying to scramble up onto the run was changed when he realized that Spots was about to bite his head off. With me holding my dog back, the cat finally made it to shore and climbed up the nearest tree to escape his tormentor.

Spots continued to bark at his treed quarry, proud of himself for keeping us safe. Finally, as I continued to admonish him that it was Murphy up there, while I practically rolled on the ground in laughter, he suddenly understood. Such a display of remorse and shame was probably never before seen in any dog. His barking stopped, his tail curled down under his hind legs, and he lowered his head to the ground with a look of deep sadness for his error. After several minutes, when the cat was sure that it was safe, he climbed to the ground and walked, still dripping wet and looking a sight, directly up to the totally humiliated mutt. Spots, with his head still lowered in remorse seemed to say with his eyes, "Gosh, I'm sorry Murphy. I didn't know it was you." Like lightning, a paw with claws extended slashed out from the highly annoyed cat, inflicting what must have been considerable pain in the poor dog's nose. His reaction to that punch in the nose was to follow behind the retreating cat, his head still bowed with an expression that tried to convey how ashamed he was of himself. I had turned Floyd around in his chair as soon as the cat had made it out of the water so that he could watch this unbelievable show. For several days both Floyd and I would tease poor old Spots about his big adventure with the mean lake creature. He somehow seemed to understand our teasing and whenever we talked about it he would look ashamed. Mr.

Murphy did not return to our yard for at least a week. When he finally came back, it was as though nothing had happened between these two old buddies.

Floyd maintained fairly regular correspondence with Edith and occasionally would place a phone call to her. She was now living with dear friends who looked after her needs at their home in a town nearby. One of his telephone conversations with her had really surprised him. He found that even though her health, which had been deteriorating for years, was very poor, once again she was back in the musical spotlight. There was a beautiful, pastoral and serene place of worship several miles away in Rindge, New Hampshire. Situated on a pine-crested hilltop with a breath-taking view, it is a place of natural beauty. It had been a center of spiritual nourishment for people of all faiths from the time of its first service in August 1945. Called *The Cathedral of the Pines*, Edith loved the place from the first moment she saw it. Back when she first discovered it she would tell Floyd how different this cathedral was since it had no stained glass windows, and not even a building at all. The floor of the "cathedral" was the fertile earth, the carpeting was made up of a myriad of pine needles, the columns typically found in places of worship were the trunks of the pine trees, and the open sky was the dome. She knew that this beautiful site had been selected by a young B-17 bomber pilot by the name of Lt. Sanderson (Sandy) Sloane as the place he would build a home for his wife, Peggy, and himself when the war was over. Sadly, he lost his life when his B-17 was shot down over Germany in 1944. The Cathedral was created by his parents, Douglas and Sibyl Sloane, as a combination place of worship and a war memorial dedicated to those men and women who gave their lives in the service of their country. Edith always felt moved when she stood near the stone multi-denominational "Altar of the Nation" overlooking Mt. Monadnock in the distance.

In the spring of 1950, Edith was invited by the founder, Dr. Douglas Sloane, to give a program of her own compositions and was told that it would be the first concert ever held there. She was delighted and honored to be asked to provide such a concert. Since she was no longer able to play her own music the way she wanted it rendered, she invited a talented pianist friend and locally well-known contralto, named Phylis Durgin to perform. On August 17th, 1950 at 3:00 PM, with many of her friends and admirers as well as younger music lovers in attendance, the air was filled with the lovely and soothing sounds of her best compositions. When the concert was over, she received many of the guests in a reception in newly constructed Hilltop House adjacent to the main Cathedral where the Chaplain's Altar and artifacts from all over the world are housed. The Chaplain's altar is a memorial to the first American Chaplain killed in action in World War I and to two noted Chaplains of World War II. It was another very special day in Edith's life; a life that had been full of special days.

By the end of summer that year, Floyd's inventory of lures and leaders had drastically diminished. There was an awful lot of unsavory stuff submerged out in the water at the end of the run. Old sunken logs, and as the days warmed up, heavy growths of tough weeds, had claimed many of his favorite lures. There really was no telling why they were his favorites, because he had yet to catch anything (except old logs and weeds) with them, but they looked deadly. But when they got hung up, his only choice was to pull as hard as possible, eventually snapping his line.

He began to voice the thought that if only he could reach a bit further to one side or the other from where the run allowed his best casts to go, he could surely do better. He had often seen fish jumping right out of the water, but always it was just too far away for him to get a lure near the spot. Before long, Richie built two new, bigger and better runs and provided hot-topped paths leading down to them. The original one, the one that Floyd had been using all along, was in a very picturesque part of our property. It was located between two huge pine trees that were right at the water's edge, with beautiful shrubs and what my dad called ironwood trees, growing nearby. It was very near the part of the shoreline that I called "the point". The cove, and Monkey Island were off to the right as you stood out on this run, while the large part of the lake which faced South towards Ashland, was around the point to your left.

The first of the two new runs was installed about 60 feet to the right of the original one and more into the cove. It jutted out a little farther and was a bit wider. Standing at its end, one could see the island off at about the two o'clock position and perhaps 200 feet away. There were several places near this run where lily pads floated on the surface. When their pure white pond lilies were in bloom, they added an extra touch of beauty to an already picturesque spot. This definitely looked like a much better fishing spot, but also had more weeds to snag lures. There were also quite a few birch trees and other types of trees and brush hanging out over the bank at this location. A partly submerged log off to the right looked for sure like it must be the haunt of "Mr. King-sized Bass". It was a couple of weeks after this run was in place before the path that led to it could be covered with hot top paving. Until then, Floyd had no way to get onto this perfect looking spot. He was very excited about the prospects of fishing from there and had a hard time suppressing his enthusiasm.

It didn't help matters any, when I landed a couple of large pickerel within a few minutes of the first time I fished from there shortly after it was built. Finally, Floyd was able to drive over the hot top, after just barely letting it cool off enough so that his wheels wouldn't sink in to it. He was grinning from ear to ear as he made his first strong, and what appeared to be, well-aimed cast from the end of this fine, new place. His new lure went straight onto the portion of the partly submerged log that protruded from the water. He had managed to hit a target of only a few square inches of rotten old wood, and buried the hooks of his plug firmly in place. He was fuming and sputtering, while I could not restrain myself from laughing at such a comical sight. In a matter of seconds, he too was seeing the humor in what had just occurred, although he obviously didn't find it as funny as I did. I quickly hopped in my little rowboat, which was tied up nearby, and in no time at all, had rescued the errant lure, dropping it in the water for him to reel in. I was less than half way back to shore, when he started sputtering again. When I looked in his direction, his fishing rod was bent nearly double. He had snagged the lure on an unseen obstacle. With some effort, I was able to get it loose and this time, he reeled it all the way in cleanly.

From that shaky beginning, he made it a point to always use floating lures such as his *Jitterbug*, or worms on a short leader from a bobber, when fishing around the old log. Being spooked by this first experience, he spent the first few days at this new run fishing mostly off to the left side, but still catching only bluegills. When he finally did go back near the log, darned if he didn't catch his first bass. It was a beauty, weighing nearly 3 pounds. He was shaking with excitement. This was what he had been dreaming of; what he worked for. I cleaned it and my mother cooked it for him. He insisted that we all share in his first real catch, promising that there would be many more like that one. It was delicious.

Spurred on by this catch to aim for greater prizes, Floyd devoted even more energy, if such a thing was possible, to improving everything about his fishing prowess. And over the rest of the summer, he had managed to land two more nice-size bass and a few pickerel. It didn't bother him at all that the latter of these fishes were loaded with bones, making them usually not too much of a joy to eat. He gobbled up the well-cooked bony fish, prepared by my mother, and gave rave reviews of the sweet taste and how nicely the meat fell away from the bones. Having such a talented cook on the premises was a pretty nice deal. Of course, someone had to clean the catch before my mother would allow it in her kitchen, so I provided this service whenever I was around. I put together a special board with a clamp mounted on it so Floyd could clean his own fish, but it was too much of a hassle for him at first. Eventually, we got it to the point where he could do a passable job of it. Mr. Murphy got more kivvers and perch than he had ever dreamed of (if cats dream) and actually walked away from one or two fresh offerings from Floyd.

The other new run my dad built was in the part of the lake that could be seen by looking straight out Floyd's door, and faced south into the large part of the lake. It really didn't have the allure of the other two, however. It just didn't look like such a promising spot, and fishing from there never did produce anything exciting. But it was a much better place from which I could dive in and swim around, even if water snakes were often seen gliding by. Floyd lost interest in that location quickly, and concentrated on the other two runs in what he thought of as the "good-looking areas".

Floyd had by this time developed a special bond with my dog, Spots. Our high-strung Dalmatian must have understood somehow that this person who never got out of his chair to walk around like everybody else, needed constant protection, or at least pretty steady companionship. It was difficult to imagine Spots protecting anybody from anything, since he made it a point to avoid danger at every turn. He lived to be loved by us. To be petted, and gently played with and made a fuss over, was all he wanted from life. But whenever Floyd buzzed around outdoors, Spots was there, watching and worrying over him. He would run in circles around his chair, sometimes nearly getting crashed into, but always expressing concern that this unusual person was going too fast, or may be headed for an unplanned drive into the lake. The first few times Floyd drove out onto one of the runs, the poor dog actually whined in fear for him. Eventually, he figured out that this was normal and not to be so worried about, but he never let down his vigilance. When Floyd would scratch Spots' ears and speak softly in his good ol' Texas drawl about what a good boy he was, the dog would sit there, with his head in Floyd's lap and gaze soulfully into his eyes. I think it was good therapy for them both.

The cat, on the other hand was still his independent cat-like self. Once in a while, he would curl up on the ground, or out on the run next to where Floyd and Spots might be parked, and permit them the privilege of his company. Then he would be off to parts and places unknown, returning sometimes days later with various parts of his anatomy in pretty bad shape. He was a hunter by nature and he was true to his instincts. One of our neighbors reported that he saw our Mr. Murphy dragging a dead rabbit through his back yard.

Floyd was only interesting to the cat when its belly was nearly empty and Floyd was fishing. I was standing next to where Floyd was parked out in the middle of our back yard on a warm, sunny day chatting about nothing in particular, when Murphy came strolling down towards us. He held his tail straight up behind him as he headed our way, looking as though he was coming for a visit. Floyd called out in a sweet, high voice, "Here, kitty, kitty, --- Here, kitty, kitty." It really looked like the cat was responding to Floyd's calls. But, as he got practically along side, he imperiously twitched his tail even further straight up and, without even looking our way, sauntered right on by. Floyd continued in the same high-pitched voice, "Here, kitty, kitty. Go to hell kitty, kitty."

When the leaves on the trees all around the lake were glowing red, yellow, and orange, with the summer having passed all too quickly, Floyd sometimes would spend his time just being outside, looking at the beauty all around him, enjoying the unique aromas that the fallen leaves gave off. He told me he had always loved New England autumns. Roy Greene had driven him, in fall seasons long ago, sometimes in a specially rigged car, to many different locations within a few miles of their home. Mr. Greene would set him up in his old portable wheelchair wherever Floyd saw something that excited his artistic passion. He had found that being outside and sketching watercolor or pastel renditions of what he saw, soothed his inner being and gave him great joy in those days. Now, sitting out in his new back yard at the edge of a lake, surrounded with trees in a blaze of color, made him think of new lures he would have to try out next year, and new fishing tackle he might buy. He had proven to the world that he could paint. Now he wanted to prove to himself that he could be a real fisherman.

When he reflected back on the progress he had made since he first dipped a line in his lake, he realized that he had indeed come a long way. But he was frustrated by the quality of his catches; too many kivvers and perch, not enough bass and pickerel. He often mentioned how he would see a nice fish jump right out of the water, but always out of his reach with even his best casts. Or he would see someone across the cove from him land a good one. Once in a while, he'd watch some kids row their boat over to the island, get out and fish from shore there and in no time at all head back, holding up a nice catch of good-sized bass for him to admire. He began to envision ways to launch his lures out many times farther than conventional casting rods would permit. He presented Richie with a half-baked idea of a spring-loaded tube from which he could shoot a specially designed fishing plug out to 50 or more feet. That ought to give him a big advantage. Maybe they could work out something that used gunpowder to propel the lure way the heck out there! Wow, this might even be something that could be patented and become a moneymaker for him.

When Richie listened to Floyd's ideas and realized what it was that Floyd really wanted, he fell silent for a few minutes. Floyd imagined that his inventive pal was mentally conceptualizing the details for a high-powered fishing whiz-bang of a device, and he would soon be the proud owner of something really unique. He was completely unprepared for Richie's next words.

"It seems to me", my dad softly said, "that what you really should have is a boat. That way, you can fish anywhere on this lake that looks good to you. What do you think?"

What did he think? When someone said the word "boat" the mental picture that went along with it in Floyd's mind was something with a pointed front, a rounded bottom, and something that could easily tip over. Something that he would have absolutely no way to get into, unless someone lifted him out of his chair and placed him in it. And it sounded like something from which he could easily topple into the lake. What in the world could Richie be thinking? Why would he suggest such an outrageous thought? He never knew my dad to be a drinker, but he thought that perhaps he had taken a couple of extra glasses of wine or something with his dinner. He'd just have to postpone this discussion about "projectile fishing" to another time, when Richie was sober.

My dad must have read Floyd's mind, because he began explaining his ideas by sketching out a rough plan for what he was envisioning. With a simple drawing and a few words, Richie soon had Floyd understanding that his boat would be more like a "barge", with a flat bottom. It would be wide enough to be very stable and could not possibly be made to tip over. It would be constructed of marine plywood and waterproof glue. There would be a ramp built into the front of it, so that when it was tied up at the end of the run, Floyd could easily drive right on down and into the boat. He wasn't quite sure just yet how Floyd would propel his boat, but he had seen something in one of Floyd's fishing magazines that might work. A little more thought about this whole project was going to be needed, but the more that he talked about it, the more excited he became.

Floyd wanted to talk about it more now - - much more. This sounded like another dream. Could this one come true also? What a fantastic idea! No more limits! The whole lake would be fair game! When Richie left Floyd that evening to go upstairs and to bed, neither man got a good night's sleep. While Floyd spent most of the night trying to picture what this unexpected discussion might actually yield, my dad was working out the details in his mind. Richie knew that safety would be the number one requirement. He was confident that he could build a flat-bottomed barge, and build it strong enough and watertight enough to meet that goal with margin to spare. How to incorporate something that Floyd could easily use to make this craft move around on the lake, was a bigger question. It was obvious that a small gasoline powered outboard motor was out of the question, being far too much for Floyd to safely handle.

After a long search through back issues of some of Floyd's favorite magazines, such as *Outdoor Life*, *Field and Stream* and *Sports Afield*, my dad found the article he was looking for in a special boating issue of one of them. It was an evaluation of a relatively new gimmick called a "Hydro-Fin". It was designed to be clamped onto the flat stern of a small rowboat as a silent substitute for a motor. A fisherman who had his boat equipped with one of these ingenious devices could move into good fishing waters in nearly total silence. It seemed that the idea was to use your motor until you got near where the fish were supposed to be, then, take it off, or move it out of the way, and attach the Hydro-Fin in its place. You could then move around a local area in relative quiet. The "fin" part of it was under water during its use, and was a thin piece of zinc-plated steel about 8 by 10 inches in size. It would be made to move in the water in a manner resembling a fish's tail. By pushing on the arm, which was above the back end of the boat and facing the user, and forcing it to move from side to side, the pivoted underwater fin would undulate like a fish, providing a solid thrust against the water, causing the boat to move forward. To go straight ahead required the fin operator to push on the handle equally as far from right to left. To steer to one side or the other, required simply pushing mostly on one side or the other, then getting back to straight travel, required equal size thrusts about the center again. This invention was meant for relatively small rowboats operated by able-bodied sailors. Would Floyd actually be able to drive his barge this way? Richie had some doubts, but it was worth a try. But the boat did not as yet exist. Details such as that could wait until next spring when, if all went as envisioned, there would be a craft on which to try it out.

Predictably, when the topic of building a boat for Floyd to use all by himself was brought up at the supper table one evening, my mother couldn't believe her ears. She quickly pointed out all the dangers such a crazy idea could pose. To say that she was not thrilled with the plan would be understating her reaction. Of course she was right to be concerned about the attendant perils Floyd would face if he had a boat. Richie had thought them all through and knew in his heart that not only could this boat be completely safe, it was something that Floyd would enjoy beyond his ability to express. For him to cruise around in our cove and fish every nook and cranny, every sunken log and every place that looked like the "perfect spot", and to do so on his own, under his own power, would be beyond Floyd's wildest dreams.

Sometime during the first part of November of 1950, a few 4 by 8 foot sheets of high quality, ¾ inch marine plywood were brought into the furnace room next to Floyd's apartment. Good quality, straight and knot-free 2 by 4s were ripped on the little table saw to make ribs 1¾ inches wide. Floyd watched closely each evening and weekend, as Richie and I (mostly Richie) worked to cut out the individual parts of his boat: bottom, sides, stern, and plow-like bow. We used Weldwood waterproof glue, which required blending and mixing just the right small amount of water with its powder to make a paste of perfect consistency. Special brass nails were driven to assemble the parts, which were smeared with liberal coatings of our fresh glue at their interfaces. It wasn't long before Floyd could see what this thing was going to look like. It was nearly a full four feet wide and close to eight feet long, with sides about 14 or 16 inches high. When looked at from above, it was a simple rectangle, not looking very boat-like at all, but putting one in mind of something that might be used to mix up a large batch of concrete or mortar.

The special ribs were attached (glue and nails) every foot or so along both sides and across the bottom. The back, or as we tried to remember to call it, the "stern" was made straight up and down and a short top of ¼ inch thick plywood about a foot long projected forward, forming a small shelf with space below. The front, rarely called the "bow" angled back about 45 degrees. This looked about right for making it easy to plow through the waves. A floor of ½ inch thick plywood was attached from front to back, over the cross-wise ribs that had been fastened to the inside of the bottom. Then a ramp of the same material, the full width of the inside of the boat was installed. It projected forward about 8 inches ahead of the sides, and met the floor at a point about halfway to the stern. This allowed the slope of the ramp to be as gentle as possible, even if it did look pretty steep.

Richie said that he'd make some modifications to Floyd's favorite run next spring, in order to accommodate the boat. What he had planned, was to add long 2 x 8s extending out on both sides of the existing run, about a foot above the water level. They would be a little shorter than the overall length of the boat and would form mooring walls. To prevent them from scratching the paint off the boat, his plan was to attach cut-up old tires to them. But this idea would also have to wait until the next year's fishing season, or more realistically right after the ice was out, to actually implement.

Visitors to Floyd's apartment were in awe of the construction that was going on in the furnace room. Several folks, even after seeing the size and shape and strength of the vessel taking shape, expressed real concern about the wisdom of completing this project. Neither Floyd nor Richie had any doubts whatsoever. Nor did Carlo and his buddies. They couldn't wait to be out there with Floyd, and they all applauded Richie's design. They pointed out to Floyd that none of them could ever have thought up such a fantastic idea, and even if they might have thought of it, they surely wouldn't have been able to make it a reality.

My dad and I turned the heavy barge upside-down on a couple of strong sawhorses. We fastened a narrow strip of wood, sawed about an inch wide from a piece of oak flooring, to the outside bottom from stem to stern. We thought that this would help allow the boat to slip through the water and stay going straight more easily than if there was no such piece there. We thought of it as a mini keel. We had no idea if this was a good plan, but figured that we could always remove it later, or even adjust its dimensions: another thing that would be resolved when the boat was actually floating.

With the vessel turned back right side up and sitting on the floor, with strips of wood under both sides to keep it from rocking on our "keel", gunwales were added along both sides. The rear deck, or shelf was finished off. Also, a long narrow compartment with a lockable hinged cover was mounted along the right side. (The "right side" in nautical terms should be referred to as "starboard side", but we paid no attention to such terminology.) This would be where Floyd would keep his fishing rods, with their reels mounted to them. We made sure that, once he was sitting in his chair in the boat facing aft, he would be able to reach across his body with his right arm and open or close the cover as well as extend his hand into this compartment to remove whatever he needed. He practiced this move over and over by reaching to his left while sitting in the middle of his room, with us measuring just where his limits were.

By Christmas, most of the boat-building job was completed. Each morning the first thing Floyd would do upon getting out of bed and into his chair, was to drive the few feet to the doorway of the furnace room and gaze at what had been born there. He spent quite a bit of time picking out a good color for his floating fishing station. He read up on what colors were least likely to bother his quarry (mostly bass) but admitted to being confused about the contradictory reports. Green seemed to be a favorite of some anglers, while blue and also gray were reported to be the best choice in the opinion of other "experts". By a stroke of good luck, the choice he made, gray, just happened to be what my dad had already purchased when he spotted a good sale on high quality boat paint somewhere.

We applied the required coats of primer on all surfaces, even removing the keel to paint under it, and ensuring that all surfaces were covered. We lifted the floor out of the bottom of the boat and removed the fishing rod compartment to paint everywhere. By the end of January, two coats of the finish gray paint had been applied. The odor permeated the house for days, but Floyd loved it. We all had to admit that by golly, the darned thing looked sea-worthy, or at least, lake-worthy.

All through the months of January, February and March of 1951, Floyd busied himself with preparations for what he anticipated to be the most exciting adventure he was to have in a long time; fishing all around the lake in his new boat. Richie suggested that once he got the boat in the water, Floyd really should limit his travels to the general confines of the cove, and not venture out into the wide open, deeper parts of the lake around the point. At least until we had some experience with how this strange looking craft would handle out there, this was a sensible plan. The natural geography of the cove provided a bit of protection from the heavier winds and waves out around the point. Besides, it always seemed that the best fishing in this pond was right out there, a little distance from his run, and around the island.

With the boat still "landlocked" in the furnace room, no one was at all sure that Floyd would really be able to handle everything it would take to manipulate it on his own. We all felt that, at least for several weeks, and maybe for all times, one or more of us would be part of his crew. Once the barge was floating at the end of the run, and tied up to it, he would have to drive his chair right on down and into it. He would need to be sure that he had taken along with him all the tackle and bait he would want. When he was all set and in place, he would have to somehow shove off and get the boat moving away from the run, and then operate whatever the propulsion mechanism turned out to be, in order to travel across the water to his destination. It would be a real plus to have an anchor so he wouldn't drift away from where he wanted to fish. How he would manage that aspect was a bit of a mystery at this time. If he managed to hook a fish, would he be able to haul it aboard and get it off the lure without having it jump or fall somewhere into the boat where he wouldn't be able to reach it? The big question at this time still was, how was he going to make this thing move in the water, and in the direction he wanted? And the even bigger question; how was he supposed to get this tub back between the mooring walls Richie envisioned, and get it securely fastened in place, since he would be facing away from the front of the boat at all times?

All these issues and more convinced us that we would be spending a lot of time taking turns helping out with all this upcoming fun. And it surely did sound like fun, paddling around and generally assisting with whatever was required. Carlo and several of his buddies couldn't wait to get out there and be part of the Walser crew. There were a few minor arguments about how many "helpers" could safely be on board at any one time. Richie was firm in the thought that it would be trouble if more than one other person was out on the boat with Floyd while he was flipping his multi-hooked lures around in all directions. He also was fairly sure that he would eventually be able to work everything out so that Floyd would in fact, with some practice, be able to safely do it all himself. I must admit that I wouldn't have been a bit surprised to find that when others were at their jobs or in school, Floyd would be spending most of his time fishing from his new boat while it was tied firmly in place at the end of the run.

As soon as the weather made it even a little bit feasible to work outdoors, my dad made some modifications to the end of the run to add mooring capability for what was soon to be launched, or at least placed in the water when the ice left for good. Carlo jokingly questioned Richie about getting the boat out of the furnace room by asking, "Hey Richie, you ain't gonna have to take that boat apart to get it out are ya? Remember the iceboat you built in my father's cellar? And the trailer you couldn't get out of your garage? It'd be a real shame to have to cut that nice piece of work in pieces to get it out!" Richie had thought this one through carefully and knew there would be no repeat embarrassments with this project, since it could easily be carried (by a couple of strong guys) on edge right out through the garage.

A Hydro-Fin was delivered in late February after having been ordered by Floyd several weeks previously. It was a very sturdily built product and looked as though it would hold up to heavy use, but would its new owner really be able to work it successfully? Richie incorporated it smoothly into the aft end of the boat, then removed all but its mounting bracket to prevent it from being injured. Provisions for supporting Floyd's fishing rods while he fished were also built into the rear end of the boat, as well as a large flat mirror. Richie thought that providing a good-size mirror, mounted at the proper angle would allow Floyd to see where he was headed while he moved the boat through the water, since he would always be facing aft. Hopefully, he would be able to navigate into the dock by watching his progress in the mirror. It would be tricky, since he would have to compensate for the reverse picture of the world that the mirror would provide, but it was worth a shot. Richie was trying to do all he could to make this vessel one that would not require the assistance of other people. Even though he knew that it might take quite a while for Floyd to learn all the techniques he would need to master, he wanted him to be able to take solo voyages so he could feel truly independent.

In March, with most of the winter's snow out of the way, some modifications were made to the run, which was now being retrofitted to be the mooring dock for this strange new craft. One of the cleverest elements of these modifications was a deceptively simple-looking addition. It was a small painted piece of ¾ inch thick plywood (about 8 by 10 inches) attached to the middle of the end of the run by means of a special hinge mounted at one end. The hinge was fastened to the end of the board farthest from the edge of the run. It was a vital component to assure Floyd a safe means to drive onto the boat. When the boat would finally be floating in its dock and securely tied in place, the large built-in ramp, which made up the forward-most part of the boat, would rest against the end of the run and project slightly over it. This little hinged board would be angled so that it lay on top of the boat's protruding front and formed a short ramp up from the run and onto the boat. The idea was that as soon as the front wheel of Floyd's chair rolled up on the hinged board and he continued to drive forward, his weight would force the front end of the boat down until its ramp was in full contact with the end of the run. He could then continue to drive the rest of the way down and to the end of the boat. When he shoved off, the hinge would allow the little board to drop down flat to the run where it would not be in the way for the returning fisherman's docking procedure. A feature of the way the board's hinge was mounted allowed it to be repositioned for proper reuse after backing out of the boat and onto the run. Simple, but ingenious. And it worked perfectly.

When this run was built, Richie had the deep-water end of it supported by means of a very clever jacking mechanism that easily allowed him to raise or lower it as the level of the water in the lake changed from spring to fall. This feature was vital to proper boarding and exiting the boat since the distance from the water's surface to the top of the run remained relatively constant throughout the seasons; so long as Richie remembered to operate the jack.

The long 2 by 8s that projected out over the water on either side of the run, had cut-up old tires mounted to them. They would protect the sides of the boat as it lay tied up there and bobbed around with the waves. They also would minimize the scraping that was bound to occur whenever the ship left port, and especially when it attempted to get back in.

Due to a combination of bad weather and other priorities, it wasn't until about the middle of April, in the year of Our Lord 1951, on a Sunday, that the boat was ceremoniously carried from the furnace room, out through the garage, down to the lake, and finally placed into the water next to its pier. Floyd was as excited as I had ever seen him. He bundled up against the cold breeze that was blowing, and drove out and around to the garage door to "supervise". He admonished my dad and me, and Carlo, who came over to help with the christening to, "Take it easy! Be careful! Watch it! Look out!" until we finally had his baby floating at the edge of the lake. He drove on the paved surface as close as he could get to where the boat was happily swimming with a guide rope fastened to her front. "Any leaks?", he wanted to know. Before Richie could reply that there wasn't so much as a drop of water in there, Carlo shook his head and cried out, "Oh my God, it's fillin' up with water! I think it's gonna' sink!" He then turned with a grin to face a somber looking Mr. Walser who did not appreciate the joke. This was serious business.

The three of us, my dad, Carlo and I, piled into the beautiful craft and, using oars from my rowboat as paddles took her out for her first short voyage. It simply wouldn't do to just drive around and into the dock. She wanted to go! We paddled out as far as the island and when we looked back, Floyd was out at the end of the run waiting for us to get this out of our system, and hoping that we would remember who it was that this was built for. As we paddled our way towards its proper dock, I realized that Floyd had parked himself at the very end of the run, but still had his hand on the chair's control handle. This run now had no barrier at its end, since it had been removed to allow the boat to slip right on in. There was nothing to stop him from plunging headlong into the lake if he should accidentally press on the forward button in his excitement. Of course, Spots was right next to him to protect him from any danger. When I pointed out to my dad the precarious position our artist friend was in, we paddled very deliberately straight into the dock. The boat slid nicely between the tire-covered planks, and bumped firmly against the end of the run. Floyd was grinning from ear to ear and was speechless.

It took a little while for us to install tie points into both the gunwales and the side planks and to figure out a good easy way for Floyd to be able to attach and loosen the ropes that would connect to them. It was very important that he be able to solidly attach his boat into its docking berth so that when he backed up in his chair, the bow would not slip off the end of the run. It was also important that he be able to get these attachments off with a minimum of effort so that he could easily be underway when he was ready.

I carried the Hydro-Fin down from the garage and attached it to its previously mounted bracket. It looked good, although it seemed that perhaps its handle was going to be difficult for Floyd to reach. The mirror was attached to its mounting bracket on the rear shelf, but its final alignment would have to wait until Floyd was actually in place. No fishing equipment of any kind was brought on board at this time. This was a sea-worthiness trial and none of that stuff was needed or wanted now.

Floyd was eager to drive on board and take the controls, but we thought it would be a good idea for us to test out the Hydro-Fin first. We needed to see if it had much of a chance of making this thing go where we wanted it to, or if another means of propulsion would have to be devised. We figured that the three of us were at least as heavy a load as there would be when Floyd in his chair and one passenger were on board. So this should be a good test. I sat on an old Moxie box I brought along for just such a purpose, while Richie knelt down at the stern to place himself roughly where Floyd would be when he finally got in here. Carlo squatted amidships and was ready to use my oars to paddle us if the fin should fail to do its job. Floyd sat there looking sullen and impatient while we cast off. Richie had clamped an old 4 by 4 to the end of the run to ensure that we would not be hearing a big splash if Floyd should absent-mindedly activate his motor.

Once the boat had cleared the end of the run, Carlo used an oar to get the bow facing out toward the island. My dad began working the Hydro-Fin handle from side to side briskly. Carlo laid the oar on the bottom of the boat. The fin was moving us along very nicely indeed. We were impressed with how smoothly the fin worked and, although there was no way to go very fast without tiring quickly, the forward speed seemed respectable. Turns were attempted and executed easily. It was time to turn the boat over to its rightful owner. We were about 75 feet away from home base when Richie turned the boat back toward the dock and continued working the handle from side to side. A stiff breeze had come up and we were now heading directly into it. Richie had to push harder to maintain forward momentum. He was getting tired. Old "Charles Atlas" was getting tired. This was going to be too much for Floyd. We would all learn sometime later, that there was simply no need to work extra hard with the cleverly designed Hydro-Fin. A steady and smooth action was all that was really required and the boat could make constant, but slow, forward progress unless a very strong headwind came up. Richie tried to dock using only the mirror to guide him, and succeeded with a minimum of bumping against the tires. We were back. We attached the ropes to securely fasten the fully checked out vessel in place. Richie did not mention how tiring the fin seemed.

Finally, after what must have seemed to Floyd to have been hours and hours, he was going to be allowed to climb aboard and take her out. The restraining 4 by 4 was removed and tossed up on the bank. We showed him how to get the hinged board properly and securely in place so that it formed its little ramp for him to drive up on. Richie coached him on what he thought would be the best technique for safely driving in, suggesting that once his rear wheels were actually on the ramp portion of the boat, he take his finger off the button. It was not obvious that the self-braking action would in fact slow him down at such a steep slope, so it was possible that he could roll the rest of the way, or most of it, without an activated motor. I'm sure Floyd understood what was just explained to him, so it came as a bit of a surprise to me that what he actually did was to jamb on the forward button and hang on to it for dear life as he rolled up the little ramp and then sped down the boat's ramp to slam into the rear deck. He was yelling "Whoa, whoa" as he accelerated the whole way down and rammed full force into the solid wood. It was good that he was securely belted into his chair, as he always was when he drove it. It was also good that the chair and not his legs slammed into the well-built deck. My dad had a hard time containing his anger at seeing how poorly this maneuver was executed, and berated him for not doing as he had been instructed, wondering out loud if this whole idea of a boat was really crazy and stupid. After a very short time, with Floyd apologizing very effectively, and promising that he would do better next time, Richie had calmed down. He only hoped that my mother hadn't been watching when Floyd went speeding, "hell bent for leather" down into his boat.

Floyd now wanted to go out and sail around the cove for the rest of the day, but his mentor insisted that he first learn how to back out of the boat and then drive back aboard correctly. Floyd was told that normally, if the boat were actually to leave the dock, even a few inches, the small hinged board on the deck would be down and out of the way. But now it was still sticking up and before he could back up, the board would need to be disconnected and laid down. Richie did that, and then told his pupil to back straight up, not turning his handle left or right, even a tiny bit. This time he wanted Floyd to keep the button pressed until his rear wheels were on the run, or he might slide back down. Did he understand these instructions? This was important. Floyd assured him that he fully understood and would execute this rearward move flawlessly. Staring straight out in front of him at his front wheel, Floyd gripped the shovel handle and pressed the wrong button. Since he was already jammed against solid wood, all that happened was that his wheel spun a little as his machine tried to respond to its command to go forward. Before anything could be said by way of reprimand, he pressed the button for reverse and smoothly backed straight up, not stopping until he was completely on the run. His pleasure at having done this so well was obvious. He pretended that the small attempt to drive a little more forward just never happened. We were all relieved to see how well he was able to back out and could tell by his look of determination, that everything else was going to be done just fine.

Richie showed him again how to set up his little hinged ramp board and told him to drive on, this time going a little more slowly. The boarding this time went perfectly.

Everyone was amazed at how quickly Floyd caught on to all aspects of using his boat. He easily adapted to the use of his mirror in finding his way back in between the mooring boards. He operated the Hydro-Fin much better than anyone would have predicted. The strength in his right arm was surprising, and he seldom complained of feeling tired, although when the wind was up, he had a hard time making progress against it. More than once on windy days, I set out in my rowboat to rescue him. I would pull up alongside and tie a sturdy rope to a hook we had installed for just this purpose, and then row my arms off to haul him back. Once in a while on particularly windy days, I would row out to him with my dad and a paddle in my boat. Once we were right up against the side, my dad would step into the bobbing craft and paddle the exhausted fisherman back to his dock. It was becoming obvious that an electric motor would be a great improvement, but none was available at the time. Richie was working on this thought and it wouldn't be too long before something was developed.

If he had been preoccupied with fishing before, now Floyd was obsessed with the boat and everything about it. All through the summer of 1951 refinements and additions to the boat were made, most of them as a result of an input from him about some issue that he found not quite the way he'd like it. Although the boat was tight as could be, and never took on lake water, it would of course collect rainwater. If a heavy rainstorm dumped a lot on us, my dad or I would bail it out for him. We soon found that it was impossible to get all the collected water out from under the floor and between the ribs, so Richie cut a piece of the floor away in one corner. This made it relatively easy to get nearly all of the rainwater out. A hand operated bilge pump made the job easier yet. We would tie a specially fitted tarpaulin over the boat in its dock when heavy rains were forecast, then remove it for him as soon as possible, even if it was still lightly raining. A little rain never kept him from getting out there to fish.

One of the additions incorporated during the summer was an anchor, which was lowered and raised by means of a hand-cranked winch. This kind of a thing was something that Floyd knew he needed right from the beginning so that he could spend as long as he wanted in one place without drifting away. Once he had his vessel outfitted with this anchor, he took to using it less and less. He said he liked the idea of slowly drifting while fishing. He could cover more of the lake with no effort that way. But I'm sure that the real reason for not using his anchor was that it was difficult for him to work the winch smoothly, occasionally being completely unable to pull it up from a muddy bottom. The first time he got stuck like that, we were surprised at how long he was spending in one place until it dawned on us that another rescue operation was needed. Richie had some ideas about how to improve the anchoring system, but had so many things to do to finish up the myriad details involved in the building of our house, that it would have to wait.

Our nervous Dalmatian was a wreck when he first saw his buddy floating around out in the cove, and he'd run along the shore barking and whining at the same time to try to alert us to what must have looked to him like a bad idea. At his first opportunity, he got on the boat with Floyd and went sailing with him. Perhaps he thought this was an even worse idea, but now he could protect him - - somehow. It wasn't long before Spots really enjoyed being out on the lake and wanted to be on the boat all the time. The only problem was that he had a short attention span and would get bored with the whole idea after a while. Maybe it was that our pooch didn't have as good a bladder as the boat driver did and needed to use a tree. Whatever the reason, when he was on board and eventually started to whine and pace around, Floyd knew there was nothing he could do but head back in so the "damn dog" could get out.

Spots learned a very helpful trick early in his boat-riding days. It was a bit of an effort for Floyd to get the boat moving out of the dock by pushing against whatever he could with a long pole provided for just that purpose. Spots found, by accident I'm sure, that when he ran out and jumped onto an untied boat, it would move out a foot or so just from the reaction of his jump aboard. Some time later he found, also accidentally no doubt, that if he were to jump back onto the dock from a slowly outward-drifting boat, that that action would result in another surge in the right direction. One more leap over open water to the front of the boat with its attendant thrust, and he would stay put since it was then too far to easily jump back to the run. Floyd found his dog-assisted take-offs to be great fun and he loudly praised his canine companion who it seemed, thought pretty highly of himself for being such a valuable crewman.

It was during one of those launching maneuvers one hot summer day, that I walked out on the pier to say something to Floyd. Spots was really into his jumping back and forth routine and was paying more attention to me than he should have been. He must have lost track of just what he was doing because when he made a giant leap over about three feet of water to get back on the run, I thought he had decided to stay there and be with me for a while. But no, he simply wasn't thinking about anything I guess. He half-heartedly made another jump out over what was by now more than four feet of open space to the front of the boat. He realized his error in mid leap and tried to compensate by stretching his front legs out as far as possible. He succeeded only in clipping his toes on the front edge of the boat and making a huge splash as he unceremoniously went for an unplanned swim. He hated the water!

By the end of fishing season that year Floyd had caught 19 bass; a few of which were pretty good size; a few pickerel and a mess of kivvers and perch. Also included in his catches were a large turtle and an eel, with the eel putting up the toughest fight that could be imagined. He thought he had a monster of a fish on his line with that one and after working it for what seemed an eternity, he was dumbfounded to find that it was not a "real" fish at all.

He pretty much confined his travels to the area encompassed by the cove, being unsure if he would be able to get back to port if he ventured out around the point very far, especially if the wind picked up. He purchased a hat-mounted flashlight that he referred to as his miner's light, and would often be out on the lake after it got dark. So long as there was a little brightness to the night sky, he could find his way back into his dock with only an occasional cry for help. We were always aware of his location when he was out there and never went to bed until he had returned to dry land and was back in his room. A few times, he would find that his battery had pooped out before he could even get off the run. He would call out to us and one of us would come to his rescue to push him and his dead-weight chair up the hill and into his charging station. Not such an easy task. By morning he was ready for another adventure.

Late in the season, he would get out of bed and into his chair at 2:00 or 3:00 in the morning, have a quick breakfast of cold cuts and pickled pig's feet, and with his miner's light firmly in place, would buzz out the door and down the 80 or so feet to his waiting chariot. He would shove off, Spots still sound asleep in his doghouse oblivious to the sound of the chair going by. Floyd would be out there when the sun came up on a misty lake with water as flat as a piece of glass. He confessed to me later that sometimes when he was out like that, he would make no attempt to fish for a while, but would simply drift, silently watching the sky slowly brighten, and feel the power of Mother Nature. He said that the first time he did this, he found a tear slowly trickling down his face and felt that he was in the hand of God. He knew that if it hadn't been for my dad, none of this would be possible, and he felt unbelievably lucky to have found such a home at this point in his life.

Although when Richie designed the boat, he was confident that it would be practically impossible for it to capsize, there were some neighbors who "remember" just such a calamity. Some even believed that Floyd had actually fallen into the drink. Neither of these potentially life-ending events ever occurred, but there was one close call. One hot late

Right: "Navigator" Spots is anxious to get underway.

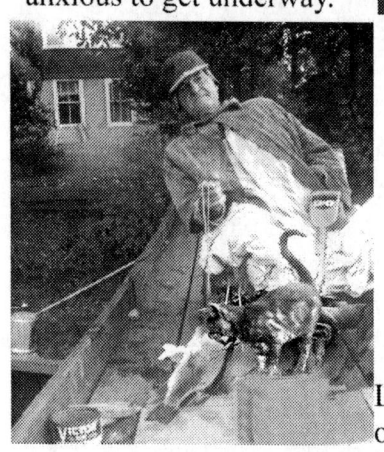

Left: "Mr. Murphy" checking out Floyd's nice catch.

Floyd in his boat, ready to land a trophy bass. (1950)

spring day, Floyd and his navigator/copilot Spots were anchored out in the cove about midway between the end of the run and Monkey Island. He had found a place he thought looked like a potentially productive bass fishing area. He had been working this location for about half an hour while his companion was stretched out, dozing in the sun on the floor of the boat right behind him. Spots loved the heat, and the gentle rocking of the boat no doubt quickly lulled him off to dreamland. For some obscure reason, Floyd at some point leaned to his right more than he should have. It may have been to untangle his lure from a lily pad, or to try to land a stubborn fish. Whatever the reason, he had leaned so far to his right that he tipped his large upper torso a little off balance. He was always careful to strap himself tightly into his chair with the belt provided for just that purpose before venturing out of the house and down to the boat. This time however, the belt was a bit loose. The result of leaning so far with a loose belt was that he got his right arm pinned under his side and was unable to push himself back up to a sitting position in his chair. With so much of his weight shifted to the edge, the boat tipped more than it ever had before, even to the point of having the opposite side out of the water. Floyd's head was inches from the surface of the lake but his belt held him fast to the chair. He began to holler for someone to help him, since there was no way he could right himself. His onboard guardian, now alerted to his charge's plight came to his aid by adding his own weight to an already precariously tipped vessel, as he stretched his neck down as close as possible to Floyd's head to see what was the matter. This move was not at all appreciated by the fisherman, whose cries for help now included some colorful language intended to make the "idiot dog" move to the other side of the boat. Their combined weight all to one side resulted in the gunwale on that side being only slightly above the water. Spots however maintained his vigilant protection, ready to attack any sea monster or whatever, that might pose a threat. Mr. Antonioli, who was working in his back yard high above the edge of the cove, heard the commotion down there and couldn't believe his eyes. He immediately called my mother to alert her to the danger. As soon as she became aware of Floyd's plight, she called the Fire Department, since Richie was at his job at Dennison and I was at school. Within a few minutes, a fire truck pulled into our yard. The firemen saw a strange looking boat out there slowly rotating about its anchor while its occupants, a large person dangling over the side, shouting for help, and a dog peering into the water seemed intent on capsizing the craft. My mother quickly explained Floyd's situation while the rescuers untied my boat and quickly rowed out to the helpless Mr. Walser. They pulled along side, calmly assessing the predicament and easily pushed him upright. Floyd thanked them for their aid as they inspected the boat and wondered if perhaps they should do something to prevent any reoccurrence of such a potential disaster. They soon realized what a stable vessel they were dealing with and how incredibly inventive the whole affair was with the special motorized chair and the way the boat was built. After they left, Floyd continued to fish for a few hours as though nothing unusual had happened. Spots, however insisted on being returned to dry land.

    As if Richie didn't have enough to keep busy what with pretty nearly constant attention to Floyd's special requirements and the many projects an unfinished house demanded, he found other challenges to keep his creative juices flowing. He had come across a descriptive article in one of his favorite magazines showing how to spruce up an old upright piano. The idea was to make it look really "modern" and to give it a complete makeover. I had been taking piano lessons for a couple of years and had an old upright whose dark-colored thick finish had craze lines running all through it. It had a good tone and the action of the keys was excellent, so I was happy with it as it was. But once my dad showed me how neat it could look if he remodeled it along the lines of the magazine article, I was hooked on the idea. In no time at all, he had removed the two legs that looked for all the world as though they supported the keyboard. When, much to my mother's surprise, that part of the piano didn't fall off, he removed the hinged top that allowed access to the sounding board's tuning pegs and threw it away. He then cut the sides down about 6 or 7 inches and closed up the opening he had just created so that there now was an indented ledge running along the top front of my piano. He completely changed the front where the sheet music would be placed so that it was strictly vertical where it had sloped previously. I began to get a bit concerned about how many more changes the poor old instrument could take before it rebelled by popping some of its tightly stretched strings. I had great faith, however that the result would be worth the worry.

His next step was to block up the two ends of the keyboard so that instead of having smoothly rounded and stepped down side pieces like most every other piano I had ever seen, they were now squared. A few other structural changes were made and then the whole piano was covered with lightly textured beige imitation leather. A mirror, about 6 or seven inches high that ran the length of the piano was set in place in the newly created recessed top. The end result was quite handsome and very "'50s" looking. I loved it. Of course my playing didn't improve any, but I enjoyed sitting at this instrument, which looked as though it should be in a smoky cabaret somewhere. The whole piano retrofit project took no more than a couple of weeks from start to finish, and that was with several interruptions.

I had assembled a small group of school chums into my own little band. We had a saxophone, clarinet, trumpet, drums, and of course my piano. This rag-tag group of serious minded but somewhat musically challenged young instrumentalists assembled for our practices where the piano was located. The fact that this room was directly over Floyd's head and we would create an awful racket while he was down there trying to watch TV, or perhaps trying to nap before venturing out to fish, never stopped us from trying to make real music. For unknown reasons, Floyd never once complained about what must have been, to him, ceiling-shaking noise with a few good notes thrown in once in a while. It is worth noting that he also never complimented me on how nicely "The Bacteria Boys" as we called ourselves, were progressing. I was sure that if he had been able to get upstairs to see how great the piano looked he would have thought the whole enterprise was quite good.

Many additional improvements to the chair and boat were made by Richie over the next few years; a steady evolution of progress resulting in even more enjoyment for Floyd. Among such enhancements was a complete redesign of the power train for the chair. The automobile starter motors and the original gearbox were replaced with a single, 12 volt motor purchased as government surplus. It was originally intended for use in small aircraft to raise and lower the landing gear. It was reversible and had a built-in gearbox that seemed to produce just the right speed and torque. The original 6-volt battery was replaced with a higher amperage 12 volt one. The old shovel handle steering mechanism was replaced with a sleek new design. It was made from stiff copper tubing with an elbow and a tee soldered to one end where the buttons for activating the motor were installed. This was a big ergonomic improvement since it allowed Floyd's thumb to press the forward button in a very natural manner while he held and steered. Activating the reverse button required a deliberate, but still simple action reducing the chance of going backward by mistake. The wires from these buttons were routed down the inside of the tubing and were out of harm's way as they made their way to the motor compartment.

The chair was equipped with a second battery contained in its rear compartment and although this did add weight to the vehicle, it was worth it considering why it was there. This extra battery was used when Floyd arrived at his place in the boat. He would reach down and back, to the right side and grasp two special heavy-duty cables that were wired into the boat and protruded enough for him to handle. He would then plug them into receptacles Richie had built in to the right rear side of the motor/battery compartment of his chair. This would provide the electrical energy to power three new additions to the boat. Floyd now had an electric motor to drive the boat, a motor to raise and lower the anchor, and a motor to pump out any accumulated rainwater. The Hydro-Fin was not removed, but was kept as a supplemental means of moving the boat if the battery should fail to hold its charge long enough to get him back to his dock. A longer handle had been attached to the fin to make it easier for Floyd to operate it. That simple addition worked out very well on its own, but incorporating a motor was dynamite. Floyd would venture out farther and farther from his landing strip and find new areas to explore. He always seemed to like the fishing best in the cove, but having the freedom to discover new territories was wonderful, and eventually he covered nearly the entire lake.

One of the things Floyd was particularly proud of was his worm farm. When he first began his new avocation of serious-minded fishing, he was generally satisfied with the worms I would dig up for him and put into earth-filled coffee cans. But now that he was into this business practically every waking moment, he felt the need for a constant nearby supply of good healthy earthworms and nightcrawlers. He especially wanted good, fat and lively nightcrawlers. I had captured them for him a few times with the help of one of my uncles. We would go out in the yard after dark with a flashlight and a soda bottle filled with a solution of a little vinegar in water and sprinkle it liberally over the surface of the area we suspected was home to some good 'crawlers. If they stuck themselves up, we'd grab hold of them and not let go. They'd try to get back into the ground, but would eventually release their tension and out they'd come. Floyd was always pleased to get a few this way, but it was difficult to harvest enough, and they didn't last long in the coffee cans. Also, they were very scarce in the hot weather. Trying to fish with a dead or near-dead worm probably amused the fish. It surely didn't produce the kind of results he wanted.

Floyd had read a lot in his favorite magazines about worm composting systems that were prized by many an experienced bass fisherman. Once he had studied the topic thoroughly, he presented the idea to Richie, who agreed that it sounded like a great plan for having a constant supply of fishing worms immediately available. Besides, someplace was needed for the batch of live earthworms Floyd had already ordered by mail from some outfit that he had seen advertised.

The area just outside and to the right of his door seemed to be a perfect spot for his worm farm. Richie built a wooden box about two feet square with sides made from old 2 by 8s and with a plywood bottom. As instructed by Floyd, who had the detail plans in front of him, Richie drilled the required aeration holes and settled this box slightly into the earth at their chosen spot near the door. A variety of materials were used as the bedding for the worms to burrow into. Some chopped up decaying leaves, a little peat moss, and some shredded newspaper were all mixed in along with a few handfuls of rich soil from the garden and the whole mess was wetted down. The information presented in Floyd's magazines suggested that a box of the size they had just made could easily be home to over 500 nightcrawlers and a whole mess of "red wigglers". Placing wet burlap on top of a layer of straw was recommended. Also, the plan was to mix in non-meat organic waste from the kitchen including vegetables, fruits, eggshells, tea bags, coffee grounds, and paper coffee filters as well as shredded garden waste. Somewhere along the way Floyd discovered that Pablum was a good food for worms, and he would liberally add some from time to time. This whole idea worked out very well, providing an excellent source of live bait, and also generating a fair amount of useful compost material for our gardens.

Having an unending supply of fresh earthworms at his disposal by no means reduced his interest in, and use of all kinds of artificial lures. He found many creative ways to use both, simultaneously. In time, his tackle boxes were jammed packed with a vast array of brightly colored spoons, spinners, jigs, rubber worms, plugs (floaters and divers), flies, jars of pork rind, crickets and frogs, and all sorts of gadgetry. He also acquired an impressive collection of split lead weights for sinkers, as well as bobbers, swivels, leaders, and hooks in all sizes. But about the most amazing thing he undertook, was the tying of his own flies. His first attempts to follow the instructions in his magazines resulted in very poor renderings of what he saw. When I first realized what he was trying to do with only one functioning hand, I tried to figure out some way to gently suggest that tying flies was perhaps just too much of a challenge. Once again, he proved me wrong about his limits. With unbelievable patience and determination, he worked out his own techniques. He asked my dad to rig up a few special fixtures that he had thought of himself, and had them attached to a lap-size board. He purchased a couple of jeweler's vises and specialized tools through mail order catalogs. After many rainy days and evenings in his room, hunched over the unique workbench on his lap, he began to turn out very respectable imitations of expensive, sought-after flies. Carlo's younger brother, Eddie was really into fly fishing and would spend many evenings after work with Floyd, helping him to improve this newly acquired talent. When they produced a couple of outstanding renditions of the popular *Royal Coachman*, they knew they had arrived.

In the early summer of 1952, the folks from Grafton who had purchased Harmony Home 2½ years previously (Mr. and Mrs. Bean) had decided to sell the charming old place. They knew it needed paint, both inside and out to improve its market appeal. In fact, the exterior cedar shingles had never been protected from the elements in any way. The Greenes loved the rustic look and the natural patina the shingles had taken on over time. The current owners were looking for a low-cost solution to hiring a painter. It just so happened that the summer job I had started working at the day after my high school graduation had abruptly ended when the construction firm that had employed me and about 35 other workers suddenly terminated everyone. I had been on the job for just over 3 weeks when the whole thing ended. This was bad news since

I had depended on that income to help cover some of my expenses at WPI where I was to start in a few weeks. Mr. Bean came to my rescue when he hired me to paint all of the rooms in the house, as well as to apply a good quality stain to the exterior. What a break for me! I could roll out of bed at a quarter to eight in the morning and be on the job at 8:00 sharp.

I worked diligently at painting all the ceilings and walls, including those in what had been Floyd's studio room. By August, I was slapping the brown stain on the cedar shingles and was amazed to watch them soak it up. The shingles on the south side, facing the lake and having been exposed to sun every day for nearly 40 years, practically sucked the stain right out of my brush.

The outside of the old house was far too big a project for me to do alone. Ladders and staging were needed to get to all the surfaces and to reach all the trim, which was to be painted a deep Forest Green. My Uncle Nick (my Aunt Rose's husband) had some available time, so he pitched in and helped me for several days with that part of the job. My father also provided considerable assistance on weekends. Between us, by the time I was ready to head off to college that September, the house looked pretty nice - - inside and out.

Not long afterwards, Harmony Home had new owners. A local couple, Louie and Anna Chouinard purchased the place. Anna had been Anna Abelli and lived on Nipmuc Road, a few houses away from our old Dow Street home. She had been in love with this gracious old house for many years. As a very young girl, she had worked for Mrs. Greene doing housecleaning chores and whatever needed doing. She was in awe of Mr. Walser and took a few art lessons from him, as did so many of the neighborhood kids. She thought Edith was gracious and kindly, and always enjoyed it when the famous composer would sit at her piano and play lovely music for her. She was particularly impressed when, in 1937 Edith took her to a movie theater in downtown Framingham on their common birthday of March 26th (Anna was 10, Edith, 62) to

Above: Floyd driving down the hot-top path to his pier. Richie and Dickie are unconcerned, since Floyd has the technique mastered. (1950)

Below: Richie, Dickie and Luigi doing a little landscaping. (1950)

Below: Richie and Dickie putting on the brick veneer. (1953)

see the just-released Walt Disney spectacular, *Snow White and the Seven Dwarfs*.

Anna would work extra diligently to clean up around the Greene household whenever she was told that a big party was planned for that evening. Then, after her supper, she would stealthily return to the gaily-decorated house, with its Chinese Lanterns lit and suspended out around the veranda. It looked enchanting to her and as she watched from behind bushes, the invited guests would arrive and be heartily welcomed by both Roy and Edith. They all looked so elegant and refined, she was sure they were very special people. Many times, she would hear some beautiful music drifting out of the house from the instruments they would be playing. She thought to herself that some day she would own this wonderful place, a thought that seemed to be a pipe dream - - until it actually happened.

Starting in about 1953, truckloads of bricks were delivered to our yard. It was time for Richie to finish the exterior of his house according to his own unique plan of applying a brick veneer, with the bricks showing their wide face. This project took a couple of years to complete since it was done mostly on weekends. There was simply too much set-up and mixing of mortar, plus clean up to attempt to accomplish much after Richie had spent a full day working at his machinist job in the factory. My involvement with the bricklaying job was limited by the fact that I was off to college for 4 years beginning in the fall of 1952 and simply was not around to help out much. Although when I was available, I did my share and enjoyed learning this new skill. I never did find out where my dad learned to do such a task, but then I had come to believe that there was nothing that was outside his ability to tackle and I never asked such questions.

My grandfather, Luigi was now living with my grandmother out in California where my Aunt Selma had moved. The old folks were very happy out there in a place that reminded them so much of Italy, with a climate that suited gardening and growing grapes over much of the year. Luigi had wanted to help put the bricks on the house for years before he moved, but the expense of actually purchasing the material forced Richie to wait until he could afford to get a few loads of bricks. By then, Luigi was in California. Both men would have enjoyed working together on this part of the house-building adventure. Luigi, in spite of the fact that he was now about 70, would have mixed the mortar and hauled bricks while his son would have set the bricks carefully in place, getting them level and even and "pointing" the spaces in between. As it was, this was the only time Richie looked even a little bit sad while working on the house. He had wanted his father to be with him during this phase because he felt he still had things to learn and would have enjoyed the special bonding that he knew would continue to have flourished.

Over the next few years, Floyd was visited by many people. Several of them had once been students of his back in the '30s and '40s. There were a few new students who showed up for lessons in the fine points of etching. Others were interested in fishing and were in awe of his boat and motorized chair. Neighborhood children, entranced by his marvelous personality and more than a little curious about his strange condition, loved to visit him. Often they would bring flowers for him to plant in his little garden next to his worm farm. They especially enjoyed bringing him books from the nearby library and then listening to his "Wild West" tales and examining his collection of real Indian arrowheads. He had a way of making everyone feel very comfortable in his presence and he truly enjoyed talking about anything and everything with each of his visitors. He felt that he was always learning something new from the folks that called on him. An expression he quoted to me more than once was, "You learn somethin' new every day if you hang around with the right people."

CHAPTER 17

IN FLOYD'S OWN WORDS
1952 - 1955

Floyd kept a journal of his fishing days in the mid-fifties. None of us knew at the time that he was writing his daily experiences. I don't think he purposely kept this diary hidden, but it was never mentioned and only found after he had passed away. He wrote his thoughts and experiences into a small bound, hard cover book of blank pages. On its cover he drew a fish and printed the words "Fishing in Waushakum Pond - -1952 - -F. N. Walser". Here, in his own words is some of what he enjoyed so much. My editorial comments, wherever I felt they were needed, are in italics.

The artist has become a fisherman.

April 1, 1952: Carlo came up this morning to help Richard fix run. Dickie painted my boat last Sun. Have been making a lot of streamers, bugs, frogs and flies. Will try them out casting line in front of plug. Fishing license cost $3.25. In 1950, I caught three bass (from "run"). 1951 fishing from boat, caught 19 bass. Kept 8, one of which weighed 5 ½ lbs. Also caught one 40-lb turtle, 1 3-ft eel, and 1 17-½ inch pickerel. This year I hope to double last year's catch. Irwin brought 2 half barrels for worms.

April 2: Carlo came with boots to help Richard place "horse" under run.

April 3: (Thursday) Richard and Dickie put my boat in at run. I went onto run for first time. Saw no fish. Cold.

April 4: Warmer. Went onto run. Saw perch.

April 5: Rain. Nick came- said he'd bring me some nightcrawlers.

April 6 (Sunday) Cold. Richard fixed boat. We went around island. Saw muskrat. New fin with long handle works great. New mirrors are fine.

April 7: Carlo came AM. Got $3.00 for old lantern. Cold & windy.

April 8: Cold & cloudy. A.M. Spots & I out 2 ¾ hrs. Saw turtle. Found nice log. Will get Carlo to help bring it in later. Went out at night alone and brought in the log - - a big one. Richard pulled it partly on bank for me. Fine full moon and a little breeze. Carlo came later with co-hogs, which we ate raw. *(The correct spelling of these Atlantic coast sea clams is quahog, but we'll stay with Floyd's phonetic spelling.)*

April 9: Still cold and cloudy. Air temp, 45. Water temp, 52. Took Spots. Caught 1 kivver for cat. Saw 2 big bass south of island. Nick sent me 3 cans of fine worms. Carlo & I plan to go for pine leaf mold tonight. Carlo and Irwin fixed up my worms in two half barrels with leaves and black mold of pine leaves. Wetted down. Sprinkled on oatmeal, and covered over with wet burlap.

April 10: Dickie painted boat mirrors and put sponge rubber across front for rods to rest upon. Cold and windy.

April 11: Cold and NW wind. Went out with Dickie after supper.

April 12: Cold. Out four hours. At 11:15 saw 8 bass. Beauties - - in one group between island and Dickie's boat. Dickie and I and Spots out around the island after supper. Caught 1 kivver for cat.

April 13: (Sunday) Air temp 45. Out with Spots 8 to 10 A.M. Caught kivver and a 14-inch pickerel on 1 worm. Light south wind. Bass: 30 – 50 feet north of island. Cat came on boat for the kivver.

April 14: Rain and cold. Out in boat short time. Shower drove me in.

April 15: Fishing season begins. Cold & cloudy. Temp 45. Barometer 31 – 30. Out 9 to 12 AM. Caught 6 perch and 1 kivver. Nick came P.M. with 7 nice trout (one 11-½ inch). I ate 4 for supper. Carlo came in evening with pheasant feathers.

April 16: A.M. Dickie and I out till 11. Called in when Miss Zimmer of B.S.S. came. Stayed for 3 ½ hours. Dickie and I out on lake again. He caught 1 perch, I caught 2. Dickie shot several turtles this AM.

April 17: Dickie and I at point. No fish.

April 18: Warm & windy. Caught 1 kivver back of island. Killed 1 turtle. P.M., windy. After supper, Richard and I at the island . Saw muskrat. Later, Carlo and I out, but no fish.

April 19: Warm but windy. Out 7:30 to 11 AM. Chair threw fit. Backed away from bed. *(This is the first of a few places where Floyd's entries in this journal show him to be a master of understatement. The chair did more than just back away from his bed. For unknown reasons, the switch that energized his electric starter motors - - one for forward and one for reverse - - caused the motors to run with no input from him. He was in the process of pushing himself backwards out of his bed and into his chair when suddenly and without warning the chair backed away several inches. This caused him to drop down between the chair and the edge of the bed. The other motor then activated, driving the chair forward, squeezing him - - or at least the lower part of him which was projecting downward - - tightly against the bed. The motor continued to run, causing the driven wheel to abrade through the linoleum flooring. He hollered for help from Angela, who was upstairs alone doing housework. She did not hear his shouts for help for quite some time. When she was aware of his plight, with the motor still running, she called the fire department. They had never encountered anything quite like this before, but quickly opened the chair's access hatch and disconnected the battery terminals to stop the motor. They helped Floyd back into his bed and moved the chair out into the middle of the room. They stayed to chat with this amazing gentleman for as long as they could, comparing fish stories and being enthralled with his entire set-up. When my dad got home, he was as surprised as anyone else that the chair could have misbehaved so badly. He very quickly isolated the problem and took action to ensure that nothing like that could ever happen again. He also knew that an entirely different drive system was needed - - one that did not use automobile starter motors. Within about 7 weeks, the new motor/gearbox system was installed. This vastly improved design used a reversible war surplus 12-volt motor with integral gearbox. It was of the type that the Air Force used to raise and lower landing gear on small aircraft.)*

April 20 (Sunday): Warm and windy, so stayed in. Wrote letters to Clara, Frank, and Edith.

April 21: Cold and windy. Out 6 to 10:30. Caught 1 kivver. Some pad leaves are within 6 inches of top of water. Saw muskrat feeding in 10 ft of water. Dickie mailed orders to S. G. & Ks. At night, Carlo came – split co-hogs.

April 22: Out with Spots 7AM. Temp @ 50. Later, wind came up strong. Caught pickerel, 14-inch, north side point. He snapped onto both hooks of plug on first cast and jumped up in the air a foot or near. Caught 2 kivvers for cat. Out at 4. Caught 5 perch back of Antonioli's place. Richard helped me into run at 6. Carlo came up at 6:30. Fished 'til 10. Carlo caught 1 kivver. He got my red & white bobber, which was lost last year.

April 23: Strong west wind. Temp 70 - - cloudy.

April 24: Out with Spots 12 to 4. Caught 2 perch north of island. Pad leaves are reaching top of water. Strong south wind after 4 PM. Fed and watered worms.

April 25: Out at 8 with Spots, but because of wind (south) and light rain, came back to run and there caught first calico bass of season. Hung 2 others, then they refused to take my worm. Air temp 43 and rain.

April 26: Cold and rainy. Temp 45. Fished 10 to 12 from unhitched boat. Caught 1 kivver. Caught a calico that got away. Received rope and vise from Sears, Roebuck.

April 27 (Sunday): Cold. Temp 45. Light rain all day. Out 2 to 4:30. Caught 1 pickerel, 1 perch and 1 kivver with worms and spinner.

April 28: Heavy rain. Temp 45. Went down to boat, but too wet and cold to fish.

April 29: Light rain. Temp 45. Out 2 to 7:30 PM. Saw big turtle north of island while fishing there. Caught 1 perch. Hung 2 pickerel and large perch. Caught 2, 9- inch perch. Came in for Carlo. In feeding perch to cat, he bit my thumb plenty hard.

(I vividly recall the incident of our cat, "Mr. Murphy" biting Floyd's thumb, since I just happened to be right there at the time. It was nearly dusk when Floyd brought the boat into its dock. The cat came aboard as he so often did to once again get some fresh fish caught especially for him, or so he must have thought. This time, Floyd held the fish, a small one, in his hand with its head not sticking out very far at all from the area between his index finger and thumb. There was very little fish protruding for the poor cat to get a hold of. To make matters worse, Floyd had started to project his thumb outward while admonishing the cat to "take it, damn you!" The somewhat intimidated Mr. Murphy took a good heavy bite out of the only thing sticking out of Floyd's hand that smelled even remotely like a fish. Unfortunately, what he sank his teeth into was Floyd's thumb. At this point, the cat was sent flying off the boat onto the shore when Floyd's reaction to the "Godawful bite" was to violently jerk his arm backwards. While Murphy was sailing through the air, the fish dropped back into the lake to be caught again some other day. In the few microseconds while all this was happening, Floyd let out a stream of the most creative cuss words I had ever heard. In all the intervening years I have yet to have

heard these words combined in quite the same way. Floyd later insisted that he never said anything more than one prolonged scream of pain. As might be imagined, it was a long time before the confused cat approached either the boat or Floyd.)

April 29, *(continued)*: Carlo dressed my thumb and we went out for an hour. He caught 2 kivvers. Carlo moved my worms under the table and fed them meal and oil. Inside we had a good supper and we split a bottle of ale. He had a "Dagwood" sandwich and laid it on the table. Spots took half of it when I wasn't looking, so outside he went. Gave Carlo my telescoping flyrod.

April 30: Sunny, but strong NW wind. Up early and down to boat, but wind too strong, so back to my pleasant and comfortable room.

May 1, 1952: Cold and strong NW wind all day. Down to boat, but too cold and windy to go out.

May 2: Cold and windy. Out 10 to 3. 5 kivvers and a couple of perch.

May 3: Cold and windy (NW) all day. Out 8 to 11AM. Caught 1 kivver and 2 perch. New rod came. Helped Dickie clean his reel. Carlo came before dark and we fished 'til 10. Carlo caught 1 hornpout. –Me; nothing.

May 4 (Sunday): Strong west wind and cold. Out 9 to 12. Dickie helped me in at run. Used new rod with plug; also spinner and worms. = 0.

May 5: Out 12:30 to 6. (Too cold and windy to go in AM.) Fine and pleasant now. Saw crane catch and eat good-sized perch. Muskrats @ island full of action looking after their business, whatever it is. Carlo up at 7. Out 'til 10; No fish.

May 6: Raw SW wind (very strong). Out 8 to 12:15. Richard got on boat and helped me in. *(I rowed my dad out in my little rowboat and brought my boat alongside Floyd's. With both boats pitching and rolling about, it was no easy feat for my dad—a non-swimmer—to scramble out of my boat and into Floyd's. He then used an oar that we brought along to propel Floyd and his boat into its dock.)* No fish, but 1 little perch used for bait. No results. Also used perch belly with spinner. Water temp is 60; only 5 degrees warmer than it was a month ago. Water plants, pads, etc. seem to have stopped growing entirely. Night, Carlo up with bus fan motor. Richard tried it out, but not powerful enough to operate my chair.

May 7: Cold, cloudy and windy. Made out order to G of 2 R etc. Wind from N.W., very strong.

May 8: Cold and 25 mph gale from NW. Mailed order for pulley for electric motor to G.

May 9: Out with Spots 8 to 1:30. Took Spots to birch trees back of Antonioli's place to get off at 12:00. Caught 2 kivvers and 1 pickerel. Put back pickerel, about a foot long. Warm, nearly 70 degrees, but strong NW wind. Dickie fixed rod holder on both sides of boat. Richard and I discussed building a new chair. (Water temp. north of island was 58 degrees.)

May 10: Out at 8 with Spots. Cast along shore for a while. No luck. Then out to midway in cove. Caught 16 ¾ inch pickerel on bottom with night crawler. Then caught 10-inch perch. In at 12 to let off Spots and to clean fish, which I did on boat. Then in house to wash fish, put in oilpaper and into refrigerator. Ate them. Out again. Beautiful warm sunny day. Shirt off for first time this year. In at 4 as wind (south) was getting strong. Dickie helped me into run. Carlo came at 7:30 PM. We went out 'til 11:30. He got 1 hornpout, I got 1 kivver.

May 11 (Sun): Rain all day. Cold.

May 12: Very strong wind from south. Painted large bucket that Carlo gave me. Temp up to 60 degrees at noon. (Wind 50 miles per hour.)

May 13: Strong wind from south and cold. Down to boat to bail it out. Fed meal to worms and wet the bag covers. Carlo up and we fished 7:15 to 10:15. I caught 13" pickerel back of Antonioli's before dark on spinner & worm. Carlo caught 0. Carlo took bucket top to fix. Light south wind and cold.

May 14: Strong northwest wind and cold. Wind went down at sunset. Irwin came and he and I went out for an hour, he using my rod and caught small pickerel, 1 perch and 1 kivver.

May 15: Rainy and cold. Out 10 to 11 = 0. Used spinner with worms @ Antonioli shore. Out 6 to 7:30. Misty northeast wind. 0.

May 16: Out with Spots 8 'til 2 PM. Disagreeable SW to N wind. Caught 2 kivvers. One 16 inch pickerel east side of island at 11. He jumped out of water five times trying to throw hook. Got around fin, so lost him. The best fighter in pickerel that I have seen. Sunny day. Used spinner and worm. Got check for $49.35 and bill for poll tax. Water temp 60 degrees.

May 17: Cold and very windy. Out 7:30 to 11:30. Caught 1 kivver and 2 pickerel less than a foot long. Then inside to await party who wants to look at etching press. Folks came at 2:30—May buy press. Out 3:30 to 7. When Carlo came, I was at landing—came in to eat. Then out near great point (west of island). Carlo and I caught 2 kivvers each; then north where I caught a 'pout. That was it. Then inside to open a bottle of Pickwick ale.

May 18(Sunday): Cold and rain. Got up at 11:00 AM. Weather cleared at 4, so out with Spots 'til 7. Caught 1 pickerel about 14" long, with pork rind on hook with spoon. Stopped by where Richard and Dickie were fixing place for my new run.

May 19: Most beautiful day. Out with Spots at 6, but him in at 7. Out to 3 PM—a 9-hour stretch. Richard got a can of worms for me yesterday. Caught 4 large kivvers and 1 perch. Two fine pickerels followed my lures in but refused to take. Carlo up at night. He caught some toads, but caught nothing but 1 kivver.

May 20: Rain. Out in afternoon. Tried out swell shiners Carlo brought, but they got only perch. Toads did nothing. Carlo up at night (rain) and cleaned reel.

May 21: Rain. Out with Spots at half past 10. Only perch and 1 pickerel. In at 4. Saw big bass north of island splashing around in shallow water; preparing to spawn.

May 22: Cold and strong NW wind, so in all day. Paid 2 boys 30 cents for about 30 nightcrawlers. They said there were 500. Cold and cloudy in evening, but some hot top for my run. Carlo back up at night with Oriole feathers and my new Neo caster stardrag reel. Carlo threw plug in tree.

May 23: Beautiful sunny day. Out at 7:30. Fed cat perch. Made Spots stay home. Tried out new reel. Caught 3 pickerel (which I put back) and 2 perch on shiners. Pickerel on spinner & worm. Saw one good pickerel and 1 water snake. Carlo, Eddie and Hazel up for a few minutes.

May 24: Beautiful windy day. Out at 7:30. Caught pickerel at Dickie's boat on 1st cast; then pickerel NW of island. Caught calico bass east of island. At hornpout spot, hung very large 'pout. Tried to lift him into boat by line and lost him. He must have weighed 1 ½ to 2 lbs. And perhaps 14 inches long. Used about 15 nightcrawlers and 10 worms all day. Caught 7 hornpout, 2 kivvers, 3 pickerel and 3 perch and 1 calico. Wind squall drove me back of island @ 7. Back in stall, fools in speedboat almost tipped boat over with me in it. I inside called police who said they would send a man up to talk to the s.o.b. party. Dickie cleaned fish for me. Out 11 ½ hours.

May 25 (Sunday): Rain. In bed 'til 12 noon.

May 26: Strong NW wind kept me in. Calmed near sundown. Carlo up and we fished 'til 10. =0.

May 27: Hung pickerel, but didn't get him.

May 28: Out 7 to 2:30. Bad day for fishing. Carlo brought fine shiners and Nick brought nightcrawlers.

May 29: Out 5:30 AM to nearly 2:00. Caught 3 fine calico. Wonderful fun. Got them in little cove near pickerel point.

May 30: Out at 7. Caught 1 pickerel, then Carlo came. We used shiners. Carlo caught 1 ½ lb. bass. I caught 14" pickerel and large hornpout. Then we came in and Carlo helped Richard raise my run after Richard moved it to new place where I can land easier, particularly on windy days. Angela cooked my 3 calicos and brought them down to my boat. Carlo went home. In after 5 and to bed. Two men using chubs caught a bass, but turned him back as both Briggs and I saw them catch it. Briggs said he caught a 2 ½ lb. bass this AM and turned it back.

May 31: Out early. Hard rain drove me in, wet. Watched Richard, Dickie and Richard's Nick lay hot top on new runway by birch trees. Then inside; bath, change of clothes and to bed at noon. Carlo came at night and put hinges on new minnow bucket top that he made.

June 1, 1952 (Sunday): Out 5:30 AM. Caught nice Calico on dead shiner, and 14" pickerel with worm and spinner. Very windy – SE. Went around back of island and over to its east shore, then along shore of cove to my new run, and in. Richard moved my worm barrels over and fixed nice place for them. Inside, Richard changed pulleys on motors so that I go faster. After noon meal, painted bucket top that Carlo made and painted Carlo's bucket inside and top. Dickie helped me on Carlo's bucket, and then we went to boat and put 5 more screw hooks on right side to hang minnow buckets, etc. Light rain. Put Pablum, etc. in worm tanks. They seem to be doing well. Released the pickerel and Calico.

June 2: Out half past 6 in the morning. Boat full of water. It tilted badly to right when I went on board. Bailed water for nearly an hour. Sunny day, but strong north wind. Caught 1 kivver. Used worm and spoon; no luck. In at 12:30 to eat and rest. After supper, Richard and Dickie fixed run; lowered it so I could get on board.

June 3: Out early = 0. In and to bed at 11. Up and out at 3:00; in at dark. Richard carried my rods in. Irwin stopped for chat; tried my new Neo caster reel. He could not catch perch so I gave him 2. Carlo went after shiners, but got only a few.

June 4: Out at 6 AM with Spots. Caught 2 large perch and one pickerel. Strong south wind. Sunny and warm in afternoon. Strong SW wind in afternoon. Out with anchor dragging NE of island. Eddie Stefanini shot redwing blackbird and asked me to let him recover the bird in my boat. I got in to shore at trees; he came on board and got his bird. He gave it to me and I got him to use the paddle and help me get back to my boat landing. What a break! Inside, I plucked feathers.

June 5: Out at 6:30 with Spots. Caught calico, perch, and pickerel. Hung a grand pickerel back of island on pollywog. The pickerel was probably 20 inches long or more.

June 6: Windy. Out with Spots AM. 0. Evening, back of island, used large frog that Carlo brought to me. = 0.

June 7: Strong wind from NW all day. Stayed in bed. Sat up in bed and wrote out order for hooks etc. to Herter, Inc. Richard down at 9:30 and worked all day putting my new motor and gearbox on chair. No solenoid switches on this motor. Get back and forward on the one war surplus motor. –A big improvement over the old starter motors. Carlo and Augie up and got shiners. *("Augie" was the nickname that everyone used for Albert Agostino who at this time lived with his wife and 3 sons upstairs in the same house I had lived in on Dow Street. He was one of Carlo's closest friends and thought the world of Floyd, visiting with him as often as possible and enjoying all aspects of their mutual passion of fishing. He was skillful at sketching and drawing, although it took a while before he actually showed any of his work to Floyd, who was quite impressed with what he saw and encouraged him to develop his talent.)*

June 8 (Sunday): Out at 4:00 AM. Used fine shiners, but only 3 pickerel (small) and 1 large perch. Disagreeable SW to N wind.

June 9: Out at 5:00 AM, fished 'til 12:00 noon. Caught 1 calico and 2 perch. South wind strong. Cat all crippled up came on boat for perch. *(Our cat was a real "Tomcat" and was very often gone from the premises for days. Many times, he would return all battered and torn from tangling with who knew what adversaries. This must have been one of those times.)*

June 10: Strong SW to NW wind. Out early—nothing. Carlo up at night. Nice and calm. We had several good strikes, but landed no fish.

June 11: Strong NW to SW winds. Out at 5:00 AM with Spots. Caught 3 perch for cat. Winds too strong to go out in afternoon.

June 12: Cold and 25mph west to north winds. Out at 7:30AM to feed and water my worms. Then on to boat to get rod. Couldn't back chair out, so sat there. Angela came down at 11:30 and when Richard came at 12:15, he helped me to get inside to my bedside. Spinners arrived from Prescott Co. Put leaders on two.

June 13: Fished with spinners = 0.

June 14: Used worms with spinners. Pickerel strikes, but caught only kivvers. Carlo up with shiners at night.

June 15 (Sunday): Very strong south winds. Out early, but caught nothing. Caught calico in evening, but it got away.

June 16: Out at 5:30 AM. Two small perch and 1 nice pickerel. Cleaned him and brought him in. Washed him and into refrigerator. Got pickerel north of island in bog with large shiner. Back out at 6:00 PM. Carlo came. Used Dickie's boat. Got first bass of season near logs east of birch grove (50ft.). It was 13 inches. Got no other strikes all evening. Brought him in and Carlo helped me clean him. My best day so far.

June 17: Out early (6:00 AM) with Spots. Hard thundershowers got us. Went in wet as rats. Changed clothes, and to bed. Back up at 11:30 AM and onto boat, but strong SW wind kept me in.

June 18: Strong winds and rain showers kept me in.

June 19: Up at 3:30 (AM) and out at 4:30. Cast a while east of island and then found that anchor wouldn't go down—hung. Back to landing and backed off boat. Used hook on anchor. Back on boat, but anchor still hung, so off again with hook Carlo made for me. Then out and down to deep water. Found anchor cable was crossed so that it would not go to bottom. South wind getting strong. Decided that it was just not my day, so in and to bed. Hooks arrived from Herter. Got a nice card from Clara.

June 20: Out at 5:00 AM. Fair sunny day, but strong north to southwest winds drove me in at 9:00.

June 21: Out with spots at 7:30. Small toad, worms and spinners. Also red and white plug got nothing. In at 1:00. Carlo up at night and got grand lot of shiners and frogs.

June 22(Sunday): Out early at first daylight. (Angela and Dickie visited me on lake in his boat.) In at 12:00. Two small pickerel and 1 perch. Wind from south and some rain and heavy clouds. Very poor fishing. Out in evening.

June 23: Grand fishing! Lots of strikes. One fat 14-inch pickerel and another same size lost at bottom in pads. Out at 5:00 AM. Heavy fog. No strikes until sun shone and SE wind. Then it was fun. At extreme other side, south of rocks. In at 12:00 noon. Cleaned fish at boat. Fish lived from 8:30 until I killed him at 12:00 on stringer. Angela brought me a couple of nice toads in a jar. Carlo up at night. We each had two strikes, but got nothing.

June 24: Fine warm day. Out at 7:00 AM. Got 4 pickerel and 2 perch. Got pickerel (13 ½ inch) with shiner and shorty No. 4 hook. In at 12:00. Cleaned 1 pickerel and 1 perch. Out again at 4:00 PM, but in at 6:00 dog-tired. Then at run, lost hook, bobber and leader in pads. Paid 15 cents to 3 boys to get them.

June 25: Used small No. 12 hook. Caught 7 or 8 kivvers and perch.

June 26: Out at 3:45 AM. Large frog and plugs = nothing. In at 9:30. Very hot. Temp = 103 degrees. To bed at noon.

June 27: Out at 7:00 AM. Hot. Nothing. In at 10:00. Back out at 1:00, then in again at 3:00 PM.

June 28: Out at 3:00 AM. Used plugs. Got strike—bass, on Jitterbug. Lost him when changing rod to left hand. Fine cool, cloudy morning. Caught 3 kivvers on no. 12 hook. In at 8:30. Carlo up at night and got a few minnows and lots of pollywogs.

June 29 (Sunday): Out early but no luck. Only perch and small pickerel. Out again at 1:00 PM in rain. Caught a perch south of island and then back in.

June 30: Out at 3:30 AM. Large perch, calico, and pickerel. In at 11:00 and to bed. Up at 5:00 PM, ate and out again. Saw Frank Mateo catch small bass on spinning rig. Said he'd select a spinning rig for me soon.

July 1, 1952: Out at 6:45 AM with Spots. Used plug and toad. = 0.

July 2: Out 7:00 PM to 1:20 AM using plugs = 0. Fine weather. Light south wind.

July 3: Slept 'til 11:00 AM. Too windy to go out. Carlo had teeth out yesterday, so he may not get up this week.

July 4 & 5: Nothing to speak of.

July 6: Carlo got nice bunch of shiners. But we got 0, except Richard caught 2 perch and I caught 2 perch and 1 pickerel.

July 7 & 8: worked hard with shiners, but got nothing.

July 21: Caught 3 ¼ lb. bass this AM at three on basarena. Out at 2:30 AM. Left fish on stringer in water for Carlo. Fish died and spoiled. Hot day. I should have cleaned him before going in and to bed. Such a shame to catch a nice fish and then waste it.

August 1, 1952: Dead weeds on water in cove, so went down to south end of lake alone. Hung one bass. Carlo came over and pulled me home. Just before dark, little Johnny Strune roared out in his red boat to talk. Later when Carlo came, he called out in dark to ask if I caught any, and I in turn asked if he'd had any luck. He said "Yes, three good ones". When I asked "what on?" he said "Two on a spinner and 1 on a worm". It sounded fishy. He then came closer and I recognized him.

August 3: Back to south end of lake Sunday evening. Stayed all night casting around pads. Early in AM about sunrise, hung large pickerel about 2 ft. long on shiner.

August 12: Augie helped Carlo get some fine shiners last night. I left for south end of lake at quarter to four. Got there at first break of day. No luck. Roamed pads. Started home around 9:00 AM, trolling minnow. First caught large perch, then got 2 lb., 15 inch bass at first land point.

August 18: Got 2 lb. bass on black Flatfish at 8:00 AM half way between our point and "Prescott's Point". Called Mrs. Stefanini and she came over for it. I had promised Eddie Stefanini a fish. *(A "Flatfish" is a particularly aggressive, banana-shaped lure with gangs of very sharp treble hooks at its front, midpoint and end. They come in a variety of colors and sizes. On retrieval, it wiggles furiously, causing those deadly hooks to lurch violently from side to side. More than once, I caught a fish using this lure and found that it hadn't even really taken the lure into its mouth, but only got up close enough for one or more hooks to snag it. When the fish actually bites the lure, it can be difficult to get it off the hooks.)*

August 21(Thurs.): Out half past 7. Caught 1 ¾ lb. bass midway between points on orange Flatfish. About an hour later, caught 1 ¾ lb. pickerel (17 inches) on white & black Flatfish. Came in at 10:00 and got Dickie to help me get the pickerel off hooks. Angela came down to see my catch. Wheels and axle came yesterday from Osborne Co. The idiots had cut the axle to 19 inches instead of 28 as what I ordered. I wrote to see what they would do about it.

August 24(Sunday): Carlo, Richard, Augie, Nick, and I left for Cape Cod for fishing trip at night. Richard, Carlo, Nick and I left shortly before midnight and reached the Cape before 2:00 AM where we met Augie. Then on to Orleans and Rock Harbor where we boarded Captain Edwin Norton's boat - - about 30 ft. long - - at 4:00 and headed out into the breakers where I wondered if the high chair that I sat in as well as myself might not roll overboard as the boat rocked about. Richard decided to take the legs off the bottom of the chair and that fixed it so my chair seat sat directly on the deck. After that, I rode the waves O.K. I caught the first fish after Nick had tied the handle of my rod to my chair and rigged it up for me. Up 'til 10:00 AM, we had caught only 2 bluefish. The captain then moved into water 30 feet deep and anchored. Carlo gave me his rod to fish with. The rest all used hand lines. The captain cracked shells from the hermit crabs - - he had a basket of them – and he baited my hook. I caught 7 or 8 nice fish - - tautogs - - 5 to 10 pounders about. When I would hang a fish, Carlo or Nick or Augie would hold the rod for me while I turned the reel handle. It was grand! I hung the biggest fish of the day, a 20 pounder, maybe. But it got off the hook, darn it! What a day! Got off the boat at 1:30. Nice trip home. Left Nick in Natick. After supper, Carlo came up, and he and Dickie and Augie cleaned fish - - 30 or 40 lbs. WOW! So tired, and then to bed. I cleaned one bluefish. The cat had a picnic! I sent Mrs. Antonioli and Mrs. Stefanini each a fish.

August 25: Went out on lake and hung a nice bass, but didn't get him. Night, Augie and Nick dropped in. Augie said he'd be back tomorrow night with some fresh clams.

August 26: Mrs. Stefanini brought some fresh corn, some hot peppers and some tomatoes. Got hangers from Helin Tackle Co. and am fixing more hooks on plugs so I hold onto the bass, I hope. Augie cooked 5 pieces of fish for me last evening – mighty good eating!

September 6: Out early using Flatfish. Telephone man out in gray boat showed me "rip" near Prescott's Point. *(At this page, Floyd drew a small map showing just where this "rip", which usually refers to a body or section of water made rough by the meeting of opposing currents, was located. He identified the location on the lake by such landmarks as "south corner of white house cuts 4th window of brown house" and "At yellow house, tree cuts middle of west side".)* Nick brought his spinning reel and fixed some Helin hooks with hangers on my plugs for me.

Sept. 16: Got 6 Flatfish lures sent to me by mail by Clara from Medford, Ore. Carlo traded the 3 duplicate Flatfish for other colors at Johnson's.

October 1, 1952: Caught 2 ¼ lb. bass on red and white Heddon plug at 10:30 AM. Warm. No wind. At the logs east of birch trees. Angela cleaned him for me. (Bass was 15 ¾ inches.) Night, Augie came and put hooks on several plugs.

Oct. 8: Frank Mateous came with his spinning rod. Went out on my boat with me for half an hour. I made 3 casts with his rod. No good casts. He caught 1 12-inch bass, 3 small pickerel and two perch. Said he'd be back Sat. afternoon.

Oct. 10: Frank came at 1:20 PM. Very cold and windy. He caught 6 pickerel and 1 perch. We got in after dark. Nick Ortenzi brought me a nice can of worms today.

Oct. 11: Caught 11-inch bass with worm and spinner.

Oct. 12: Augie came. I loaned him my reel to use when we go fishing some night soon.

Oct 16: Augie and I out for 'pout. No fish around. He caught 1 'pout, I caught 1 kivver. Carlo came later so we went in and called it a day.

November 10, 1952: Our meeting here in my room. Burdick brought *(illegible name)* around 8:30. Fourteen people attended. We are to try for more fish in this lake. Augie and Carlo here.

1954
(There are no entries at all in Floyd's diary for the year 1953)

(No date given, just the year, 1954 for the following entry)
Eddie *(Belloli)* gave me the propeller of his gas motor and Richard fixed electric motor on it and placed it at end of boat, and it works out great. Carlo came up and helped Richard paint the boat.

March 21, 1954: Sunday. First day of Spring - - Cold and windy. Richard has my boat all ready - - just waiting for some warm days. Last Friday AM broke ice (1/4") with pole to get 40 feet to open water. Saw 2 ducks. Saw no fish. Sat. Strong south wind. Went out with little David. Later, Eddie Belloli. Out in boat again to show him how nicely the little propeller he gave me works on my electric motor. Trouble with buttons, but Richard fixed them. Nick Ortenzi looked at my rods - - says he's ordered a spinning outfit.

Mar 22 (Mon): Cold, and north wind. Augie brought up his drawings which were quite good. Carlo came later and cut mats for the etchings that I gave them. Earlier, I called Edith and wished her a happy birthday, (26th of March).

Tue, Mar 23: Temp 50. Strong south wind. Out on lake 2 to 5 PM. Several weak bites on worms and got one kivver, **(First fish.)** Two geese flew from north of island, passed near me and landed on water near Prescott's point.

Wed, Mar 24: Fine sunny day. Out 10 to 5. Great day. Caught 4 kivvers with worms inside notch north of island.

Thurs. Mar 25: Cold and raw. Out north of island. Two kivvers, and a calico bass - - on earthworms. My etching pupil, Mrs. Ungvary, came at 1:30 for lesson. She paid me $15.00 for five lessons. Brought me the I. Shore catalog, which she got for me last week in N.Y.C. At night, Augie came and we discussed fishing, etc. Around noon, rain and the two Canada geese were swimming all around in our cove. I enjoyed watching them thru my window. And so, to bed!

Fri. Mar 26: Up early to go out but very windy, 'tho temp. @ 60 degrees. Dug in my worm farm. Angela brought coffee grounds, which I worked into the earth along with cornmeal and oatmeal. The worms are fat and sassy and I filled up a can to keep them handy for fishing. Sent inquiry letter on prices to I. Shor. Received letter from Jack Barnett.

Sat Mar 27: Cold, but out to notch and caught 4 kivvers. Letter from Clara.

Sunday, 28th: Up early to make trip in boat to far end of lake, but strong south wind came up to change my plans! Richard put in new board at boat run. Worked most of day on trolling rigs.

Mon., 29th: Strong wind, so inside to get ready for opening of fishing season. Fed worms.

Tues. Mar 30: Below freezing all day. Dorothy and her man came in A.M. They live near Washington, DC. She asked for a picture of mine, so gave her a watercolor of

Hastings House. Went out and covered with paper the cans containing worms so they will not freeze. Carlo up and finished cutting mats for and framing the 4 pictures that I gave him. (One watercolor and 3 etchings.)

Wed Mar 31: Another cold, raw day.

Thurs. April 1, 1954: June Ungvary over at 1:00 PM for etching lesson. She paid me $10.00 for paper. Another cold day. (First day of April.)

Fri. Apr 2: Cold, (45 degrees) and strong wind from south. In afternoon, Lynn Sherill, Mary Ellese came in. Lynn wanted to know if I wanted more books from library. Plan to watch Olson – Gavilan championship fight on TV tonight.

Sat Apr 3: Cold northwest wind up to 50 mph. About 4:00 PM went out and looked after my worms.

Sun. April 4: Temp to 14 above this AM. Up to 40 at 4:00 PM. Went out and down to boat, but too cold to go out on lake. Angela fixed good chicken dinner. Wrote letter to Clara.

Monday Apr 5: Temp up to 40 @ 2:00 PM. Strong raw SE wind. Dickie home all week. Put porcelain etch dish in my drawer. Hope crumbs will drop in it as I eat there in the future. Dickie brought lad on crutches. I invited him to go fishing on my boat with me later on. *(The "lad on crutches" was my friend Gene Salti, who was stricken with polio at a very young age. I knew him from early elementary school and all through high school, graduating together in 1952. He wore heavy metal braces on his legs and back and used crutches to get around. He was amazed at all Floyd had done in his life considering how severe his handicap was. Gene admitted to me later that he was afraid to go out on Floyd's boat with him, since if he ever were to topple out, he'd sink like a rock due to his heavy leg braces. Then he jokingly added that maybe he could be a good anchor. Not too long after this, Gene was to die in the crash of a small private airplane. The only other person on board, the pilot who was a good friend of his, was also killed in the crash.)* Eddie Belloli spent a couple of hours with me in the afternoon. We dug into my worm bed and found lots of them. Eddie left when

Dickie came down with my supper. Augie came later. We talked fishing. He left at 8:00 PM. Carlo came at five past eight. Rigged up his spinning outfit. Marked up his rod from $2.98 to $22.98.

Tues. Apr 6: Very cold and windy. Dickie helped me work up some gadgets for my boat.

Wed. April 7, 1954: Temperature up to nearly 60. Up at half past 5. Richard looked in on his way to work to comment on the beautiful day. AM; 5 kivvers, (In at 11) Cast bobber on to bush. Broke leader leaving hook, lead, and bobber in bush on island. Anchored east of island. Big bass came toward me, about 4 feet away. Seeing me, he turned into reverse instantly. In for Dickie to work on boat. Reply and prices from I. Shore. Out and caught 2 kivvers and 1 perch. Eddie B. came for feathers to tie flies and so I changed my bedding after eating supper, and so to bed. While I was watching fight on TV, Richard came to say that phone call from his sister, Selma in Sacramento, California said his father in coma at hospital.

Thurs.: Strong south wind. Temp @ 60. Down to boat to get rod and hook stick. Richard in at 11:00 AM to say that round trip fare to Calif. is $250, which I loaned him. He and Angela wanted to give me an IOU, but I said no. Richard leaves Friday at 6 PM. Hope that he finds his father better.

Fri. Apr 9: Temp 43 @ 12 noon. Wind NW. Richard in to show me his plane tickets to Calif. He leaves for Boston at 4:00 PM today. Richard put my new $30.00 Lifetime battery in my chair. After they left for Boston, I went down to boat. Gave cat a kivver. Wind felt cold, so came back inside.

Sat Apr 10: 35 mph S. wind. Up early. Got worms to fish, but cold and wind drove me back into my room. Dickie helped me fix fishing reel handle. I painted top of Angela's new birdhouse and Dickie put it up. Dickie in after I went to bed to say that Richard had phoned from Sacramento.

Sun. Apr. 11: Strong south wind and light rain.

Mon. Apr 12: Up early and out around island. Became windy, so back in at 10. 35 mph wind. Eddie came at 4 with flies he made. Carlo in for visit after supper. Took his spinning rod and reel.

Tues. Apr 13: Out after 9 but strong south to southwest wind dragged my anchor, so came in.

Wed Apr 14: Lynn in with kids. Strong south wind all day. Cloudy and rain.

Thurs. April 15, 1954: Battery went dead while on lake. Used fin to reach boat landing. There 2 to 5 PM and my $30.00 self-recharging battery failed to recharge. *(This so-called self-recharging battery, also referred to in this document as "Lifetime" battery was unreliable. It was presented to my dad as some sort of a break-through in the state-of-the-art of batteries at that time. It was supposedly able to completely recharge itself after being thoroughly run down in use, by the simple act of waiting an hour or so for it to do so on its own. Needless to say, it was to prove very disappointing to all concerned.)* Angela got "Chi-chi" who, with Antonioli's help got me off boat by pushing. Eddie and Louie also came. Mrs. Antonioli brought me some chrysanthemums. At night, Eddie came and we made a good Royal Coachman. *(This was one of the most sought-after flies that experienced fly-fishermen truly prized. It remains very popular even now. The fact that Floyd, even with some help from Eddie, could develop the technique for tying this and many other flies, was another testament to his determination and drive.)*

Fri. Apr 16: Temp. 42. Light rain. Planted my chrysanthemums, and the mist and rain should make them grow.

Sat Apr 17: Went to boat in rain to pump it out.

Sunday 18th April: To boat early, but heavy rain through night had filled boat again, so could not get on boat. Around noon, got Dickie to raise "run" so that I could get on boat to pump it out.

Mon. Apr 19: Out before 6. Augie came to fish about 6:00 AM and stayed 'til 10. Augie got 6 kivvers in notch, which I fished with perch bellies (0). "G" came and took battery - - is to replace it.   To bed early, but Carlo came at 7 PM, so up and out 'til 10:00 PM. (0!)

Tues. Apr 20: Strong south wind. Sunny and warm. Stayed inside. Herter package arrived. To bed early.

Wed Apr 21: Up ¼ past 4 AM. Temp 55 - - gentle breezes. Saw big bass east of island. Caught 4 kivvers, 2 perch, (one perch on spinning fly). Trouble getting into boat stall due to strong south wind at 10:30. Gave Bunky F. 3 big kivvers. Geese came along and Angela got bread and fed them. Inside, made double spinner with streamer hook. Down to boat to try it out. Perfect! No twisting of line on retrieve. Changed worms in cans - - put in new earth and feed.

Thurs Apr 22: Warm, but very windy. Watched Senate committee hearing on TV. McCarthy vs. army head. Very interesting in spots. *(The senate committee hearings that Floyd watched with such interest over the next several days, were truly spectacles to behold. Senator Joseph McCarthy got into a confrontation with the United States Army and its secretary, Robert Stevens. With a television audience of twenty million Americans, the flamboyant senator randomly fired accusations of Communism toward certain Army officers. With assistance from his faithful aid, Roy Cohn, he put together enough evidence to give him at least slight credibility. But McCarthy went too far. President Eisenhower helped the Army mount an impressive counter-attack. Over the span of thirty-six days, there were thirty-two witnesses, 71 half-day sessions, 187 hours of TV air time, 100,000 live observers, and two million words of testimony. Every day, millions of TV sets showed McCarthy pointing his finger yet again at another man. When he was attacking an associate of Joseph N. Welch, chief attorney for the Army, Welch stood up, faced the senator and said: "Until this moment, Senator, I think I never really gauged your cruelty or your recklessness. Let us not assassinate this lad further, Senator. You have done enough. Have you no sense of decency, sir, at long last? Have you no sense of decency?" and with that, the hearings ended, and so did McCarthy's witch hunting career. On December 2, 1954, the senate voted 67-22 to condemn him for "conduct contrary to Senatorial traditions." - - No wonder Floyd watched this real-life drama so often!) (Source for the preceding information partially excerpted from "The Fight for America: Senator Joseph McCarthy" by Jesse Friedman.)*

Fri. Apr 23: ("G" returned "Lifetime" battery!) Augie came at ½ past 7 o'clock. I still in bed because of light rain. On with plastic waterproofs and down to far end of lake. Lake full of water and we fished the water near brush and weeds. Large fish, many of them scooted around in the shallow water in the brush and weeds. Rained most of the time while we were out, but we had a grand day and reached home at 4 PM. Sears battery pushed motor the entire trip. Our bag- - 5 shiners, 9 perch, 25 kivvers and Augie got a 17" pickerel on a spoon. Otherwise we used worms.

Sat Apr 24: AM Rather tired today. We are looking for Richard via plane from California this eve. Dickie put my "Lifetime" battery back in chair. Richard in after supper - - gave me 2 lures Selma bought in Sacramento. Richard left his father feeling well and working in his garden. Gave me a drink of his father's wine. Later, Carlo came for his worms, as he goes trout fishing tomorrow AM. Geese have made nest on north end of island. I watched one working on nest.

Sun Apr. 25: Cloudy and cool. In most of day putting tackle in order.

Mon. Apr 26: Keeping battery charged up so it will take Carlo and I to inlet at far end of lake tonight. To boat at noon. Richard came on boat to toss bread to geese who came within 6 feet of boat. Then Angela came and watched me back off "run" so I would miss the large hole caused by the muskrat and last big rain. Watching McCarthy senate committee hearings on TV. On boat waiting for Carlo. Eddie and little Eddie came and little Eddie caught 4 kivvers with my rod. Carlo came at dark. Went to far end of lake. No luck - - no fish.

Tues. Apr 27: Out to island and found geese OK. Was afraid that they had been taken. Cat came aboard and took a fish. Back in to eat and watch senate committee on TV. Angela in with $150. She put a hundred in bank. Wrote orders to Sears and to I. Shore.

Wed Apr 28: Rain. E. Belloli stopped his loaded truck and spent the afternoon. When rain stopped at 4 PM we went out on lake - - he with fly rod. I got a perch and he a kivver. In AM I talked with News office about geese having nest on island. Asked them to notify game warden.

Thurs. Apr 29: Up early to take advantage of beautiful day. Propeller conked out near Prescott's point, so fished using fin to move around 'til 11. Then in to senate comm. on TV. After supper, Richard took off motor to fix propeller. Angela and Mrs. Stefanini and I watched Richard lay cement at entrance to boat run. Later, Eddie up to make out order to Herters. (He took order to mail tomorrow.)

Fri. Apr 30: Another fine day. Out fishing 8 to 10:30, (2 kivvers) then in to watch senate comm. on TV. Fed goose and gave kivver to cat. Theresa and Anna over with their babies. Angela put some leaves on my worm bed and Theresa got a couple of pails of earth and helped me to put it on top of the leaves. Card from I. Shore, which I answered while listening to committee hearing on TV. Phoned Eddie and he came up just before dark. We went around island with male goose scolding us as Eddie tied rope to his boat. Shidpoke attempted to land on island, but goose threw a fit - - flapping his wings and Shidpoke beat it. *(It seems that the word "shidpoke" is a colloquialism used by Floyd for some type of heron.)*

Saturday, May 1st, 1954: Up early - - beautiful day. Fed goose. Richard came and took fish for cat, then shoved me off. Went to far end of lake. Caught 21 kivvers and 3 perch during AM. Saw wakes of several good fish. Saw muskrat. Pads almost up to top of water in places. H. Sheppard came out in canoe and we talked ½ hour or more. He had a spinning outfit - - said he caught 6-lb. small mouth last Saturday and put him back. Forgot his canoe oars, went back 20 minutes later and they were gone. He said the big motorboat crowd would not be out for some weeks. Talked with man at far house. Said he and his two boys were learning to cast with their new rods. South of Prescott's point, stopped to let motor cool. Large blimp passed near overhead. East wind getting strong, so back to landing. Goose came beyond P. point so I gave him bread. Vises from I Shore and battery lantern (8) – 12 volt. Vises are fine and Richard put batteries in so looks like light will fill my needs perfectly. **Letter from Tom told me of Ben's passing.** *(The "Ben" referred to here was Floyd's oldest brother, Benny Haden. They had always been very close. This was the one who traveled all the way from their hometown of Lampasas, Texas to Fargo, North Dakota in 1909 to bring his younger brother home upon learning that he had suffered heat stroke and had fallen from his horse. There is no doubt that hearing of Ben's passing in a letter from his half-brother, Tom [of whom he was also very fond] must have been very difficult for him. However, the journal has only this one sentence to document it. - - The emphasis in the words is mine - -)* Two Eddies and Lorraine up after supper and fished an hour - - they caught no fish.

Sun. 2nd May: Carlo and Elaine up at 9 to get worms to trout fish. Said we may go to Spag's tomorrow night. *(Spag's was - - and still is - - one of the most famous and unique retail outlets in New England. Technically it is in Shrewsbury, but it has always been thought of as being in Worcester. It has been a family business since the day it opened in 1934 when Anthony Borgatti, who was nicknamed "Spag" set it up. He pioneered the concept of discounting in a building that had every conceivable item priced at what appeared to be rock-bottom prices, with all of it jammed into far less space than any "sensible" retailer would have thought prudent. With very little space for the hundreds of excited shoppers, all looking for bargains, to squeeze between the seemingly random piles of merchandise of all descriptions and categories, it was an experience to shop there. Customers loved it and many would travel considerable distances for the chance to pick up something they didn't even know they needed until they saw it wedged in between other items at what they thought of as an unbelievably low price.)* Temp 50 - -light rain. Tony up - - brought me a few worms. Turned them loose in bin for them to grow larger.

Mon. May 3: Temp 50 - -light rain. Carlo called at 6 to say he'd be up later for trip to Worcester. Later, he came with George and The Engineer. They loaded me in auto and we took off. I bought lurecast Langley reel. 15 @ $11.25. Also bought screwdriver, coat and hat. Very interesting to watch crowd at Spag's. George bought cap, spinning reel - - also a rod. Back home at 10.

Tues. May 4: Rain - - temp 45. Watched senate comm. on TV.

Wed. May 5: Temp 45. Lynn and Bunky brought book from library and some chrysanthemums from her grandmother. I planted them in worm bed. After supper, gave 2 kivvers to cat. Arthur Perrini put boat on water. Told me his name - - said he used to come over for lessons. Goose ate bread as I laid it upon boat edge.

Thurs. May 6: Temp 45. Cold and damp. Watched TV senate comm. hearings.

Fri. May 7: AM temp 50 degrees. Up early and out on lake. Sun out around noon and fine and warm then. In near 4 PM. Angela put log by birches and laid brick along edge of my trail to boat. Got 6 kivvers and 4 perch - - had to work for them. Pads are reaching top. Got Richard to tighten motor clamps.

Sat. May 8: Out at 8:30. Put bucket of earth on worm bed, then inside before it started to rain. Finished book "Eight Bailed Out".

Sun. May 9: Rain. To boat to pump water out. Battery ran down, so was stuck. Mr. Chiavarini standing on bank holding umbrella to keep off rain. Spoke to me so I asked him to go tell Richard, who came out and pushed me inside. Called "G" later to say that I would continue to use battery after Richard changed plug of electrical charger which had gone bad. Big gray boat raced into cove. I called police Officer Kelly. Said to call again if big boat comes in again. Later, Carlo up with his spinning rod. Then Eddie up so we came in for him. Eddie got a perch - - I got a calico. In after dark. Eddie stayed to tie flies 'till 11 PM. Let him have H's fly tying book.

Mon. May 10: To boat - - right rope off. Blackbirds have eaten all the bread I had on boat for geese! Angela put rope on boat hook. Carlo up at 7:45. Very cold and raw, but out to fish. Carlo got a fine 16 ½ inch pickerel - - also a perch. I, 5 kivvers and 1 perch. In house after 10. Carlo cleaned pickerel while I on way to bed. After putting pickerel, (skinned) in my freezer, Carlo left for the evening. And so to bed at 12:30.

Tues. May 11: Temp 50. Very cold and windy. Two fine things happened in AM. Cat came cruising for a fish to eat. I went on boat and raised minnow bucket partly out of water to get a kivver. With cat on my shoulder (right) I heard "auk - - auk" and looking back to my left saw goose with his long neck sticking out over boat urging me to give with the bread! Two Boy Scouts with bunch of cowboy books and 3 magazines, (Collier's and Look) - - (Guy Clemon's troop). Two fine boys, I'm sure. I tried to give them a dollar, but they refused - - they being more interested in getting a merit badge for their good deed. *(Guy Clemons had been Floyd's helper during the time, in the mid-thirties, when he was working for the WPA giving art lessons to the local children.)* A cold, windy, yet a most pleasant day with Angela bringing a splendid supper of lamb, ham, fried potatoes and spinach; yum yum! Later, Nick Scianna in to say that he could get me a 21 inch Philco TV set for my set and $150.00. Do not think much of the idea as J. DeCollibus offered me a $55 to $65 allowance on my set, while Nick would take it in return for making the deal.

Wed. May 12: Another cold, windy day. Angela brought Herter package, so I called Eddie's wife. Later, two Eddies in. We divided our things. Gave little Eddie silver ring.

Thurs. May 13: Watched senate comm. hearing on TV. Out at 11:30. Four kivvers and perch in 4 hours. Redheaded boys threw rocks at goose and threw net, etc. off boat.

Fri. May 14: Sunny day! Caught 1 kivver. In at 11. Took paint etc. and painted on boat landing, "KEEP OFF! YOU!" "PRIVATE - -KEEP OFF!"

Sat. May 15: Good day - -got 4 kivvers and 2 perch. Saw waves of big fish north of island.

Sun. 16th of May: Heavy rain all night and AM. Richard bailed out my boat for me. Out 3 to 7. Beautiful weather - - got 2 or 3 perch and 15 or 20 kivvers in notch north of island. Waves of big fish near muskrat den. Two big boats into cove, so in to talk to police. Kelly said he would be up. Later, Chief and an officer up. Showed them my boat. Going on to it, Sergeant Mehegan seemed rather stupid about the workings of my motors. He asked if the trouble with big boats was with some of the boatmen with whom I have a deal (made last year). I told him that it was new men that needed to be told to stay out of the cove. He was OK, but didn't like the dandelions growing about. Said that he spent a lot of time digging them out of his garden.

Mon. May 17: Out early using spoons. Two good strikes on brass hammered spoon.

Tues. May 18: Propeller clattering like a thrasher. Richard fixed it partly in evening.

Wed. May 19: Good day - - used fin to move around. Large waves north of island made by big fish. Snake came for my bait buckets. He must have a good nose. Fish took worm on hook on 10-lb. leader. Leader cut without tightening line.

Thurs. May 20: Good day - - out 9 AM to 5. Cloudy and cool but very little breeze. Got big hornpout south of island. 12 kivvers and perch. Watched boys catch turtle.

Fri. May 21: Rained all night and most of day. Down to pump water out of boat at noon.

Sat. May 22: Up early, but rain kept me in 'til 9 AM. Heavy, dark clouds. Turtle almost took my bait. Boy rode horse down to lake. I asked him what he would take for it. He said, "Not a million bucks". In to boat landing. Gave cat a fish. Richard brought plants and put in my worm bed. Inside, Dickie showed me his grinding machine that he made at Worcester Tech. Watched "You Asked For It", Stu Irwin & Jackie Gleason who was a riot.

Sun. May 23: Up early, but light rain kept me in 'til 8. Three kivvers and 1 perch in 4 hours of fishing! Temp 52 - - dark high clouds. Light rain in the afternoon. Listened to Red

Sox ball game in NY. Carlo up and we went out fishing - - 10 kivvers. Got 4 kivvers in 3 hours. Dark, cloudy all day.

Mon. May 24: Watched senate comm., then on lake. Caught 7 tiny perch (4 to 5 inches). After supper, out south of island. Fishing with 4" perch, got big turtle. Pulled it in. He had perch by its middle - - tail sticking out on one side of mouth and head (with hook) on other side. Called Richard - - he got in his boat and up to me. Got gaff hook out of my box, took line in hand, pulled up turtle and gaffed him. Then brought him in and put it in metal can. Later, Carlo up. We got a few fish. Then, in. Carlo took turtle to Columbus Hall. Carlo brought me wool jacket and 4 golf club handles.

Tues. May 25: Strong south wind. Watched senate comm. Out after supper - - poor fishing. Eddie up with 3 dozen chubs. Eddie got calico and I got 15" pickerel west of island. Inside, E. cleaned fish. I gave him fly rod and reel, (Salmon). Ed's birthday.

Wed. May 26: Up at 4:30 AM. Out to point and around island. One pickerel.

Thurs. May 27: Caught 2 pickerel between 15 and 16 inches on Eddie's chubs. Later, turned them loose.

Fri.: --

Sat. May 29: Strong south winds. Replanted 2 chrysanthemums and 2 rhubarbs from worm bed.

Sun. May 30: Out at 5 AM. Bucket-full of big kivvers.

Mon. May 31: Out at 5. 25 or 30 kivvers. On way in from notch near point got 20-inch pickerel with plug trolling. Called Richard who came out to help me net it. Called Carlo and he came for it. Talked with Bratica who came down to shore. He said geese with 1 little gosling were there the evening before.

Tues. June 1, 1954: Strong south wind all day. Carlo up after supper, then back home for my pickerel, Ed's calico, and Carlo's pickerel and his 9 trout, which Hazel had cooked very nicely for our fish feed. Eddie brought beer and a bag of cohogs. Augie, Carlo, Eddie and I enjoyed ourselves 'til 12:30.

Wed. June 2: Strong south wind and showers. Listening to senate comm. hearing.

Thurs. June 3: Out AM at 6. Fish hard to get. Battery down at door, so Angela pushed me inside. Charged battery 10 to 4. Then out 'til sundown. Perfect weather. Good catch of kivvers - - about 15, some very tiny ones in shallow water. Geese with gosling along Antonioli's shore. Boys came by on way to hunt turtles.

Fri. June 4: Light showers. Watched senate comm. hearings. At noon, down to boat to try new spoon tails. Antonioli says gosling is gone. That accounts for honking of geese all AM.

Sat. June 5: Out early - - in at noon. Got a lot of kivvers for garden fertilizer. Little breeze. Cloudy and hazy. Talked with Bratica and dog's owner. Also boys in green canoe came by for chat. Used motor to get to landing where battery failed, so called Richard who pushed me inside, where I made out order for battery charger, ($32.01) from Sears, Roebuck. Listened to Red Sox game.

Sun. June 6: Got out of bed at 11 AM. Out cultivating rhubarb. Got Dickie to bring water from lake for worm bed. Weather cool and windy. Watched ball game on TV.

Mon. June 7: Strong west wind - - cool and cloudy. Gathered worms. Watched McCarthy Senate comm. hearing on TV. Mostly monitored telephone calls. Called Edith on phone. She said that she is feeling somewhat better. After supper, rear wheel of chair went off floor of boat at right side. Richard helped me get back onto floor of boat and put down a new strip on right floor. In to landing as Carlo came, so out again east of island. Carlo got 4 kivvers and I got 1 kivver. Then in house. Battery failed, so Carlo pushed me inside. Carlo put some treble hooks on 3 spoons - - order to Sears.

Tues. June 8: Again cold NE wind - - dark and cloudy. In bed 'til 11 AM. Watched senate comm. hearing on TV. Cohn *(Roy)* is witness. Order to Herter for fishing items.

Wed. June 9: Cool and cloudy. Watched senate committee hearing on TV. Senator McClellen is my favorite and I like Cohn and McCarthy least. Out on lake at 12:30. Mrs. Stefanini came and sat on box near boat. Angela came for fish for cat. I put it in bucket so she could take it to cat. Later, I came in after anchoring only once, as battery stays down. Angela pushed me in, although battery did not fail this time. Again listening to S.C.H.

Thurs. June 10: Warm and cloudy. Out at 11 to 2:30. 16 kivvers in 50 feet of boat landing. Pauline's husband out in Richard's boat - - had 4 perch.

Fri. June 11: Listening to S.C.H. McCarthy on stand, being cross-examined. Out at 12. Hot and sultry. Two kivvers. In at 2:30 to watch S.C.H. on TV.

Sat. June 12: Beautiful day. Out west of island. Got a few kivvers - - in at 11AM. Shirt off in sun, first time in '54. Sears battery charger fixed and connected up by Richard and so, to bed early to charge battery all night.

Sun. June 13th: Up early and out after the shower. Got to pads south west of island when battery gave up. So, in to landing. Dickie pushed me in. "Lifetime" battery just no damn good. Called "G" and he came for the useless and worthless so-called <u>lifetime</u> battery. Said he'd be back in a few days. He'd better bring my $29.95.

Mon. June 14: Out in AM - - got a tiny perch. Out again 3:30. Took boy named Richard south of island. Boys in canoe saw turtles. Brought Richard in to landing, then out. Put on perch. Almost immediately got big something on. I think it was a bass. He got off hook while I put net in water.

Tues. June 15: Rain. Went to boat and pumped it out. Old Sears battery going great with help of new battery charger. Watching S.C.H. on TV. Richard brought letter from the old jerk, "G". I phoned him. Then wrote letter. He is totally crooked and unreliable, so I probably will not get back the $29.95 that I paid him for the worthless battery on March 1st.

Wed. June 16: Strong east wind. Listened to S.C.H. Out at 11 - - in at 2:30. Fed cat a couple of kivvers. Watching TV.

Thurs. June 17: Senate committee hearing ended.

Fri. June 18: Beautiful day.

Sat. June 19: Out early - - in at ½ past 11.

Sun. June 20: Wrote to Clara.

Mon. June 21: Strong south wind.

Tues. June 22: "G" and his pal came. Admitted the battery I had, had been found to be worthless. I gave them merry hell. "G" said that he would return my $29.95 this coming week! We'll see.

Wed. June 23: Out at 6, but wind came up, so in at 9 AM. Wind eased up, so out at 11. Cloudy - - began to rain about 1 PM, so in again. Wrote to Edith.

Thurs. June 24: Out AM. Fine day. Kivvers for cat.

Fri. June 25: Out early. Saw large turtle walking along on the bottom near my boat. "G" came and brought my $29.95 that I had paid him for the so-called "lifetime" battery that was faulty and that proved to be such a headache for me the 3 months that I tried to use it. Am now using my old Sears battery and my new Sears charger, and it is working fine.

Sat. June 26: Cloudy with a little rain - - finally, a shower drove me in from the lake.

Sun. June 27: Out early. Beautiful day. Got Louie to check the stump under water near main pad opening.

Mon. June 28: Out before 6 - - cloudy and cool, with sprinkles. Richard took kivver from my hook for cat. Out, but found unable to anchor down, so came back to run.

Tues. June 29: Up and out at 4 AM - - just faint break of day. Carlo up at night - - rain.

Wed. June 30: Used perch - - got big turtle on, but he ate the fish and let the hook come up bare. In at 1:30. **Open bass season!**

July 1st, 1954 Thurs.: Out at 4 AM. Temp. Upper 50's - - cold - - no fish.

Fri. July 2: Out at 5 AM. Cloudy and cool. In at 1 PM and to bed. Up at 6:30 PM and out at 8. "Swoosh!" near island at 1 AM. Strike at 1:30 on plug that I made. *(Here, he drew a small sketch of the plug he made.)* After jerking rod from my hand, he got off. Another "Swoosh!" near log. Started in at after 2 AM. Rain showers. Trouble getting into "run". In and to bed at 4 AM.

Sat. July 3: Up at 12, noon and got Dickie to fix nails so my rod will not slide across again and lose another bass. Plan to go to bed early and out about 2 AM tomorrow.

Sun. July 4: Up 12:30 AM - - out at 1:30. Weather cool - -westerly breeze. No rise and no strikes. In at 10. Carlo came with Elaine. Took big minnow pail, net, etc. and, with Augie got some shiners. Then got an old 50-gallon wine barrel, bored ½ inch holes, put it down in water by boat landing and dumped in shiners. Hope they live.

Mon. July 5: Out early with shiners. Carlo up after sun-up. Out 'til after 1 PM. Good shiners worked themselves to death - - little luck. Carlo got best fish - - 16" pickerel. Carlo put bobber and shiner in top of tree! Then climbed after it and brought it down. Carlo got lilies for two ladies. A jerk on shore threw rocks in water, so I called him names.

Tues. July 6: Eddie came about 10 AM - - out 'til 4:30. Got some small perch and some shiners, which I plan to use for bait tomorrow. Told Eddie that he could add my old shotgun to his collection anytime. His new house is being built.

Wed. July 7: Out 2 AM - - strong wind came up - - disagreeable! Shiners all dead, and perch weak and useless when I went to use them after daylight.

Thurs. July 8: No bass! To bed at 1:30 PM.

Fri. July 9: Up before 12 midnight and out around 1 AM. Motor went bad - - used fin - -arm sore. Richard fixed propeller gears and removed piece of brass.

Sat. July 10: AM out after daylight. Got first bass - - around 14 inches. Put him back.

Sun. 11 of July: Out before 2 AM. Cold with fog rising from water. Nothing in the way of fish.

Mon. July 12: Out after 6 AM. Great weather - - cool, but sunny. Used some worms - - hung very large perch (13" or more, I think). In at 1 PM. Augie in before supper to show me his new reels, casting and spinning. Augie is selling out and will move soon - - sorry.

Tues. July 13: Strong south wind. $1.00 to Helin for trebles. Letter to Edith. Talked to Eddie on phone - - said he'd be over tomorrow @ 7 for some night fishing.

Wed. July 14: Got some fish for cat and rested for tonight. Fine warm, sunny day. Eddie and Augie up after super. Eddie brought me some pepper plants. Out fishing, but thunderstorm drove us inside.

Thurs. July 15: Cold. Out at 2 AM. 52 degrees - - nothing.

Fri.: Cold

Sat.: Out 8:30 AM. Beautiful sunny day - - in at 1 PM.

Sun. July 18: Strong south wind.

Mon., Tues., Wed.: No bass.

Thurs.: Hung big bass near pines on red & white plug. He straightened hook out and got away.

Fri.: No bass.

Fri. July 30: got bass about a foot long - - put him back.

Sat.: AM early over to point on other side of lake. Got my first white perch - - 9 ½ inch trolling, and 18" pickerel on night crawler.

Sun. August 1, 1954: Threatening weather, so rested up a bit.

Mon. Aug. 2: Up early - - anchored at point near pines. Got white perch and big kivver at one time!

White perch took big fly on spinner ahead of worm hook. Eddie over at 7 PM, so I got up out of bed and we went to far end of lake at Hollis Street. Casting, but no bass. On way home, plane pilot flashed his lights on us in reply to Ed's flashing signals. In home after 11.

Tues.: Rain all day.

Wed. August 4: Got first good bass of season. Fish took entire plug into mouth, so hooked himself. Louie weighed him - - almost 2 ½ lbs. - - 16 ¾" long. What a job cleaning him! Into freezer. Plenty of fish now with the pickerel and white perch, for our fish fry - - Carlo, Eddie, Augie and I.

Thurs. August 5; Up early - - 3 AM - - out at 4. Wind whipping in different directions, but light. Over to Prescott point. Cold and windy there, so went past point and anchored. Casting with plugs. Wind stronger. Used fin to move about to cast. When the sun came up clear and red, I decided to call it a day and started home - - and with God's help my little motor pushed the propeller thru the waves. Plenty of "juice" in battery.

Fri.: COLD - -56 degrees. On lake for little while.

Sat. & Sun. 8th: No Soap!

Mon. August 9: Mailed letters to Clara, Herter, and Montgomery Ward. Called J. DeCollibus to fix TV set and aerial. Out short time on lake in early AM, but rain began and lasted all day. Painted some plugs (4). If the bass don't bug their eyes out when they see these, then nothing will make them. To bed early, then Augie came to say that Carlo and Eddie were on the way so we'd have the fish fry now. But my fish were frozen, so talked them into making it next Monday night. Eddie came with 8 bottles of Haffenreffer. Later, Carlo came. Eddie put bag of cohogs in my refrigerator for next Monday. Carlo, Augie, and I chipped in a dollar each for next week's refreshments.

Tues. Aug. 10: Rained all day.

Wed. Aug. 11: Up at 5 AM and out at 6 and over to troll over the reefs. Got 2 kivvers and 2 white perch. Weather very cool. Painted some plugs.

Thurs. Aug. 12: Cold - -strong wind all day.

Fri. Aug. 13: Cold, but sunny. Out on lake AM. - - nothing.

Sat. Out AM.

Sun. Aug. 15: Out AM. Irwin in with me and I loaned him my Heddon rod.

Mon. 16th: Out at 8 AM - - warm and foggy. Got 16 ½" pickerel between "points" with large brass spinner spoon. Cleaned it to add to our collection of fish for fish fry tonight. Phoned to Edith. Angela defrosted the fish and took them up to cook for us tonight. Eddie came about 7. He and I took a little jaunt on lake, using my rods to cast. Then Augie came with refreshments and put 6 quart bottles of ale in my refrigerator. Ed held my flashlight for me to see how to back off boat, then inside to open a bottle. Called Carlo who had got in from work late, (8 PM). Carlo arrived at 9. A good time of drinking, eating good fish, and joshing 'til the break-up of party at 12. Rain shower about 10.

Tues. Aug. 17: Very cold and windy. Used brush to put rubbing alcohol on plant lice on my chrysanthemums. Killed the lice - - hope there is no injury to plants.

Wed., Thurs., & Fr.: Richard built plank fence to hold loam for my new garden. On Friday, went with Richard up to look at his garden.

Sat. Aug. 21: Mr. Stefanini brought chicken & rabbit manure in wheelbarrow. Out using spinning outfit, got fat 19" pickerel. Angela went down to boat to weigh it - -2 lbs. - - My best pickerel.

Sun. Aug 22: Fine, cool day. Hung big turtle on spinning outfit. Talked with Roberge and Irwin.

Mon. Aug. 23: Cold in early AM - - later, beautiful warm sunny day. Boy in green canoe got me two frogs.

Thurs. Aug. 26: Got large pickerel - -19 or 20" - -on spinning rig. Laid rod down to put net in water - - smart pickerel threw goldfish lure from his mouth and wrapped it around end of rod - - - - -.

Sat. Aug. 28 : 13" bass on S.M. plug. Got man in big boat with blue top to unhook bass and put him back.

Sun.: Aug. 29: Irwin and I looked over the brush piles. He will try to learn what the large transparent balls attached to sticks are. Might be frogspawn.

Mon. Aug.30: Caught 13" bass - - put him back to grow. Around pickerel point, hung bass at #2 pads, (on S.M.) Back between points with spinning rig, got bass on goldfish in splash out of water. Judge bass 15 or 16" - - hung up on brush pile that Richard put in, so had to break line and lose fish and goldfish. What a day! Dickie fixed my hoe and got dead fish out of boat. Carlo up after 7. He and I out 15 or 20 minutes, but wind rising from NE, so in. Carlo took my 2-lb. pickerel. Raining when he left for home.

Tues. Aug 31: Raining hard from NE. Hurricane came about 10 AM. Ended about 3 PM. Latter half wind was from SE. Richard home at 12:15 and fixed Carlo's radio to battery so we could get radio news. About 4 PM, I went up hill where there were men sawing up trees and limbs. Richard's fine tomatoes lying flat on ground. My TV antenna flat on roof. Two Eddies came - - big Eddie stung by hornet. Electricity out completely.

Wed. September 1, 1954: Moving around in chair very little to save battery.

Thurs. Sept. 2: Out on lake in AM. Irwin moved roll of weeds from in front of my boat landing. Richard pushed me back inside at noon.

Fri. Sept. 3: Inside, hoping the electric company will have power on soon. Changed reels.

Sat. Sept 4: Richard pushed me to boat in AM and back in at noon. Hung a bass south of island and caught one nearly 14" near boat run.

Sun. Sept. 5: Thank heaven the electric power came on about 20 minutes past 7 AM. Richard in soon after. Able to sit up once more by motor instead of having to get Richard or Dickie to boost me into a sitting position! Strong wind from SE - - cloudy.

Mon. Sept. 6: Up 2:45, out 3:40 AM. Mild, calm weather 'till after sunset when wind became strong from north. Got no bass, 'though one snapped at plug near my fin. Got big perch on plug near tree downed by storm. In early.

Tues. Sept. 7: Out at 6:30 AM. Got 16 ½" pickerel at "downed" tree. Cleaned him and started to the far pads - - got a big kivver on a plug. Rain drove me in. Electric storms and rain beginning at 10. Angela down and washed my apples and put fish in freezer. Checked plugs and sharpened hooks.

Wed. Sept. 8: Got bass on twice south of island, (shiner minnow). Lost it in weeds - - straightened hook. Carlo and his pal, Jim up at night - -brought goldfish.

Thurs.: Nothing.

Fri.: Bad weather.

Sat. Sept. 11: Watched TV from 2 to 6 AM. Telling of hurricane progress. About 9, Richard and Louie in to watch TV with me. We had a few drinks. Raining very hard - - wind strong from north. Hurricane winds began about 11 AM, but big blow came about 5 PM from north. My boat would have sunk, but Richard took Louie and they bailed it out with buckets. Electricity out! Eddie Belloli and his father up in evening. Helped Richard and Dickie put the boat in order. Water very high.

Sun. Sept. 12: Up at street watching Richard and Dickie clear trees ruined by storm.

Mon. Sept. 13: Electricity back on. Richard raised run so I could get on boat.

Tues. Sept. 14: Rain. Out about 10 AM- - in at 1. Windy. Lake very high. Mrs. Stefanini waved from shore.

Wed. Sept. 15: Rain & cold. Eddie Belloli over at night with old gun and 2 quarts of Pickwick Ale.

Thurs., Fri., & Sat.: Cold, rainy, and raw.

Sun. Sept. 19, & Mon., Tues. Wed., and Thurs.: Cold & windy or rain.

Fri. Sept 24: Temp 40 degrees. Up and got "catch" on left side of chest, so decided to call D.A.A., then Dr. Dodd, who said he would be up Monday AM.   Hope my heart keeps ticking.

My Daily Prayer:
I pray to my God that
You will help me to use
good judgment always
and I pray that You will guide
and comfort me and all
kind and good people everywhere.

Mon. Sept. 27: Dr. Dodd came. Looked over my boat. Stayed and talked a couple of hours. Said my trouble in back was bursitis. Later, Carlo and Augie came and took me to

Spags. Carlo brought me a bag full of nice apples. They stopped at center and got ale for a drink.

Tues. Sept. 28: Rain.

Wed., Thurs., & Fri.: Watched World Series - - NY vs. Cleveland. Warm weather, so out all mornings. Got a dace and shiner Tues.

Sat. October 2, 1954: World Series ended - - Giants winning 4 straight.

Sun. Oct. 3: Got big pickerel almost into net. He regurgitated the kivver.

Mon. Oct. 4: Caught 17 ½" pickerel on kivver as it touched water. Then hung big bass who got loose after jumping high out of water. (Using 6" perch.) In PM, got 2 more heavy strikes.

October 5, Tues.: After spending about 3 hours fishing with #4 hook for proper size kivver finally got one and put it on hook. Soon got the big pickerel, and what a beauty! Measured 22 inches and very fat. This is best pickerel this year by far. Carlo up at night.

Tally of pickerel caught

1 - - 22 inch

1 - - 20 inch

2 - - 19 inch

2 - - 18 inch

1 - - 17 ½ in.

3 - - 16 ½ in.

Wed. Oct. 6: Out for a little while in PM. Frost at night.

Thurs. Oct. 7: cold & windy.

Fri. Oct. 8: Out for a little while at temperature of 45 degrees. Too cold to fish.

Sat. Oct. 9: Strong south wind - - cold. Worked with garden earth getting ready to bed down my worms for the winter.

Sunday, October 10, 1954

My God, I thank you for the privilege of being alive, and I thank You for my good fortune in feeling well and carefree and content.

I am very thankful for my home, for my chair, and for my boat.

And I thank you God for the few friendly people who help to make living more pleasant for me.

(The above is my daily prayer)

Tues.: Oct. 12. Got up at 3 and to boat 4 AM. Temperature about 70. Medium south wind. Water cold. No luck as to fish, but enjoyed the beautiful moonlight. About sun-up, a big pickerel followed my red & white plug to boat and splashed his big tail clear of the water as he went down.

Wed. and Thurs.: Very warm weather. No small bait-size perch and kivvers can be found. Thurs. AM early went over to the reefs on far side of lake, but got nothing trolling over or fishing there.

Fri.,Oct 15: Out near island - - used large bait, (5"). Fish bit it about half way up its body, then turned bait loose. (Bass, no doubt.) Hurricane due tonight, so winds getting up and so in at noon. Feeding cat a fish and taking all my rods (3) home.

1955

Angela went to Natick hospital March 29th for operation. Mr. & Mrs. Antonioli and Louie & Anna came in to see that I was OK during the following few days while Angela was away.

Very cold and windy spring. Richard got boat in water April 9. Louie and Nick Ortenzi helped put it in water. 10th, (Easter) I went out. Got 5 kivvers for cat. Cold and windy, so out but few times - -2 or 3 times and got a few kivvers for cat before opening day, April 16th, which was very windy. Carlo up a couple of nights after I got boat in. Went out with light and saw 17" bass, pickerel and 'pout. Richard and I out with him following Thursday night. Saw 18-inch pickerel. Richard fixed a new pump. Have new light anchor (extra) at front of boat.

Sat. 16 April: Bought new 4 year Sears battery. Ed & little Eddie up for an hour or two. Had new flyrod.

Mon. Apr. 18: Up early and went to far end of lake where I spent the day. Got 2 perch and kivvers. Canadian goose without mate honked considerably. Talked with lady and girls in boat about goose, etc. On way home, stopped to talk with boys in deep water cove. In home at 4 PM. Strong wind came up about 5 PM. Pleasant, sunny day. Took lunch of cheese, salami, and a banana!

Tues.: Cold and windy. Out to look after my garden and worms.

Wed.: Good day! Eleven kivvers and 6 perch.

Thurs.: Cold and windy.

Fri. Apr 22: Light rain. Out 11 – 2 after rain stopped. Tried small perch and worm - - 1 kivver. Cold and cloudy, so inside listening to Red Sox game from NY.

Sat. Apr. 23: Windy, but out anyway. Got 3 kivvers. Another large dead bass drifted to the lake shore and Richard buried him in my garden. I wrote Sheppard about the 2 dead bass.

Sun. Apr. 24: Cold, damp and windy.

Mon. Apr. 25: Temp. at 43 all day. Strong NE wind with light rain. Went to pump out boat but couldn't get pump to work. Brought the 5 tomato plants in separate pots inside as cold weather made them look sick. Wrote letter to Edith.

Tues., Wed., Thurs., Friday - - Rain and cold: 42 to 45 degrees.

Sat. Apr. 30: Sunny and cold. Went to back of lake, but no fish.

Sunday, May 1, 1955: Took David out. 12 kivvers in AM, 19 in PM along north shoreline.

Monday: Very windy!

Tues. May 3: 23 kivvers. Beautiful day. Night, Carlo, Eddie, Augie and Joe up with beer. Made me an Honorary member of their N.H. Sportsman's club. Eddie brought cooked trout - - a nice one!

Wed. May 4: 25 kivvers, some perch and shiners.

Thur: 23 kivvers, two of them 9 ½ inches long. Saw big bass feeding.

Fri. May 6: 23 kivvers.

Sat.: 20 fish in AM, 10 of them shiners. In afternoon the 2 boys west of island got 28 'pout. I caught 4.

Sun. May 8: Rainy, but out. Hornpout gone, but got 4 shiners and 3 kivvers. Carlo came up in afternoon to clean the 4 hornpout. Richard got fine tomato plants in Natick. He planted 10 plants in my garden. Put scrap fish at roots of plants. - - Cold.

Mon. May 9: Cold and windy - - temp 54 degrees at 1 PM. Dug some small worms to put in boxes to feed them and use them later when they are grown. Also, some larger worms to use tomorrow. Rigged up my spinning outfit for use some warm day. Eddie up in evening to join in order for hooks from Herter's.

Tues. May 10: Cold and windy, but out at 8 AM to 4 PM. Got 17 mixed including 5 shiners. Gust of wind blew my brown jacket into water and it drifted to nook north of island. Carlo came up at night and got my coat. We made out hook order.

Wed. May 11: 14 fish. Hung pickerel and bass on bait fish. Called Augie. Carlo up at night with Elaine. I in bed. They went fishing in my boat.

Thurs. May 12: Up at 5 AM and on boat waiting when Augie arrived about 7. Went down to far end of lake, and came in at 2 PM. We got 70 fish. Fine sunny and warm day.

Fri. May 13: Fine day. Got 20 kivvers, etc. before noon. In the afternoon, Angela and I transplanted Sweetpeas, pinks and asters. Dug some worms. Tired.

Floyd getting ready for another day of fishing. Note details of boat construction and rigging. Photo taken in 1952.

CHAPTER 18

THE FINAL YEARS
1956 - 1966

Although there are no further entries in his journal, Floyd maintained his full-time involvement with all aspects of fishing. He continued to enjoy the company of his old pals as well as a special bond with my parents and me. When Edith Rowena Noyes Greene passed away at the home of her dear friends in Maynard on June 23, 1956, he felt a deep sense of loss. He arranged to have a beautiful basket of her favorite flowers sent to the funeral home and had it signed,
" 'Brother', Floyd Niles Walser".

For the next three years he continued to enjoy the freedom to get around in his room, his yard or his lake whenever the mood struck him. A freedom he constantly felt so fortunate to have had bestowed upon him by my dad, a man who had really been a stranger to him until he built his house at "Lucky Point". Floyd knew of my nickname for our property and mentioned to me more than once that he thought I had come up with a very appropriate name, since he too felt especially lucky there.

On his 70th birthday, January 29, 1958 Floyd was thrilled to have a special visit of his pals to honor the event. Carlo, his brother, Eddie, and Augie came over after work that evening and were joined in Floyd's room by Richie. Carlo brought a cake and bottles of beer to share. When Carlo presented the cake, Floyd said something about not having any birthday cake candles to put on it. Someone produced a tabletop size candle, stuck it into the top of the cake and lit it - - perfect! The combined resources of the birthday party visitors presented Floyd with a fifth of his favorite bourbon, as well as a bottle of wine. They all knew that at the rate at which Floyd consumed hard liquor, the whiskey should last

Floyd's 70th birthday celebration:
Top: Carlo, "Birthday Boy", Augie, Richie
Bottom: Richie, Eddie, Augie

him at least until his 90th birthday. They all agreed that they were looking forward to another fishing season during which Floyd would catch a nice mess of bass and pickerel that would wind up in another fish fry in his room; just like they had come to enjoy in the past few years.

By the end of fishing season in 1958, he was beginning to slow down a bit and to tire out more easily after even a partial day of chasing after his gamefish. One evening, after coming in from a particularly blustery day on the lake, during which all the fish were still safely swimming and eluding his lures, he commented that he wished he could plug himself into a recharger the way he perked up his battery. He said that then maybe his 70 year-old body would be revitalized so he could keep up with himself. He realized that he was finding it more and more difficult to do all that he wanted, and felt as though he would have to start cutting back on the amount of time he spent out on the lake.

He must have been totally unprepared however for the news that Richard and Angela delivered one Sunday in February 1959. They had decided to sell the house and build a new, smaller one in the neighboring town of Natick. A combination of factors had made this change necessary. The increases in real estate taxes were becoming difficult to manage, and the size of the house and yard were becoming a bit too much for my mother to take care of without getting run down. They had put their hearts and souls into the planning, design and construction of this, their dream house, so it was a difficult choice for them, but one that they felt they must make. They would, of course build him a room of his own in the new basement, which like his current home would have full length windows and a door that opened out to ground level around back. But unlike his present accommodations, there was no lake anywhere near there. He would be able to take all of his personal stuff from in his room. But there would be no point in bringing his fishing paraphernalia, and his beloved boat would become only a memory.

As the new house neared completion in July, 1959 with Richie once again doing the lion's share of the work, one of the last items to be completed was the cesspool for Floyd. This was identical in design and construction to what had been successfully used in the past, and was located just outside one of the windows that were planned to be next to Floyd's bed. However, when the Board of Health in Natick and the Welfare/Disability agency that had been following Floyd for years, found out about this installation, they would not permit it to be put to use under any circumstances. This was devastating news for all involved. No way could be seen to get around this obstacle. Floyd would not be able to continue to live downstairs from his good friends, Richard and Angela.

The Welfare people decided that the only thing to do was to put Floyd into a nearby Veteran's Administration hospital/nursing home. The facility was checked out thoroughly and the staff was interviewed, especially by Carlo and Richie, in the hope that they would understand the unique and very special person who may be soon joining them. Floyd was driven out to see the place for himself to help minimize the feelings he must have had as a result of having to leave his comfortable and exciting lakeside home. It was with great reluctance on the parts of all concerned that he was moved into a room of his own in this place along with his motorized chair and a minimum of his belongings. The many items that simply could not be accommodated in the nursing home room were moved from the old lakeside apartment into the room that Richie had intended him to use in his new home in Natick. Carlo brought some of the surplus personal items to his home to store for Floyd.

The staff at his new home did allow him to bring a fair amount of his painting supplies and equipment. Carlo had shown them some of the fine work that his buddy had done over the years and they were duly impressed. They felt that it the fabled old elm had just recently been cut down added to the timeliness of his entry.

Over the next few years he began experimenting with a very different (for him) use of color. He was reaching for a modern style, but tried to make it a style of his own. Some of his friends and visitors, familiar with his old work, were taken aback by the garish and wild colors he was putting down. Most thought the work so different as to be called "awful" or "weird". No one, however voiced any negative criticism directly to him, but would agree in private that he was becoming sort of "off-the-wall". Then every once in a while, he would produce something that most would say was his best work yet, with brilliant colors and fine brushwork.

As he aged, the number of paintings he attempted reduced dramatically. He read, watched TV, especially boxing and baseball as well as variety shows and drama, and otherwise kept himself busy. He continued to exchange letters on a regular basis with his sister, Clara, in Oregon. They would update each other on events in their lives. Painting became less and less of an interest for him. Or perhaps the effort it would take for him to set up everything and to get the inspiration for a new painting had become too tiring, even if he still have the desire to express himself with his artwork. To help him continue to realize that among the many paintings he had done in his lifetime, there were still several that should be seen and appreciated, Carlo got him into another venue. Framingham's Temple Beth Am had put together what they called "Art '65", which included paintings and sculpture from dozens of local artists and which ran from October 31 through November 7, 1965. That this was a special honor for the old artist was borne out by the way in which the show was described in the local newspapers. The core for the show was made up of 3 prominent figures in the art world; Arthur Hoener, Iso Papa, and Jane Kay. Their careful screening of the submissions insured that what would be shown would represent the best in every school of expression; the best that "Art '65" could bring to Framingham. Some of

would be excellent therapy and a great way for him to relax if he could continue with this artwork. They would not, however allow any etching acid to be brought into their facility, so creating etchings was a thing of the past. Realistically, he hadn't done many etchings once he had moved into our basement apartment, so that part wasn't a big adjustment. What was a difficult transition was being in the hospital-like surroundings with many residents who were desperately ill. He was not the least bit ill, and couldn't seem to imagine himself as having to spend his last years in such a place.

As could well be expected, this move did not suit the independent and still very sharp Mr. Walser one bit. He was unhappy there from the start and the staff didn't know quite what to make of him. Here was a man who in some ways had a more serious disability than many of the other residents, and yet he insisted that he required a minimum of help from them. Everyone, residents and staff alike were in awe of his motored chair and his ability to drive it out of his room, down the halls and wherever he wanted to go. Richie, after a long talk with the person in charge to convince him that it was safe, saw to it that the battery charging station was properly set up where the new arrival could recharge his battery as often as it might be needed. Floyd morosely noted that it most likely would only need to be recharged once a week, if that, since he wouldn't be going anywhere very often.

The nursing staff insisted that they provide him with more care and attention than he wanted or needed. His unhappiness with his new surroundings reflected in his mood and the way he would react to minor annoyances. The principal result of his unhappiness was that several of the nurses reacted negatively to his flip remarks and caused him even more discomfort.

He did try to paint, but had a hard time getting into it. He asked Carlo, who continued to visit 3 or 4 times a week to please try to find him somewhere else to live; somewhere that didn't have nurses running around and patients who needed so much care. Most of the residents in his ward were men in their upper 80s and 90s and the majority of them were very frail, sickly and often demented. Very few of them ever had any visitors. Seeing them daily upset him greatly. He could look after himself if given half a chance.

It took about 6 months, but finally one evening early in 1960, during one of Carlo's very frequent visits, some exciting news was brought to the gloomy Mr. Walser. A room was located in a house on Waverly Street in South Framingham in an area know as Coburnville. Carlo had been talking to everybody who would even half listen (and he knew a lot of people in Framingham and surrounding towns) about how much his old pal needed a place to live. This location was only about a mile or so from Carlo's house, so frequent visits would continue to be no problem. There was a railroad track right out practically in the back yard instead of a lake, but there was not a lot of traffic on it. The room was neat and clean and had a nice front porch where he would be able to sit on good days and paint or simply watch the world go by. The rent was within reach of his limited resources and the owner of the house was someone Carlo knew and liked and was thought to be a good person. Floyd would be safe there in this mainly blue-collar neighborhood of dependable, hard-working people. As could be expected, Floyd was ready to move with no questions asked, except "How soon can I get in there?"

What a tremendous difference the new apartment made on Floyd's happiness! Once again he was in his own place with no sick people or hospital smells to assault his sensibilities. The room was large enough for him to have all his old belongings back surrounding him, comforting him just by their presence. Here he felt that he would in fact be interested in resuming his painting and drawing. Working hard at recapturing his old first love would go a long way towards helping him to miss Waushakum Pond a little less. He felt that after the VA hospital, this was like heaven.

Once again, his biggest helper in moving in and adjusting to his new surroundings was his faithful old friend, Carlo.

There is little doubt that without that fine and good-h[earted] man to look after him so well, Floyd's life at this point [would] have been very different indeed. Richard and Angela d[rove] into visit when they could, but it was Carlo now, w[ho was] Floyd's principal benefactor. I, by this time had gr[aduated] from college, gotten a job, gotten married and had s[tarted a] family. I was so busy with my own new life that I ra[rely vis]ited the man who only a few years ago had lived do[wnstairs] in my house and whom I had come to think of as [a] "relative" and good friend.

Once he had really settled into his new place, a[nd no] longer "distracted" by a lake in his back yard, h[e got back] into his artwork. The first few watercolors and [etchings he] cranked out did not please him and he realized [he was] out of practice. However, after a few months of re[viewing the] basics, with his characteristic single-minded de[termination] he was once again turning out art that he found a[cceptable. In] early 1962 in one of his frequent letters to Clar[a he wrote:] "... I have now switched from etching to water[colors] and am turning out better paintings now than [I have ever] done before. I am 74 years old now and can on[ly work a few] hours a day. Usually I do the drawing the first [day and paint] it the second day. On larger watercolor picture[s it takes 3] or 4 days to finish them."

It had been several years since his work h[ad appeared] in various art shows and exhibits and he mis[sed] being invited to participate and to have his e[fforts seen by] people who knew art. So he was more than [ready to] feel that excitement once again. His recentl[y finished wa]tercolor painting of the Gates Street Elm, [titled The] *Framingham Elm*, was accepted by the jur[y of the Eastern] States Exposition in Springfield, Massa[chusetts. He had] painted, sketched and produced etchings [of this] giant for many years and from many vanta[ge points. In this] latest rendition, he had worked from one [of his old draw]ings and added some of his latest techni[ques] would be excellent therapy and a great way for him to relax if he could continue with this artwork. They would not, however allow any etching acid to be brought into their facility, so creating etchings was a thing of the past. Realistically, he hadn't done many etchings once he had moved into our basement apartment, so that part wasn't a big adjustment. What was a difficult transition was being in the hospital-like surroundings with many residents who were desperately ill. He was not the least bit ill, and couldn't seem to imagine himself as having to spend his last years in such a place.

As could well be expected, this move did not suit the independent and still very sharp Mr. Walser one bit. He was unhappy there from the start and the staff didn't know quite what to make of him. Here was a man who in some ways had a more serious disability than many of the other residents, and yet he insisted that he required a minimum of help from them. Everyone, residents and staff alike were in awe of his motored chair and his ability to drive it out of his room, down the halls and wherever he wanted to go. Richie, after a long talk with the person in charge to convince him that it was safe, saw to it that the battery charging station was properly set up where the new arrival could recharge his battery as often as it might be needed. Floyd morosely noted that it most likely would only need to be recharged once a week, if that, since he wouldn't be going anywhere very often.

The nursing staff insisted that they provide him with more care and attention than he wanted or needed. His unhappiness with his new surroundings reflected in his mood and the way he would react to minor annoyances. The principal result of his unhappiness was that several of the nurses reacted negatively to his flip remarks and caused him even more discomfort.

He did try to paint, but had a hard time getting into it. He asked Carlo, who continued to visit 3 or 4 times a week to please try to find him somewhere else to live; somewhere that didn't have nurses running around and patients who needed so much care. Most of the residents in his ward were men in their upper 80s and 90s and the majority of them were very frail, sickly and often demented. Very few of them ever had any visitors. Seeing them daily upset him greatly. He could look after himself if given half a chance.

It took about 6 months, but finally one evening early in 1960, during one of Carlo's very frequent visits, some exciting news was brought to the gloomy Mr. Walser. A room was located in a house on Waverly Street in South Framingham in an area know as Coburnville. Carlo had been talking to everybody who would even half listen (and he knew a lot of people in Framingham and surrounding towns) about how much his old pal needed a place to live. This location was only about a mile or so from Carlo's house, so frequent visits would continue to be no problem. There was a railroad track right out practically in the back yard instead of a lake, but there was not a lot of traffic on it. The room was neat and clean and had a nice front porch where he would be able to sit on good days and paint or simply watch the world go by. The rent was within reach of his limited resources and the owner of the house was someone Carlo knew and liked and was thought to be a good person. Floyd would be safe there in this mainly blue-collar neighborhood of dependable, hard-working people. As could be expected, Floyd was ready to move with no questions asked, except "How soon can I get in there?"

What a tremendous difference the new apartment made on Floyd's happiness! Once again he was in his own place with no sick people or hospital smells to assault his sensibilities. The room was large enough for him to have all his old belongings back surrounding him, comforting him just by their presence. Here he felt that he would in fact be interested in resuming his painting and drawing. Working hard at recapturing his old first love would go a long way towards helping him to miss Waushakum Pond a little less. He felt that after the VA hospital, this was like heaven.

Once again, his biggest helper in moving in and adjusting to his new surroundings was his faithful old friend, Carlo.

There is little doubt that without that fine and good-hearted man to look after him so well, Floyd's life at this point would have been very different indeed. Richard and Angela dropped into visit when they could, but it was Carlo now, who was Floyd's principal benefactor. I, by this time had graduated from college, gotten a job, gotten married and had started a family. I was so busy with my own new life that I rarely visited the man who only a few years ago had lived downstairs in my house and whom I had come to think of as a special "relative" and good friend.

Once he had really settled into his new place, and was no longer "distracted" by a lake in his back yard, he got back into his artwork. The first few watercolors and pastels he cranked out did not please him and he realized that he was out of practice. However, after a few months of reviewing the basics, with his characteristic single-minded determination, he was once again turning out art that he found acceptable. In early 1962 in one of his frequent letters to Clara he reported "... I have now switched from etching to watercolor painting and am turning out better paintings now than I have ever done before. I am 74 years old now and can only work 5 or 6 hours a day. Usually I do the drawing the first day and paint it the second day. On larger watercolor pictures I may take 3 or 4 days to finish them."

It had been several years since his work had been shown in various art shows and exhibits and he missed the thrill of being invited to participate and to have his efforts praised by people who knew art. So he was more than a little happy to feel that excitement once again. His recently completed watercolor painting of the Gates Street Elm, which he called *Framingham Elm*, was accepted by the jury for the Eastern States Exposition in Springfield, Massachusetts. He had painted, sketched and produced etchings of this sprawling giant for many years and from many vantage points. For this latest rendition, he had worked from one of those old paintings and added some of his latest techniques. The fact that the fabled old elm had just recently been cut down added to the timeliness of his entry.

Over the next few years he began experimenting with a very different (for him) use of color. He was reaching for a modern style, but tried to make it a style of his own. Some of his friends and visitors, familiar with his old work, were taken aback by the garish and wild colors he was putting down. Most thought the work so different as to be called "awful" or "weird". No one, however voiced any negative criticism directly to him, but would agree in private that he was becoming sort of "off-the-wall". Then every once in a while, he would produce something that most would say was his best work yet, with brilliant colors and fine brushwork.

As he aged, the number of paintings he attempted reduced dramatically. He read, watched TV, especially boxing and baseball as well as variety shows and drama, and otherwise kept himself busy. He continued to exchange letters on a regular basis with his sister, Clara, in Oregon. They would update each other on events in their lives. Painting became less and less of an interest for him. Or perhaps the effort it would take for him to set up everything and to get the inspiration for a new painting had become too tiring, even if he did still have the desire to express himself with his artwork.

To help him continue to realize that among the many paintings he had done in his lifetime, there were still several that should be seen and appreciated, Carlo got him into another venue. Framingham's Temple Beth Am had put together what they called "Art '65", which included paintings and sculpture from dozens of local artists and which ran from October 31 through November 7, 1965. That this was a special honor for the old artist was borne out by the way in which the show was described in the local newspapers. The jury for the show was made up of 3 prominent figures in the art world; Arthur Hoener, Iso Papa, and Jane Kay. Their careful screening of the submissions insured that what would be hung would represent the best in every school of expression; the finest that "Art '65" could bring to Framingham. Some of

Floyd's best work was selected by this jury. Once again, much praise for his talent was heaped upon 'ol Tex and he felt proud and content.

In early 1965 he had arranged for a youngster who lived nearby, to come in each afternoon when school was over for the day and check up on him. This capable 12-year-old, named Arthur would do whatever needed to be done. He would take care of the bedpan, change the bed linens once a week, bringing the soiled ones home to be washed, open a can of soup or other food and heat it for him, run quick errands such as buying a few groceries, mail a letter, and generally make himself useful. Arthur enjoyed his brief afternoon visits with Mr. Walser, as he always called him. He felt more like a friend than an employee, earning 25 cents a day.

February 16, 1966, a Wednesday, was cold and blustery. When Arthur showed up to do whatever needed doing, he walked right in through the unlocked door as usual and announced his presence. Floyd was in his trusty old motorized chair at the sink, the water running and his right arm extended to hold an apple being washed. His back was to Arthur and with the sound of the water running, it appeared that he hadn't heard his helper enter. Arthur walked up closer saying, "Hi, Mr. Walser. What's up for today?" When Floyd failed to respond, the young fellow knew immediately that something was very wrong. Floyd had died. Right there at the sink. Washing a piece of fruit for a snack.

Arthur immediately called Carlo and told him what he had just discovered, not believing the words as he said them. In a few minutes that seemed like hours to the poor kid, Carlo and two Framingham police officers showed up. Carlo did not want to believe that his good old friend was suddenly gone. They had planned to play cards that night with a couple of other local pals. It was too sudden, too quick. In fact, just a few days ago, on February 1st Floyd had written what was to be his last letter to Clara. In that note he expressed optimism for the upcoming springtime, indicating that he was feeling better and wished Clara and her second husband, Carl Hanson, a good year ahead.

A few days later, Floyd Niles Walser, cowboy, artist, fisherman, and most of all, good friend was laid to rest in a grave in Edgell Grove Cemetery in Framingham Centre. A small rectangular stone with his name and the dates of his birth and death was placed on the ground to mark the grave. Edith and Roy Greene, who had passed away 10 and 20 years ago, had been buried a short distance from there in the same cemetery.

This man who had touched the lives of so many over the years, who had taught what he loved and loved what he did was gone. His art, which by this time had been appreciated by so many, was his legacy. But for me, the memories of his courage and determination to achieve what others may have thought to be beyond his reach will remain. He is greatly missed.

* * * * * *

Floyd's chair, in addition to his many beautiful works of art, also lived on after he was gone, at least for a short while. Richie had heard of a fellow worker at Dennison whose young son was severely disabled due to a crippling birth deformity. The youngster had all the spunk and spirit of any of his peers, but had no way to get around on his own, since his father simply could not afford to purchase any type of electrified wheelchair. By the late '60s there were several models of such chairs on the market, all of which were very expensive. When Richie had developed his unique solution to Floyd's lack of mobility back in 1950, he knew of no products that could be purchased or modified, so he developed his own specific answer to the need. Now, with its original owner deceased it seemed a shame for the chair to be idle. Practically unthinkable was the idea that it should be dismantled and discarded.

Richie met with the youngster and his family and quickly sized up what few modifications should be incorporated into Floyd's well-used chair so that this little driver would be comfortable and safe in it. When he presented it to the family and explained how the battery charging system worked, as well as a few other important features, they were overjoyed and choked with emotion that this man whom they knew only slightly, would be so generous. He refused any money for his invention commenting that he had been repaid many times over in simply seeing how much it had meant to that wonderful Texan whose daily prayer had included his thankfulness.

Once Richie was sure that the new operator of this famous machine could safely handle it, he drove slowly home taking the long way so he could drive by Lucky Point. His eyes misted slightly as he could almost see and hear Floyd once again zipping all over the place and out to his boat, his fishing rods waving from the back of the chair as he drove across the hot top. He smiled to himself as he wondered if the kid could use a boat.

ACKNOWLEDGMENTS

This story could not have been put together without the help and support of several people, and I am grateful for the significant input of so many. For years, I had wanted to describe the unique way in which my father's innate talent for all things mechanical had so dramatically improved Floyd Walser's life. It remained an elusive goal until my Aunt Selma made it abundantly clear to me that I needed to get to work on this true story and that I needed to do it now rather than later. I have her to thank for providing not only many insights into her brother's early days, but also for providing the impetus to get cracking. She has reviewed much of the manuscript and has given her approval to those parts of the story that she knew to be factual.

Of course my mother was consulted frequently and through my retelling of parts of her own experiences, she has enjoyed reliving those heady days.

My mother's sister, my Aunt Rose, also provided some memories and helped reconstruct portions of the courtship and marriage of my mom and dad.

Hazel Belloli (Carlo's widow) provided a wealth of background information and much of Floyd's original artwork as well as his captivating journal that is recounted in chapter 17. Corinne (Belloli) Mannarino and her husband, Joe also provided memories and insight that were of real value in capturing additional parts of the story.

I owe a great debt of gratitude to Gordon Walser of Blanco, Texas, who is the youngest son of Benny Haden Walser, Floyd's older brother. Gordon has become a long-distance telephone friend over the many months it has taken to capture the story. He has accurate recall of many key events and was able to provide some marvelous old photographs as well as some old Texas lore. He has taken the time to read and comment on much of the book as it was developing.

Some extremely valuable material was provided by Jacquie Molé of Oregon, the daughter of Floyd's sister, Clara. In addition to providing me with copies of letters Floyd wrote to Clara as well as some newspaper clippings, she also recounted her own limited meeting with the artist when he drove out to Oregon.

Billy Walser, Tansey's youngest son, recalled some details of the time that Floyd stayed with his parents and him in Abernathy, Texas.

The granddaughters of Erie (Walser) Risinger were a wonderful source of photographs and other valuable material. They are: Mary Mills, Polly Kiker, and Bobbie Skelton, daughters of the late L.V. Risinger; and Cheryl Huffman, whose late mother was LV's sister, Ouida. It was difficult to track them down, but once I located them, with some help from their cousin, Thad Risinger, they were exceedingly helpful and I thank them for their time and effort.

Leaton Clark, whose mother is a Walser from a different branch of the family, has been a great source of genealogical material from which I was able to develop the correct timeline of the lives of many of Floyd's relatives.

The staff of the Framingham Historical Society and Museum has been very helpful. Especially supportive in my explorations of their files were Frederic Wallace and Bonita Bryant who really know their way around the archives.

Susan Lee, genealogist with the Harvard Historical Society, provided a wealth of detailed background material on Roy Greene's family and his early days.

Leah Cramer, of the Horseheads Historical Society, provided an amazing amount of wonderful information about Floyd's correspondence school instructor, Zim. Included in the material she supplied was a most informative book entitled *ZIM, The Life Story of Eugene Zimmerman, Horseheads Cartoonist* by Jan Strausser-Kather. I thank Mrs. Cramer for her permission to quote freely from the material she supplied.

Information on what it was like to harvest wheat at the turn of the last century was provided by Al Durtschi, of

Walton Feed, Inc. who also reviewed what I had written on that subject and helped me to get it right.

John W. Enz, State Climatologist in the Soil Science Department of the University of Fargo, provided specific meteorological details of temperature and humidity in that city in August 1909.

I received a considerable amount of help on getting the facts correctly stated concerning Floyd's car from Judith Kirsch, Researcher at the Henry Ford Museum in Dearborn, Michigan. My request to the Ford Motor Company for details on what I believed to be a 1930 era Ford was forwarded to her. Even though the car turned out to be a Chevrolet, the amount of information she and her Ford Model A experts provided was impressive and very useful.

Tom Huber, a map librarian at the Illinois State Library, provided me (at no charge) a tabletop-size national road map for the year 1931. It is titled "Paved Road Map of the United States" and was published by the National Map Company of Indianapolis. It allowed me to accurately describe the route Floyd took on his 1932 trip to Texas.

Material about the "Bonus Army March of 1932" was gleaned from a presentation, found on the Internet, by Brian R. Train, in his welcome to the students of History 151 at the University of Massachusetts.

A marvelous resource that helped me describe what gasoline stations were like in the '30s was the book *The American Gas Station* by Michael Karl Witzel.

Louis and Anna Chouinard, who have lived since 1953 in what had been "Harmony Home" and have been good friends since before that time, invited me back into their home. It was more than a little nostalgic to be in the place that so many years ago was Floyd's studio and the Greene's special haven. They provided one of Floyd's self-portraits, "Tex", and the original sketch he made of the house in 1936.

David Carlson provided me with some details about the time his older brother, Skippy, rode along with Floyd in the 1943 trip to Texas, as well as recollections of time he himself spent as a youngster visiting with Mr. Walser.

Shirley Mahoney, of the Cathedral of the Pines, sent me information about Edith's 1950 memorial service concert at that place of beauty and inspiration.

Arthur Stucchi, who was the 12 year-old who had been doing errands for Floyd and found him on the last day of his life, reviewed that portion of the manuscript and confirmed its authenticity.

Ginger Esty, a Selectman in Framingham, whose grandmother was Lillie Fuller Merriam, Edith's librettist for the opera Osseo, provided additional insight into that aspect of the story. She also provided some excellent copies of a few of Floyd's etchings.

Fred Bortolussi ("Freddie") provided a useful collection of material that his mother had kept over the years commemorating the close relationship she had with Edith.

Dr. Alden Gagnon, MD reviewed the paragraphs that dealt with heat stroke and polio and confirmed that the descriptions were accurate.

Susan B. Pickford took the time to read the manuscript in various stages of completion and provided valuable editorial input. Her contribution to the finished product is much appreciated.

I wish to thank my good friends, Larry and Judy Pumfrey, both of whom are talented artists, for the suggestion to incorporate into the front cover, Floyd's marvelous oil painting of Henry Ford's Grist Mill in Sudbury, Massachusetts. They also were a great help by reviewing the entire manuscript to validate my descriptions of art-related material.

Raymond Nelli took digital photographs of the painting of the mill for the front cover, as well as the picture of Richie's early family.

Charles Mitchum put together all the photographs included in the book. His skill with the computer allowed marginally useful photos to really tell a story. His creative input into the design of the covers is genuinely appreciated as are the many hours he spent fine-tuning the interior photos and their captions.

Of course, with me from the start of this project and constantly helpful and supportive is my wife, Pat. She was the sounding board for the entire book, as I would read a few pages at a time as they developed, for her comments and input. She carefully read every page of the manuscript, making note of incorrect spellings and twisted sentence structure, as well as suggesting areas for improvement and key episodes from the story she knew should be included. Her enthusiastic support and willingness to let some of our priority projects get pushed aside for the duration, has been wonderful.

Whatever errors of fact or of any other type, which may remain, are totally my responsibility.

Richard L. Rotelli
Chelmsford, MA